MARION HUSBAND

MARION HUSBAND

OMNIBUS

THE BOY I LOVE

&

PAPER MOON

Omnibus edition published by Accent Press Ltd – 2008

ISBN 9781906373344

The Boy I Love
First Published 2005
Copyright © Marion Husband 2005

Paper Moon
First Published 2006
Copyright © Marion Husband 2006

The right of Marion Husband to be identified as the author of this work has been asserted by her in accordance with the Copyright, Designs and Patents Act 1988.

The stories contained within this book are works of fiction. Names and characters are the product of the author's imagination and any resemblance to actual persons, living or dead is entirely coincidental.

All rights reserved. No part of this book may be reproduced, stored in a retrieval system, or transmitted in any form or by any means, electronic, electrostatic, magnetic tape, mechanical, photocopying, recording or otherwise, without the written permission of the publishers: Accent Press Ltd, The Old School, Upper High St, Bedlinog Mid-Glamorgan, CF46 6RY

Printed and bound in the UK

Cover Design by Red Dot Design

For my mother, Margaret Donkin

The Boy
I Love

Chapter One

November 1919

Hiding in Adam's pantry, Paul remembered how he was once forced to eat marmalade at school, a whole pot of marmalade, Jenkins twisting his arms up his back as Nichols held his nose and clattered the spoon past his teeth. He stared at the jar on Adam's shelf. Its contents were all but finished; only a dark orange residue speckled with toast crumbs and marbled with butter remained. He unscrewed the lid, wondering if marmalade could taste as bad as he remembered. The scent of bitter oranges assaulted him as outside the pantry door his father's voice rose a little, as close to anger as he ever came.

'He's not well enough to be out on his own.'

'Doctor Harris, I swear I didn't even know he was home.'

'He writes to you.'

'He wrote occasionally.'

Paul placed the marmalade back on the shelf, listening more carefully. That pinch of truth would help the lie down – that "occasionally" held the right note of disappointment. His father might almost believe his letters to Adam were infrequent.

George sighed. 'If you do see him …'

'I'll bring him straight home.'

Paul listened as Adam showed George out, waiting until he felt sure his father had gone before pushing the pantry door open. In a stage whisper he asked, 'All clear?'

Adam sat down at the kitchen table. Taking off his glasses he ground the heels of his hands into his eyes.

'Jesus, Paul. He knew you were in the pantry. He bloody knew.' He looked up. 'He didn't speak to me. He spoke to the

1

bloody pantry door.'

Sitting opposite him Paul reached across the table and took his hand. 'At least you didn't give us away.'

Adam drew his hand back. 'He could smell your cigarette smoke.'

'Maybe he thought you'd taken up smoking. Maybe you should.' Paul shoved his cigarette case towards him. 'Calm your nerves.'

'You know I hate it.'

Lighting up, Paul blew smoke down his nose. 'Hate what? Lying, smoking or having a one-eyed lunatic hiding in your cupboards?'

'Smoking.' Adam sighed. 'No point hating the rest of it, is there?'

Adam polished his glasses on the corner of his shirt. Hooking the wire frames over his ears he smiled at Paul. 'Cup of tea?'

'I should go. He's had enough worry, lately.'

'Haven't we all.'

'I'd better go.'

'Yes. Of course. Better go.'

Neither moved. Paul's bare toes curled against the cold lino. The kitchen of Adam's terrace house was always cold, always smelt of yesterday's frying, always made him want to take boiling, soapy water and a scrubbing brush to the sink and stove and floor. He thought of the stale-biscuit smell in the pantry, the damp in the corners, the nagging suggestion of mice. He shuddered and wiped imaginary marmalade stickiness from his fingers.

That morning he had turned up on Adam's doorstep, leaving his father to his breakfast, using up another lie about needing fresh air. He had seen Adam only yesterday, his first day home, and all he could think about was seeing him again, of lying down in his bed and breathing in the fug of sweat and come and cigarettes as he slept. Adam would work downstairs, marking his piles of ink-smudged essays. Later he would slip under the covers beside him, warming himself against his body. As the room darkened they would make love whilst in

2

the street children called to one another and dogs barked and church bells closed the day. There would be none of yesterday's fast, furious fucking, the sex that came from relief and awkwardness and lust. Adam would make love to him and he would be loose-limbed and lazy. Afterwards he would sleep again. He would sleep all night in Adam's bed, Adam's legs entwined with his, Adam's breath warm on his face. He had wanted this day and night for years.

Adam, however, had wanted to feed him – eggs and bacon and thick slices of bread, cups of sweet tea, a rice pudding he'd made especially for him. He was an invalid to be fattened; he was too thin by far, a bag of neglected bones. Quick with embarrassment Adam had fussed between sink and stove and table. Later they had fucked routinely and Paul had left his eye patch on although he had planned to take it off. Taking off the patch would have been a kind of unveiling. Such theatrics had seemed inappropriate after the ordinariness of rice pudding.

Paul stubbed his cigarette out, crushing it into a saucer so that it all but disintegrated and Adam ducked his head to smile into his face.

'Paul? You've gone silent again.'

'I'm fine.' He smiled back. Like George, Adam needed constant reassurance. 'I've left my shoes and socks upstairs.'

Adam laughed. 'You know, I half expected to see you in uniform. I almost didn't recognise you, standing there in civilian clothes.'

'Disappointed?'

'No, of course not.'

'You said once I suited the uniform.'

'Did I? You suited the cap, I think.'

'I'll keep it. Wear it in bed.'

'I'm glad you're back.' Adam laughed again. 'Glad. Christ, what kind of word is that, eh? Glad. Bloody glad.'

'I'm glad to be back.' Paul stood up. 'I'll go and get my shoes.'

As he went past Adam caught his hand. 'I love you.'

'I know. I love you too.'

3

Paul took a shortcut home through the park that separated Thorp's long rows of back-to-back terraces, its steel works and factories from the small, middle-class ghetto of Victorian gothic villas where his father lived. He sat down on the graveyard wall opposite his house and lit a cigarette, imagining his father in the kitchen toasting cheese, his usual supper. Cheese on toast then cake made by a grateful patient, then tea, strong, just a little milk, no sugar. George was a man of habit. Paul looked at his watch; it was later than he'd thought – the tea would be drunk, the cup and saucer and plate washed and dried and put away. His father would be reading the *Telegraph* in front of the kitchen fire. In France, and later during his months in St Steven's, he had remembered his father's rituals and almost wept with homesickness. Now, as the cold from the wall seeped into his bones, he wanted to walk away from the smallness of them, back to one of the pubs he had passed along the back streets. At the Stag's Head or the Crown & Anchor he would order beer and share a joke with the hard men of Thorp. Paul smiled to himself. He would get his head beaten in along a dark alley, called a fucking little queer as boots smashed his ribs. He had only to look at one of them in the wrong way. Best if the fucking little queer went home and faced his father's disappointment. Tossing the half-smoked cigarette down he crossed the road towards the unlit windows and locked door of his father's house.

Margot said, 'He's home.'

'Who, dear?' Her mother looked up from her knitting, rows of grey stitches that were beginning to take the shape of a mitten. Mitten production hadn't stopped just because the war had. There were orphans' hands to keep warm now. Absently she repeated, 'Who's home?'

'Robbie's brother. Paul.'

'Oh?' Iris Whittaker laid the knitting down on her lap. 'That poor boy. He was so handsome, wasn't he? I remember how handsome he looked at your birthday party. Such a beautiful face. It must be quite dreadful for him.'

'It would be dreadful for any one. Even an ugly man.'

'Yes, of course, but worse, somehow, for such a good-looking boy. Such a courteous boy, too. So charming. Poor George. I thank God every night you were born a girl. If we'd had boys like poor Doctor Harris …'

They would be dead, Margot thought, and considered saying it aloud. Dead as dodos. Dead as doornails. Stone, cold, dead. No one said the word dead in this house, although whichever of the vicarage windows you looked from you could see the weeping angels and floral tributes that marked out dead territory. Dead was such a stark word when death was so close, so her father, when he'd told her of Robbie's death, had cleared his throat and said, 'That boy's been taken from us.'

She knew, of course, exactly who and what he meant. That boy: Robbie. Dead.

Her mother picked up her knitting. 'He'll have a glass eye, of course. It might look real, from a distance.'

'Look but not see,' Margot said quietly.

'Pardon, dear?'

'Didn't you think he was horribly vain?'

'Vain?' The wool was held taught and crossed over the needles. 'All men are vain, dear. At least he had the right to be.'

Margot closed her eyes. Robbie had said, 'It's amazing that Paul and I have leave together.' He'd grinned. 'I can show you off to him – introduce you as my fiancée.'

'I thought we weren't going to tell anyone.'

'We can tell Paul. He's so self-centred he'll have forgotten by tomorrow.'

Margot remembered how Robbie had pulled her into his arms, holding her tightly so that her cheek felt the scratchiness of his uniform. Khaki smelt of dry hessian, of sweat and metal polish that she imagined was the stink of gunpowder. Beneath the khaki his body felt hard and spare. She tried to remember how she had responded, if she had drawn away a little or pressed herself closer. She remembered he groaned. Perhaps she had encouraged him.

5

'I think I'll go to bed.' Margot closed the book she'd been pretending to read and stood up.

Iris glanced at her. 'Say goodnight to your father.' The knitting needles picked up speed. 'Tell him if that sermon isn't finished by now it's too long.'

In her father's study a picture of Jesus surrounded by children hung above the fireplace. Christ was white and pale gold, the children dark and dressed in bright colours. A lamb knelt at Jesus's side, a garland of flowers around its neck. The picture was titled *Suffer the Little Children.* Robbie had frowned at it. 'I was in Palestine before the war. The children wore rags.' She tried to remember the tone of his voice. Not quite so pompous, maybe, just matter-of-fact.

Her father looked up from his desk. 'Margot. Off to bed?'

She sat down opposite him on one of the chairs arranged for those about to inform him of marriages, births and the passing-on of loved ones. Placing his pen down the Reverend Daniel Whittaker smiled at her.

'Sermon on the Mount. For the memorial service tomorrow.'

'Oh.'

'Blessed are the peace-makers.'

'Yes.'

'It's so important to strike the right note. So difficult.' He sighed. 'I've asked Mr Baker to read the lesson.'

Mr Baker: three lost sons. Margot nodded. 'That's good.'

'I hope it won't be too much for him.'

'Daddy …?' she began. More quietly she went on, 'I'm going to have a baby.'

'Sorry, dear?' Looking up from the sermon he frowned. 'You do look peaky, my dearest heart.' He sighed again. 'You should go to bed. Up the wooden hill.' He smiled. 'Remember how I used to say that when you were small?'

'Yes.'

'Yes.' After a moment he said, 'Go to bed, Margot. Try not to worry.'

As she was about to close the door behind her he called out, 'Say your prayers, Margot. God always listens.'

On the stairs she looked back towards the study door. She had deliberately left it ajar so she might spy on him from the wooden hill. He was lighting his pipe, packing the tobacco down with his thumb as he sucked on the stem to draw flame. She knew he knew. For now it was their secret, stored against her mother.

Her mother had no idea how wicked she was. Although Robbie had said I love you only once, she hadn't stopped him when he slipped his hand under her camisole. She had lost her voice; the shock of his cool, hard palm against her breast seemed to cleave her tongue to the roof of her mouth. He had drawn away, smiling at her hands clenched into fists at her sides. 'You're not going to box my ears, are you?'

'No!' She remembered blushing.

Robbie laughed a little, his eyes avoiding hers. 'I wish you were older, sometimes.'

Her blush deepened and she dug her fingernails into her palms, a counterpoint to the pain of humiliation. 'I'm old enough!'

'Then try and behave as though you are!' Vehemently he said, 'Don't look at me as though you want to eat me alive, then turn stiff as a corpse the minute I touch you.'

Later he was penitent, his head bowed as he held her hands. She'd been afraid that he might cry. A little later still and he was pushing her down into the long grass beside the Makepeace tomb, covering her face with frantic kisses as his hand scrambled beneath her petticoats. When he had pressed his hand between her legs she hadn't protested. 'Let me,' he whispered, and she'd nodded, not knowing how to refuse him: the war had made him strange, an infectious strangeness, she realised now.

She splayed her fingers over her belly. She would show soon and even her mother would notice. Then there would be tears. All the listening Gods in the world wouldn't help her then. She thought of nunneries; a nunnery would be her mother's solution. Nuns with hard hands and stern voices would take charge and smooth it over and send her home a sinner still, but a sinner whose sin was taken away, a Mad

Hatter's riddle. She wouldn't think about it anymore. Turning away she climbed the stairs to bed.

Paul had vomited twice that morning. Once just after his father told him they were going to church and again as they were about to leave, when he told him that it was to be a special service of remembrance and they were expected for lunch at the vicarage afterwards. That second time had exasperated George.

Placing his hand firmly on his son's forehead he barked, 'Any stomach pain?'

Paul twisted away. 'No.'

'Bowels moving normally?'

'Dad! For Christ's sake.'

George ushered him out. Locking the front door behind him he said, 'You smoke too much. It's enough to make anyone sick.'

Across the road St Anne's Church loomed from the leafless trees. Sunday-best parishioners snailed their way towards the church doors. Paul began to worry that he would be expected to talk to these people, that they would tell him about lost sons and husbands and brothers as though they expected some kind of comfort from him because he survived. He felt the bile rise in his throat again and he closed his eye.

'Paul.' George's voice was sharp. 'Pull yourself together. Remember what your doctors said.'

'They said, "Lieutenant Harris, we've dug out your left eye with a rusty spoon. Any questions?"'

'Don't be idiotic. And I wish you wouldn't hide your glass eye behind that patch. You look like a pantomime pirate.'

They crossed the road. George took his elbow and steered him like a very old man along the graveyard path, past the angel weeping over his mother's grave, past the urns and obelisks of those who had died comfortable deaths. Frosted leaves crunched beneath his thin-soled shoes and the cold kept his hands deep inside his trench coat pockets, making him a sloppy civilian from capless head to ill-shod foot. In some hospital or another he'd lost the leather gloves Rob had given him. He thought about the gloves, concentrated on remembering their beautiful stitching, the way they kept the shape of his hands when he took them off, the expensive, masculine smell of them. He thought about the gloves as George led him up the aisle and gently pushed him down on to a pew. Only when his father pressed a handkerchief into his hand did he realise he'd been weeping over their loss. From the pew in front a child turned to stare at him and was slapped on the legs for her rudeness.

'Have you met Reverend Whittaker, Paul?' Standing in front of the vicarage fireplace George was forcing himself to smile.

Paul nodded. 'We met during my last leave, at Margot's party.' He held out his hand. 'How are you, sir?'

Daniel Whittaker shook his hand briefly. 'Would you like a drink before lunch? Whisky or sherry?'

'Oh, whisky, I think.' George seemed to relax a little. 'Lunch smells good.'

Whittaker turned towards an elaborately carved sideboard crouching against the dining room wall. 'My wife's cooking beef.'

Handed his own short measure of Scotch Paul said, 'Do you mind if I smoke, sir?'

'I presume you smoke cigarettes?'

'Yes, sir.'

'Then would you mind if I asked you to smoke them in the garden?'

George said, 'It's a disgusting habit, dirty and disgusting.'

'I smoke a pipe myself.'

To hide his smile Paul bowed slightly. 'Would you excuse me?'

'Don't be long, Paul. I don't want you catching cold.'

To avoid catching cold Paul walked back to the hallway where Whittaker had hung his coat. He put it on, turning up the collar and buttoning it, trying not to think of those wretched gloves that once lived in the pockets.

As he fastened the belt a voice behind him asked, 'Are you

9

leaving?'

Paul turned round, his fingers going to check that the eye-patch hid all it was supposed to.

The vicar's daughter smiled at him, her own hand going to the blush that was spreading over her throat.

'Hello, Margot.'

She was standing on the stairs, so much higher than him he had to tilt his head back to look at her. Touching her left eye she said hesitantly, 'The patch … it makes you look dashing.'

He laughed.

'No. Really. It suits you …' Her blush deepened. 'Sorry, I didn't mean that, exactly. It must have been horrible.' She came down. 'Are you leaving?'

'Leaving? Oh, no. No, not leaving. I wanted a cigarette.'

'Daddy wouldn't let you smoke in the house?'

'No.'

'I smoke.'

'Really? Well, if you'd like one of mine …'

'Yes, thank you.'

She had thought he was Robbie, returned from the grave, wearing the same coat she imagined they buried him in, the same coat he had spread on the grass behind the Makepeace tomb. He had lost his captain's cap, and those strips of cloth like khaki bandages he wrapped around his shins, but it was Robbie, not dead, only lost. She'd stood on the stairs watching him, holding her breath to be as silent as possible until slowly she realised that this was only Paul, the boy who had looked so close to weeping as her father spoke of the importance of remembering, everyone had seemed embarrassed for him. Afterwards, when he was in the queue to shake her father's hand, most people had kept their distance, as though madness was contagious.

In the garden Margot watched as he fumbled with a cigarette case and matches. His hands shook and he smiled apologetically as first one match and then another broke.

'Let me,' she said, and took the matches from him.

He stepped closer, accepting the light she held out. Just like

Robbie, he blew smoke down his nose and smiled at her. 'When did girls start smoking?'

'Same time as boys.'

'1914?'

She felt her face flush. 'Probably.'

They stood side by side, smoking in silence. From the corner of her eye she noticed his fingers go again and again to the eye-patch as though checking its straightness. Tossing her finished cigarette down she pulverised it into the crazy-paved path.

'I have to help my mother serve lunch.'

'Margot ...' He caught her arm as she turned away, immediately releasing her as she faced him. 'I'm sorry about Rob.'

'I should say that to you, shouldn't I?'

'I know how close you and he were.'

'What do you know? What did he say about me?'

'That you were going to be married.'

'Yes! We were!' She laughed harshly. 'He promised me. We would have been married by now.' She began to cry and he took a handkerchief from his pocket and handed it to her. 'I'm sorry.' Dabbing at her eyes she said, 'I don't know what came over me.'

'Misery? That's what comes over me, anyway.'

She gave back the handkerchief. 'Thank you for the cigarette.'

As she walked away she had a feeling he was watching her. When she looked back she saw that he had turned away and was staring out towards the graves.

Chapter Two

In Parkwood's kitchen Paul slumped into the armchair by the fire. He took off the eye-patch and threw it at the hearth where it caught on the coal scuttle handle.

Hanging up his coat George asked, 'How are you feeling?'

'Tired.'

'Why don't you go and lie down for an hour?'

'I'd rather stay here, if you don't mind.'

'I don't mind. Glad of the company.' He sat down in the armchair opposite him. 'You can smoke, if you like.' As Paul lit a cigarette George said, 'Margot's a pretty girl, isn't she? She sent me such a nice letter after Robbie was killed … reading between the lines she seemed quite fond of him.'

Paul remembered Robbie's own description of Margot's feelings. Shyly he had told him, 'She loves me. In fact …' He had glanced away. 'She allowed me to, well, you know.'

Allowed. Paul shuddered.

'Are you cold?' George got up and put more coal on the fire, delicately placing aside the eye-patch. Sitting down again he pressed on. 'Margot's such a sensible girl, a nice, sensible girl.'

'I'm not interested, Dad.'

'Why not?'

'She's a fat little girl.'

George was silenced, gazing into the fire as the room's clutter was tidied away by the dusk. Nothing had changed in this room since Paul's childhood. Even the bookcase was still full of his grandfather's books, their spines cracked with age, their titles fading. Paul wondered how long it was since anyone had unlocked the glass doors and taken a book down.

Not since his last leave, probably, when he had taken *A Tale of Two Cities* on the journey back to the front. He frowned, trying to remember what had become of it, and saw Jenkins hunched against the cold, a candle dripping wax on the thin pages.

Jenkins snorted. *'A far, far better thing* my arse. Bloody fool that's what I say.'

Jenkins. It was dangerous how the most innocent thoughts could remind him – he should have learnt that by now. All the same, each reminder was a jolt, as though he'd been suddenly woken from sleep walking. Unable to sit still, Paul got up. 'I think I will have that lie down.'

Jenkins sang *The Boy I love*. *'There he is, can't you see, smiling from the bal-con-neee...'* He made the words up as he went along. Some of the words were filthy.

Lying on his bed in his room, Paul blew a smoke ring, squinting as it disappeared into the gloom. The wind roared in the chimney and threw the bare branches of the trees against the window. He lifted his hand and its enormous shadow played in the candlelight as Jenkins's catchy tune played inside his head. Jenkins, in balaclava and muffler, grinned at him.

'The boy I love is up on the balconee. The boy I love is ...'

'For Christ's sake, Jenkins.'

'You're a miserable bastard, Harris. But then having to read the men's pitiful letters would make anyone a miserable bastard.'

'I'm censoring, not reading.'

Jenkins laughed. 'Of course! One's mind becomes numb to the blather, eventually.' He put on a Tyneside accent. *'Me darling lass. I hope this letter finds you as it leaves me: utterly, utterly buggered.'*

Paul closed his eyes, smelt the burnt patties and boiled potatoes they'd eaten that evening. He could taste them still, greasy as mutton, salty as sea water. He thought of icecream sundaes, eaten with long spoons from tall glasses in Robinson's café, of the cold lemonade that always accompanied them. He groaned softly. Next to him on the table made from planks and barrels, the yellow flame of a candle drowned in its pool of wax.

Jenkins came to sit next to him. He rested his hand on Paul's thigh. Paul's skin crawled beneath his fingers and he fought to keep from shuddering. He should have shoved him away but something held him back, some idea about protesting too much, of being the obvious queer pretending to be appalled by queerness. He waited for Jenkins to tire of this game and felt his leg tense with the effort of not moving. Jenkins looked at him, digging his fingers into his flesh before lifting his hand away.

Staring at his bedroom ceiling Paul flicked ash into the saucer balanced on his chest. He remembered the day Jenkins joined his platoon, his shiny boots yet to be broken in and creaking with each step, his trench coat and uniform stinking of newness. He remembered his own stink: damp khaki and sweat overlaid with lousy sweetness. As Captain Hawkins introduced them, he could have sworn Jenkins's nose wrinkled as he held out his hand. Jenkins hadn't recognised him for a moment. Plenty of men called Harris, after all, and he supposed he'd changed a little, grown up. Paul shook his hand, all the time his heart hammering as he grinned like an idiot to hide his shock. Not used to seeing him smile, Hawkins had eyed him suspiciously. 'Are you all right, Harris? You look like you've seen a ghost.'

'I have that effect on people, sir.' Jenkins at last let go of his hand, his eyes questioning. Finally recognising him, he laughed, a short, startling burst of noise that made Paul want to vomit with fright. 'Harris! Jesus – *Paul* Harris?' Jenkins looked at Hawkins. 'We were at school together, sir!' He turned back to Paul. 'Good God! Harris! I'd have thought they'd let you sit this one out!'

Paul exhaled sharply. His room was becoming colder and he thought of getting up and drawing the curtains against the chilly moonlight, of climbing fully dressed beneath the slippery eiderdown and blankets George had piled on his bed. Too much effort. He thought about having a wank and his

14

hand plucked faintly at his fly buttons, but all the familiar filthy images evaded him. He thought about Jenkins in school, twisting his arms up his back, forcing his face down into the nest of dead, newly hatched sparrows he'd hidden in his bed. His nose had brushed the fragile flesh and he'd closed his eyes tight, trying not to breathe the green-meat smell. Later, he'd carried the nest to the bins outside the school's kitchens, feeling responsible for the little corpses that looked so dismayed by their pointless deaths. Around that time, Jenkins's bullying had become more inventive, and he remembered the sense of dread of what might come next. Constantly afraid, he'd felt as disgusting and powerless as the birds.

To stop himself thinking about Jenkins he made himself think about the vicar's daughter, the way she'd smoked her cigarette like Jenkins at his most needy. Robbie would have shown her how to smoke like that, reluctantly at first, then amused by her efforts, then taking it for granted that she should smoke as he did, the whole process taking place over the weeks of his sick leave, during that last summer of the war.

'Don't you think she's marvellous?' Robbie had grinned at him from the foot of the bed. His sleeves were rolled up and his forearms were deeply tanned. His smell of outdoors invaded the comforting stuffiness of his room, making Paul pull the bedcovers over his head.

'Go away, Rob.'

Rob had tugged the covers away. 'I've been up for hours. I've mowed the lawn. What are you going to do? Waste your leave sleeping?' Sitting on the end of the bed he said, 'Margot *is* marvellous, isn't she? We're going to be married.'

'Congratulations.'

'What do you think of her?'

What had he said? Something that had made Rob sulk. That she was too young, or too plump, that when he'd danced with her at her birthday party she'd smelt of steamed roses.

Paul frowned as this memory came back. Dancing with her he had wanted to bury his nose in her hair, to hold her closer and breathe her in, so distracted by her scent she must have thought he was touched.

He covered his face with his hands. Imagine, linking her arm through his as they strolled around the graves. Imagine, taking off his coat and spreading it out beside the Makepeace tomb, laying her down on its black silk lining. Imagine, whispering endearments and lies, promises and reassurance as the Makepeace dead listened impotently beneath the hard earth. He imagined the words Robbie said when he finished: 'I'm sorry.' Knowing Robbie he would have apologised. The rest he knew for definite, Robbie had told him.

'She cried,' Robbie said.

'I should think all girls cry, the first time.'

He had been sitting opposite him on St Stephen's lawn and Robbie had looked away, fumbling in his tunic pocket for his cigarettes. Fiercely he said, 'Bloody hell.'

'You haven't asked me to be your best man.' Paul leaned forward in his invalid's bath chair to light his brother's cigarette. 'Should I be polishing my best eye, or not?'

'Of course I want you there ... when you're better, of course.' He shifted uneasily, glancing at some of the other patients wandering the grounds in their pyjamas and plaid dressing gowns. Stiff and correct in his captain's uniform, his fingers went to the knot of his tie, adjusting it minutely. At last he said, 'We won't be married for a while. Plenty of time for that when I'm discharged.'

The war had been over for ten months. For the first few weeks of peace Paul had been blind on his back in an army hospital bed, under orders not to move in case what remained of his sight should be dislodged for good. It would be his own, careless fault if he lost the use of his right eye as well. He'd kept silent, refusing to acknowledge responsibility, wanting to be deaf, too: deaf, dumb, blind, the ultimate retreat.

Halfway recovered that day in September, he'd smiled at his brother. 'You don't have to hang around, Rob. Thanks for coming to see me.'

Robbie frowned at him. 'You're better now, aren't you? Properly, I mean. In the head.'

'Maybe.'

'They should let you go! It's idiotic keeping you here! Good God, Paul. You're so bloody *thin*!'

He remembered laughing – being thin seemed the very least of it – and Rob had frowned again, further discomfited. He stood up. 'I'd best be off. Take care of yourself, Paul. Tell them they should send you home, where you belong.'

Paul watched him as he walked away, remembered how his brother adjusted the fit of his cap with both hands before brushing a speck of lunatics' dust from his tunic. He had pulled on a pair of gloves, preparation for his ride home on the borrowed motorbike. Later Paul was told that the bike had skidded on spilled oil. He imagined its wheels slowly spinning as it lay on its side, sun glinting in its spokes as his brother bled into the earth from the gash in his skull. The farmer who found his body had thought at first that he was only sleeping, peaceful on his back in a verge of grass and poppies.

There had been unspoken irony in the condolences. Rob had joined the army in 1913 – was one of the first to fight. It seemed wrong that he should die on an English road, that there should be some natural law against it. Told he was too frail to attend the funeral, Paul had spent the day completing a jigsaw of Buckingham Palace with another lieutenant who believed the war was still raging and in an hour or two they'd be out on patrol. The fantasy was oddly comforting; he'd gone along with it until the last piece of the jigsaw was fumbled into place, imagining a close crawl across no-man's-land instead of his brother's burial.

His room was completely dark now. George called him for his supper and he got up, fumbling like a truly blind man towards the door. Downstairs, he realised that he'd tricked himself into forgetting about Jenkins for almost half an hour.

Every Wednesday and Saturday Thorp held a market along its High Street, a choppy sea of white canvas stalls from the Georgian cube of its town hall to the medieval stone cross outside the Shambles. Catholic martyrs had once burned at that cross, Margot had been told, but although she had examined the pitted stone she didn't believe it. Thorp had

17

always seemed too sensible a place for such carrying on, a commercial, agnostic place half way between the cities of Durham and York, with no tradition of mining to ally it with its neighbours.

The Wednesday streets were littered with cabbage stalks and bruised apples, the stalls strung with lanterns to light the late afternoon. Margot walked quickly past the butcher's stall. Lately, all smells had intensified and she covered her mouth and nose with her hand so that she smelled only her own woolly mitten smell instead of the cold-blood stink of freshly slaughtered chickens. The creatures hanging from their scaly feet stared at her with dull slits of eyes in the yellow light. She looked away and bumped into Paul.

'Oh, I'm sorry …'

'Hello, Margot.'

She hadn't realised who it was until he spoke. The voice was unmistakably Robbie's. She jerked her head up in shocked recognition, her heart pounding fiercely. Paul Harris frowned at her.

'Are you all right?'

Disappointment tasted like metal against her teeth. She nodded breathlessly.

Paul took her arm. 'Perhaps you should sit down.'

Where the make-believe martyrs had once burned stood a pair of wooden benches. Paul sat her down then crouched in front of her. 'You look terribly faint.'

She sat up straight, breathing deeply to try to subdue the nausea she felt. When she was almost certain she wasn't about to be sick, she said, 'I'm fine.'

Sitting next to her he took out his cigarette case. Opening it, he held it out to her but she shook her head.

'Not in public, eh? We have to care what people think. People will think we're a courting couple. They'll think isn't it marvellous how she's standing by the poor soul, some girls wouldn't look at him again in that state.'

Margot looked around, exaggerating an interest in passing shoppers. 'Aren't they thinking about what to buy for supper?' She turned to him. 'You're not a poor soul.'

'No, I know. I'm a very lucky boy.' He held her gaze. 'May I buy you a cup of tea?'

She hesitated. Paul got up and waited expectantly in front of her. It seemed rude to refuse him. Getting to her feet she said, 'All right. A cup of tea would be nice.'

In Robinson's Department Store café they were shown to a window table. As Paul passed other tables Margot noticed how heads turned to watch him go by, their conversations pausing only to resume in more hushed tones. She felt like a chief mourner at a funeral, ostracised from normal society. For a moment the urge to reach out and take his hand was so strong she curled her own hands into fists inside her mittens.

They sat down and he glanced at a menu. 'Toasted teacake? How about muffins? They used to do marvellous cream cakes here. Éclairs, meringues, that kind of thing.'

'Nothing for me, thank you.'

He closed the menu and placed it down beside him. 'Just tea, then.'

'You have something.'

A waitress hovered, pencil poised. Paul's fingers went to the eye-patch. 'Tea for two, please.'

Margot took off her hat and gloves and placed them on the chair beside her. Self-conscious suddenly, she glanced out of the window to the street. Three floors below them, the lamps on the market stalls twinkled. A hurdy-gurdy man turned the corner into view. She could just make out the red of his monkey's fez as the man stopped his machine and began to wind its handle. She heard Paul strike a match and turned to look at him.

He was beautiful, as beautiful as she remembered Robbie to be, although his dark hair was cut brutally short, his skin pale against the black of the eye-patch. If she were honest she would say he was more beautiful than his brother. He made her feel large and solid. She looked down at the starched white tablecloth.

Paul said, 'There's a monkey dancing in the street.' He was looking out of the window, his face reflected in the dark glass.

'I think its owner only has one arm. Poor devil.' He turned to her. 'I've been wondering what I should do for work. Perhaps I should ask him where I might buy a monkey.'

The waitress came back with the tea and Paul turned to stare out of the window again as she set out the cups and saucers. Margot waited until she had gone before asking, 'What if there are no monkeys to be had?'

He turned to face her. 'Trays of matches? Or newspapers. I could sell the *Gazette* outside the station.'

'That spot's already taken.'

'Then I don't know.'

'What do you want to do?'

'Nothing.'

'What did you want to do before the war?'

He frowned as though trying to remember. At last he said, 'I should go and give that man some money. He'll be freezing, he should get some hot food.'

Margot looked out of the window. The hurdy-gurdy monkey had climbed on to the man's shoulder; the music had stopped and they were walking away. An excited band of children ran after them and Margot found herself remembering the picture of Christ and the children in her father's study. She closed her eyes, the hot metal smell of the teapot making her feel suddenly sick.

Gently Paul said, 'Are you really all right, Margot?'

'I'm pregnant.'

She half expected him to change the subject, to pretend not to hear just as her father had. Instead he said flatly, 'Oh.'

'Oh?' She almost laughed. 'You said oh!'

'Did Rob know?'

She looked away, unable to face his concern, wishing she hadn't told him but at the same time wanting to talk about Robbie's baby. She forced herself to look at him.

'You won't tell anyone, will you?'

'What will you do?'

'Sit in a hot bath and drink gin? I tried, it doesn't work.'

The gin had tasted of perfume and had cost most of her savings. She hadn't allowed herself bath salts. The water was

20

so hot she had cried out, half-drunk, self-pitying mews of pain as her feet were scalded. She'd grasped the side of the bath, arms quivering with the strain of supporting her bottom just out of the water. When she finally sat down she expected to see blood cloud between her legs. That evening, red-faced and giddy, she'd almost told her mother.

Hesitantly Paul said, 'Margot ... have you seen a doctor?'

'Your father?' She heard her voice rise incredulously.

'There are other doctors.'

'I don't know any.'

'Margot ...'

'Stop saying my name like that!'

'What will your parents say?'

'That God always listens? Do you think he does?'

'No.' The sharpness in his voice made her look at him. He was paler than before. His hand went to the eye-patch, all five fingers checking its position. Just as sharply he said, 'They'll send you off somewhere, won't they? The baby will be taken away?'

She thought of nuns, of the black crucifix on the white wall and the high, barred windows of a room she had imagined so often it had become real. A tear rolled down her face. She wiped it away quickly but he had already taken a handkerchief from his pocket and handed it across the table.

'I'm sorry, I didn't mean to make you cry.'

She laughed, snivelling into his handkerchief. 'I cry all the time. Haven't you noticed?'

'Do you want to give the baby up?'

His handkerchief smelt of Robbie. She wanted to cover her face with it and weep great abandoned sobs that would have the fox-furred old ladies on the next table tut-tutting in disapproval. Instead she stifled her tears, making her sinuses ache.

Softly he repeated, 'Margot, do you want to give the baby up?'

She looked down, watching her fingers crumple the handkerchief. 'What else can I do? What? There's nothing else I can do!' Her voice rose and he seemed to cringe. Taking a breath she said, 'I shouldn't have told you. I'd better go.'

As she made to get up he caught her hand. 'Don't go.'

He sounded too much like Robbie, just like Robbie when he said, 'Did I hurt you?' She remembered how he'd rolled on to his back, his fingers scrambling to button his flies. The uneven ground bruised her back through his coat; a smell like flour and water paste leaked from between her legs.

She pulled her hand away from Paul's, desperate now to get away. 'I have to go.'

'Then let me walk you home.'

She nodded, too concerned with the nausea watering her mouth to protest.

He'd decided almost as soon as she'd told him about the baby that he would ask her to marry him. All the way down the stairs from the café he wondered how she would react, although it seemed an obvious solution to him; he even felt a sense of relief. He thought about the ordinariness of being married, remembering the fellow officers who'd shown him their carefully staged photographs of their wives and babies. He remembered that occasionally he had envied them, imagining an easy, undemanding state of domesticity, safe and shameless. Their wives probably respected them, looked to them for support; at the very least there had been a settled air about such men, they'd seemed calmer and more self-assured, although some of them were younger than he was. Most of them spoke to him of their wives with smiling pride. He had written to one such wife, her photograph, salvaged from her husband's corpse, propped beside him. Struggling with inadequate sentiments, he had finally turned the photo face down, feeling as though he was trespassing in a world he knew nothing about. His letter was brief and no doubt of little comfort. By then, words had already begun to fail him; even his letters to Adam were becoming shorter.

He thought of Adam, his reaction. Perhaps he would see such a marriage as a smoke screen for their relationship, a trick to play on the gullible. He glanced at Margot and at once felt an overwhelming pity for her. He had an idea what kind of husband he would make.

The market traders were dismantling their stalls as they walked along the darkening High Street. Behind them someone dropped part of a stall's metal skeleton, the iron pole clattering to the pavement with a din like broken church bells. Paul felt his heart leap. Fighting the urge to throw himself to the ground, he stopped and lit a cigarette, shielding the match with cupped, shaky hands. Margot stopped too, glancing away in embarrassment when he caught her eye.

He smiled awkwardly. 'Still not good with loud noises.'

'Robbie told me about how poorly you were.'

Poorly. That was a nice, Robbie word. 'Well, I'm better now. Officially.'

Looking along the street again she said hurriedly, 'You really don't have to walk me home.' Quicker still she added, 'Don't tell anyone, about what I told you.'

On impulse he took her hand. The words came on a rush of breath. 'I could marry you.'

She stared at him. 'You?'

'Yes.'

'It's ridiculous!'

'Why?'

'*Why?* We hardly know each other. Why would you want to do such a thing?'

'Why did you tell me?'

'What do you mean? I don't know why!' She seemed lost for words. At last she said, 'It wasn't so you'd propose! It wasn't that! I'd never have thought of such a thing.'

'I would have, if I were you.' He glanced away, awkward now, his small store of bravado exhausted. He watched the market traders load their trucks, the clangs of metal poles punctuating the noise of her breathing. Eventually he forced himself to look at her. 'I'm sorry if I've upset you. It seemed the best solution.'

'You'd really marry me?'

'Yes, if it meant we could keep Robbie's baby.'

Her face was white in the darkness, her relief obvious, and she stifled a cry with her hand. Putting his arm around her shoulders he held her as she wept.

Chapter Three

'Dear Lieutenant Harris,' Patrick wrote. 'Congratulations on your forthcoming marriage.' He paused, tapping the pen against his lower lip. Should he congratulate him? He read the words again; they were too formal, too distant. And how should he address him now he had lost his army rank? *Dear Paul.* Patrick smiled to himself. *Dear Paul, remember me?*

'Mr Morgan!' From the front of the shop Hetty shouted, 'Mr Morgan, we need more sausages.'

The shop was packed. A queue snaked past the window. Dull, patient faces stared in at the trays of pork pies and the grinning, winking plaster of Paris pig that was Morgan's High Class Butcher's mascot. Putting the pen down, Patrick walked through from the back with the sausages and the queue shuffled forward. A few of the women smiled at him. He smiled back obligingly.

Pointedly Hetty said, 'Thank you, Mr Morgan.'

Patrick looked to the next customer. 'Mrs Taylor. How can I help?'

From beneath the rim of her black straw hat Mrs Taylor eyed him suspiciously. 'Not like you to be so cheerful, Patrick Morgan.'

He thought of Paul, suddenly brought back to life by that short marriage announcement in the *Gazette,* and he smiled. 'Mrs Taylor, today I've reason to be.'

At six o'clock Hetty turned the sign to 'closed' and leaned back on the bolted door. 'Oh my aching feet.'

Patrick laughed. Counting the takings, he glanced at her over his shoulder. 'Go home. Give them a good soak.'

'I'll stay, if you like. Help you clear up.' Standing beside him she said shyly, 'It's been a good day.'

He handed her a ten-shilling note.

'What's this for?' She frowned at him.

'Christmas bonus.'

'It's too much.'

'As you said, we've had a good day. Besides, you deserve it. I couldn't do without you.'

The note was folded into her skirt pocket. Without meeting his eye she said, 'Thanks.'

He sensed her hesitation. Quickly, before she could say anything more, Patrick said, 'See you bright and early in the morning?' He turned back to the till. After a moment he heard the door close and knew that she had gone.

Slamming the till drawer he thrust the money into a cloth bag, folding it so that it would fit neatly in the inside pocket of his coat. He wouldn't go home, not straight away. He'd go to the Castle & Anchor and drink two pints, one after the other, and then a whisky to warm him. He would think about the letter he'd started. The excitement he'd been trying to disguise all day burst out of him and his laughter echoed off the white-tiled walls.

It had been Sergeant Thompson who first pointed out Lieutenant Paul Harris. Walking to the pub Patrick remembered how, on the day he joined Paul's platoon, Thompson had leaned close, lighting their cigarettes behind a cupped hand.

'See that officer?' Thompson had nodded in Paul's direction. 'Fucking little Nancy.'

A Very light lit the indigo sky, showing up Thompson's filthy smile. Patrick stared into the exploding darkness, excitement stirring inside him. Mirroring Thompson's leer he said, 'Bent over for you, has he?'

Thompson threw back his head and laughed, 'I'd split him in two, man.'

Smiling now, Patrick pushed open the door of the Castle & Anchor and was bombarded with light and noise. He

26

remembered Thompson naked in the de-lousing queue. He'd scratched his balls with all the casualness of someone who knows he's watched. Patrick had gone on watching, knowing he was above suspicion.

'Patrick. What can I get you?' Maria held a polished glass up to the smoky light, squinting at streaks. 'Pint?'

Patrick nodded. In the mirror behind the bar he saw that he was still smiling – an unfamiliar expression was suspended maniacally between the *S* and *T* inscribed in the glass. Placing the beer in front of him, Maria jerked her head towards a group of men in the corner of the bar.

'Mick's holding court again.'

His smile disappeared. 'Who brought him this time?'

'Jack Watts, but he says he hasn't the strength to push him back home.' She laughed. 'Mick organized a draw to see who'd get that honour.'

'There's no need for that now.'

'Oh, let someone else do some work for a change!' She turned to the bottles ranged in front of the mirror and poured a small measure of Scotch into a glass. 'Here. On the house.' She glanced towards the group of men, wincing against their burst of loud, dirty laughter. 'Go home, Patrick. Get a bit of peace before they wheel him back.'

He downed the Scotch in one. Picking up his pint he turned towards the still laughing men. 'Wish us luck, Maria.'

She smiled grimly. 'Good luck, pet.'

In confession he'd told Father Greene he hated his twin brother. Behind the intricately carved screen the priest had remained silent for a while before sighing, 'You must pray for patience, Patrick. Remember Mick's difficulties.' There had been no penance. He had wanted a penance. Greene's leniency had seemed like an insult.

I don't hate him, Patrick thought as he sat beside his brother's wheelchair. Not hate, exactly. Mick grinned drunkenly at him, lifting his glass and clinking it against Patrick's.

'I'm pissed.'

'I'd never have guessed.'

27

Leaning towards him Mick said in a loud, mock whisper, 'I also *need* a piss.'

Men on either side of them shifted uncomfortably. Patrick finished his pint and stood up, manoeuvring the chair around the table, careless of feet that weren't quick enough to get out of harm's way. As he wheeled him towards the pub doors, Mick turned back to his drinking partners. Putting on a high-pitched, frightened voice he called, 'Help! The bastard's kidnapping me!'

Awkward laughter followed them into the street, where Patrick stopped and walked around the chair to button Mick's coat against the cold.

Sullenly Mick said, 'I said I wanted a piss. I didn't say I wanted to go home.'

Patrick looked up at him. 'Don't call me a bastard in front of other people.'

'Can I call you a bastard at home?' He groped in his pocket and took out cigarettes. Without offering them to Patrick he lit one and blew smoke into his face. 'Can I call you a bastard now?'

Patrick began pushing the chair towards home. 'Did Hetty's mother come?'

'That useless bitch, she knows I hate liver and onions. I threw the disgusting mess at the wall.'

Patrick sighed and wondered if he really had, and if Annie had stayed long enough to clean it up. Carefully he asked, 'Did she stay?'

Reading his mind Mick said, 'Don't worry, Jack's dog ate it. Cleaned up better than that old hag would.'

'What will we do if she refuses to come back?'

Mick hunched further into the chair. After a while he said, 'I can look after myself.'

Patrick stopped at number six, Ellen Avenue, unlatching the gate and wheeling the chair up the black and white tiled path of their Edwardian villa. Stooping for the key hidden beneath the smiling Chinese lion that guarded the front door, he turned to Mick.

'Hungry?'

Mick nodded.

'Scrambled egg and bacon, how's that sound?' He tipped the chair back, lifting its front wheels over the step, and pushed his brother into the dark house.

Preparing supper, Patrick added up the months since he'd last seen Paul. It had been thirteen months in all, over a year of missing him.

He'd been one of the lucky ones, discharged only five months after the end of the war. He'd returned to Thorp, to his childhood home, empty since his parents' deaths in a road accident a year earlier. Walking through the house he'd thrown the windows open, imagining he could still smell his father's brassy scent, that odd mix of fresh blood and copper coins. In the garden he'd made a bonfire of their clothes, even the brushes and combs on the dressing table that were still matted with his mother's hair. As he'd carried bundles of their belongings to the fire, he'd fantasised that he was preparing the house for Paul's return, that they could live together quietly and that no one would think it unnatural or improper that he should take care of him.

As it was, he brought Mick back from hospital, to a house cleared of their parents' effects. Even the ashes of the bonfire had been raked over.

He'd begun on the shop next, scrubbing away the stink of its neglect with bleach and boiling water. A pile of sacks squirmed with maggots, the rotting hessian disintegrating under his brush. Maggots and all were swilled down the yard drain, along with the sweetly rotten residue from a butcher's shop that hadn't been properly cleaned since he'd joined the army in 1915. He saw a rat escaping beneath the yard wall and sure they'd be more laid down poison, his lip curling in disgust as he remembered the rats in France.

When the first batch of pigs was delivered the flurry of activity attracted old business associates of his father, the pretence of paying their respects a thin cloak for their curiosity. The animals' squeals drowned out their rheumy-eyed reminiscences and he'd allowed them to drone on about

29

how sorry they were about his parents. Some even bothered to be sorry about Mick, too. As he poleaxed pigs, as he disembowelled and dismembered, he wanted to tell them to save their breath, he wouldn't do business with any of them: they were all too tainted by association with his father.

With Hetty newly employed behind the shop counter, Patrick went to bed and slept for fifteen hours. He'd dreamt of Paul, bloodied and disfigured in Thompson's arms.

Patrick arranged bacon and scrambled egg on to plates. About to call Mick, he hesitated, thinking of Paul's marriage announcement in the paper. The wedding was to take place on Christmas Eve, a week away. There was nothing to stop him going to the church. He would see him, even if only from a distance. Wondering why he hadn't thought of it before, he smiled to himself. His appetite killed by excitement, he spooned more of the eggs on to Mick's plate and called his brother to the table.

'I dreamt my legs grew back last night.' Mick looked up from mopping bacon fat from his plate with a slice of bread. 'I dreamt Mam was still alive and when I saw her I just got up and walked.' As though he had just thought of it he said, 'Let's visit the grave tomorrow. Take some flowers.'

'If you want.'

Patrick began to stack the plates as Mick lit a cigarette and deftly manoeuvred his chair away from the table and over to the fire. Reaching up to the mantelpiece he took down a book and began to read. He became absorbed almost at once, his expression becoming softer and losing the anger that so often animated his face. About to carry the plates through to the kitchen Patrick asked, 'Can I get you anything?'

Mick barely glanced at him. 'Nothing, thank you.'

'Call me when you want to go to bed.'

In the kitchen Patrick held a plate under the running tap, remembering Paul sleeping beneath a lilac tree. He remembered squatting beside him, watching as his chest rose and fell, fighting the urge to kiss his mouth, to run his hands beneath his shirt. He breathed the scent of white lilac blossom, heavy as gas on the warm air. Grass grew high, brushing pollen against his puttees and his cock's aching hardness. He groaned.

Paul woke, squinting against the sun. Drowsily he said, 'Sergeant Morgan?' His hand went to shade his eyes as he sat up. He frowned. 'Morgan?'

'Captain Hawkins wants you, sir.'

He knew he sounded sullen. His Thorp accent made even ordinary words sound like a threat. Paul had fallen back on to the grass, pushing his hand over his face as if to rub the sleep away. 'I'll be along in a moment, Sergeant.'

Patrick hesitated, still squatting at his side. Paul had frowned up at him. 'Was there something else?'

Patrick loosened his grip on the still running tap. It had left a star shaped imprint on his palm and he pressed it hard against his erection. Thinking about Paul he could bring himself to climax in no time, come right here at the kitchen sink and swill the evidence straight down the drain. Remembering Mick in the next room he turned off the tap and began on the day's dirty dishes.

Hetty said, 'What do you want for Christmas, Mam?'

'Peace and quiet.'

'What would you like really? I've seen a lovely scarf in Robinson's.'

Her mother grunted, 'You keep your money.'

Hetty fingered the ten-shilling note in her pocket. The scarf was thick and soft, a rich navy blue; it would go with her mother's wardrobe of black; it wouldn't upset her invented rules of mourning. All the same she knew her mother wouldn't wear it. Taking the note out she placed it on the kitchen table.

'He gave me this as a bonus.'

As her mother held the money up to the light Hetty laughed. 'He's a butcher, Mam, not a master forger.'

She placed the note down on the table again where it looked dull and insignificant against the bright greens and reds

31

of the new oilcloth. 'It's got something nasty stuck to it.'

Hetty hadn't noticed the small clump of sausage meat sticking to one corner. She picked it off. 'It'll still spend.'

'Then spend it on yourself.' She turned back to the stove where her husband's supper of mince and onions was boiling noisily.

'What about Dad. What would he like?'

Her mother laughed harshly. 'A crate of beer?' Looking at the clock on the dresser she said, 'He promised he'd be home by now. He'll be sat in that pub, laughing and joking. How can he laugh and joke, eh? How can he behave like … like …'

'It's his way of coping, Mam.'

Her mother stared at her scornfully. '*Coping*! How do I cope, eh? How do I cope with it?'

Badly, Hetty thought. Next to the clock her brother Albert's photograph was draped in a square of black crepe. In the parlour a candle was kept burning in front of another, larger photo of Albert in uniform, a crucifix propped against the ornate frame. Bertie's shrine, her father called it once, and never mentioned it again.

Her mother sat down at the table and picked up the ten-shilling note. Holding it out to Hetty she said, 'He must think a lot of you.'

Hetty took the note and crumpled it into her pocket. 'He says I work hard, that's all.'

'It's a pity you have to work at all for riff-raff like him. I remember when his father ran that shop, so filthy you wouldn't have set foot in it.' She got up again. Going to the back door she opened it and peered out into the yard. 'Where's your father got to? His tea's ruined.'

'Shall I go and fetch him?'

'I don't like you going in pubs.'

'I don't mind.'

'Are you sure?' She twisted her apron in her hands, looking from Hetty to the door and back again. 'Maybe just walk up the street and see if you can see him.'

Hetty put her coat on and stepped past her mother into the yard. 'I won't be long.'

32

At the corner of Tanner Street Hetty saw her father walking towards her.

Joe Roberts sighed. 'She sent you out to look for me?'

'She was worried. Besides, it was my idea.'

'Was it?' He smiled at her. Linking her arm through his he patted her hand. 'How's my girl? That big bruiser of a butcher asked you to marry him yet?'

'I'm working on him.'

'Good. Plenty of money, the Morgans. No harm marrying money.'

'Mam says he's riff-raff.'

Joe laughed. 'Patrick Morgan might be but she thinks the sun shines out of that brother of his. Him being a major has gone to your mother's head. Anyone would think he'd won the war single-handed, if they listened to her. What's she cooking for tea?'

'Mince.'

'God love us. Can't you smuggle a nice bit of sausage home, pet?'

They had reached the back yard gate and Hetty drew her arm away from her father's. Joe pulled at the hem of his jacket and straightened his tie. He grinned at her. 'Once more into the breach?'

She grinned back. 'Once more.'

As she was about to go in Joe caught her arm. 'I was joking just now. Money's nowt – you marry for love. Life's hard enough with it.' He sighed. 'Come on. Let's not keep your Mam worrying.'

When she told Elsie and the others she was leaving the sugar factory to work in a butcher's, Elsie had summed up the general feeling.

'You must be bloody mad.'

'It's better money.'

'You'll stink of meat.'

'Well, I'm sick of stinking of sugar.'

Elsie smirked. 'He comes as a set, you know. Him and that

crippled brother.'

'I'm going to work for him, that's all.'

'Of course you are.'

Lying on her side in bed, Hetty pretended that Patrick was beside her, his body fitting together with hers, close as two spoons in a drawer, and her hand moved to rest between her thighs. She lay still, waiting.

Through the wall came her parent's furious whispering, the usual row fuelled by her mother's anxiety and her father's exasperation. She listened, not wanting to, wishing they had found Bertie's body. They should've told them he was dead rather than only presuming. The shrine was just a pretend acceptance.

She heard their bed creak and held her breath to listen to the sudden silence. After a while all she could hear were her father's snores.

Chapter Four

Her mother said, 'You've made your bed, you lie on it.'

Her father said, 'Margot, please think carefully about this. There are three lives involved.'

The doctor said, 'My dear, you are a fit, well young woman and I don't envisage any problems.' He had pushed her knickers down so that they gathered beneath the hard bump and pressed his hands over her in a blind search for problems he had decided wouldn't exist. He gave her iron tablets and told her to eat liver. She craved oranges. To Paul, who waited outside, he said, 'Congratulations, young man. Please give your father my best regards.'

'You look tired,' Paul said, and handed her a cigarette as they waited for the tram home.

When they arrived at the vicarage Margot led Paul through the house to her father's study. For the first time in her life, she tapped on the door. Turning to Paul she smiled nervously as her father called, 'Come in.'

The study was filled with the smell of pipe tobacco and Margot breathed it in greedily. The pipe itself lay extinguished in the ashtray. He never smoked in front of his parishioners. He glanced at her briefly. 'Sit down, both of you. Now.' He looked down at his open Bible. 'I thought we'd have the reading about Christ turning the water into wine. Have you chosen some hymns?'

Before Margot could tell him they hadn't Paul said quickly, '*All Things Bright and Beautiful*, sir.'

'And the others?'

'*Praise My Soul the King of Heaven*,' Paul said. 'And because it will be Christmas Eve we thought *O Little Town of*

Bethlehem. If you think that's appropriate.'

'No, I don't. Think of another one.' Writing the accepted titles down he said, 'Now, I shall give you away, Margot, of course, and the Reverend Collins will conduct the service. We don't want any fuss, so your mother and I have decided to hold just a small reception here at the vicarage.' To Paul he said, 'Mrs Whittaker would like a guest list from you.'

Paul took a folded piece of paper from his pocket and handed it across.

He frowned at it. 'Only one guest apart from your father?' For the first time he looked at Paul directly. 'Adam Mason? Is he your best man?'

Paul looked down at his hands clasped together on his lap. Margot guessed he wanted a cigarette as much as she did. Her father repeated his question and Paul stood up abruptly. 'Would you excuse me, I need some fresh air.'

As he left the room Daniel sighed. He sat back in his chair, pinching the bridge of his nose between his fingers. 'Are you absolutely sure about this?'

Sullenly she said, 'What else can I do?'

'You could do as your mother said.'

She had been wrong about the nuns. Her mother's solution had been worse. She would go to Aunt May's in Carlisle and stay there until the baby could be given up for adoption. Margot remembered the aunt from childhood visits, a spinster who smelt of camphor and attended spiritualist meetings. There were cats, she remembered, and shuddered.

'Do you honestly think that boy is fit enough to marry you?'

'He's fine. You make him nervous, I think.'

'He makes me nervous. At least he's given up wearing that eye-patch. He looks almost normal, at least.'

The patch had been abandoned the day they'd told her parents. She remembered how startled she was, for a moment imagining he'd been miraculously healed. The dead glass, a paler green than his eye, was horrible, and so she ignored it.

'Has he found a job yet? You can't live with his father forever.' Bitterly Daniel added, 'Even in a great big mausoleum like that.'

Hesitantly Margot said, 'He's found a house to rent. In Tanner Street.'

'Tanner Street's a slum!' He shook his head. 'I'll talk to him. I'm not having you and the baby living there.'

The baby. It was the first time he'd referred to it directly. She felt herself blush. Looking down to hide it she heard her father sigh. 'Oh, Margot. How did this happen? I thought it was Robbie you were sweet on, but then this, this *other* one comes along and ...' He closed his eyes and his face became pinched with anger. At last he said, 'How could he? He hardly knew you ...'

The door opened and Paul came in and sat beside her. He took her hand. 'Is there anything else you want to talk to us about, sir?'

The Reverend dropped the pretence of civility. 'Do you have a job yet? How do you intend to pay for a decent home for my daughter, because she won't be moving into Tanner Street, I'm telling you that now.'

'If you saw the house yourself, sir, I think you'd find it's not as bad as you imagine.'

'For heaven's sake stop calling me sir, boy! You're not in the army any more!' He glared at Paul. 'And I have been inside those houses. Members of my congregation live in those streets.'

'Then you'll know decent people live there.' Releasing her hand he stood up. 'Is that all, Reverend Whittaker?'

'Yes. So what do I say now? Dismissed, lieutenant?'

He was never sarcastic. For a moment he looked ashamed of himself and Margot blushed for him.

Paul took her hand again. 'Goodnight, Reverend.'

He waited. When there was no reply he turned and led her out of the room.

She saw him outside.

'I'm so sorry,' she said. 'He's upset.'

Paul took out his cigarettes and lit two at once. Handing her one he said, 'He'll get over it, they all will, eventually.'

'I think Mummy likes you.'

He looked at her. 'Did she like Robbie?' Her silence made him laugh. 'Mothers usually did like me best.'

Margot leaned back against the vicarage wall, tilting her head to rest on the cold bricks, wanting to press her hot face against them. A bright moon shone its ghostly light and the air was sharp with frost. She shivered.

Paul said, 'Dad's out at a patient's.' He hesitated. 'We could go to Parkwood …'

She glanced back. 'I should go and tell Mummy where I'm going.'

'Do you have to? She knows you're safe with me.' Taking off his coat he put it over her shoulders. 'Come on. I've set the fire in the kitchen – it only needs a match. We might even stretch to a cup of cocoa.'

Paul wondered if she'd been in the house before but she looked around her with such curiosity he guessed she hadn't. Picking up a pile of newspapers from one of the kitchen armchairs he tidied them on to the floor.

'Please, sit down. Would you like some cocoa?'

She nodded absently and went to stand in front of the bookcase, tilting her head to read the spines of those books too large to stand upright. Opening the case she took a book out.

'*Health During Pregnancy.* Do you think your father would let me borrow it?'

He took it from her only to hand it back immediately, hating the shrivelling feel of its dust-dry cover. 'Keep it. Dad never looks at books.'

She sat down on the edge of the chair he had cleared, holding the book on her knee and watching him as he whisked cocoa powder into the warming milk. At last she said, 'You chose hymns.'

'I remembered them from school. You can change them if you want.'

'No, they're fine.' She laughed awkwardly. 'I remember them from school, too.' She blushed. She blushed often and he wondered if this was as much a symptom of pregnancy as the sickness she suffered from. He didn't know. *Health During*

Pregnancy was the only book in the house he hadn't read.

He handed her the cocoa and sat down. After a moment she got up suddenly and took a framed photograph down from the mantelpiece. She smiled at it and then at him.

'When was this taken?'

'1915.' He remembered how George had wanted a studio picture of them both in uniform. To please him they had gone to Evans, Society Photographer, and posed in front of a turquoise backdrop that developed as a grey, Flanders sky. Evans posed them standing back-to-back, heads tilted towards each other, arms folded across their chests. Paul had tried hard to keep a straight face, concentrating on the sharpness of Rob's shoulder blades through the thickness of their tunics. Neither smiled, and because their caps shaded their eyes they didn't look ironic as they had intended, only fierce. Noble, Evans said, his two noble warriors. Paul had wondered if Evans was queer or just patriotic.

Margot replaced the picture and sat down. 'He talked a lot about you.' Her blush deepened. 'He told me he never thought he'd see you in uniform.'

Paul sipped his cocoa, aware that she was watching him. Sitting on the edge of the chair she held her cup in both hands, her face still hectic with colour. Her mouth opened, only to close again. He saw her bite down hard on her lip.

He said, 'He called me a fool when I volunteered.'

'But he was so proud of you...'

He laughed. 'I'd just started medical school. Robbie said they needed doctors more than they needed foolhardy boys. Well, he was right. I just couldn't wait, though. Couldn't wait. The day that photograph was taken was the happiest of my life. I didn't care that Rob was angry. He took me for a drink anyway.'

'Where did you go for a drink?'

He glanced at her from lighting a cigarette and she smiled slightly. 'I like to picture him in different places. Make more memories of him, I suppose.' Staring down into her cocoa she said, 'Sorry. It must be painful for you to talk about him.'

'We went to the King's Head. Afterwards he went into

39

Morgan's butchers and bought two pork pies and a pound of sausages. We ate the pies on the way home. He had the sausages for breakfast, before he went back to France.' Looking over his shoulder he said, 'He stood there, at the stove, pricking the sausages with a fork. His sleeves were rolled up and his braces hung at his sides. Afterwards I walked with him to the station and I didn't see him again until your party.'

'He was so pleased you had leave, he even told Daddy.' She laughed, 'I think Daddy was expecting Alexander the Great, the way Robbie built you up.'

'He was disappointed, then.'

Avoiding his gaze she said, 'I didn't know you wanted to be a doctor.' Quickly she said, 'I'm ruining your life, aren't I?'

'No. Don't think that.'

'I can't help thinking it. You don't have to marry me if you don't want to. Mummy can arrange for me to go away.'

'I want to marry you, Margot.'

'Why? I mean, apart from the baby …'

'Isn't that a good enough reason?'

Tears ran down her face. 'It just seems so unfair on you.'

Taking her cup he put it down and crouched in front of her. 'Have you thought it might be unfair on you? After Robbie, having to marry a one-eyed, nervous wreck isn't every girl's dream, is it?' He took her hands. 'It's pointless talking about fair and unfair. It just *is*. Besides, believe it or not I'm happy. I feel settled for the first time in my life.' Squeezing her fingers he laughed a little. 'Maybe I should ask if I'm ruining your life?'

'No, of course not! Please let me tell them it's Robbie's baby. Daddy won't be angry with you then.'

'He won't be angry for long.'

She wiped her eyes, avoiding his gaze, and he ducked his head to look up at her. 'Margot, I don't want this baby to grow up and find out from someone else I'm not its father.'

She began to cry more desperately and he helped her to her feet. He caught her scent, that smell of rose petals seeped in a hot bath, and he thought of Rob, wondering if he had been

40

astonished by it too, or if all women smelt like her. Wanting to catch her scent again he pulled her into his arms and held her tightly. Desire stirred inside him, sweet and surprising.

Later, after he'd walked her home, he wondered how long they had stood there. Eventually she'd stopped crying and her arms had moved cautiously around his waist. As she rested her head on his shoulder he could see the way her hair had been combed and held into place. There was something affecting about it and he touched her head lightly so that she wouldn't feel it but would go on standing still and quiet in his arms. He had closed his eyes and allowed himself not to remember anything.

The memories came back when he woke in the night.

He was blind; both eyes were covered in gauze and bandages that smelt of his father's surgery. They might save one eye, if he could lie very still. That was very important. He had to lie very still on his back and not move. The sheets became creased and uncomfortable, a pungent heat seeped from the rubber mattress and from time to time a nurse would slide a bedpan beneath him or wash him with brisk thoroughness. Whatever they did they warned him in advance, breaking from their private conversations to explain what they were about to do. Only when they changed the dressings on his eyes did they give him their complete attention. Then their voices were quiet, their commentary frighteningly precise as what seemed like yards of bandages were unwound.

The last person he'd seen was Sergeant Thompson, an ex-miner with coal dust tattoos etched beneath his skin. The sergeant smiled into his memory, showing off the gold tooth that looked too soft to break skin and made his breath smell of gun barrels. Thompson had held him in his arms screaming, 'Get the bastard stretcher bearers!' And then, remarkably tenderly, he'd heard him whisper, 'It's all right, sir. Take your hands away from your face and let me see.'

Paul closed his fingers into fists, crumpling the sheets. Across the landing his father coughed. He too was wakeful and soon

41

Paul would hear him get up and pad to the bathroom in his felt slippers, not flushing the lavatory, not closing the bathroom door in case these sounds might wake him. The noise of his father pissing was proof of his love.

He'd asked only, 'It's Robbie's baby, isn't it?'

'No.'

'I don't believe you.'

He listened as George made his way back to his room. He imagined leaving his own bed and climbing into his like he had as a child. Those excursions had been rare; his father suffered them only so long before carrying him back, kissing his forehead with quick finality as he tucked him tight between cooling sheets. And if he did climb in beside his father, if he buried himself in the stuffy sleepiness of his double bed and said, 'I'm scared, Dad,' what could George do? He was scared, so what? Being scared was normal. Scared had its own peculiar comfort.

Lying on his bed, Paul curled on to his side. Closing his eye he forced himself to concentrate on sleep, trying to ignore Jenkins's quiet humming of *The Boy I Love*.

Chapter Five

'Are they staring at me?'

Standing beside Paul at the front of the church, Adam turned very deliberately and looked at the bride's side of the congregation. 'No,' he said. 'They're just whispering amongst themselves.'

'About what a bastard I am.'

'A handsome bastard, though.' He touched Paul's hand discreetly. 'Listen – if you look round they'll all smile at you. They think this is terribly romantic.'

'I look idiotic, don't I? Should I have worn the eye-patch?'

'No.'

'I'm so sorry, Adam.'

'Hush. Don't say that now. Try and calm down.' He frowned at him. 'You're not going to faint are you?'

'I don't know. Maybe. I need some air, I think.'

'I'll come out with you.'

'No.' He smiled, hoping to reassure him that he wasn't going to run away. 'I need to be on my own for a while.'

He'd told Adam he was going to marry Margot the day after he'd proposed to her. They had been in bed, feathers from Adam's pillows and eiderdown curled into the dusty corners of the room and drifting in the draught beneath the door. There were so many feathers it was as though he and Adam had been pillow fighting. Beside the bed a pillow slumped like a weary, defeated body, its insides poking through its worn ticking. He had picked it up and hugged it to his chest. Very quickly he'd said, 'I've asked a girl to marry me.'

'What?' Adam had laughed, a harsh burst of noise that had

made him cringe. Adam had sat up and reached for the spectacles he always removed before sex. Hooking their metal arms over his ears he'd repeated, 'You've *what*?'

Paul had actually quaked, and that had been the worst part of it, feeling so afraid that the ordinary contempt Adam felt for him would finally erupt into something vicious. Adam had stared at him, his face suspended above his so that he could smell his own scent on his breath, and at last he'd said coldly, 'Did this girl say yes?'

To his shame he had began to cry because he cried too easily, even now when he was supposed to be cured of crying. Adam hesitated a moment too long before pulling him into his arms. He held him awkwardly as though sex had made him unclean. 'It's all right,' he said unconvincingly. 'Just tell me how it's happened.'

Adam had believed he was being told the truth. He believed the story that he'd laid down with Margot in the long grass of a meadow beyond the asylum's grounds. He believed that she'd allowed him – a lunatic – to push her skirts up and shove her legs apart. He believed they had both been overcome by a passion that stemmed from their shared grief over Robbie and it was this last shameful invention that stopped Adam short of hating him. He'd said he could understand, he knew all about grief and passion. He said that it could even work out for the best if one of them was married – who could suspect them if he had a wife and child? He'd held him tighter and it seemed he was almost excited at the prospect of fucking a married man. 'I'll talk to the headmaster about getting you a job at the school,' he'd said. 'Don't cry anymore. Everything will be all right.' Suddenly Adam had planned a life for him: he was a family man and schoolteacher and undercover queer. He had an urge to tell Adam the truth just to see him look ashamed.

The fact that Adam believed him, that Margot's parents believed him and hadn't simply laughed at such patently obvious lies, seemed bizarre. He wondered what their belief said about him and about Margot, who surely deserved better. He'd considered telling the truth only to realise that if he did

44

no one would allow them to marry. They would say it was too much of a sacrifice on his part, meaning that he wasn't fit to be a husband, let alone bring up another man's child.

Margot and her father appeared at the entrance to the churchyard. They paused, the Reverend glancing at his watch, angry and impatient as ever, as Margot nervously adjusted her veil. The plain, old-fashioned white dress she wore made her look pale and frightened and the shiny material strained across the small bump of her belly, guaranteeing that all eyes would be drawn to it. He could hear the tongue-clicking already. Moved by the sight of her, he swallowed back the ridiculous tears and went back quickly inside the church before she saw him.

In the vicarage dining room, Paul looked down at the glass of sweet sherry he'd been nursing since Margot's mother had ushered him into the house. The feeling he was being stared at persisted, along with the idea that everyone knew where he'd been for the past year. They would be speculating on the nature of his madness, whether he was a potential danger or mere nuisance. Lunatics were usually one or the other, aside from embarrassing, of course. He sipped the sherry, relieved that Whittaker had decided to do away with the formality of speech making. Beside him Adam said quietly, 'Don't look now.'

'Ah, Paul!' His new father-in-law smiled with forced heartiness. 'Won't you introduce me to your best man?'

Whittaker shook Adam's hand. 'Now Adam, let me introduce you to a few of the other guests. Paul, shouldn't you be with Margot?'

To be with Margot he would have to edge his way through a group of women. Margot stood quietly amongst them, holding the small bouquet in front of her like a shield. The women's voices rang around her, rising in pitch before their sudden laughter made her look down at the carpet. Side-stepping through the women, Paul took her hand.

She smiled at him shyly and from the corner of his eye Paul saw the women exchange knowing looks. One of them reached out and touched his arm flirtatiously. 'We were just saying what a very handsome pair the two of you make.'

He turned away, leading Margot through the crowded room.

When they were alone in the garden he lit her cigarette. 'Are you all right?'

'I think so.' She glanced away from him, blowing smoke towards the graves. 'Better when it's over, I think.'

She had put her hair up, making her look older. Fine tendrils escaped, curling at the nape of her neck and around her ears. Her veil had been discarded as soon as the ceremony was over, leaving the top of her hair flat where it had been gripped in place. She shivered. 'Handsome pair, eh? Silly woman.' She drew deeply on her cigarette. 'When shall we leave?'

'Now?'

'I have to get changed.'

'Hello, you two.' Stepping forward Adam said, 'Sorry, I wasn't eavesdropping. I just came out to say your mother's looking for you, Margot.'

She threw her cigarette into the bare brown soil of the rose bed. 'I'd better go and see what she wants.'

Adam watched her walk towards the house. 'Childbearing hips.' He glanced at Paul. 'Funny, I imagined she'd be ever so fragile looking. A frail, delicate doll with an obscene little bump. But she has tits *and* an arse. I'm surprised at you, Paul.'

'Are you?'

Taking off his glasses Adam took a handkerchief from his pocket and polished the lenses vigorously. 'Sorry. I suppose I'm just a bitter bastard.' He sighed. 'She seems sweet, really. And she smokes! You've one thing in common, at least.' Quickly he said, 'I've left you both a bite of supper in the pantry – just cheese and bread, that kind of thing. Milk and tea of course – I presume you're not going away anywhere?'

'No.'

'Probably best, this time of year. Not much fun.'

'Thanks for standing by me today.'

'We coped, didn't we?'

'Yes. We coped.'

Adam stepped forward and hugged him, the stiff, awkward embrace of an ordinary best man. Stepping away hastily he said, 'Shall we go in? I think you have to cut the cake.'

From the house George called, 'Paul, for heaven's sake boy, come in out of the cold!'

Adam laughed emptily. 'He's always wanted you in out of the cold, hasn't he? Well, at least someone's happy.'

They turned to walk back to the house. Startled, the graveyard rooks hurled themselves into the sky.

In the house on Tanner Street, Margot stood in the bedroom doorway and looked around the little room. Paul had brought furniture from his father's house, a chest of drawers and a bedside table made from some dark expensive wood, recently polished and smelling of beeswax. On top of the drawers stood a jug and basin, decorated with the cheerful faces of blue and yellow pansies. Tucked discreetly under the bed was a chamber pot in the same pattern. Beside the jug was a vase full of holly, heavy with berries.

Placing her suitcase beneath the sash window Paul said, 'Sorry about the smell of paint.'

'That's all right.'

'I kept the windows open for a while but I didn't want the place getting too cold.'

'Really, I can barely smell anything.'

'Right, well, I'll go and light the fire downstairs. Would you like a cup of tea?'

'Tea?'

'Unless you want something stronger?'

'No! I mean I just thought...' Lamely she said, 'Tea would be nice.'

He went downstairs. Margot took off her new, going-away hat and tossed it at the chair in the corner of the room. Suddenly exhausted, she lay down on the bed. The stink of fresh paint hung heavily in the air and she tried to breathe only through her mouth, turning to bury her nose in the eiderdown. Smelling lavender she tugged the quilt back to reveal freshly

47

laundered sheets. He had taken care with their wedding bed. She shivered.

That morning, as she'd twisted and tugged her hair into place, her mother said, 'Your father's not a good judge of character, for all that he's supposed to be.' She'd met her eye in the mirror. 'I like Paul. You should consider yourself lucky to catch him.'

'I didn't *catch* him.'

Her mother had laughed grimly, pinning a lump of hair with a quick stab. 'Perhaps you should put a little lipstick on. You look far too pale.'

Paul returned with a cup of tea and placed it on the bedside table. He sat down at the foot of the bed. 'I've made up my bed in the other room.'

'Oh.' She felt herself blush and busied herself reaching for the cup of tea, only to spill some of it on the eiderdown. The stain spread darkly. 'Sorry.' She looked up at him. 'I'm so clumsy.'

'It's nothing, don't worry.'

To the tea cup she said, 'You don't have to sleep in the other room, if you don't want to.'

A silence grew between them, going on and on until she hardly dared look at him. At last he took her hand, holding it between both his own. After a while he said, 'You're tired, I'll sleep in the other room tonight.' He smiled shyly. 'I'm making some sandwiches. Come down when you're ready, if you're hungry.'

When he'd gone she got up, going to the mirror above the chest of drawers. She pushed her fingers through her hair. In the vicarage bathroom she'd rubbed away the last of the sticky lipstick and she looked pale, more like a mourner than a bride. Catching sight of the holly from the corner of her eye she touched the prickly leaves, imagining their sharpness might pierce her skin, that the pain might shock her out of her numbness. Instead the leaves gave against her touch, soft and glossy as funeral lilies.

Chapter Six

Patrick watched the bridal party from his hiding place behind a yew tree, close to the church porch. He watched as Paul smiled for the camera and turned to kiss his bride at the photographer's insistence. A reluctant kiss, Patrick thought. The girl on his arm didn't even close her eyes. All kisses should be received blindly, but this girl stared wide-eyed at some point beyond Paul's shoulder. Behind the newlyweds, the doctor, the vicar and his wife forced smiles. Patrick had witnessed few weddings in his life, but those he had attended he remembered as exceptionally joyful compared to this sad little gathering. He smiled to himself, grimly satisfied.

Earlier he had watched Paul and another man walk up the path to the porch and wait outside the church while Paul smoked a cigarette. The other man was weedy and bespectacled, nervously checking his watch and smiling fleetingly at guests who hurried past them into the church. Paul ignored everyone. Later, Paul came out on his own and the sudden conviction that he had changed his mind and wouldn't be going through with it had made Patrick's heart race with the idea that he might step from his hiding place and take him home. Eventually, however, he went back inside the church and Patrick had noticed how his hand went to his face as though checking on a non-existent eye-patch.

'He's blinded.' He remembered the pity in Thompson's voice as they watched the stretcher-bearers take Paul away. He'd been about to run after them, all sense and discretion lost to grief and shock, when Thompson had caught his arm to hold him back. 'Leave him be. Someone else can look out for the poor little bastard now.'

49

Walking back to the shop Patrick remembered how until then he'd always thought he'd been so careful, that no one would ever guess except Paul himself. He day-dreamed that Paul would one day notice and then, during some routine business, would catch his eye, would smile that all too rare smile of his and lead him to some quiet, private place where a sergeant could fuck an officer senseless.

In the shop, Hetty glared at him. 'Where have you been?'

He ignored her but she caught hold of his sleeve. 'It's Christmas Eve, our busiest day!'

'Be quiet!' He glared back at her, keeping his voice quiet and immediately turning to the customers. 'Right. Who's next?'

She didn't speak to him for the rest of the afternoon until, as she was about to leave, she said grudgingly, 'Have a nice Christmas, Mr Morgan.'

'Hetty...' She glanced at him from buttoning her coat. 'I hope you and your family have a nice Christmas, too.' From beneath the counter he brought out the chicken he'd put aside. 'I kept this back for you.'

'What is it?'

'A pound of apples – what do you think?' He bundled the cold, heavy parcel into her arms.

Looking at it suspiciously she said, 'I thought I'd had my bonus.'

He sighed. 'Leave it, if you don't want it.'

'I didn't say that.' She readjusted the parcel in her arms. 'It's heavy.'

'Would you like me to carry it home for you?'

She hesitated only briefly. 'Would you mind? I don't want to take you out of your way.'

He took the chicken from her. 'You live on Tanner Street, don't you?' She nodded. 'It's on my way home.'

Her mother had made no preparations for Christmas, just as last year. The year before that Albert had been home on leave from the training camp, still yet to go to France, and they had decorated the house with paper chains and Chinese lanterns and lined his favourite pink sugar mice along the mantelpiece. Now the only thing on the mantelpiece was Albert's shrine. Its candle leapt in panic as Hetty showed Patrick into the parlour.

'Take a seat. I'll make you a cup of tea.'

'Really, Hetty, I should be getting along.'

'Stay. Mam'll want to thank you for the bird.'

'It's nothing.'

'It was very generous. Now,' she pulled out a chair. 'Sit down. Shan't be long.'

In the kitchen Hetty took the best willow pattern cups and saucers from the dresser and set them out on a tray. She worked quickly, afraid that if she took too long he would come and find her, making his excuses to leave. As the kettle boiled she cut a slice of the plain, yellow rice cake her mother made for her father's bait, and then, as an afterthought, cut another slice. They would eat cake together. Hetty smiled to herself, her anger at his disappearing act that afternoon already forgotten in the novelty of having him in the house. Remembering the chicken, still wrapped in its newspaper, she patted it gratefully.

With everything laid neatly on the best doily, she carried the tray through, kicking the parlour door open with her foot. Patrick stood up at once, crossing the room quickly to hold the door open for her.

The little room seemed even smaller with him in it. Tall, broad men looked out of place in these little houses, Hetty thought; they were made clumsy by the mean proportions. Expecting him to knock over one of her mother's china dogs she said, 'Sit down, I can manage.'

As she poured the tea he said, 'Is that your brother's picture?'

Hetty glanced at the mantelpiece. 'Yes.'

'Were you and he close?'

'Not really.' She hesitated before saying quickly, 'Not close like you and your brother.'

He laughed. 'You think we're close, Mick and I?'

'Aren't you?'

51

'Sometimes.'

'I always wanted a twin.' She pushed the plate of cake a little closer to him. 'I thought a twin sister would always be a friend, no matter what.'

'Sometimes twins don't get on.'

'But blood's thicker than water, isn't it? And a twin, well...'

'Their blood is thicker than most?'

'Yes, I suppose so.'

He took a piece of cake that looked like a doll's portion in his huge hand, and ate it in two bites. Finishing his tea he placed his cup back in its saucer. 'I have to go, my *twin* will wonder where I've got to.' He stood up. 'Thank you for the tea.'

'Stay till Mam gets back, at least.'

He was already buttoning his coat. He smiled at her. 'Happy Christmas, Hetty.'

She saw him to the door, standing on the front step and watching until he turned the corner out of sight. He'd been in the house all of fifteen minutes. No ground had been won. In the parlour she cleared away the cups, and noticed that he'd left his gloves behind. She lifted them to her nose, breathing in his familiar scent, before hiding them away.

Patrick and Mick spent Christmas day alone together, eating turkey and fried potatoes from their mother's best china and drinking beer from her crystal glasses. Crackers were pulled in a series of loud bangs that had them both screwing their eyes up tight in a parody of fear. Mick wore a pink paper hat rakishly over one eye and read cracker mottoes in an exact impersonation of Father Greene. The room became hot from the many candles that dripped wax on to the mahogany sideboard and table and illuminated the sepia faces of the unsmiling dead: mother, father, two little sisters, a grandmother stuffed into black bombazine; all stared disapprovingly from their gilt frames.

In his own voice Mick said, 'Here's to us.' Pouring the last of the port, he clinked his glass against Patrick's. 'God bless us, everyone.'

'To the future,' Patrick said.

'Forget the past.'

'Seconded.'

'Although it had its moments.'

Thinking of Paul asleep beneath the lilac tree, Patrick nodded. 'It did.'

Mick frowned at him, his dark eyes smiling questions. 'It did, did it? Tell me more.'

'You first.'

'Nothing to tell.' Mick looked down at his glass, swilling its contents and splashing a ruby stain on the white tablecloth. 'Major Michael Morgan has never been kissed.' He glanced up at him. 'There. Tell the truth and shame the devil.'

'I don't believe you.'

'No?' He laughed. 'Well, it *is* hard to believe, me being so handsome an' all.'

'Never?'

'For Christ's sake.' Reaching across the table Mick pinched his cheek. 'Don't look so appalled, Patty. It's not so terrible, is it? I just never got around to it. Too busy being promoted.'

Mick drained his glass then wheeled his chair away from the table and over to the fire. Taking off the paper hat he screwed it into a ball and tossed it into the flames. The fire flared, sending flimsy charred scraps up the chimney. On the mantelpiece their parents scowled from their wedding portrait. Reaching behind it, Mick produced two cigars. 'So,' he smiled. 'Tell me who made your war bearable.'

Patrick drew out the ritual of trimming his cigar and lighting it, sitting back in his chair and stretching his legs out in front of him. He blew smoke rings at the ceiling. Mick watched him, smiling indulgently until he said at last, 'Did I know her?'

'*Her*!'

'Him, then.'

Patrick studied the tip of the cigar, a good, Havana cigar, the best that could be bought in Thorp. It was sweet and delicious. He poured himself some of the brandy used to fire the pudding, offering the bottle to Mick who shook his head. Taking a large sip Patrick said, 'I think Hetty's sweet on me.'

Mick laughed. 'Poor thing. Well, when she gets tired of barking up the wrong tree, send her home to me.'

Patrick thought of Paul outside the church with his new wife. 'Perhaps I should get married.'

'And perhaps I'll grow new legs, but it wouldn't be what you'd call natural, would it?'

Patrick drained his glass and poured himself another. Knowing Mick was watching him he snapped, 'I can get drunk, can't I?'

'As long as you can stand to put me to bed later.' Mick held his gaze and Patrick laughed drunkenly.

'Have I ever let you down? Ever? Remind me.'

Mick drew on his cigar. 'You've never let me down. Never. Not yet.'

The room had become even warmer. If Patrick squinted the candle flames danced and the frozen faces of his family blurred into one. He had meant to burn the photos, along with the rest of his mother's favoured possessions, but in the end he couldn't bring himself to do it, his own superstitions surprising him. Getting up, he took his parents' wedding photograph down, slamming it on the table in front of Mick.

'When I heard they were dead I told the officer who broke the news, "I'm an orphan." I laughed – we both laughed. It was bloody ironic.'

Mick picked up the photograph and frowned at it. He looked at him. 'You laughed, eh?'

'Didn't you?' He felt drunk, more drunk than he'd ever been in his life. He thought of Paul walking towards the church with that unknown runt of a man and jealousy swept over him. Because he was drunk he said thickly, 'Paul Harris got married yesterday.'

'So?'

'So nothing, I'm just telling you.'

'I knew his brother, Rob.' Mick gazed at him. After a while he said, 'Paul was the *very* pretty one, wasn't he? I mean, Rob was handsome, but Paul...it's a wonder he got past the recruitment sergeant. Crying out to be gang raped, that one.' He smiled slowly. 'You wear your heart on your sleeve, Patty. So, I'm listening, tell me about Paul. How you met, his first words to you, everything.'

'Fuck off.'

Mick held his hands out to the fire. 'It's cold in here, isn't it? I'm always freezing cold.'

'Have a brandy, that'll warm you.'

'I've had enough. How did you know he got married?'

'It was in the paper.' Patrick hesitated. Sullenly he added, 'I went to the church. I watched him as he went in and waited until he came out again.'

'Did he see you?'

'No. I don't think so.'

Mick turned back to the fire. 'Be careful.'

'I'm so fucking careful he's forgotten I exist.'

'Are you going to remind him?'

Patrick stared down at his drink. He thought about the letter he'd written and hadn't sent, a stiff, formal letter as though he was still playing sergeant to his officer. It wouldn't do at all. He had to be bolder. Remembering Paul asleep beneath the lilac tree he said, 'Yes, I'm going to remind him.'

Not wanting to disturb the pain expanding inside his head Patrick lay stiff and still in bed. He could hear Mick snoring and he opened his eyes only to close them again against the winter sunlight. He was still dressed, stinking of yesterday's cooking and cigar smoke. Reaching out, his hand covered Mick's. He had put him to bed only to fall asleep beside him.

Mick stirred, crying out soft, unintelligible commands and flinging out his arm so it rested on Patrick's chest. Patrick lifted it aside and sat on the edge of the bed, holding his hangover carefully in both hands. Slowly, more and more of last night's conversation came back to him and he groaned. Mick always had to know everything – everything had to be told, discussed, resolved; there'd never been a single thing he could keep to himself.

55

For a while he watched his brother sleeping, making sure dreams no longer disturbed him. At last he stood up gingerly, going to close the curtains so that he'd sleep on.

Chapter Seven

The headmaster himself showed Paul around the school.

'Of course you realise you'll be teaching only the most junior boys.'

'Of course, sir.'

The school smelt as his own school had, of sweaty plimsolls and damp gabardine and Paul wished he could smoke as he struggled to keep up with the headmaster's impatient quickness. A cigarette would at least be a distraction, something to keep the memories at bay. He remembered Jenkins lying in wait at the end of long school corridors and the bowel-loosening fear of what he might have in store for him. The memory made him feel ashamed but he willed himself forward, even as he imagined himself running back the way they had come, the startled headmaster staring after him.

Adam had arranged this interview with the headmaster. The man had opened the school especially for him, taking a day from what he called "the wasteland" between Boxing Day and New Year to interview him. He raced a few steps ahead of Paul, his shoes squeaking on the parquet floor of the corridors and from time to time he flung open an empty classroom door, briskly shouting out its form number. To Paul each room appeared identical to the last: rows of desks facing a huge blackboard, the teacher's desk raised on a low platform. He tried to picture himself behind such a desk, controlling thirty or so boys. Half of them would be on his blind side. Perhaps he could rig up a mirror.

In the Headmaster's study Paul watched him shuffle through his references before tossing them down on his desk.

The reference Adam had written was on top and he tapped it with his index finger, smiling at Paul.

'Our Mr Mason thinks very highly of you. He seems to think you'll make a very good teacher.' He sat back in his chair, putting on a show of studying him. At last he said, 'In the army for how many years?'

'Three, sir.'

'And you're quite well, apart from …' He waved his hand vaguely around his own left eye.

'I'm fine.'

'Well, that's good. A lot of my staff are past retirement age – certainly not as fit as they used to be. But with so many of you youngsters away … to be blunt, we need fresh blood pretty desperately. I've got classrooms full of boys with no one to teach them.' He got up and went to the window that looked out across the playing field. 'You were in university for a short time, before the war?'

'I was taking a medical degree.'

'Yes, quite. Well, you're certainly educated. In normal times, of course, I would expect more, but these aren't normal times …' He sighed as though the seriousness of the decision he was about to make weighed heavily. At last he said, 'I'm sure we can work something out, come to some arrangement … term begins again on January sixth.' He looked at Paul over his shoulder. 'Shall we see if we suit each other?'

They had been married five days. Every night Margot lay stiffly in bed, waiting and listening. Every night Paul sat downstairs, reading and endlessly smoking until midnight or later when she would hear him climb the stairs. As he reached the landing her heart would pound so hard she imagined he could hear it. She wondered if he would stop and tap on her shut-tight door and she would tense, listening intently as she slowly counted to ten. It usually took around ten seconds before she heard his bedroom door close behind him. It seemed sometimes that he listened, too, standing outside her door as shy and awkward as she was, so that idiotically she had begun to imagine ways to seduce him, knowing she was too clumsy and gauche to make a success of such absurd plans. She remembered how tightly he had held her that evening in his father's house; she should have kissed him then and got it over with.

He had gone out that morning in his wedding suit, washed and shaved and shoes polished. As he'd combed his hair in the mirror above the sitting room mantelpiece he'd caught her watching him and smiled at her reflection.

'How do I look?'

She had blushed, caught out in her act of spying, wondering if he realised how beautiful she thought he was and whether he would be offended by her use of such an unmanly word to describe him.

The house still smelt of paint. She wandered from sitting room to kitchen and back again, half-heartedly dusting the furniture Paul had brought from Parkwood: a table that dominated the little room, a sideboard intricately carved with bowls of fruit and flowers, empty apart from a cheap, wedding-present tea-set. The furniture was even more depressing than the dark, poky house and she trailed upstairs, only to pause outside the closed door of Paul's bedroom.

Telling herself she didn't want to intrude on his privacy, she hadn't been in his room, shy of his underwear, his pyjamas, his shaving things, everything that made him real and ordinary and disappointed. Now boredom mixed with curiosity and she opened the door, hesitating only a moment before going in.

The room was freezing, the curtains drawn back and the window open. He had made the bed, turning back the sheets and blankets as she imagined he had been taught to in the army, so neat and precise it looked as though a ruler had been taken to the edges. Beside the bed a book lay open, face down on the floor, a stack of books beside it, bookmarks inserted between the pages. On top of the books was an ashtray containing a single cigarette stub and a spent match. His clothes, his shoes, everything was put away. The only things to be shy of were books and cigarettes.

Sitting down on the edge of his bed, she remembered watching Paul at her birthday party. Standing next to her, watching too, her friend Edith – older and more worldly than she – had said, 'He's so handsome, isn't he?'

'I suppose so.'

Still looking at Paul, Edith smiled. 'He's probably having a passionate, unhappy affair with a Parisian actress. She's very neurotic and threatens to kill herself if he ever leaves her.'

Margot laughed, but was ready to believe that some beautiful, willowy French woman would throw herself at his polished boots. When Robbie came back with their glasses of punch he frowned.

'That's Paul over there. What's he doing on his own?'

'Smoking.' Edith grinned and Robbie turned his frown on them.

'He looks lost. Has he been introduced to anyone?'

'He's only just arrived.'

It was the first time she had seen Rob angry. Coldly he said, 'I'll go and fetch him.'

Her father had brought the gramophone out of the house and Edith and her other friends were gathered around it. Across the lawn she watched as Robbie embraced his brother, only to hold him at arms' length as through inspecting the correctness of his uniform. She heard them both laugh and as one they turned to her. She looked down, her face burning, knowing she had been the subject of their laughter. In a moment they both stood in front of her.

Robbie was smiling now. 'Darling, this is Paul, my brother.'

'Pleased to meet you, Margot.' Paul glanced towards the makeshift dance floor laid out on the lawn. The gramophone had begun to play a waltz and he smiled at her. 'Would you like to dance?'

She was still blushing, aware of everyone watching them as he led her on to the floor. With his back to the on-lookers he bowed slightly. Only she could see his grin. Holding her in his arms he said quietly, 'Are they watching?'

'Yes.'

'Good. Happy birthday, by the way.'

She had tried to keep a little distance between them,

keeping her body stiffly away from his so that she danced badly. All the same, she remembered that he had a pimple on his chin, that there were dark rings under his eyes, that his wrists protruded stick-thin from the sleeves of his tunic. He had smelt of coal tar soap and cigarettes and seemed too frail to wear a uniform. She had thought him vain and arrogant and was glad when the dance was over.

Duster in hand, Margot stared out of Paul's bedroom window. Girls turned a skipping rope in the street, their chanting carrying on the still air as the rope lashed the cobbles. She thought of Paul dancing with Edith, remembering how Robbie had squeezed her hand too tightly.

'I'll start to get jealous if you don't stop staring at my brother.'

'I wasn't!'

He laughed, his own eyes on Paul. 'It's all right. He has the same effect on everyone.'

'And what effect is that?'

'You were the one staring at him, Margot. You tell me.'

Bristling she said, 'I was only thinking how arrogant he seems – can't even be bothered to hide his boredom.'

Robbie lit a cigarette, shaking the match out slowly as he watched Paul dance. After a while he said, 'He only got home yesterday. He goes back the day after tomorrow. I expect he's exhausted.' He looked at her. 'I would expect so, wouldn't you?' After a moment he laughed. 'Don't look so sulky. I want you to like Paul. I know you and he will get on fine.'

A week later Robbie was back in France. Just before the armistice he wrote to tell her Paul had been wounded. *Would you write to him? He gets so few letters. Dad tells me the nurses read our letters to him and it's the only diversion he has. I can only imagine how truly bored he must be ...*

She had tried to compose a witty, entertaining letter fit for an unknown nurse to read to a bored, blind man. The task had been too difficult. The half-page she wrote had lain abandoned on her desk. Eventually she threw it on the fire.

From the kitchen Paul called her name and she ran downstairs too quickly, making herself breathless.

Standing in the passage he frowned. 'Are you all right, Margot?'

'I'm fine.'

'Are you sure? You look pale.'

'Never mind me. Tell me how you got on.'

'I start next week. Scary, isn't it?'

'It's wonderful. Congratulations.' She stepped towards him, only to stop, unsure of herself.

With sudden decisiveness he said, 'I think we should go and celebrate.'

'Where?'

'I don't know. We'll take the train somewhere. The seaside.'

'It's winter.'

'So? Come on, I'll buy you lunch in the Sea View Hotel.'

The sea was out, the beach a wide expanse of dull yellow sand they shared with only a few seagulls. She walked ahead of him, from time to time stooping to pick up a shell. Her dark wool skirt brushed the sand and a strand of hair escaped from her navy blue tam-o'-shanter. She tucked it impatiently behind her ear, turning to smile at him before looking out at the still, grey sea.

'I feel like we're playing truant,' she said. 'No one knows we're here and they'd disapprove if they did.'

'I've felt like that all my life.' He lit two cigarettes and handed her one. 'In the army, even at boarding school, I was always expecting someone to tap me on the shoulder and say, "Harris, you idiot, what are you doing here? You should be somewhere else"'

'I would've hated boarding school.'

He thought of Robbie holding on to the sleeve of his brand new blazer in the school hall. George had told him to hold his hand but that wasn't done. With each word Rob spoke he jerked his sleeve until he thought he would pull it from its seams. *Don't cry. The others will think you're a baby if you cry.* He was seven. Despite Jenkins's best efforts over the next fourteen years he hadn't cried once.

They began to walk again, keeping to the firm, wet sand at the edge of the water and following a trail of spiky seagull footprints. When the headmaster had offered him the position he'd almost told the man he'd changed his mind, that the very thought of setting foot in a classroom again made him want to throw up. Instead he'd heard himself accept, meek as ever. He sometimes wondered if he'd agree to anything. Such a sense of duty he had! From the corner of his eye he glanced at Margot. He knew she'd be pleased that he'd got himself a nice, middle class profession. He smiled to himself bitterly, hoping she was the type who could manage on the slave-wage he'd agreed to.

Above them on the front was the Sea View Hotel, its grand Edwardian façade shuttered for the winter.

Paul said, 'Sorry about lunch.'

She glanced up at the hotel. 'I was wearing the wrong hat for it, anyway.'

'I imagined it would be decked up for Christmas, all lights and flunkies.'

'Perhaps next year.'

'The Grand Hotel is holding a New Year Dance. Shall we go?'

She looked down at her bump. Hesitantly she said, 'Would it be seemly?'

'Are you supposed to hide away?'

'No, but …'

'I think I'd like to go dancing.'

'All right.' Avoiding his gaze she nodded. 'I'd like that, too.'

'Good.' He slipped her arm through his. 'Now, let's find a nice warm café and have a cup of tea.'

All the cafés were closed, their windows opaque with condensation, their doors locked. They walked up and down the promenade and along side streets lined with little shops advertising candy rock and ices, their windows decorated with miniature Union Jacks for the victors' sandcastles. All were closed. The whole town seemed deserted, all life stored away for the winter beneath a dustsheet of grey sky.

'There's a pub along there.' Margot smiled. 'You could buy me a port and lemon.'

'Are you sure? It looked a bit rough.'

She laughed. 'That's all right. I've got you to protect me.'

The King George was as hostile as he'd suspected, the landlord eyeing them suspiciously as he settled Margot at a table furthest away from the men leaning against the bar. Taking off her hat and mittens and unwinding her scarf, she looked around curiously. Her face was pink from the cold sea air. She looked too young to be in such a place.

He bought a port and lemon and a pint. As he went back to the table, Margot lit a cigarette, shaking the match out and tossing it into the ashtray like a practised smoker. Picking up her drink she laughed. 'Down the hatch.'

'Down the hatch.' He clinked his glass against hers.

'I've never been in a public house before.'

He lit a cigarette. 'They're usually a bit nicer than this.'

She looked around her again, at the dark brown walls, the spluttering gaslights that made the absence of comfort or warmth even more obvious. Too lightly she said, 'I suppose you've been in lots of places like this.'

'A few.'

'In France?'

'They're different over there.'

'How?'

'Just different.'

'You don't want to talk about it. That's all right.'

He laughed. 'Over there they call them cafés. They put tables on the pavements outside and serve wine and food.' He looked at the barman slowly twisting a dirty cloth into a pint glass. Turning back to Margot he said, 'You can order a cup of coffee and a glass of cognac and sit and watch the world go by.'

'And French women go by?'

He took a long drink. Wiping away a beer froth moustache he caught Margot's eye and smiled. 'Thirsty.'

'You've almost finished it!'

64

Draining what was left in the glass he stood up. 'I'll have another while you finish that.'

As he returned with a second pint Margot asked, 'Have you ever been to Paris?'

'No. I haven't been anywhere, really.' He laughed shortly, lighting another cigarette. 'Nowhere exciting, anyway.'

'I've never even been to London.'

'Then one day we'll go. Perhaps if you're with me I won't get so lost.'

'You got lost?'

'Hopelessly.' He smiled at her. 'Didn't you go on holiday when you were a little girl?'

'Once. We went to Scarborough for a week.' Quickly she said, 'What did you do in London? Were you on your own?'

'Yes, on my own. I was on leave, early in the war, ages ago. I didn't have enough time to get home and back so I got lost in London.'

'All on your own.'

He laughed. 'Yes, completely. Very sad.'

'But on your other leaves, what did you do?'

'I didn't have many. There was that one, in London, one other when I came home and slept for two solid days, and that last one, when I met you.'

'But the army sometimes held receptions for officers, dances, that kind of thing...'

He frowned at her. 'Who told you that?'

She blushed. 'Robbie.'

'I think that was before the war.' He gazed at her, her sweet embarrassment making him smile. 'Margot, I left school and like an idiot joined the army almost at once. Unlike Rob, who was his regiment's pride and joy, I was never invited to balls or the General's parties.' Gently he said, 'You were the first girl I danced with in my life.'

She looked down, running her finger around the rim of her glass. 'But you're such a good dancer.'

'We were made to dance together, at school. I was usually the girl.'

She smiled at her drink. 'May I have another of these?'

As he took Paul's money the landlord jerked his head in Margot's direction. 'On honeymoon, are you?'

'Visiting.'

The man laughed. 'Visiting, eh? We don't get many *visitors* this time of year.' Handing him an overflowing pint he said matter-of-factly, 'We've a room here. I do a nice cooked breakfast if she's up for it.'

Paul sat down and Margot said, 'What were you talking about with that man?'

'The weather.'

She smiled, closing her eyes as she took a long sip of her drink. 'I feel quite light-headed.'

'We should get you something to eat. You shouldn't drink on an empty stomach.'

She smoothed her skirt over the small bump. After a moment she said, 'That man was talking about me, wasn't he? Saying what a hussy I must be for drinking and smoking and...'

'And?' Paul smiled.

'And going out with soldiers.'

'Soldiers?' He looked around the darkening, shadow-filled pub. 'I don't see any soldiers.'

'You.' She sighed. 'You know what I mean ... anyone can see you were a soldier ... especially when you wear that coat.'

Finishing his drink he hauled her to her feet. 'I think we'd better go and find you something to eat.'

Along with everywhere else, the fish and chip shop was closed and they walked towards the station, both sobered by the cold evening air. Margot looked at him sheepishly. 'He wasn't talking about the weather, was he?'

'He thought we were on honeymoon.'

'Honeymoon? Here?' She looked at him, astonished. 'Who would come here on honeymoon?'

Carefully Paul asked, 'Would you have liked a honeymoon?'

'I don't know.' She blushed. 'I suppose I thought it wasn't appropriate somehow.' Brightening, she smiled at him. 'I'd like to go dancing at New Year, though. I think that would be nice.' She laughed slightly. 'Remember when we danced together at my party?'

He remembered the feel of her in his arms, her body so stiff, as though he repelled her. Although he'd bathed in almost scalding water he'd imagined he stank, that itchy, lousy smell, sweet as decay. She had smelt of steamed roses. He smiled to himself, remembering how much he had wanted to lead her away to some quiet place just so he could breathe her calming scent in private.

Margot was laughing. 'When we danced you looked so pained and bored, I told Robbie I thought you were very rude.'

Recollecting himself he said, 'And Rob agreed.'

'No. No, he didn't.'

'He told me I should buck up.'

'It was a terrible party, anyway. You had every right to look bored.'

'I wasn't bored.'

'No. I realise that now. You're just shy, like me.'

She stopped walking and turned to face him, holding his gaze for so long he imagined he could see himself in her eyes, a slight, shy boy trying to live his brother's life. At last she reached up and touched his cheek. 'You look so sad, sometimes. I'm so sorry, Paul, for all this.'

Her hand was cold and he pressed his face against it, turning to kiss her palm. She groaned softly, a low needy sound and he pulled her into his arms. He kissed her, tasting the sweetness of port wine as she held him tightly. She must have felt his erection through their clothes because she made that same raw noise again.

Holding her face so that she'd meet his gaze he said, 'Let's go back there ...' He searched her eyes, smiling because they were so bright and large. Kissing her again he said, 'Let's have a honeymoon.'

'Shall we?' She seemed shy suddenly, glancing away towards the dark sea and the distant lights of ships. Managing to look at him she said awkwardly, 'I think you're terribly handsome, you know.'

Taking her hand he led her back along the street towards the lighted windows of the King George public house.

The bed was hardly wider than a single bed, its sheets smelling of rainy back streets. There were thin, satin-trimmed pink blankets gathering in deep furrows at their feet and trailing on to the floor. The room was too warm for blankets; it seemed to have sucked up the heat from the room below, drawing it through the cracks in the floorboards just as it drew the laughter and chatter from the bar. Naked, with only a sheet covering her, Margot lay still, listening. Laughter rose and fell; greetings and insults were exchanged. Paul slept on, mumbling anxiously at a sudden burst of noise.

The landlord had been deadpan when they arrived back at his pub. Taking a key from a hook behind the bar he had led them up a steep flight of stairs and along a short corridor, its carpet as sticky as his pub tables. His swinging lantern cast his huge shadow on the wall ahead of them, a hunched, scary monster, intensifying her nervousness. Unlocking the room he'd stood back, smiling broadly at Paul only to resume his poker face as he handed him the key.

Paul turned to her as soon as the man had left. 'You don't have to go through with this.' Taking out his cigarette case he sat down on the bed and lit two cigarettes at once. He handed her one and she noticed his hands were shaking. 'We can still go home, if you want to.'

There was a chest of drawers beside the bed, the only other piece of furniture in the room. Balancing the cigarette on its wooden edge she took off her hat and began to unbutton her coat. Without another word Paul got up, keeping his back to her as he began to undress. Naked, he climbed into the bed, lying on his back and staring at the ceiling until she climbed in beside him. The sheets were cold and she shivered.

He turned on his side, drawing her close to him. His erection nudged her belly and she was shocked into stillness, afraid as she remembered the hot, tearing pain of that first time with Robbie. From the pub came a shout of laughter and he held her even tighter.

He smelt of musk, nothing like his usual scent. The smell made her want to bury her face in his chest and the pits of his arms. He was hairier than she had expected, his chest covered in coarse, springy hair, jet-black against the paleness of his skin. She curled her fingers into it and he pressed her hand flat against his chest. His heart beat steadily beneath her palm and he kissed her.

'You taste sweet, of port and lemonade. It's delicious.'

'You taste of cigarettes.'

'Sorry. Such a filthy habit.'

'You were smoking the first time I saw you. Just standing in our garden, staring out into space, smoking. You looked so sophisticated.'

'And you thought "What an arrogant boy".' For a while he was silent and she shifted in his arms until her head rested on his chest. He stroked her hair steadily. At last he said, 'I feel clumsy, a bag of sharp bones.' He hesitated, then, 'Should I just hold you? Would you prefer it if I just held you?'

Her disappointment surprised her. Carefully she said, 'We're married, now.'

'I've never done this before.'

He shuddered and she sat up a little, causing the sheet to fall away from her. Daring herself to be bold she took his hand and pressed it against her breast. Her nipple hardened against his palm and he closed his eyes, before pulling her down on top of him.

Going home on the train Margot fell asleep, her head resting on his shoulder. Paul avoided eye contact with the other passengers. Dishevelled and unshaven, he imagined he stank of sex, that everyone must surely be able to smell it on him. He closed his eyes, Margot's body a weight against his. She smelt only as she always did, of fat, blowsy roses.

As the train trundled towards Thorp, he thought of Adam, feeling the same guilt he always felt on the very few occasions he'd been unfaithful to him. He opened his eyes, staring out of the window, remembering.

He'd been sleeping in a chair beside his hospital bed, and

had woken, startled at the sound of Adam's voice.

'I'm sorry,' Adam said, 'I didn't mean to make you jump.' He'd stood over him, smiling with all the awkwardness of any visitor to an asylum, although he'd visited often. 'Here.' He held out a package. 'I bought you some sweets.' Pulling up another chair Adam sat down, watching uncomfortably as, one after the other, Paul ate all the toffees he'd brought.

'You'll be sick.'

'Would you like one?'

'No, I bought them for you. I just didn't expect you to eat them all at once.'

As though he thought he wouldn't be heard above the rustle of wrappers, Adam waited until the last sweet was finished. 'I heard about Rob. I'm so sorry, Paul. I don't know what to say.'

The toffees had made his tongue raw. All the same he craved another. He looked down at the empty wrappers on his lap, feeling through them for one he might have missed.

'Paul? Did you hear me?'

'Yes.' He looked up at him. 'Robbie's dead. There's nothing to say.'

After a long silence Adam said, 'How are you?'

He lit a cigarette, wanting a contrast to the burning sweetness. Pinching a stray strand of tobacco from the tip of his tongue he said, 'You know how I am. They cut my eye out. Other than that, I'm fine.'

Adam sighed. 'I'm still missing you, counting the days until you're home.'

'Do you really miss me?'

'What kind of a question is that? Of course I do! I love you, you know that.'

He thought of Jenkins, his body slumped against his own. At last, remembering Adam's presence, he said, 'You wouldn't love me, if you knew what I'd done.'

'What? Paul, I can't hear you if you mumble.' Frustrated, he said. 'Paul, won't you *try* to pull yourself together?'

The train began to slow. Fellow passengers folded their newspapers and collected coats and briefcases. Margot smiled at him, sleepily. 'Are we home, already?'

He nodded. Getting up he busied himself with buttoning his coat so that he wouldn't see the fragile happiness on her face.

Chapter Eight

Her mother found the gloves Patrick had forgotten on Christmas Eve. She laid them on the kitchen table in front of Hetty, silently waiting for an explanation. Unable to keep the exasperation from her voice, Hetty said, 'If you must know he carried the chicken home for us on Christmas Eve.'

'Who did?'

'You know who. You know they're Patrick's gloves.'

'Oh, it's Patrick, is it? Not Mr Morgan any more? I suppose you're all free and easy with him now you've asked him into our home? Well, next time, Madam, you ask me if you can bring men into this house. You don't do it behind my back.'

'It would have been rude not to ask him in. Especially after he'd given us the chicken.'

'I didn't ask for his charity. Tough as old boots, anyway. I've told you before I don't want meat from that shop.'

Hetty picked up the gloves, turning them over in her hands, wanting to press them to her face to see if they still smelt of him. He hadn't missed them, as far as she knew. Planning to return them to his house each evening, each evening her courage failed and the gloves remained in their hiding place.

She said, 'You shouldn't go looking through my things.'

'Looking through your things?' Her mother laughed scornfully. 'Tidying up after you, don't you mean? Putting *things* away. If you want to keep secrets you should keep them more carefully.'

Hetty put her coat on, thrusting the gloves into the pocket.

'Where're you going?'

'I'm taking them back to him.'

*   *   *

She would say, 'You left your gloves at our house on Christmas Eve. I'd forgotten all about them until this evening, and as I was passing your house anyway ...'

Hetty sighed, nervously fingering the gloves in her pocket. With luck he'd be home. If she missed all the cracks in the pavement he would smile and ask her in and his brother would be safely tucked up in bed.

Outside his house she stood at the gate, surprised to hear music coming from the lighted room that looked out over the small front garden. A man spoke above the music that came to a sudden end with the sound of a gramophone needle being scratched across a record. Another voice, unmistakably Patrick's, decided her. Walking up the path she pulled the front door bell.

'There's someone at the door, Patty. Go and see.'

'I'm not expecting anyone.' Patrick slipped the gramophone record into its sleeve and put it away. 'They'll go away if we ignore it. It's time for your bath, anyway.'

The bell rang again and Mick wheeled himself over to the window. Lifting aside the lace curtain he peered into the darkness.

'It's that little shop girl of yours.'

'Are you sure?' Patrick caught sight of Hetty over Mick's shoulder. He groaned. 'I'll get rid of her. Wait there.'

Hetty said, 'Oh, Mr Morgan ... you're home, then.' She looked surprised to find herself there. Her usually pale face was even paler against the dark scarf wrapped around her throat. Awkwardly she said, 'I hope I'm not bothering you.'

Behind him Mick said, 'Hello, Hetty. Please, come in. You must excuse my brother keeping you on the doorstep. He's not used to visitors.'

Patrick ignored him. Still standing in the doorway he said, 'There's nothing wrong, is there?'

'Oh, no. No!' Hetty laughed as though the idea was outrageous. 'I was passing and ...'

'For God's sake, let the girl in. You can see she's freezing.'

'It's all right. I'll go if it's inconvenient.'

Patrick stood aside. 'You'd better come in.'

Mick poured her a glass of sherry; he even cut her a slice of the last of the Christmas cake. He talked too much, as he always did when he felt others were embarrassed. Eventually, as Hetty calmly sipped her drink, Patrick realised that it wasn't Hetty who was embarrassed, but Mick himself. His stream of words had dried up and he smiled desperately at Patrick, willing him to end the silence.

Patrick cleared his throat. 'That's a pretty scarf, Hetty.'

'Thanks. It's Mam's. I bought it for Christmas but she lets me borrow it.'

Mick said, 'Did you have a nice Christmas?'

'Quiet.'

'Ours was quiet, too. Wasn't it, Patrick?'

'Very.'

Mick laughed, a short, embarrassing burst of noise. 'We should all have a rowdy New Year to make up for it. We should go dancing ...'

'That would be lovely.' Hetty grinned. 'Somewhere posh with a nice band.' She looked at Patrick, adding, 'Somewhere they let balloons down from the ceiling at the stroke of midnight.'

'The Grand used to do that kind of thing, didn't it, Pat?'

'I don't know.' Turning to Hetty he said, 'I was just about to help my brother to bed, Hetty.'

She fumbled in her coat pocket. 'Oh! Nearly forgot.' Handing him a pair of gloves she said, 'You left these at our house the other day. I was passing and I thought ...'

'It was kind of you.' He stood up. 'Well, if that was all.'

'Yes. Right.' Placing her glass on the table she smiled shyly at Mick. 'Thank you for the drink, Mr Morgan. And the cake.'

'My pleasure, Hetty, and call me Mick, please.'

Patrick held the door open. 'I'll see you out.'

As Patrick came back into the room Mick glared at him. 'You shitty, bloody bastard.'

Gripping the arms of the wheelchair Patrick brought his face up close to his brother's. 'I told you I'd get rid of her, didn't I? But no, you had to ask her in *and* show me up as well! Thanks, Mick. Was that little charade worth it?'

Mick took his cigarettes from his pocket. His hands shook as he struck a match. 'You were rude.'

'Rude!' Patrick laughed. 'That's bloody priceless coming from you.'

'She's a nice girl.'

Patrick stood up straight. 'I don't want to encourage her. She's an employee, not a friend.'

'Of course! God forbid we might have any friends!'

Patrick gazed at him, his anger slowly ebbing away. 'You're tired. She could see how tired you are. She wasn't going to stay long, anyway.'

'All the same you had to remind her how bloody helpless I am.'

'I'm sorry.'

'No, you're not. You like everyone to know you do everything for me. Well, what a great big bloody selfless bastard you are! I wish you'd left me in the hospital. At least there …'

'Go on. At least there what?'

'I had people to talk to.' Sullenly he said, 'I wasn't alone all day, every day.'

'Shall I take you back there? You can take up basket weaving again. So, seeing as you miss it so much, first thing in the morning off we go.'

'All I'm saying is she could have stayed a little longer.' He bowed his head. 'She could have stayed. We were getting along.'

Patrick sighed. 'She came to see *me,* Mick. You know what she's after.'

'So? Marry her. Once she finds out you can't get it up for her maybe she'll find her way into my bed.'

'Don't be so disgusting.'

'You're disgusting. A lovely girl like that showing an interest and all you can think about is buggering some whey-faced, lisping boy.'

'He doesn't lisp.'

Mick laughed. 'Doesn't he? I could have sworn....'

'What do you know?'

'Oh, we've met, *Paul* and I.'

'When? When did you meet?'

'Oh, sometime. Can't remember.'

'Liar! Fucking Liar!' Patrick seized Mick's arms, digging his fingers into the flesh. 'You're just lying now.'

'Let go.'

'And what can you do about it if I don't?'

Drawing his head back Mick spat in his face.

'You filthy bastard.' Patrick wiped the spittle away, glaring at his brother as he stepped back. 'I think I will take you back to that hospital. I really think I will.'

'And close the shop for a day? I don't think so.'

'No? Well, wait and see.'

Mick tossed his cigarette stub into the fire. He smiled slowly. 'I suppose you could always dump me there on a Sunday when the shop's closed. Bit of a bugger getting there on a Sunday, though. And on Sundays there'll be no one at the hospital to do the paperwork. They're very strict about their paperwork.'

'Well, they can just leave you sitting in the drive until Monday, then, can't they?'

'Oh dear.' Mick lit another cigarette. 'You *are* cross. Poor me.'

'You're pathetic.'

'You and me both.' He looked up at Patrick through a haze of cigarette smoke. 'I bet Hetty's got gorgeous tits. Not too big. Just nice. You didn't have to be so off-hand with her.'

'Yes, I did. Now, do you want that bath or not?'

They were identical twins, a novelty act dressed up in matching outfits: sailor suits with beribboned caps, blue velvet breeches with white knee socks. Their mother spent too much time brushing their hair, smoothing it into exactly matching neatness. She wanted others not to be able to tell them apart, a

76

trick she played on the world until even their own father couldn't be bothered to tell which was which.

Patrick stooped over the bath, dipping his hand in the water to test its temperature.

Mick smiled at him. 'Just the right degree of boiling?'

'Just. Ready?'

Mick nodded, putting his arm around Patrick's shoulder as he was lifted from the chair. He closed his eyes, sighing as the water covered him.

'Hot enough?'

Mick nodded.

'Call me when you've finished.'

'Pat … don't go for a minute. I've been thinking …' He laughed, frowning down at the water. 'What have you put in this bath? It smells like one of Mother's handkerchiefs.'

'Lavender. It's supposed to help people sleep.'

'People? How about bad-tempered cripples?'

'It might help. You never know.' Patrick sat on the edge of the bath. 'So, what were you thinking?'

Drawing a deep breath Mick said quickly, 'I was thinking maybe we could go dancing, Hetty and I. Oh, you could come too.'

'Could I? Thanks. Where shall we go? Paris?'

'The Grand Hotel.'

Patrick laughed. 'The Grand Hotel? The Grand Hotel with all the steps leading to the doors?'

'We could manage a few steps.'

'You mean I could.'

'All right. You could.'

'You're joking, aren't you?'

'They're holding a New Year Dance. I saw it advertised in the paper. And Hetty said she'd like to go.'

Patrick stared at his brother. The lavender-scented steam seemed to blur his features, making him look younger and less like himself. His eyes were wide with hope.

Shaking his head Patrick said. 'She's made quite an impression on you, hasn't she?'

'I can't stop thinking about her tits.'

'Mick …'

'Oh, don't *Mick* me. I don't want your sympathy. I just want to take a girl out.'

'To a dance? You know how people stare at the best of times.'

'I stare back.'

'Hetty will want to dance.'

'You can dance with her.'

'Which will give her the wrong idea entirely.'

'Not if you behave as you did tonight.' After a moment he said, 'We still look alike, don't we? Even now. If she likes you…'

'No, Mick.'

Mick sank lower into the water. 'Fuck off, then. Fuck off so I can have a wank in peace. After all, it's the only relief I'm ever likely to get. I knew you wouldn't agree to it. So fucking scared of a few stares! Just keep me hidden away till I rot.'

'You go out sometimes.'

'And you wheel me back again.'

'Because you get drunk and spew your guts all over me.'

'Once.'

'I get scared for you, when I'm not there.'

Mick looked at him. The cold tap dripped like the measured tick of a clock, timing the silence. At last he said, 'Please, Pat.'

'I don't know …' Patrick sighed, unable to think of a good enough reason why they shouldn't go. Knowing he would regret it he said, 'All right. I'll ask her.'

Mick exhaled a long breath. 'Thanks.' He closed his eyes and Patrick recognised this as his cue to go.

Cleaning the bath, hanging towels over the clotheshorse to air, Patrick tried to imagine asking Hetty to the hotel's dance. He saw her face brighten only to fall when he said, *'Mick's coming as well.'* He hoped she would turn him down, certain she wouldn't.

He ran cold water into the bath, sluicing away the last of the lavender suds. As children they had bathed together, their mother sitting where he had, on the edge of the bath, watching them with rapt indulgence.

No girl would ever have been good enough for her boys, but she would have hated Hetty more than most. So common, so coarse, with her rough hands and scrawny features. Such women didn't even wash properly. Involuntarily Patrick curled his lip in disgust. Hetty would smell of milk and blood and bone. All women did.

He remembered the whore's room, papered with a pattern of abstract flowers and Chinese dragons, hump-backed, serpent-like creatures with manic, goggle-eyed smiles. He had stared at them, counted their repeat around the walls and tried to imagine such creatures breathing fire as the girl worked on him. Her hands were small and brown with half-moons of dirt beneath her fingernails, her fingers surprisingly strong around his cock. She frowned over her task, tipping her head to one side so that he imagined her as a bird, poised over a half-buried worm. He'd closed his eyes. Reaching out he'd grasped her wrist and lifted her hand away. 'I can't.'

'Don't worry, pet, it happens.' Her voice was singsong Geordie. Into his silence she laughed. Lowering her voice she said gruffly, 'Not to me it doesn't.'

'What?' He opened his eyes to look at her.

'You all say it. I say *it happens* and you say *not to me it doesn't.*'

She had been kneeling at his side on the bed and she got up, the flimsy robe she wore falling open. A trickle of blood ran down her thigh and she drew the robe tighter around her. All the same he caught her scent, his mother's scent, ripe and fecund and suffocating. He gagged, stumbling to the basin in the corner of the room, vomiting Dutch courage under the grinning eye of dragons.

Chapter Nine

Her father had a new curate: a stocky, cheerful redhead who shook Paul's hand too vigorously, studying his face as though trying to decide which eye was real. As the curate, Martin Peters, asked Paul if he had accepted Jesus into his life, her father smiled at Margot as though some need for revenge had been partly satisfied.

Taking her to one side her father said, 'Your mother tells me he's found a job. Will he cope with a class full of boys, do you think?'

'Of course he will.'

'Well, I hope so, Margot. I hope he can take care of you.'

'He can.' She looked at Paul. Without thinking she said, 'Isn't he like Robbie? He even laughs like him.'

He frowned. 'I don't see Robbie in him at all. Robbie was a fine boy. And perhaps you've forfeited the right to mention his name.'

Humiliated, she looked away so he wouldn't see her eyes fill with tears. Her father sighed heavily.

'Have you a handkerchief? Then use it. We have a guest, please don't embarrass him.'

Margot walked out through the French doors into the garden, ready to cry as much as she liked. Once outside though she only felt childish, shivering in the cold without even a cigarette to occupy her. She glanced back into the brightly lit dining room. Her father stood with the curate and Paul, his expression still pained and angry. After a moment he touched the curate's arm, excusing himself.

Standing beside her in the garden he said, 'I'm sorry. Of course you can talk about Robbie if you wish.'

Unable to speak she smiled tearfully, taking his hand.

'Oh, you're cold!' He rubbed her fingers. 'Let's go in.'

'Not yet.'

'Don't cry, Margot. I'm sorry.' Exasperated he said, 'I'm just so angry still.' He looked back at Paul. 'What he did to you makes me angry. But I'm trying. I'm trying to get over it.'

'He's not as bad as you think – I really like him …' She thought of the night in the seaside pub and blushed.

'Like! You should be head over heels in love with him. Instead you're crying alone in the garden.'

Quickly she said, 'He's taking me to the New Year Dance at the Grand tomorrow.'

'And so he should! Now, dry your eyes and let's go in. Your mother's serving the tea.'

The curate reminded Paul of a sailor he had once fucked in the lavatories on Darlington Station. The sailor had a short, stubby cock nesting in the most vividly coloured pubic hair he'd ever seen. His skin smelt of hot, dry canvas and a mermaid tattoo swished her tail over his coccyx. He thought often about that mermaid. He was thinking about it now as the curate said, 'I'm afraid I spent the war in Blighty. Spent a lot of time pushing paper around in the War Office.'

The sailor hadn't been wearing underpants. He still wondered why this had seemed shocking. The mermaid had long, golden hair, of course, her tail undulating as he fucked him. Suddenly ashamed, he closed his good eye, leaving only the glass eye to look at the curate.

'Paul?' Margot slipped her hand into his, squeezing his fingers hard. She laughed awkwardly. To the curate she said, 'His eye gets tired.'

'Yes, of course. I understand.' They both blushed.

Placing a trifle in the centre of the table her mother called, 'Now, everybody, come and sit down. Help yourselves to tea.'

'Have some more trifle, Paul.'

Paul smiled at his mother-in-law. 'No, thank you, Iris.'

He hadn't used her name before and she smiled back at

him, pleased. Her plump, pink hands reached for the curate's bowl and spooned in another wobbling helping of raspberry sponge and yellow custard. Still smiling at Paul she said, 'You won't say no, will you, Martin?'

'No indeed, Mrs Whittaker.'

'Paul's about to become a teacher, Martin, we're very pleased.'

'A teacher?' He raised his eyebrows at Paul. 'That's important work.'

'Isn't it?' Iris beamed. 'I do think you'll make an awfully good teacher, Paul.'

'Do you, dear?' Reverend Whittaker frowned as though surprised. 'What makes you think so?'

'Daddy …'

Whittaker ignored Margot's anxious look. 'I think teaching is going to be quite a challenge for him.' He turned to Paul. 'Perhaps you should think about a less demanding career.'

'What would you advise, sir?'

'Clerical work? I don't know. What has the army equipped you for?'

'Oh, Daddy. Please …'

'No, Margot, let Paul answer. He's always so quiet, listening, watching.' He laughed shortly. 'We hardly know anything about you, boy, nothing at all, in fact.'

'What would you like to know, sir?'

'Don't call me *sir*. Are you deliberately trying to anger me?'

Coldly Iris said, 'What should Paul call you? Father? Reverend? Or Daniel, even?'

Whittaker stood up, tossing his napkin down on the table where it knocked over a jug of cream.

Paul set the jug upright again and used the napkin to mop up the spill. No one else at the table moved as Whittaker turned and walked out, slamming the door.

The curate laughed nervously. 'Oh dear. I'll go after him.'

'Yes,' Iris snapped. 'Go after him. I'm sure none of us can be bothered to.' She turned to Paul. 'He liked your brother, I'm afraid. He liked him very much.'

Paul said, 'We should take this cloth off the table before the cream stains.'

Quickly Margot said, 'Don't worry about that, Paul.'

Iris stood up. 'No, Margot, Paul's right. Help me clear the table.' She touched his hand. 'Why don't you go and have a cigarette? We can manage here.'

In a ruined church in a village close to Arras, Jenkins had sat down beside him. 'If you could eat anything, Harris, anything in the world, right now, what would it be?'

Walking along the path leading from the vicarage to his mother's grave, Paul remembered how Jenkins had reminded him of the hunger he'd been trying to ignore all day. Knowing Jenkins wouldn't leave him alone until he replied, he'd said. 'I don't know. Anything.'

'God – you've no imagination have you, Harris? You're no fun at all! Think about it, man! I know what I'd have – my mother's mince and dumplings. Custard for dessert. Just very thick custard, skin an' all. Mother's brilliant at custard.' After a moment he said, 'Your mother's dead, isn't she?'

Above their heads starlings darkened the sky, ready to roost amongst the charred rafters. Jenkins looked at him questioningly. 'That's right isn't it? I seem to remember you had a dead mother. What was that like, having your mother die on you?'

Brusquely Paul said, 'I don't know.'

'You don't know? Really? Your mother dies and you haven't a thing to say about it?' He moved closer to him, his forehead creased in mock puzzlement. 'And I would have thought you were quite the Mummy's boy, Harris. Yet you don't seem to care about her at all. You really are the limit, aren't you?'

He had wanted to keep silent to prove to himself that he didn't always have to rise to Jenkins's bait. Instead, hating the pompousness in his voice he said, 'She died when I was born.'

'Oh.' Jenkins turned away. Huddling further into his trench coat he stared straight ahead at the overturned altar. 'You killed her, then.' He laughed suddenly, making Paul jump.

'You know, Smith's custard tastes of onions. Christ knows what he does to it.'

They'd been marching to the forward trenches. Hawkins had seen the church and allowed them to stop for ten minutes. The men sprawled out on what was left of the pews, some sleeping, others staring into the spaces the shells had made, their faces grey with exhaustion, their uniforms caked in drying mud. From time to time one of the men coughed harshly, breaking the unnatural quiet as the crucified Christ looked down on them, his face and body taken up with his own agony. Paul stared at the cigarette smouldering between his fingers. The food Jenkins had conjured made his stomach growl with hunger and Jenkins glanced at him, and patted his knee before getting up. Paul kept his head bowed feeling every inch a coward as Jenkins stood over him. He heard him snort and flinched as Jenkins nudged his foot with the toe of his boot. 'Come on. Best foot forward, eh? Before you burst into tears.'

Crouching now at his mother's grave, Paul rested his hand on the angel's hip as he took the dead chrysanthemums from the urn at her feet. He turned away from the stink of their water, holding the slimy, dripping stems at arm's length as he carried them to the bin. Walking back to the grave, he pulled up a dandelion that had braved the cold, raking back the disturbed chips of white stone with his fingers. The angel wept into her hand, and he remembered his grandfather standing here next to her, weeping for his daughter. As a small child he'd imagined that the old man and the angel were trying to out-grieve each other.

'Paul?'

He turned around and Margot smiled at him shyly. She stepped towards him. 'I was looking for you.'

'The flowers had died. I didn't want to leave them for Dad.'

She stepped closer. 'Are you all right?' She stood across the grave from him seeming to read and re-read the names and dates inscribed on the stone. At last she said cautiously, 'Let me tell them about the baby.'

'No.'

'I want him to like you.'

'He wouldn't have liked me anyway.'

'That's not true! He liked Robbie.'

He looked at the angel, imagining the bodies of his mother, brother and grandfather buried beneath her feet, only to remember other bodies at the side of a French road, a neat row covered in blankets. Care had been taken for those particular dead; nothing for the camera to see but small differences in the lengths and sizes of the corpses. His men stood behind their shovels, posing solemnly, and the photographer, fussing over his equipment, caught his eye and smiled at him, queer to queer. Paul had only stared back, angered at the man's lack of respect for the dead, hating that he should capture their images inside the camera's black box. Even now he worried whether faces had been sufficiently well hidden.

He grasped the angel's wrist, wanting to pull her hand away from her face. The stone was worn, as though other fingers had worried it. He thought again of Jenkins. He remembered sitting in that ruined church, glancing at him surreptitiously from the corner of his eye, trying to work out if his growing paranoia was justified. Whether it was or not, he'd decided then that the only defence against him was to be silent, to give nothing of himself away.

The familiar paralysing guilt returned. He closed his eyes, appalled all over again at his own wickedness.

'Paul? I think we should go home.'

He had forgotten Margot and looked up in surprise. She smiled anxiously and took his hand. Curling it up in her mittened fist she led him towards the cemetery gates.

Chapter Ten

Hetty's father said, 'Do you think they should be taking that crippled lad out on a night like this?'

Her mother sniffed. 'He'll catch his death. I just hope he wraps him up warm.'

Smoothing down her freshly washed, misbehaving hair, Hetty said, 'Do I look all right?'

'You'll do.'

Behind her mother's back her father winked at her. 'She'll do, will she, Mother?'

'If she has to go at all.'

'Dancing at The Grand!' Joe shook his head in mock amazement. 'My little Henrietta.'

There was a knock on the front door and Hetty jumped. Wearing a dress in the new, shorter style and new, heeled shoes instead of her usual button boots, she felt less like herself than she had ever done in her life, her chilly ankles indecently exposed. Even her underwear was new and too scratchy; the new-fangled, flesh-toned silk stockings she'd squandered her savings on seemed to rustle with each move she made. Too late to change into something else, she wished she'd worn at least one thing that was soft and quiet and reassuringly hers.

Hetty felt the cold air as her father opened the door on to the street. Her heart beat faster as she heard him invite them in. Nervously she went to the door herself, finding the three of them on the pavement, a gang of neighbours' children gathered around Mick's chair.

Mick smiled at her. 'Hetty. You look lovely. All set?'

The wheelchair made Joe awkward and he grinned too

broadly. 'Doesn't Major Morgan look smart, Hetty?'

'I'm not a major any more, Mr Roberts. Please, call me Mick.'

Tersely Patrick said, 'Are you ready, Hetty?'

'Yes.' She smiled as brightly as her father had.

'Have a nice time, pet.' Joe squeezed her arm. 'Burst a few of those midnight balloons for me.'

Mick lit a cigarette and handed it over his shoulder to his brother before lighting one for himself.

'What do you think, Hetty, quails' eggs on the buffet or pork pies? How grand is The Grand these days?'

'I don't know.' She stumbled beside them, her shoes pinching. Mick exhaled sharply.

'Patrick. Please, it's not a race.'

Patrick slowed a little.

Hetty had often imagined holding her wedding reception in The Grand Hotel. She had thought carefully about the reception, the cold hams and salad, the trifle bobbled with whipped cream. There would be roses in tall vases and a cake with four tiers. Lately she'd imagined Patrick in a morning suit, a carnation in his buttonhole, brilliant white against feathery green fern, matching her trailing bouquet.

They stopped at the hotel steps. There weren't many; Hetty counted each one as she stood beside Patrick, five in all. Patrick drew on his cigarette heavily as he too seemed to count the steps like an athlete gauging the size of the challenge. Turning the wheelchair around so that Mick faced away from them he said, 'Ready? Here we go.'

That afternoon, for the first time as a married man, Paul had visited Adam. They'd gone to bed at once, Adam leading him wordlessly up the stairs. Afterwards Adam held him too tightly. Paul could feel his breath against his shoulder as Adam whispered, 'Do you love me, still?'

He hesitated a fraction too long because he felt Adam's body stiffen and knew that he was holding his breath. For a moment he felt as though he could kill him simply by

87

remaining silent and so he said quickly, 'I love you, of course I do.'

'Of course?' Adam's laugh was strained. 'Your marriage hasn't changed anything?'

'No.'

Adam hugged him even closer. 'I've been so jealous these past few days, thinking of you and her.'

Paul struggled from his arms and turned on his side to face him. Desperate suddenly to reassure him and ease his own guilt he said, 'Don't be jealous. I don't want you to think like that.'

'Like what? It's normal, isn't it? My lover sleeps with someone else every night, therefore I'm jealous.' He sighed, taking off his glasses and rubbing his hand across his face. 'I thought this Christmas we'd be together. For the first time in years I thought we could spend Christmas together.'

'I'm sorry, Adam.'

'Yes.' He sat up and put his glasses back on. Sitting on the edge of the bed he glanced at him over his shoulder. 'You're sorry, I know.'

Paul reached out, placing his palm flat against his back. Adam's skin was soft as a child's, and so white it was almost translucent. In the summer the freckles on his arms would darken and auburn would show in his hair. In the sun he would burn easily and if they placed their arms side by side his own skin would appear dark as an Indian's in comparison. Moved to tenderness, Paul sat up and slipped his arms around his waist. He kissed his shoulder and Adam turned to look at him.

'Remember our first Christmas?' Adam laughed shortly. 'God, I was nervous! If it hadn't been for you taking charge … I never could quite believe my luck, you know. 1914. Best Christmas of my life.'

'Mine too.'

'It could be like that again, you know.'

Paul laughed. 'Could it?'

'Yes!' Adam twisted round to face him. Becoming animated he said, 'Make an excuse to her – we could spend a whole day and night together. We could make up for all that time we lost.'

Paul lay down on the bed. He held his arms out. 'Lie down, eh? Let me hold you before I have to go.'

Adam lay down, resting his head on his chest. 'You don't take me seriously.'

'Things have changed, that's all.' Paul lifted his head to smile at him. 'I'm not sixteen any more, Adam.'

'Don't I know it.' He sighed. 'At least we'll be together at school, eh? At least we have that.'

Paul stroked his hair, thinking of his interview with the Headmaster, the sense of panic he'd felt as he'd accepted the offer of a job. Perhaps he'd been too hasty, there had to be other work he could do. Shop work, he thought, and tried to picture himself behind a counter in Robinson's, earning even less money than the school offered. It would be difficult enough to keep a wife and baby on a schoolteacher's salary, impossible on a clerk's. And of course it would be different teaching boys rather than being one of them. At least he wouldn't be entirely at their mercy.

He let his hand rest on Adam's head. 'At school – you'll show me the ropes? Make sure I'm not too much of a new boy?'

'You won't need me to mother you! Standing up in front of a class of twelve year olds?' He laughed. 'Christ – it's nothing compared with everything you've been though.' Smiling up at him he said, 'You're not worried, are you?'

'No. I suppose not.'

'I can't wait. Seeing you in the staff room, being able to talk to you without worrying about what other people might be thinking. I don't think I've ever been in a normal situation with you.'

'Normal?'

'You know what I mean.'

Paul resumed stroking his hair, remembering the first time they'd met and whether that situation could be considered normal. The day he left school for good Robbie and George had met him off the train, bringing Robbie's new friend Adam along for the ride. He remembered being light-headed with the relief of never having to see Jenkins or his gang again, that he'd greeted his father and brother with uncharacteristic joy, like a long-jailed prisoner finally released. Some of that joy had spilled over to Adam, who'd seemed bemused by this manic boy. They'd shaken hands and for a moment Paul had become still, the noise of the station retreating. Adam had held his gaze, his hand dry and cool in his. Paul remembered some detached part of himself noting how handsome he was.

Adam shifted in his arms, drawing him closer. 'How will I be able to keep the pride from my face when I introduce you in the staff room? Half of the old crocks will fall in love with you at once, of course.'

'Only half?' Paul gently disentangled himself from his embrace and got up. Beginning to dress he said 'I think you have a skewed idea of my attractiveness, Adam.'

'No. I just think you're the most gorgeous boy that ever lived.'

Buttoning his flies Paul looked up at him. 'You'll be all right tonight, won't you?' Hesitantly he said, 'You could still come with us, if you want. Margot's friends will be there, you wouldn't be out of place.'

'Yes I would. Besides, I hate dancing. And dancing with her friends … Christ! I'd rather have my toenails pulled out.'

Dressed, Paul leaned over the bed and kissed him. 'Goodbye, Adam.' He kissed him again, drawing away as gently as he could when Adam curled his fingers into his hair. Paul remembered how much he'd looked forward to this afternoon in his bed. Now the sex was over with he couldn't wait to get away, wanting only to be alone. He thought of Margot waiting for him to take her to the hotel's dance and sighed miserably.

Adam caught his hand. 'When you're dancing with her remember I adore you.'

The dress Margot had worn for her birthday party didn't fit any more. She had tried it on but the buttons along the side seam wouldn't fasten, the material stretching obscenely across the bump even when she breathed in. Now the dress lay in a

90

blue silk puddle on the floor and she realised she had nothing else to wear for the dance that night.

She stood aimlessly in front of her open wardrobe, staring at clothes she had riffled through again and again as if a suitable dress might magically appear. At last she reached for the old-fashioned long black skirt and pale green blouse she had worn to the memorial service. The skirt would have to be held together at the waist with a safety pin.

Laying this dismal outfit on the bed she sighed. She was twenty and would look forty. Paul, wearing the evening jacket now hanging alongside her clothes, would look young and dashing and all heads would turn towards him. They would wonder what he saw in such a dowdy girl.

It was easy to imagine that there had been a sophisticated, older woman in his past. Paul had a gentleness that she imagined could come only from experience; that night in the pub he was slow and careful, making her feel she was as much in control as he was. Robbie, on the ground beside the Makepeace tomb, had acted so quickly that the shock had made her frigid. Although his kisses had softened her, even though she instinctively opened her legs, no one had explained the mechanics of it, that penetration had to be forced to overcome her body's resistance. She'd felt something give inside her and heard Robbie's gasp of triumph. Frightened, she'd laid still and stiff beneath him, hating the way he screwed his eyes tight closed as though he was the one being hurt. It was over quickly, that one and only time with Robbie. She had bled a little and in her innocence the idea of pregnancy hadn't even occurred to her until she'd realised she hadn't bled since.

After that night in the seaside pub, Paul had moved into her room, although he hadn't made love to her again. Lying beside him as he slept his troubled, talkative sleep, she worried that he might be repelled by her pregnancy; she felt huge beside him, fat and unlovable although he treated her with the type of kindness that could easily induce self-pity. She had an idea that Robbie would have been sterner with her. She wondered if Paul would be easier to love than his brother, suspecting that he might be.

Going to the window she looked out on to the street, straining her eyes against the dusk to see him. She had expected him home an hour ago and she began to worry. He still seemed frail to her; he may have fallen or fainted, he may have stepped out blindly in front of a tram. She exhaled sharply, afraid all over again for her future.

He appeared then, as though she had conjured him, walking quickly. Margot stepped back from the window. She would pretend not to have noticed the time. Drawing the curtains she began to dress for the dance.

Chapter Eleven

In the hotel lobby Patrick looked around, trying to guess which corridor would lead them to the ballroom. It would be too bloody easy for the bastards to put up a sign. But then this whole expedition was a crazy idea. They probably didn't even allow wheelchairs into the hotel. There was bound to be some regulation excluding them. He breathed deeply, trying to control the anger that had been building inside him all day.

Evenly Mick said, 'Patrick, perhaps we should ask that porter over there.'

'People are going in that direction.' Hetty smiled at Mick, her pinched little face white with cold and nervousness. 'I'm sure it's that way.'

Mick began to wheel himself along the corridor that Hetty pointed at. He smiled over his shoulder. 'Come on, you two. Looks like they've started without us.'

Outside the ballroom a table had been set up. A girl sat behind it. Ignoring Mick she turned to Patrick. 'Tickets?'

Patrick rummaged in the pockets of his dinner jacket, disturbing the smell of mothballs. At last the three squares of thick, jagged-edged card were found and handed over. Inspecting them as though they might be forgeries the girl said, 'If you want to hand your coats in, the cloakroom's along there.'

'Do you want to hand your coat in, Hetty?'

'Of course she does!' Mick laughed. 'And so do we.' To the girl who was adding their tickets to a small pile he said, 'Thank you.'

She ignored him 'It's two pence for each coat.'

Handing in their coats, Patrick looked back at the girl.

'Miserable little bitch.'

Mick frowned, glancing at Hetty who was preoccupied with peering into a tiny hand mirror taken from her bag. 'Don't talk like that in front of her. And cheer up. We're meant to be enjoying ourselves.'

'She didn't even look at you. Bloody rude!'

'I don't care! You're just making it worse by going on about it. Now smile, you're upsetting Hetty.'

Tables were arranged around a dance floor, a candle flickering on each one. Above the floor a net was suspended, captured balloons bumping against each other in the rising draught. On a stage at the far side a five-piece band played American Ragtime.

Mick grinned at Hetty. 'I'd ask you to dance, but …'

Hetty smiled back. 'I think we should find a table first. Catch our breath for a bit.'

'Good idea.' Manoeuvring his way towards the tables Mick looked back at them. 'What are you waiting for?'

Quietly Hetty said, 'It's nice to see him so happy.'

'Isn't it?' Patrick looked at his brother grimly as Mick pushed a chair out of his way, apologising to the party whose table it belonged to. No one moved to help him – they all seemed too shocked. Surprisingly, Hetty laughed.

'Come on,' she said. 'The cavalry's cleared a route for us.'

I look all right, Hetty thought. I look nearly pretty and I'm sitting with the two most handsome men in the whole place. She smiled to herself and surreptitiously glanced at Patrick. He was staring at the dance floor, his face as poker-straight as his back. She wouldn't worry that he hadn't smiled this evening, he was obviously concerned about his brother. They'd overheard a woman tut-tutting that such people really shouldn't be out in public places. Mick had pulled a face at the woman's back and she had laughed out loud.

Mick leaned a little closer to her. 'Has it lived up to your expectations?'

'I think it's lovely.'

He laughed. 'I'm pleased. I would have to complain to the

94

manager if the hotel had let you down.'

'Have you been here before?'

'Once. A cousin's wedding.' He lit a cigarette. Tossing the spent match into the ashtray he smiled at her. 'Have you been here before?'

'Me? No, never.'

'But you knew about the balloons.'

'Our Albert used to work here. He told me.'

He nodded, keeping his gaze fixed on her face as though trying to memorise her features. She found herself gazing back at him and he smiled slowly before looking down at his cigarette. 'Why don't you ask Patrick to dance?'

She laughed awkwardly. 'He should ask me.'

'He should.' Leaning across her he tapped his brother's arm. 'Patrick, dance with Hetty.'

As though he had been given an order, Patrick stood up and held out his hand, wordlessly leading her on to the dance floor.

The Grand Hotel was just as Paul remembered it when George would take him and Robbie for lunch on the last Sunday before the start of a new term. His father imagined this was a great treat. Neither he nor Robbie could bring themselves to tell him they were both dreading the return to school too much to enjoy it.

The porter remembered him, asking after his father as he took Margot's coat and led them along a corridor. They by-passed what looked like a queue to hand in tickets and another queue for the cloakroom and were ushered into the ballroom. The porter grinned as though he had shown them into the Palace of Versailles. He shook Paul's hand, 'Very glad to have you safely home, sir.'

Margot scanned the room. When the porter had gone Paul asked, 'Have you seen someone you know?'

'Edith Briggs. You remember her from our wedding? And Catherine Taylor. She said Ann would be here too.' Smiling suddenly, she pointed at two girls dancing together. 'Yes. There's Ann and Winifred.'

Paul lit a cigarette, taking his time so she wouldn't notice that his hands were shaking. Watching the two girls dancing together he realised with a sinking heart how few men there were to partner the women and that he'd be expected to dance with all her friends. His hand went to the glass eye and he drew on his cigarette deeply.

Margot smiled at him, her eyes bright with excitement. 'Shall we go and sit with them?'

Hetty said, 'This is nice, isn't it?' She'd been concentrating on her dance steps, looking down at her feet. Now she looked up at him, smiling anxiously.

She smelt of violets, sickly as cheap sweets; even her hair, a frizz of mousy curls, smelt of violets. She wore a dress of brown crushed velvet, reminding him of the skin of small rodents; he could feel her bones though its thin pile and imagined that he could hear her heart pounding fast as a vole's. He had forgotten how tiny she was, or perhaps he hadn't realised; in the shop she was quick and capable, larger than life in that enclosed space behind the counter. Here, on this half-empty dance floor, he felt like a giant dancing with a small child.

He looked up at the balloons. They would float down and be burst under foot with deliberate violence. It would take all his courage not to hide from the explosions under the table. He imagined cowering behind the cover of the starched white tablecloth. Mick would pull him out by the hair.

Smiling, Hetty waved at Mick. Mick waved back and went on watching them through a haze of cigarette smoke, his hand beating time to the music on the arm of his chair. Patrick remembered that dancing the waltz had always been one of the few things he could do better than Mick, that and slaughtering pigs.

Hetty laughed, still smiling at Mick. 'Mam said he could be charming when he wants to be, when he's not getting upset.'

'He treats your mother badly.'

'You heard about the liver and onions, then?'

'He told me. I'm sorry.'

'It's not your fault.' She smiled at him. 'No onions, next

time, eh?' He laughed and her smile broadened. 'That's better. You've looked ever so worried since we got here.' Very briefly she put her finger on his lips. 'And don't say sorry again. It's all right. I was worried, too.'

'About?'

'Showing myself up. Not being posh enough.'

'Posh enough?' He laughed. 'Posh enough for what?'

Nodding her head towards a group of young women giggling amongst themselves she said bitterly, 'Them. I bet none of them ever worked a day in a shop. See that one laughing? She's just moved in a couple of doors down. Newly wed and at least four months gone. She's nowt to be snotty about, that one.'

Patrick frowned at the girl. 'Is she snotty? She looks like a good sport.'

'Good sport?' Hetty snorted. 'You sound like one of them.'

He looked again at the girl. She stood next to a young man, only slightly taller than she was so that her head rested easily on his shoulder as she leaned into him. They held hands, he supposed that's what newly weds did, but then the girl snaked her arm around her husband's waist, drawing him closer. It was a sensual display for such a public place and Hetty laughed.

'No wonder she had to get up the aisle double-quick.'

The girl's husband looked around, as though he sensed they were watched. He stared straight at Patrick.

Later Patrick wondered how he managed to find his voice but at that moment he heard himself say, 'I know him. He was an officer in my platoon.'

'Oh? Should you say hello?'

He barely heard her. He was staring at Paul, a taste like gunmetal on the tip of his tongue, that sweet softening of his guts already starting.

Margot was saying, 'Oh, the new curate's awful! He has *red* hair!' She laughed, showing off, making him want to lead her away somewhere quiet so that she might calm down. 'Most curates are dismal, but *Martin!*' She laughed again. 'Martin's just awful.'

Edith said, 'What a pity,' and blushed.

Paul smiled at her absently, still shocked at seeing Morgan. He forced himself to watch him walk off the dance floor. It was definitely him: not many men carried themselves like Sergeant Morgan. He walked as if he owned the world.

Jenkins had said, 'Have you seen the new sergeant, Harris? I think we should send his photograph to the Kaiser. Immediate German surrender.'

Lying on his bunk Paul said, 'He's surly.'

'Surly, eh? Just your type, I'd say.'

Margot and her friends laughed, startling him back to the present. He lit a cigarette from the butt of the last, remembering Morgan lying beside him, still as stone as German voices joked in the nearby trench. His face, like his own, was covered in mud, like a blacked–up minstrel, only the whites of his eyes showing. A shell exploded and the minstrel eyes had fixed on his, mirroring his own fear. As the earth rained down he felt Morgan's arm on his back, his huge hand protecting his head by pressing him down further into the stink of those killed before them.

He looked up to see Morgan leave. Excusing himself to Margot, he followed.

Morgan sat on the hotel steps, his hands clasped together between his knees. Standing a few feet away, Paul hesitated. Shock had made him forget what his Christian name was. All he had ever called him was Morgan or Sergeant. Using either would make him sound like a prig.

He took a step down so that his feet were at the same level as the other man's thighs. After what seemed like a long time Morgan said, 'Hello, sir.' He got up. Even standing on the step below Paul, he still towered over him. He took out his cigarettes and lit one, tossing the match down. Seeming to make a great effort to look at him, only to look away again, he said, 'How are you?'

Paul cleared his throat. 'Fine. You?'

Quickly Morgan said, 'What do you think about all those

balloons?'

'Balloons? Oh … I suppose they'll make a few bangs.'

Morgan sat down on the steps again. 'It's too hot in there, I felt sick.'

Paul sat beside him, judging a careful space. 'Do you feel all right now? You look a bit green.'

Morgan laughed shortly, flicking cigarette ash at the space between his feet. 'I'm all right. Pulling myself together.'

He hadn't changed very much over the months. His hair was a little longer and he was cleaner and more closely shaved. He was the type that could shave twice a day, the type that would always have the shadow of a beard. Types like Hawkins cursed him as a ruffian. The fact that the army couldn't find a uniform big enough to fit him properly only added to the look. Now, however, his evening suit appeared to be tailor-made, cut so that it showed off his broad shoulders and narrow waist. He'd undone his collar stud as though about to undress and the bow-shaped ends of his black tie lay flat against his starched white shirt. The cloth of his trousers strained across his thigh and Paul's cock hardened despite himself. He remembered how attracted he'd been to this astonishing man, how difficult it had been to be around him and the tension in the air whenever he, Jenkins and Morgan were together. Jenkins's innuendoes had never let up; he'd felt like smashing his teeth down his throat.

After a moment he said carefully, 'When did you get home?'

'June.' Morgan dragged his eyes away from the middle-distance to look at him. 'I heard you got married. Congratulations.'

'Thank you.'

Morgan hesitated, then, 'I'm glad you're all right, sir. Recovered. After that business with Lieutenant Jenkins we thought ….'

Paul stood up quickly. The shock of hearing Jenkins's name spoken after so long set his heart pounding. His voice broke as he said, 'I have to get back to my wife.'

Morgan stood up too. Facing him he said, 'Don't rush off.'

He touched his arm and Paul flinched. Smiling slightly Morgan said, 'Sorry. You followed me out – I thought...'

'I have to go back inside.'

'Yes, of course.' He stood aside. As Paul was about to go in, Morgan said, 'I sometimes have a drink in the Castle & Anchor. Sunday lunch times.'

Paul nodded, and walked back into the hotel.

Margot sat alone at the table, watching her friends dance with each other. Flushed from the single glass of dark, sweet sherry she'd drunk earlier, blotches of red spread over her face and neck and she fanned herself ineffectively with her hand. Her waistband cut into her and she tugged at it, wondering if she dared unfasten the safety pin holding it together. Beneath her fingers the baby stirred, a faint rippling response. She pulled her hand away.

She had wanted to dance. She had wanted Edith and the others to watch her dancing with Paul and she had wanted them to be jealous. Instead, she watched her friends dancing, forcing herself to smile as they passed by. If they were jealous, they weren't going to show it. Ann had told her how good she was for not minding about Paul's glass eye. They all agreed on how delicate he looked, like an invalid. St Steven's asylum was mentioned – madness alluded to in questions dressed up as concern. From the corner of her eye she saw them exchange sly smiles. She had become the butt of their joke, and she'd looked away, searching for Paul.

Alone at the table she found her gaze drawn to the striking-looking man in the wheelchair two tables away. He talked constantly to the girl beside him, using his hands eloquently. Throwing his head back he laughed and the people on the table between them turned to stare. He stared back. After a moment he said loudly, 'I'm sorry – did you miss the punch line? I'll tell the joke again, if you like. *What's the difference between a nun on a bicycle and a whore on ...*' He stopped, frowning at the girl beside him. 'You know, now *I've* forgotten it!'

A man got up from the other table, outrage making his voice quaver. 'Can't you see there are ladies present? If you weren't in that chair I'd …'

'You'd what?' Motioning at the man with his cigar he said evenly, 'You're making a fool of yourself. Sit down.'

He sat, blustering, as the man in the wheelchair caught Margot's eye and smiled. She looked away quickly.

Behind her Paul said, 'Margot, I'm sorry … if I'd known you were on your own …' Margot turned to look at him. Sulkily she asked, 'Where have you been?'

Paul sat down and lit a cigarette, forgetting to offer her one. Eventually he said, 'I needed some fresh air.'

Bitterly she said, 'You missed all the excitement. That man over there nearly got into a fight with the man in the wheelchair. The crippled man was very rude.'

'Was he? Perhaps he had cause.'

Margot frowned at him. 'Are you cross with me?'

'No, of course not!' He got up, crushing his cigarette out. She noticed again that his hands were shaking. 'Come on. Let's show them how to dance.'

Chapter Twelve

Each Sunday morning Paul walked Margot to church, kissing her goodbye at the churchyard gates before crossing the road to Parkwood. This was the fourth Sunday of their marriage. Already a pattern was emerging, a structure to his life of work, home and weekends spent working in Parkwood's garden, neglected since he joined the army. Outside this respectable structure was the occasional evening he spent in Adam's bed. Further outside the boundaries were his thoughts of Patrick Morgan.

Digging out a diseased rose bush, Paul exhaled sharply. He'd been afraid of seeing Morgan again, knowing that one day he could turn a corner and he would be there. He'd always imagined that if he did see him he would walk away in the opposite direction, terrified of the memories that would be stirred up. But, of course, reality was different. In reality he lay awake at night imagining seeking him out at that pub he'd mentioned. He imagined taking him to some quiet place, Parkwood, perhaps, when his father was out, somewhere safely private where Morgan could do just what he wanted with him.

The first time they'd met Morgan had saluted him, bringing himself smartly to attention and making him feel small and weedy, unwashed and stinking after four days and nights in the front line trenches. At that first meeting he'd been too exhausted to notice just how staggeringly beautiful he was. Only later did his skin bristle whenever he stood close to him. Whenever they lay together in the waste of no-man's-land, beneath the once all-consuming fear, he felt protected.

Back in the relative safety of the trench he tried to believe that Morgan was only a competent sergeant, a hard man who cracked filthy queer jokes behind his back just as the other men did. In his heart, though, he knew what Morgan was; he gave himself away, at least to him. And to Jenkins, of course: Jenkins had an unwavering nose for queers.

Paul pulled at a dead rose and a thorn sliced through his gloves and into his finger. He cursed, tossing the glove down and sucking at the bright jewel of blood.

In Parkwood's kitchen George cleaned the wound, tut-tutting as he dabbed on stinging iodine. He glanced up at him. 'You should be more careful, I don't want you getting a blood infection.'

'It's nothing.'

'Oh, I know. No doubt you've seen worse. *Had* worse.' He sighed. 'It doesn't stop me worrying.'

Paul drew his hand away from his father's inspection. 'Don't worry. You don't need to any more.'

George made a pot of tea and set a large slice of cake in front of him. 'Mrs Calder made it. It tastes better than it looks.'

To please him Paul took a bite and surprised himself by finishing it. George smiled. 'I'm impressed. Another slice?' Watching as he ate he said, 'You're getting your appetite back, good. Only normal, in a boy your age.'

Paul laughed through a mouthful of cake. 'You make me sound like a child.'

'You are my child.' George sipped his tea. After a while he said carefully, 'Does Margot mind you not going to church with her?'

'No. I think he minds, though.'

'Whittaker's a fool.'

'Oh?' Surprised, Paul said, 'I thought you liked him.'

'I don't like the way he looks at you.'

Paul grinned. 'Neither do I.'

'I'm glad you think it's amusing.'

Paul got up and went to the window looking out over the garden. The lawns sloped down to the summerhouse, bordered on both sides by flower beds and high brick walls. Behind the summerhouse, sycamores and horse chestnut cast shadows over the kitchen garden where brambles and dock had taken over, strangling the gooseberry and currant bushes. Some of the glass in the greenhouse had been broken and the ashes from his last bonfire were a blackened, solid mass.

Certain he would be killed, Paul had burnt Adam's letters on that bonfire during his last leave. Calm, he threw the letters into the flames one by one. The wind blew charred fragments straight up into the sky and scattered endearments across the neighbours' tidy gardens.

Coming to stand beside him George said, 'The garden was too much for me when you and Robbie were in France. I hated seeing it go so wild knowing how much you loved it, the care you took with it when you were home. I just never seemed to have any time.'

'Perhaps it needed a fallow time.' He smiled at his father. 'A rest from my fussing.' He turned back to the garden. 'You don't mind me taking it over again, do you? I'm not intruding?'

'Intruding? For goodness sake, Paul! This is your home!'

'It's *your* home, Dad.'

He heard his father sigh, knowing what was coming next. At last George said, 'Why don't you and Margot come and live here? It seems silly spending your money on rent when I've so much room.'

'We're happy where we are, Dad.'

'Tanner Street isn't the best place to bring up a baby.'

'You sound like Whittaker. I'll find somewhere better, in time.'

'On a teacher's salary?' He hesitated before saying quickly, 'Paul, please change your mind and finish your degree. You wouldn't be away from home for that long and if you wanted to you could see Margot at weekends …'

'If I *wanted to*?' He frowned at him. 'I don't want to go away again. I've been away from home all my life.' He turned from the window. 'I have to go. I told Margot I'd meet her after the service.'

He was early; hymns were still being sung. Paul sat down on a bench outside the church to wait. He lit a cigarette, staring down at the gravel path, promising himself he would think about Patrick Morgan only for a little while, until the next hymn finished. The congregation drew breath and launched themselves into *Jerusalem*.

He thought about Patrick in evening dress, his tie loose, his cigarette held nonchalantly between his knees as he sat on the hotel steps. He could see that he had cut himself shaving; he could smell his beer breath, see that his teeth were white and straight and put his own to shame. There was a slight kink in his jet-black hair – with a gold hoop in his ear he would be a gypsy. He wore a signet ring on his little finger. He had always despised men who wore rings.

Paul flicked cigarette ash at the ground, remembering. They lay together in no-man's-land, Morgan's arm and hand heavy on his back and head, causing his helmet to cut into the back of his neck. He could hear him breathing, deep and steady as a fit man running, and he was afraid the Germans would hear. Their patrol was almost over. In a few minutes he would be drinking tea laced with rum, trying not to shake too obviously in case it disturbed the child sent to replace the last Second Lieutenant to have been killed. His teeth would chatter uncontrollably, causing Jenkins to make some bloody remark. Eventually the shaking and chattering would stop. The rum would make him feel light-headed. He had all this to look forward to, in a few minutes.

Morgan whispered, 'All right, sir?'

Paul nodded into the mud. The weight on his back and head lifted. He signalled that they should move on.

There wasn't any rum. Instead Hawkins saw to it that he was served tinned peaches and condensed milk, a reward for not being dead. Wide-eyed and silent, the replacement watched him eat until Paul paused, his spoon half way between his mouth and bowl and dripping peach juice. Meeting the boy's gaze Paul said, 'I've forgotten your name.'

'Davies, sir.'

'Stop staring at me, Davies.'

'Sorry, sir.'

Behind the boy's back Jenkins laughed. 'Don't mind Harris, old man. He's aloof with everyone. I've been trying to crack a smile from him for weeks now – he's just too serious-minded for ordinary chaps like us.' He looked at Paul, eyebrows raised. 'Can't seem to see the joke, can you, Harris?'

'Maybe you should explain it to me.'

'Oh, I don't think you're that slow, Harris. You'll catch on in your own time.' He'd looked at Davies. 'By the way, don't call him *sir*. It rather goes to his head.'

In the churchyard Paul frowned. Of course it was inevitable that in remembering Morgan he should also remember Jenkins. A rook hopped and flapped across a grave and he watched it, telling himself he must stop thinking about both.

Jerusalem ended.

'So, what next?' Mick looked out over the park lake. Closing one eye he made a pistol of his hand, taking aim at a swan swimming towards them. As if it really had been shot, the swan dived into the water. He turned to Patrick. 'Are we going home or are you going to go on staring into space like a love-sick girl?'

Patrick went on watching the birds on the lake. Thinking of Paul he said, 'We'll go home. It looks like rain.'

Mick began to wheel himself along the path. Over his shoulder he called, 'You could always knock on his door, you know. Knock knock. Oh, hello, Mrs Harris. Is your husband at home? It's just that I want to fuck him so badly I think I'm going to burst.'

Patrick had to run to catch up. Taking hold of the chair he swung it around so Mick faced him. 'Why don't you keep your filthy mouth to yourself?'

'It's only the truth, isn't it? Bugger the boy and forget him. You're beginning to get on my nerves.' He held his gaze for a while before manoeuvring the chair round and wheeling himself away.

*   *   *

Pushing the wheelchair along the street towards home, Patrick thought back to the time when he'd first realised he loved Paul. He remembered crouching close to a brazier as he brewed tea at the end of the trench furthest from the officers' dugout with Collier huddled beside him, his baby face blank from exhaustion. The shelling had kept up all day; Lewis, Anderson and Smith had been killed. He'd liked Smith. Pouring tea into a tin mug he handed it to Collier who cupped it in both hands. Tea slopped over his boots as the mug rattled against the boy's teeth. Patrick remembered thinking it would be better in a baby's bottle – less would be spilled.

He'd looked up to see someone emerging from the officers' dugout, adjusting the strap of his helmet tighter around his chin. Patrick stood very still, squinting into the darkness. From this distance all the officers looked the same. After a moment another emerged. The first officer turned to the second and adjusted the other man's helmet, too. Patrick watched more carefully. The first officer could only be Paul; only Paul would care enough to do such a thing.

The two began to walk towards the brazier, stooping slightly to keep their heads below the sandbags. He watched as Paul turned and smiled reassuringly at the other man, Davies, the new Second Lieutenant. He looked down at his tea. The two passed by with only the briefest acknowledgement. A shell exploded. Paul shoved the boy against the sandbags, shielding his body with his own.

He wondered if he'd loved him from that moment, or earlier as he'd watched him adjust the boy's helmet, if it was his tenderness or his bravery that made him feel as he did. Whenever he saw Paul he felt soft and sentimental, as though pity and desire had become confused. Perhaps it wasn't even love he felt but something far more basic: an overpowering desire to fuck him. First Lieutenant Paul Harris was by far the most fuckable man he'd ever seen. He wanted to keep him safe so that he might have him all to himself.

Mick said, 'Why have you stopped?'

'I need a cigarette'

'Here. Give it to me. I'll light it.'

'I can light my own.' His hands were shaking and he dropped the box, scattering matches over the pavement. He scrambled over the freezing flags, chasing matches that jumped away from him or fell between cracks. His fingers were clumsy, numb with cold, blotched pink and red and white like raw sausage.

As he stood up straight Mick held out his hand. 'Give them to me.' Lighting two cigarettes at once he handed one to him. 'Do you want to know what I would do if I were you? I'd forget him.'

Patrick laughed harshly. 'Would you? Fancy!'

'All right – what are you going to do? It's been weeks since that dance.'

'Three weeks, that's all.'

'Three weeks. He knows where you work, Pat. He knows where you *drink*. Don't you think if he was interested …' He exhaled sharply, exasperated. 'Jesus – I can't believe I'm even talking about this, as if he was some coy bloody girl playing hard to get! For Christ's sake, why can't you just forget him? Carry on like this and one of us will end up in the condemned cell.'

Patrick turned his back on him. They had stopped outside the Church of the Blessed Virgin. Beside the porch was a statue of Mary cradling the crucified Christ in her arms, a larger-than-life-sized portrayal of misery. The sculptor had concentrated on the agony of Christ's dying, his back arched so that each rib strained against the blue-veined marble skin. His arm stretched long fingers to the ground as his head lolled against his mother's thigh. Mary raised her face to heaven, betrayed.

Sighing, Patrick said, 'Do you want to go in and light a candle for Mam?'

Mick nodded, tossing his half-finished cigarette into the gutter.

On New Year's Eve, on the steps of the hotel, he'd had the urge to brag, 'The shop's up and running again now. Of course, it's in a good position – good passing trade, and I'm earning a reputation for quality … *There are rooms above. Empty, private …'* Thank God he'd kept his mouth shut.

Lying on his back in bed, Patrick slipped his hand beneath the waistband of his pyjamas, resting his palm flat over the warmth of his groin. He curled his fingers into his pubic hair, tugging the curls straight. He would allow the fantasy to build slowly. First, Paul in uniform, cap and polished boots, tapping a swagger stick against his thigh. Holding the image for a while he smiled, watching this fancy-dress Paul walk up and down outside the shop, waiting for him, of course, anxious, impatient. Once in the room upstairs he would hold Paul's gorgeous little face between his hands and kiss him roughly, backing him hard against the wall and tugging at the buttons of his tunic as Paul groaned, his eyes big with fear. It would be his first time.

Patrick's fist closed lightly around his cock. Opening his eyes, he stared at the ceiling. Of course Paul wasn't interested in him, Mick was right. He thought of him, dancing with his pretty wife, smiling into her eyes as though he loved her. Rolling on his side he cursed and brought himself to a quick, unsatisfactory climax.

Chapter Thirteen

Hetty said, 'Me Mam's poorly. She won't be able to see to Mr Morgan this dinnertime.'

She watched as Patrick went on jointing the pig. Its head sat on the counter beside him, its soft, dead eyes watching her above its broad grin. Wondering if he had heard she started again.

'I'm not deaf, Hetty.' He glanced at her. 'What's wrong with your mother?'

'A bad cough – she didn't want Mr Morgan catching anything.'

'No, of course.' He sighed, laying the cleaver down gently. 'He's expecting her. I don't like leaving him on his own all day.'

As she'd planned to she said, 'I'll go, if you like, the shop's quiet.' Even to her own ears she sounded reluctant and she expected him to dismiss the idea at once.

Instead he asked, 'Are you sure?'

Already anxious, she managed to smile. 'As long as you can spare me.'

'I'll pay you the same rate as your mother, on top of your normal wage, of course.' He turned back to the carcass as though the matter was settled. 'Twelve thirty, then. The key's underneath the lion. Let yourself in.'

Between outbreaks of coughing her mother had said, 'If he's left soup for him see that it's piping hot. He'll only make you heat it up again if it isn't. And he likes his tea strong, almost black. Don't chatter – he hates it. Set his tray with the good silver and a serviette. You'll find them in the third drawer of the dresser in the back room, all starched and ready.'

'I won't remember all that.'

'Yes, you will. He'll soon tell you, anyway. Soon lets you know when it's not right.' She smiled a rare, soft smile. 'He's a gentleman. Such good manners.'

'Except when you serve him liver.'

Her mother sighed. 'Aye, well. We can all lose our tempers sometimes.'

Crouching beside the hideous lion, Hetty fumbled for the key, shuddering at the woodlice that scattered in panic from her fingers. Nervously she opened the front door, squinting into the gloom as she stepped into the hall. 'Hello? Mr Morgan...?'

A door at the end of the hallway opened, banging against the wall as Mick wheeled himself towards her. He frowned, stopping a few feet away. 'Hetty? What are you doing here?'

'Mam's poorly. I've come instead. If that's all right?'

For a moment he seemed lost for words. He took off the glasses he was wearing, folding them into his shirt pocket and closing the book on his lap. Taking out his cigarettes he lit one, exhaling a long plume of smoke before finally looking up at her. 'Shouldn't you be at the shop?'

'He's spared me.'

'Right. Well, good ...' He wheeled himself towards her, awkwardly pushing open another door and waving her through. 'Please, come in. Sit down.'

This was a different room from the one she'd been shown into last time. The other room was cramped, busy with wallpaper and furniture and bric-a-brac. This room was empty except for a desk, a bookcase and a single armchair. There were no pictures or photographs, only the spines of books to look at, rows and rows so that the bookcase was full and still more were stacked on the mantelpiece and floor. Despite her nervousness Hetty asked, 'Have you read all these?'

'There were one or two I couldn't finish. Take your coat off, Hetty – sit down. Would you like a drink? Is it too early for a drink?'

He looked younger. His hair was washed but not combed

and there was a stain of something that looked like jam on his collarless shirt. The tartan blanket that usually covered him from the waist was missing, the legs of his grey flannels neatly folded and tucked beneath his thighs. Realising she had been staring she looked away quickly, unbuttoning her coat and draping it over the back of the armchair. 'I'd best get on, Mr Morgan, you'll be wanting your dinner.'

'I'm not hungry. Look, sit down. There's no hurry for any of that. Sit down and tell me what you've been doing today.'

She sat down on the edge of the chair, feet and knees together, hands folded in her lap, making herself as neat and demure as possible to hide the awkwardness she felt. She promised herself that in a moment she would make her excuses and escape to the kitchen.

He laughed self-consciously. 'I don't bite, Hetty.'

She made to get up. 'Mr Morgan, Mr Morgan told me I should see you get something to eat …'

'Too many *Mr Morgans*, Hetty. It might be less confusing if you call me Mick, as you did at the dance. We had a good time, didn't we? I didn't expect to enjoy it so much.'

'It was lovely.'

'Have you kept your balloon?'

'It's shrivelled up quite a bit.'

'I know the feeling.'

Noticing her blush he looked at his cigarette. 'Sorry. Always was hopeless in mixed company.'

She smiled. 'You've jam on your shirt.'

'Oh?' He frowned down at himself. 'Blast it, so I have.'

'Is that why you've no appetite? Filled up on bread and jam?'

Picking at the stain he said. 'Just the jam, actually.' When she laughed in disbelief he said, 'Don't tell Pat. He thinks it's decadent not to spread it on bread first. So,' he cleared his throat. 'Was the shop busy today?'

'Mondays are quiet.'

'Then he won't want you to rush back?'

'He didn't say.'

Patrick hadn't said anything, only nodded curtly as she

112

called goodbye, raising the meat axe to bring it down hard on a carcass. He'd been silent all morning. Earlier she'd dropped a tin tray on the tiled floor and its clatter made him jump so badly a woman in the queue had mouthed, 'Nerves. They're all bad with their nerves.' The rest of the queue had nodded sagely.

Hetty glanced at Mick. Nerves didn't seem to affect him very much. She wondered how he had lost his legs, imagining the horror of it. Ashamed of her gruesome thoughts she said quickly, 'Would you like me to make you a cup of tea?'

'No, thank you. Father Greene made me some earlier. I get the feeling he only ever makes tea when he comes here. He seems so keen to do it I haven't the heart to tell him I'm capable of boiling a kettle. Pat doesn't like me to, of course. He worries I'll scald myself reaching up.'

'I'd worry, too.'

He looked down at his cigarette, burnt almost to nothing between his fingers. Tossing it into the fire he said, 'Don't worry about me, Hetty. Waste of time. Now, tell me how you came to work for Pat.'

'I fancied a change from Marshall's.'

'From sugar pigs to real pigs? I would have thought the sugar pigs were pleasanter.'

'I like the shop.'

'Do you?' He lit another cigarette, frowning. 'I hated it. Dad made me work there every minute I wasn't at school, helping with the slaughtering out the back. Patrick and I were the only boys from Thorp Grammar who knew how to wield a meat axe.' He looked at her through a grey screen of smoke. 'As soon as I left school I joined the army to get away from it. Dad called me all the names he could think of. I told him I'd be a general. Shame he got himself killed before I was even a major – I would've liked to see his eyes pop one last time.'

'Don't you miss them?'

'I miss my mother.'

'I remember her. She was always so lady-like in her lovely clothes, so tall and elegant. I could never look like that.'

'Yes you could.' He held her gaze, just as he had at the

113

dance. As she was about to look away he said, 'I think you're very pretty. And you looked so lovely at New Year. I was proud to be with you.'

She blushed.

After an awkward silence he cleared his throat. 'You know, I've been stuck in this house for days. If Pat isn't expecting you back at the shop perhaps we could go out? The park is just at the end of the road ... we could take a turn around the duck pond.'

'Oh, I don't know ...'

He grinned. 'I look pale, don't I? As though I need some fresh air? And Father Greene said I'd go blind reading so much.'

'Did he?'

He nodded solemnly. 'Terrible blind. Now you don't want that on your conscience, do you?'

She stood up, taking her coat from the back of the chair. 'Once round the pond then straight back.'

Patrick locked the shop door, turning the sign to *Closed*. He'd had enough of customers, their grumbles and inane chatter, the way their fingers scrambled secretively in their purses like misers begrudging every dirty penny. The last one had wanted three sausages. Three bloody sausages. Her hands had been filthy.

He took the day's takings from the till and walked along the High Street to the bank where the grey-faced little snob of a clerk counted the pennies and half pennies as though they stank. Patrick stared at him, willing him to say a wrong word as the queue shuffled impatiently behind him. He noticed that the bag of copper had speckled the counter with grains of sawdust. He smiled to himself, gratified.

As the clerk weighed the coin he found himself thinking of Paul, remembering the first patrol they went on together. His beautiful face had been daubed with mud and all badges, all indications of rank, stripped from his tunic. Snipers shot at officers first. Paul had smiled at him encouragingly and he remembered having to look away. Lust, on top of such fear, was too much. He wouldn't look at him directly again until they were safely back.

Hawkins always sent Paul on these patrols because Jenkins was such a useless little get. Patrick had suggested once he would go alone with one of the corporals, no need to risk an officer. The man laughed his terrible, braying laugh. It was as if he believed Paul enjoyed these expeditions into no-man's-land.

The clerk was saying, 'Sign this, please.'

A slip of paper was pushed under the grille. Patrick signed it absently, thinking of Paul's slow, practised squirming through the ruts and furrows, how he kept his face close to the mustard-gas stink of churned earth. He had wanted to protect his body with his own as they crawled, covering his full length. He screwed his eyes closed.

Shoving the empty cloth bag under the grille, the clerk said pointedly, 'Good day, Mr Morgan.'

Patrick started, opening his eyes. He glanced over his shoulder and the next in line glared at him. Bundling the bag up he pushed it into his pocket and walked out.

Patrick wandered the maze of narrow alleys that ran off the High Street and were lined with second-hand bookshops and pawnbrokers and poky, beer-only pubs. Stopping outside a junk shop he gazed through its grimy window. Amongst the battered furniture and bric-a-brac a hollow elephant's foot bristled with crutches. Next to it stood a wheelchair, a luggage label displaying its price. He wondered what had become of its owner and found himself staring at the suggestion of an indent on the chair's seat, as though whoever it was had only recently been lifted from it. He shuddered.

He walked on until he came to the high walls embedded with shards of glass that shielded Marshall's sugar factory from sweet-toothed burglars. The factory backed on to the railway line. He could hear the trains rumbling their way west to Darlington or north to Newcastle. If it weren't for Mick he would steal a ride; he would lose himself in a larger place than Thorp, if it weren't for Mick.

He remembered the army doctor watching him as he signed Mick's discharge papers, his cool, condescending voice as he said, 'I hope you understand the enormity of what you're taking on.' This dapper little colonel in his pristine white coat and polished riding boots, and himself, a rough, awkward sergeant who imagined he could look after such a severely disabled man. Smiling the doctor said, 'Major Morgan isn't the easiest patient.' He should've told him to stick his stethoscope up his arse.

A train whistle screamed. Patrick stopped on the embankment a little past the factory and watched the train speed north into a tunnel. He'd been to Newcastle once during leave in the middle of the war. He remembered liking its vastness, nothing like the pitiful villages of France and Belgium, or the closed-in narrowness of Thorp. Imagining himself living and working there, he'd strolled along its streets. Girls had smiled at him. He must have looked happy, he supposed.

He walked on towards Thorp Station. Cheap cups of tea could be had from the station buffet where Bath buns sweated under their glass domes and a coal fire burned in an ornate grate. The buns were soft and sugary and delicious. Decisively, he crossed the street and bought a platform ticket from the station's front office.

Leaning into the doorway of the classroom Adam said, 'Well, you look the part, at least.'

Paul turned to him from wiping the blackboard. 'Looks are deceptive.'

'Oh dear.' Adam came in and perched on the edge of his desk. 'Bad day?'

Placing the blackboard duster down Paul said, 'I got through it. I don't think I taught them very much but at least there wasn't a riot.'

'Did you expect there to be?'

'I keep expecting them to spot what a weakling I am.'

'You're not weak.'

'Aren't I?' Wearily he said, 'Are you going home? I'll

walk back with you.'

'I was thinking we could ...' Adam laughed awkwardly. 'You know ... if she's not expecting you I could squeeze you in before Henderson arrives for his Latin tuition ...'

'I'm tired, Adam. All I want to do is crawl home, eat and go to bed.'

Adam followed him out of the classroom. As they walked along the corridor he said, 'How about after supper, after Henderson?'

'Not tonight, Adam.'

'It's been a while, that's all.'

'Less than a week.' Paul looked at him. 'I don't want Margot to become suspicious.'

'Why should she? We're friends, aren't we?'

They walked out of the school and into the yard. Boys still milled about. A football rolled at Paul's feet and he kicked it back in a curving arc. Adam raised his eyebrows. 'Impressive. Tell the boys you were a football player and all your worries will be over.'

Paul frowned at him, knowing from the brittle edge to his voice the mood Adam was slipping into. 'I'm sorry if you're disappointed.'

'Disappointed! Don't flatter yourself.'

They walked almost to Tanner Street without speaking. Finally Adam said, 'I suppose she'll be waiting with a meal on the table, little house all spic and span.'

'I doubt it.'

'Oh? She looks like the domesticated type to me. So, will you have to fry yourself an egg, or something? Christ, if I had a wife ...'

They stopped outside Paul's door. Hesitantly Paul said, 'I'll see you tomorrow.'

Adam ignored him and went on walking towards his own house five doors away.

There were no Bath buns, just a few rock cakes, yellow as sulphur and studded with dead-fly raisins. Patrick carried his cup of tea to a table by the window, rubbing a view-hole in the

117

condensation to look out at the platform. Two sailors were waiting, their huge kit bags lolling at their feet. He watched them, jealous of the easy way they stood and talked together. He had never been easy around other men, only Mick, and Mick didn't count.

After he had signed the papers in the doctor-colonel's office, a nurse had showed him along a corridor. He remembered glancing inside the open doors of the first ward he passed, catching a glimpse of five or so men playing cards around a table. All of them were double amputees, like Mick. All of them turned to look at him as he passed, defiantly dismissive of visitors with legs.

When the nurse left them alone together Mick said, 'Have you come to take me home?'

Patrick nodded. He sat down beside the cumbersome, institutional wheelchair that took up too much space in the bare little room deemed suitable for visitors. They hadn't seen each other for two years. Mick reached out and touched his face, sweeping his thumb under his eye.

'Don't cry, Patty. I'm all right.'

'I felt it, when you were wounded, the pain...'

'No.' Mick leaned closer. Taking his hand he ducked his head to look up into his downcast face. 'You only think you did, afterwards, when you found out. The shock ... it must have been the shock.'

'It was terrible.'

Mick smiled slightly. 'They gave me morphine so quickly, and then the doctors put me to sleep ... the pain was in your head, Pat. It wasn't real.'

'I thought I was going to die.'

Mick sat back in his chair. 'I'm so sorry, Patty. I tried not to think of you. I couldn't help it.'

The sailors climbed aboard their train. His tea had gone cold but he drank it anyway. Lighting a cigarette he thought of Paul again, idle, unfocused thoughts: Paul in dress uniform or in black tie and dinner jacket, a doll to dress up as the fancy took him; Paul as bridegroom, a yellow rose in his buttonhole. He saw again the girl on his arm and fought against the sudden surge of jealousy.

The tea finished, he walked out on to the platform. Suspended on a chain outside the waiting room a large clock face showed five o'clock. Patrick watched as the minute hand jerked past the Roman numeral twelve. He looked along the platform, anxious now even as his cock stirred in anticipation. Taking a deep breath he walked purposely towards the public toilets.

The man said, 'Not here.'

Boldly as he dared Patrick said, 'Where, then?'

'Follow me.' The man turned away from him. 'It's not far.'

He followed him out of the station toilets, keeping a few steps behind. They walked through the dark back streets, the man's furtiveness acting like a magnet, drawing him along. He didn't once look back. He's a fool, Patrick thought. Only a bloody fool would put himself in such danger.

The man pushed open a back yard gate and beckoned him inside. As soon as Patrick was in the yard the man shut the gate quickly, and hurried to unlock the door into the house. Even then he didn't stop. Patrick saw only a brief glimpse of a chaotic kitchen, pans in the sink and on the stove, their contents left to congeal. He breathed through his mouth against the smell of cold grease and damp.

The stairs creaked and he felt he should tiptoe to avoid the noisiest boards and that he should've taken off his shoes. He knew these poky terraced houses – the neighbours could hear a dog fart through the walls. At the top of the stairs the man glanced at him before pushing open the bedroom door. He went at once to the bedside table, picked up a photograph frame, and slipped it under the bed. Patrick almost smiled; the man had a sweetheart, then. He didn't want her pretty little face smiling out at him as he was fucked.

Neither spoke, only undressed by the light of a full moon shining through threadbare curtains. Naked, they lay down on the bed. Patrick stared up at the cracks in the ceiling and gently rested his hand on the man's thigh.

'Maybe you should take your glasses off,' he said.

'I'm blind without them.'

'Take them off.'

He sighed, taking off his spectacles and placing them on the floor.

Patrick rolled on to his side. Propping himself on his elbow he looked down at the skinny, hairless body beside him. The man smiled slightly and for the first time Patrick saw that he was handsome, perhaps even a little younger than himself. The smile stayed in his eyes, wry and intelligent, as though he understood the absurdity of their situation.

Kneeling now, the man bowed his head and closed his mouth around his nipple, biting gently as Patrick drew a sharp, surprised breath. His hand moved down Patrick's body, past his leaping, greedy cock, to rest on his thigh before pushing his legs apart. Lifting him slightly, he pushed a finger inside him, biting down harder on his nipple as Patrick arched his back and clenched his fingers into his hair. He would come too soon. Twisting away he sat up, leaning back on his elbows.

The man looked up at him myopically. 'Relax.'

'Sorry.'

'You're married, aren't you?'

'No!'

'You're being unfaithful to someone.'

'No. There's no one.'

'Then relax.'

'I'm sorry.'

The man laughed. 'Jesus.' Taking Patrick's hand he closed it around his cock. 'I've been hard since I first saw you. You don't have to apologise to me.'

His penis was small, like a boy's, its skin smooth and soft as fine kid. Patrick held it gently, his fingers reaching down to stroke his balls. The man groaned, a deep, sexy noise full of that knowing smile, and he kissed Patrick deeply, his hands moving over his body. After a while he broke away, sitting on his haunches beside him. 'Ready now?'

Patrick nodded.

The man took one of the many pillows and placed it beneath his groin as he rolled on to his belly. He laughed a

120

little. 'Be careful. I've not seen many as big.'

He'd imagined he would think of Paul. Instead he thought of nothing but the effort of pushing himself inside this stranger's body. As he tried and failed the man reached back, taking hold of his cock to guide him. Finally he said matter-of-factly, 'You'd best use some spit.'

Patrick spat on his fingers, rubbing the spittle over his cock before trying again. The resistance gave. Beneath him the man cried out, bracing himself against Patrick's thrusts. His head banged against the metal bars of the bedstead, which in turn banged against the wall. Patrick gritted his teeth, holding back from the release of orgasm, wanting to go deeper and deeper as hard and as fast as he could. Eventually the body beneath his lost its tension and collapsed down on to the mattress. Patrick's own orgasm followed quickly.

The man rolled on to his back, throwing his arm over his face and panting heavily. He laughed. 'Christ.'

Patrick lay still, closing his eyes against the sound of his breathing. In a moment he would get up and dress. He wouldn't touch him or look at him again. Now though he felt too drained to move. The familiar despair crept over him and he covered his face with his hands.

'Are you all right?'

Patrick heard the bed creak and tensed, not wanting to be touched. He knew the man was leaning over him. Forcing himself to speak he said, 'Yes.'

'What's your name?'

From downstairs came the sound of someone knocking on the door. Patrick glanced at the man but he only frowned as though he might have something to do with the caller. When he made no move Patrick said, 'Answer it.'

'I'm not expecting anyone...' He frowned again. 'Jesus! I forgot about Henderson!' He got up, pulling on trousers and shirt. Buttoning the shirt swiftly he said, 'Stay here. For God's sake stay out of sight.'

Patrick began collecting his clothes from the floor. Feathers tumbled across the bare boards, the small, white and brown feathers used to stuff pillows. He wondered how anyone could

121

live like this. The rosebud-patterned wallpaper was peeling from a damp corner, the bedding was stained with mildew and the feathers collected in balls of dust. On the bedside table was a teacup containing half an inch of cold, muddy cocoa, and he remembered the picture frame the man had hidden under the bed. Curious, Patrick knelt down, stifling a sneeze caused by the thick layer of dust. His fingers closed around the frame and he picked it up, peering at the photograph in the dim light.

Paul gazed back at him. Dressed in cap and trench coat, its collar turned up to frame his face, he was unsmiling, as beautiful as ever. Patrick placed the picture down gently on the bed and stood staring at it before lifting it up again. He turned it over, easing out the cardboard holding it in place. On the back of the photograph Paul had written, *Adam, I really think I should have smiled – don't you? (What a prig I look!!) My love always, your Paul.*

Your Paul. Setting the picture down on the bedside table, Patrick looked towards the door and the sound of voices in ordinary conversation carrying from the kitchen. He remembered the man as the one who had stood beside Paul outside the church. How could he not have recognised him? Of course they were lovers, the two of them. On the back of the photo another hand had written *January 1916.* They were lovers and had been for years. Anger rose inside him. Sweeping his arm across the table he scattered its contents across the floor.

The glass in the picture frame cracked in two. Next to the broken cup a puddle of cocoa sat proud, too glutinous to soak into the bare floorboards. An old shoebox that had been behind the cup spilled its contents of bundled letters. Patrick crouched beside them, recognising Paul's handwriting on the torn envelopes.

He crouched there for what seemed like minutes, the voices downstairs a low, background drone as he imagined reading each letter. To his eyes each envelope seemed thick, each letter pages long, nothing like the short notes he'd sent and received. He reached out and picked up one of the bundles. Seven or eight letters weighed heavy in his hands. He held the bundle to his nose, wanting to smell Paul on the stiff envelopes, but there was only a faint smell of dry earth. The bundles felt gritty, the blue and gold cord they were tied with fraying at both ends.

The cocoa had soaked into the floor. Patrick stooped and picked up the broken cup, slipped the picture back under the bed and put the letters in their box, before beginning to dress. He put on his jacket and chose a bundle of letters, thrusting it into his inside pocket. One bundle among so many wouldn't be missed.

The man appeared in the doorway. 'I heard a crash.' He smiled awkwardly, glancing over his shoulder towards the stairs. 'I had to tell my visitor I have a cat.'

'I knocked the cup over.'

'Doesn't matter … you don't have to run off because of a broken cup.' He smiled that same wry, condescending smile, making Patrick want to punch him. He turned away. Touching the letters to make sure their bulge wasn't obvious he heard the man, *Adam*, laugh. 'Well, perhaps we'll meet again?'

Brushing past him Patrick ran from the house.

Chapter Fourteen

January, 1918
Dearest A – Thank you for the chocolate, and the socks – I
gave the marmalade away to one of the poor kids they've been
sending us recently. He tells me it was delicious and sends his
very best wishes. (He hopes for strawberry jam next time).

Remember I told you about Captain Hawkins? Today he
showed me a photo of his wife and baby. She is called Agnes
and the baby is called May and we both stood looking at their
photograph and smiling like fools for what seemed ages. I told
him she was very handsome and the baby very sweet and felt
sorry for him as he put the picture away. He's only just back
from England and baby's first Christmas.

Dad sent me my copy of Robinson Crusoe. *Do you*
remember how I told you Granddad read it to me when I was
eight and was sent home from school with whooping cough?
George thought the story too difficult for me but Granddad
said I was just like my mother and nothing was too difficult for
her. Reading it now I find that it is too difficult. I find myself
thinking about Robinson and Friday too much for my own
good. The pages are becoming damp as it hasn't stopped
raining for days – already there is mildew on the cover. I know
Dad meant well but I'm afraid the book will be destroyed by
this bloody weather.

How is school? The boy you told me about, Brownlowe, I
do remember his brother from Christmas parties and such. I
was sorry to hear what happened. Rob knew him quite well, I
think. I'll let him know, as he'll want to send condolences to
the family. I agree it's unlikely he's alive if they've listed him
as missing, but being out here makes you pessimistic – they

may be right to hope.

Remember the shrine I told you about on the side of the road? We passed it today, blown to smithereens. Later Smith said what a pity it was because the little statue of the Virgin had such a pretty face. Jenkins laughed so much the poor man took offence. I tried to apologise to him, but it was difficult with Jenkins crying with laughter. It wasn't that funny really – it was just the sad, serious way Smith said it.

We're having a quiet time of it at the moment. I read Crusoe *and think of you (and Friday). I sleep a great deal, and dream all kinds of idiotic things. Last night you were here with me. Hawkins gave you a dressing down for not having the right kit. You asked if I had a spare pistol you could borrow. It all seemed very normal but then I woke up missing you so much I couldn't go back to sleep. I walked out into the trench and ended up drinking tea with Smith and Sergeant Thompson, although I wouldn't normally bother the men. Thompson with his gold-tooth-grin sees right through me and I can't decide whether his smirking behind my back bothers me or not. Mostly not, I think. His tooth is fascinating. It makes his breath smell of gun metal, as though he sucks on the barrel of his rifle. Am I smirking behind his back, now? Yes, definitely.*

Write soon, won't you? My very best love – P

PS: I've suddenly realised that I don't have a photograph of you. I thought you could go to Evan's studio in your Sunday best and have your picture taken beneath the artificial rambling roses. Look pensive. Don't smile. Right profile would be best, I think. Next time Hawkins shows me his wife and family I can produce you from my wallet, my own true love.

Patrick folded the letter back into its envelope and placed it beside the others. He remembered the demolished shrine, the Virgin lying in a ditch amongst splinters of wood, her hands still clasped to her chest, her head a few feet away. It had made him remember the statuette of Saint Francis kept in his mother's dressing table drawer because its head had broken off. Whenever the drawer was opened the bearded face rolled towards the light, exhaling the stink of lavender.

At the French roadside Paul had hurled the Virgin's head into the sky. Watching him, Patrick had crossed himself. Rain came down in sheets, blurring Paul into a grey smudge as he stared after the head's trajectory. The cobbled road ran with water, the countryside disappearing under the flood. He thought of the head drowning.

Mick's voice shouted up the stairs. Patrick jumped, expecting him to burst into his room just as he used to. Gathering the letters together he left them in a pile by his bed and went downstairs.

Sitting at the bottom of the stairs Mick said angrily, 'I've been shouting for you for ages. What were you doing up there?'

'I must have dozed off.'

'Liar!'

'Don't call me a liar.' He edged past into the kitchen. 'Do you want some supper?'

Mick followed him, banging his chair on the door; he damaged it in exactly the same place every time so that a groove had appeared. He glared up at Patrick. 'Where were you this afternoon?'

'You were all right. You were with Hetty, weren't you? I didn't think you'd miss me.' He began looking through cupboards, finally bringing out a tin of corned beef. 'Will this do? I'll make you a sandwich.'

Mick knocked the tin out of his hand, sending it scuttling across the floor. 'I asked you where you were today!'

'Nowhere.'

'Seeing Harris?'

Patrick laughed bleakly.

Taking a fistful of his shirt, Mick yanked him down so that their faces were level. 'The fire in my room went out – do you know how cold it is in this morgue?'

Patrick pulled away. 'Hetty should have …'

'Well she didn't! You had no right to send her here like that.'

'I thought you'd be pleased.'

Mick gazed at him as though he couldn't believe his ears. 'I

126

don't want her skivying for me! I can look after myself!'

'Then go and light the fire in your room.'

'I would if you left some fucking coal in the scuttle!'

'You know where the coal is, Mick. Down the cellar steps, first door on your left. Remember? We've always kept it there.'

'Piss off.' Mick turned the chair round, banging it against the door again. The book that had been on his lap slid to the floor and Patrick stooped to pick it up, then followed him into his room.

The cold came as a shock after the warmth of the kitchen. Placing the book on the hearth he squatted in front of the dead fire and cleared the ashes from the grate.

'Give that book to me. It'll get filthy down there.' Without looking up Patrick handed it to him. Snatching it Mick barked, 'Now get out.'

Patrick sighed. 'I'll light the fire first.'

'I want to go to bed. I don't need a fire if I'm asleep.'

'It's early yet.'

'I'm tired. And I don't need your help, either, so just get out.'

Patrick straightened up, dusting ash from his hands. 'You haven't eaten today, have you?'

'So?'

'Why don't I make you a sandwich? I'll bring it to you in bed.'

Mick bowed his head, fumbling in his pocket for his cigarettes. After a while he said, 'She didn't light the fire because we went for a walk. To the park. We had a nice time, really. The kerbs were a bit difficult for her, but she's quite strong. Didn't complain.' Lighting the cigarette he said, 'I asked her to visit me again.'

'Did she say she would?'

'Yes.'

'So what's wrong?'

'Nothing.' He laughed bitterly. 'Everything's tickity-boo.'

'I'll light the fire, shall I? Then get you something to eat?'

'Do you think she said yes out of pity?'

Crouching in front of the fire Patrick looked at him. 'I don't know, Mick.'

'If it's pity I'd rather she didn't bother.'

Patrick turned back to the grate. 'Maybe pity will become something else.'

Mick exhaled as though he'd been holding his breath. 'Maybe. Corned beef sandwiches then? I'll go and make a start in the kitchen.'

Margot made supper of eggs and bacon and black pudding and Paul ate it without comment. He was always quiet when he came home from the school, as though he was too exhausted even to make conversation. She would have liked to hear about his day, to talk about the other masters and their wives and families. All day she tried to think of things they could discuss over supper, ordinary gossip that would make their marriage seem normal, but nothing very much happened to her. She cleaned the house, she shopped with the little money he gave her and from time to time she visited her mother, short, stilted visits in an atmosphere still crackling with her mother's anger. Since New Year's Eve and that disastrous dance, she had felt friendless. As she went about her chores, aware of the baby moving inside her, she tried to be proud of the fact that she'd out-grown the girls she'd been at school with.

So far their neighbours remained strangers, although she could hear their children's cries and shouts through the walls. Often she left the house just to get away from the nagging feeling that the women in the street were deliberately snubbing her. She'd go window shopping, avoiding the haberdashery with its display of lacy Christening gowns, and wished she'd saved even a little of the weekly allowance her father used to give her.

She knew that soon she would have to ask Paul for money to buy clothes and underwear, replacements for items that were becoming too tight or too threadbare. She had begun to worry about this, of being even more of a burden, noticing that Paul's cuffs were becoming frayed and that he spent nothing on himself apart from the cheapest cigarettes. She thought of her father, who wouldn't settle for anything but the best pipe tobacco, a little treat that had always seemed unremarkable; now, compared to Paul, he seemed like a spendthrift.

She cleared the table of the supper dishes. Unable to stand the silence any longer she asked, 'How was school?'

'Fine.' He looked up from the *Evening Gazette*. 'It was fine.'

She rinsed a plate under the single cold tap. 'And Adam, is he all right?'

'Yes.' He returned to the newspaper. 'He's fine, too.'

She felt compelled to persist. Making her voice light she asked, 'Is he courting?'

Paul flicked over a page. 'No.'

'No? That's a pity, he could bring his girl to supper, if he had a girl, of course.'

'He hasn't.'

'Oh well. It was just a thought. You know, I realised today that he lives next door to that girl, the one who was with that crippled man's brother at the dance.'

He looked up at her, frowning. 'His brother was with a girl? Are you sure?'

'Yes!' She laughed. 'I thought I recognised her when she was dancing with him.'

He turned back to the paper. After a while he said, 'I don't remember a girl.'

Sighing, Margot scrubbed at the greasy frying pan. She thought of the slight, sharp-faced girl she sometimes passed in the street. She looked about her own age and sometimes she felt that she should introduce herself but so far she'd been too afraid; the women who lived in the terraces seemed unpredictable, too quick to make friends and enemies.

Paul stood up. 'I'll dry, shall I?'

'No. You should sit down, you've been working all day.'

He took a tea towel from the drawer and began to wipe the plates. Earlier he had taken off his jacket and tie and unbuttoned his collar so that the dark hair of his chest was just visible. There was ink on his hand. As usual when he stood close to her, she was surprised by how much she wanted him.

He smiled at her and she looked down into the grey washing-up water. Summoning courage she said, 'I may need a few shillings extra, soon.' She felt herself blushing. 'There are some things I need.'

'Of course. How much would you like?'

'I don't know … not very much.'

He began to put the plates away. 'You must tell me if I'm not giving you enough housekeeping.'

'Things *are* expensive.' Awkwardly she said, 'How much more could you give me?'

'Enough to go mad and buy you a new dress? I'm sorry, I didn't realise you were worrying about money. Tomorrow make a list of everything you need, for the baby as well. I'll draw the money out on Saturday.'

Relieved, to her horror she began to cry. At once Paul drew her into his arms, kissing the top of her head as she pressed her face to his chest. 'Oh, Margot, hush, please don't cry over money. Money doesn't matter.'

She drew away from him, hurriedly wiping her eyes. 'Yes it does … you work so hard.'

He laughed. 'I've worked harder.'

'You always look so exhausted.'

'Well, that's just me – pale and interesting, I can't help it.'

She blew her nose, then stuffed her handkerchief into her pocket, avoiding his gaze. 'I know you don't sleep well.'

'I can't help that, either.'

'I'm never sure whether to wake you or not.' Her voice rose and she tried to fight back the tears, remembering how frightened she was when Paul woke shouting in the night. Last night she had found him crouched in the corner of their bedroom, his arms covering his head as though protecting himself from blows. Managing to meet his eye she said, 'What happened last night, for instance …'

He frowned. 'Last night?'

'You got out of bed, you were shaking.'

'I don't remember.' He sat down at the table and lit a cigarette. Exhaling smoke he said, 'I'm sorry. I'll sleep in the other room, if you like.'

'No. I don't want you to do that.' She blushed again because she said the words too hastily, making herself sound brazen. 'You wake me anyway. It's better if I'm there with you.' Sitting down beside him she said, 'Don't you think it's better?'

He laughed, looking down as he rolled his cigarette around the rim of the ashtray. 'I think it's much better. I don't want to scare you, that's all. I know how horrible it is, being woken like that.'

'It's all right. I don't mind.'

He smiled, reaching for her hand and squeezing it gently. 'Try to wake me, next time it happens. Give me a good kick.' Still holding her hand he stood up. 'Shall we have an early night?'

Paul stared at the bedroom ceiling and lit a cigarette. Beside him Margot snored quietly, soft little rasps of breath that made him feel protective of her. A moment ago he had covered her more snugly with the eiderdown, watching her for a moment to make sure she slept on. He considered getting up and spending the night in the spare room to save her from the horror of his nightmares, but the thought of that monastic, freezing little room filled him with dread. He closed his eyes, torn by his need for the comfort of Margot's presence and the guilt that he might wake her.

They had made love and afterwards she had held on to him, smiling sleepily. She seemed to enjoy sex, although they were both made awkward by the feeling that sleeping together was somehow illicit. That first time, in the room above the pub, he'd conquered his nervousness by losing himself in the kind of foreplay he practised on Adam during those long Sundays spent in bed together before he left for France. It was the kind of sex he liked best: no penetration but slow, engrossed caresses and long, deep kisses, lips and tongue and fingers all intent on one purpose. He could make time stand still that way, he could make the whole world recede until all that was left was touch and taste and he'd press his fingers to Adam's lips

131

so that even the silence would be pure. It only took concentration, a single-minded forgetting.

That first time with Margot had been his first time with any woman and he'd been afraid of hurting her, afraid, too, of his own reactions. In the end it seemed he'd wanted her too badly; after the foreplay, the silent, astonishing exploration of her body and her own shuddering climax, he'd entered her with what seemed too much force against too little resistance and he'd come too quickly. Only afterwards did he think about the baby and for a moment he was swept by a terrible sense of guilt. She would miscarry; the baby couldn't survive such violence. He'd talked himself down from the sickening height of fear, trying to convince himself with rational arguments. Still he remained afraid, and it became another reason why he hadn't made love to his wife again until tonight. And there was Adam, of course, and the pestering voice in his head reminding him of his faithlessness.

He stubbed his cigarette out and rolled over on to his side. Unable to sleep, he remembered what Margot had said about Morgan being with a girl at the dance. He knew he shouldn't be so surprised – it would be normal, sensible even, to put on a front and take a girl dancing. All the same, he felt jealous, a bitter feeling none the less real for being irrational. Patrick Morgan was the one person he could retreat into fantasy with: a strong, gorgeous man uncomplicated by all the disappointments and compromises of reality. In his fantasies Morgan had eyes only for him and never thought of hiding behind a fearful front of heterosexuality. In his fantasy world he believed that Patrick Morgan was invincible, a compelling superstition he'd held since the first day they'd gone on patrol together.

Jenkins had said, 'You know, Harris, some battalions don't send men out. Not even to inspect the wire.' After a moment he went on, 'You always go, too. You and Morgan – our own David and Goliath – there must be quite a feeling of comradeship out there, between you and the mighty sergeant.'

Writing a report at the dugout table, Paul made himself look up. 'What would you know about it?'

'Nothing, of course, seeing as you keep all the glory for yourself.'

'Hawkins has ordered I take Sergeant Morgan out on patrol tonight. Why don't you come with us, see how glorious it really is?'

He laughed as though astonished. 'Would you really want me there, spoiling your fun? Surely you want to be alone with him?' Slyly he added, 'And I'm sure he feels the same way – he just can't seem to stand to let you out of his sight.'

Morgan had appeared in the doorway then. He looked from Jenkins to him and back again. Jenkins smirked. 'Well, I'm sure you two have lots to discuss about tonight's jolly. I'll leave you to get on with it in private.'

Paul remembered that Morgan had sat down opposite him and had turned to watch Jenkins step out into the trench. When he seemed certain he was out of earshot, Morgan said gently, 'Are you all right, sir?'

'Why shouldn't I be?' For the first time he had met Morgan's gaze directly. Morgan leaned forward and for a surreal moment Paul imagined he was about to kiss him. Instead he picked up a box of matches from the table. 'May I?' He struck a match, illuminating his face for a second before he lit his cigarette. Paul remembered feeling a sense of melodrama, a sense that he had added to the over-wrought nature of a scene that should have been ordinary, if only for the sake of his own sanity.

Margot shifted beside him, rolling over so that her body nudged his, and he moved away a little. Her belly was hard, the skin stretched too tightly over the life inside it. He expected a tiny fist to break through the thin barrier and punch him. He stubbed the cigarette out and closed his eyes in an attempt to sleep.

Chapter Fifteen

'You going out, Hetty?'

Adjusting her hat in front of the hall mirror, Hetty turned to her father. 'I'm going for a walk.'

'Oh?' Joe smiled. 'Who with?'

'No one.'

'No one called Morgan?'

She turned back to the mirror, the ratty little face under the ugly cloche hat. Harshly she said, 'I'm going for a walk, that's all.'

Joe sat down on the stairs and took a bag of sherbet lemons from his pocket. Holding out the bag to her he said, 'Here. Save me from eating all these myself.'

'No, thanks.'

'No?' He returned the sweets to his pocket. 'I'll keep them for later then, when you get back.' Looking at her he said, 'Your Mam said you had to see to the Major the other day?'

'I didn't *see* to him.'

'Then what did you do?'

Talked, Hetty thought. Laughed and talked. She had never laughed so much with anyone. Sighing she said, 'I sat with him, that's all.'

'And then you went for a walk in the park.'

She frowned at him. 'How did you know?'

'Mrs Carter saw you.'

'Nosy old bag. What did she say?'

'What was there to say?'

'Nothing. We went for a walk, that's all.'

'I'll tell you what she said.' He took a sweet from its bag, contemplating it for a moment before popping it into his mouth. 'She said you were laughing and joking and carrying on like bairns.'

'We were feeding the ducks.'

'Well, there's no harm in that.'

'Why shouldn't he laugh and joke, anyway?'

'No one's saying he shouldn't.'

'I can just imagine her tut-tutting, all disapproving, thinking he should be in a home, out of sight so he doesn't offend …' She drew breath and Joe smiled at her.

'Who does he offend?'

'You know what I mean.'

Joe took the sweets out again. Shaking the bag a little he peered into it, selecting carefully. 'He's a handsome lad, though. What happened doesn't stop him being a handsome lad.' He looked up at her. 'Are you going to see him now?' She coloured and Joe exclaimed. 'Oh, Hetty, don't. Don't. Don't get involved. It's all right your Mam doing her bit and helping out, she can take it.'

'Take what?'

'I don't blame him for getting frustrated, any man would. But it's bad enough your Mam having to put up with it. I don't want him taking it out on you an' all.'

'He's lonely.'

'Is he? Well, that's not your worry. And what about his brother? What does he have to say about it?'

She looked at her reflection. 'He doesn't say anything.'

Carefully Joe said, 'Are you trying to make him jealous?'

'No!' She turned on him. 'That would be a terrible thing to do.'

'Yes. It would.'

Hetty laughed bleakly. 'Nothing would make him jealous anyway. He looks right through me.'

'Hetty …' He sighed. 'Have you thought about going back to Marshall's? You liked it there.'

'I like it where I am.' She took her coat from the hook. 'I'll see you later.'

In the shop Patrick had said, 'Mick enjoyed going to the park yesterday. Thank you for taking him out.'

'It was no trouble.'

'It was very kind of you. He tells me you're going to visit him again?'

'On Sunday.'

He'd smiled as though relieved. 'He's looking forward to it.'

Unable to stop herself she said, 'You don't mind, do you?'

'Mind?' He'd laughed. 'I'm pleased. He thinks a lot of you.'

Now outside the Morgan's front gate, she hesitated. She could go home and tomorrow she could apply to Marshall's for her old job; she could decide never to see either of the Morgan brothers again and it would be sensible and easy, like loosening a too-tight corset. The Chinese lion grinned at her. Sighing, she walked up the path to the door.

Nervously Mick said, 'You are going out, aren't you?'

'I thought I'd play gooseberry.'

'For god's sake, Pat!'

Patrick laughed. 'I'm joking. Don't worry, I'm going to the pub. You and Hetty can have the house to yourselves.'

'Perhaps she's expecting you to be here.'

'She's coming to see you, Mick. She won't want me hanging around.'

'Won't she?'

Patrick sighed. 'Well, if she does and I'm not perhaps she'll get the message.'

'Maybe you should stay. It's not seemly, is it? A young girl alone with a man ...'

The knock on the door made them both jump. Patrick smiled at Mick reassuringly. 'I'll go and let her in.'

Lying on the bed Adam watched as Paul took off his trousers and folded them over the back of the chair. 'God, I've missed you.'

Paul glanced at him. 'Aren't you getting undressed?'

'Not yet, I like seeing you naked when I'm still fully

136

dressed.'

'Really?' Unbuttoning his shirt Paul said, 'Get undressed, eh? We haven't got long.'

'And you want to get straight down to it? Christ.' Adam sat on the edge of the bed and began untying his shoelaces. 'Very romantic.'

Naked, Paul climbed beneath the bedcovers. The sheets felt damp and smelt of sex. Unable to help himself he thought about Margot. She would be in church now, listening to her father's sermon. Afterwards, Daniel would tell her again how worthless her husband was. Later still, as he sat opposite him at lunch, the Reverend would make a point of cross-examining him about his prospects as a teacher or ask how much nearer he was to finding a decent place to live. All the time he would look at him as though he was some sub-species of human, an offence to nature. Paul covered his face with his hands, desperate for a cigarette.

Adam knelt beside him. Lifting his hands away he kissed Paul's mouth lightly. 'I have missed you.'

'I know, I miss you too.'

'Do you?' He laughed slightly, sitting back on his heels to look at him.

'Yes. Look, Adam, do you mind if I smoke?' Paul got up and went through his jacket pockets for his cigarettes.

Adam said, 'What's the matter?'

'Nothing.' He exhaled smoke, looking down at the tip of the cigarette. 'Lunch with Margot's parents.'

'Oh. Well, do you have to think about it now?' Adam lay down and held out his arms. 'Come here. Let's have you thinking about something more entertaining.'

Paul lay down and rested his head on Adam's chest. He felt Adam's fingers curl into his hair and begin to massage his scalp. Paul closed his eyes, trying to concentrate on his touch. Instead he saw himself facing Whittaker across the vicarage table. He drew deeply on the cigarette.

'Get up.' Adam pushed him away. 'There's ash all over the bed, all over *me*.' Grasping Paul's wrist he frowned. 'You're shaking. What's the matter with you? It's lunch with your in-

137

laws, not some dawn raid! For Christ's sake, Paul, grow up.'

Paul got up and began to dress. Aware of Adam watching him he said, 'The sheets need changing.'

'So you're going home in a sulk?'

'I don't think either of us are in the mood now, are we?'

'Come back to bed.'

'They're expecting me there at one o'clock.'

'Then we have a couple of hours. Please, Paul. I've waited all week for this.' Adam held out his hand. 'I just want to hold you. You can smoke all over me if it helps.'

Half dressed Paul lay down beside him. 'Whittaker really hates my guts.'

'You got his daughter pregnant, Paul.'

'And I married her.'

'Shotgun weddings tend to be a bit embarrassing, especially if the bride's father is a vicar.' Adam squeezed his hand. 'He'll get over it. And if he doesn't, so what? You don't *have* to go there for lunch.' He pulled Paul into his arms and kissed him. After a moment he took the cigarette from him and stubbed it out before rolling him over on to his front. Paul was still wearing his shirt and Adam pushed it up, exposing his backside. Paul heard him sigh and felt his lips on the base of his spine. He closed his eyes as Adam entered him, counting the strokes until he climaxed.

Adam fell on to his back, breathing heavily. Finding Paul's hand he kissed it. 'Sorry. Sometimes all you need is a quick, hard fuck.' He looked at him, smiling. 'Not shaky anymore?'

'I shake all the time.'

He laughed. 'No you don't. You're over all that now.'

Paul lay on his stomach. He went over the process of dressing, of going out into the street and walking to the church. In the graveyard Margot would come out to meet him, kissing his cheek and taking his hand while her father glowered and her mother smiled. Her parents should unite against him and have done with it, but they had taken sides, making it worse.

Feeling Adam's hand on his back he rolled away and got up.

'What are you doing now? Don't rush off. I want to make love to you.'

'You just did.'

'Not properly ...'

'It felt properly to me.' On impulse he said, 'Do you want to go for a drink?'

Adam laughed, astonished. 'A drink? Where?'

'The Castle and Anchor's closest.' He thought of Patrick. He might be waiting for him at the bar at this moment. Tempting fate, he decided to press Adam into going with him. 'Come on, just one pint.'

'The Castle and Anchor's a dive. We can't go in there.'

'Why not?' Paul looked at him from buttoning his flies. 'Why shouldn't we go in there?'

Adam shook his head. 'We'll get such a warm welcome, won't we?'

'It's not stamped on our foreheads, Adam.'

'Isn't it?'

'I'll go on my own.'

'Do that. The smoke in those places brings on my asthma.'

Dressed, Paul leaned over the bed and kissed him.

Adam caught his wrist. 'Try and come back tonight?'

'I'll try.'

Patrick had always liked the look of the Castle & Anchor public house. He liked the way its double doors straddled the corner of Tanner Street and Skinner Street, its shape like the prow of a ship sailing out over a cobbled sea. He liked the gothic script etched into its opaque windows: *Fine Wines & Spirits. Snug & Private Rooms.* Snug. He liked that word best.

Patrick crossed Tanner Street, glancing at Hetty's house as he passed by. He thought of the photograph of the dead boy on their mantelpiece and tried to remember what he had looked like. Something like Hetty, he supposed.

Before he reached the pub he could hear the piano playing. As he pushed the door open the playing stopped and into the sudden silence a voice called, 'It's the big man himself! On your own today, Patrick?'

139

Patrick nodded at the group of men playing dominoes. The one who had spoken said, 'The Major's all right is he? It's marvellous how you cope with him.'

The others nodded, their eyes fixed on their game. One of them looked up briefly. 'You're a saint, Patrick. Not many would do what you do...Oh, look at that! I'm knocking.'

The first man laughed. 'And I've won. There. Another game?'

The dominoes were turned over and shuffled; the piano started up again. Patrick imagined taking a couple of heads in each hand and banging them all together. The din from the piano would drown out the cracking of thick skulls.

At the bar a pint was already pulled and waiting for him. Maria smiled. 'All right, Patrick?'

He made to get his money out but she shook her head. 'Already paid for.'

To his right a voice said, 'Patrick. Hello again.' Paul smiled at him. 'Did I give you a start? I'm sorry.'

Patrick exhaled sharply. 'Sir ...'

Paul took a cigarette case from his pocket. He opened it and held it out. 'I really did startle you, didn't I?' As Patrick took a cigarette Paul said, 'Do you want to sit down?' He caught his eye, holding his gaze for what seemed like an age before Patrick broke away. Patrick picked up his drink and carried it to an empty table.

Sitting opposite Paul took a long drink from his own pint. Lighting a cigarette he said, 'So, this is your local?'

'Yes.'

Paul looked around. 'It's different from The Grand Hotel, anyway.' He blew smoke down his nose. 'How's your brother?'

'He's fine.'

'Did he enjoy himself at New Year?'

'Yes, thank you.'

'Good.' He took another long drink, almost draining his glass.

Patrick stood up at once. 'Let me get you another.'

'Thanks. I'll have the same again.'

Maria raised her eyebrows in Paul's direction. 'Who's that, then?'

'One of the officers I served with.' So she wouldn't notice the tremble in his hands Patrick gripped the edge of the bar, turning his knuckles white. When he'd seen Paul he'd thought his knees would buckle, that he'd collapse on the floor. His heart was pounding even now.

Maria was smiling at him quizzically. 'An officer, eh? I thought he sounded posh. Slumming it, is he?'

'Something like that.' Fumbling with the coins he paid her quickly and carried the two pints back to the table, slopping beer over his shoes. He sat down, watching as Paul took another long drink. Nervously he said, 'It's strong stuff, the beer they serve here.'

Putting his glass down Paul said, 'Isn't it'

'You should go easy.'

Paul lit another cigarette. 'Was that your fiancée, the girl you were with at New Year?'

'No. She works for me.' Patrick voice quavered and he cleared his throat. 'I have my own butcher's shop. It's on the High Street.'

'I know – Morgan's, the butcher's with the happy pig in the window.'

'Happy pig, eh? I suppose it is. I always thought it was sinister.'

'Then why do you keep it?'

'I don't know … people recognise it, I suppose.'

Patrick tried to ration himself to looking at Paul for only a few seconds at a time. All the same he noticed that the glass eye was a shade darker than it should be and there was a faint white scar below it where the shrapnel had cut. He was thinner than he remembered and less boyish. In the army he'd been serious, weighed by responsibility. Now he smiled and the smile changed him, made him more attractive, if that were possible. Hardly able to believe he was sitting across a pub table from him, Patrick stole another look.

Paul's hand went to his face and he laughed awkwardly. 'I lost the eye.'

'Yes.' Patrick looked down at his drink. 'Sorry.'

'Worse things happen.'

Forcing himself to meet his gaze he said, 'It's the wrong shade of green.'

Paul smiled. 'I rather like that. It draws attention.'

'What does your wife think about it?'

He stubbed his cigarette out. 'She likes it, too.' Finishing his pint, he put the empty glass down. 'Another?'

Patrick watched him at the bar, allowing his eyes to linger on his neat little backside until the beginnings of a hard-on made him look away. He wondered if he would be drunk enough to take back to the shop. Three pints of beer in quick succession might make a man his size just pissed enough. He looked down at his own half-finished drink. In all his fantasies Paul had always been stone-cold sober, an awkward, vulnerable boy, not this self-assured man. Perhaps a dingy room over a butcher's shop wouldn't be good enough for him. Thinking of the soiled mattress left behind by the last tenant, his hard-on shrivelled.

As he sat down Paul said, 'Cheers.'

'Cheers.'

Paul lit another cigarette, offering him the open case. When he shook his head Paul laughed. 'I smoke too much. They wouldn't let me smoke in the first hospital and I nearly went mad. One of the nurses used to take pity on me occasionally, but Matron caught her and gave us both a frightful row. I couldn't see at the time and I thought this Matron was enormous, a real battle-axe. She wasn't, of course.' After a moment he asked, 'Do you know what happened to Sergeant Thompson?'

Patrick nodded. 'He stayed on. I told him he was mad.'

'Didn't you ever consider it?'

'Never. Did you?'

'Sometimes.'

Patrick stared at him incredulously. 'You'd have stayed in the army?'

Paul stared back. He smiled slowly. 'I liked the uniform.'

'It suited you.'

'Heads turned.'

'I'm sure.'

Holding his gaze Paul said, 'So, you have your own pork butcher's shop. Do you sell everything, right down to the squeal?'

'Everything.'

'Drink up.' Paul drained his glass.

'Where are we going?'

Standing up, Paul said, 'You're going to show me round your shop.'

Chapter Sixteen

'This is inexcusable.'

Daniel went to the dining room window, lifting aside the lace curtain to look again for Paul. Turning to Margot he snapped, 'Did you tell him to be here for one o'clock?'

'Yes.' Anxiously she said, 'Can you see him?'

Iris sighed. 'He's probably staying at home until this rain stops. Lunch can wait a few minutes.'

'He's half an hour late, Iris, half an hour.' Daniel looked at his watch. 'Almost forty minutes, now.'

Standing beside her father, Margot looked out at the path leading from the vicarage to the churchyard. Rain bounced off the ground, hammering on the roof of the bay window and running down the glass. 'Perhaps I should go and look for him.'

'You'll do no such thing!' Daniel frowned at her. 'Go out in your condition in weather like this simply because he's forgotten the time? We'll eat without him.'

'I'm worried, I've never known him be late.'

'You hardly know him at all. I should imagine this is typical behaviour.'

Her mother laughed sarcastically. 'Typical.'

'I suppose you think this kind of thoughtlessness is acceptable? That's it's all right to keep everyone waiting?'

Iris snapped, 'I'm surprised he agrees to come here at all the way you treat him.'

'How do I treat him? How does one treat a person who hasn't the grace to meet one's eye or make even the smallest effort at conversation?'

'You should make allowances.'

'Allowances!' Daniel snorted. 'He should pull himself together.'

Her mother laid down her knitting and stood up. 'I'll go and turn the oven down.'

'No, we'll eat now.' He turned back to stare out of the window as though keeping a vigil. 'Margot, go and help your mother.'

The rain began slowly, a few fat drops that gradually became a downpour. Patrick turned his collar up, shivering as rain trickled down his back. Half way along the deserted High Street he stopped at the entrance to an alleyway. To Paul he said, 'It's down here, the back door to the shop.'

Paul smiled at him, the rain plastering his hair flat. 'So what are we waiting for?'

'It's not much...'

He laughed. 'Patrick, I'm getting wet.'

Once again Patrick checked for the shop keys in his pocket. His fingers closed around them, the key to the back yard gate already warm from his touch. Exhaling he said, 'All right. Let's get out of this rain.'

The bones were massive, their bulbous ends pink and white and shiny as newly shelled pearls. Standing in the doorway at the back of the shop, Paul turned away from them quickly, breathing through his mouth to avoid their cold-iron smell. On the wall above them hung knives and cleavers, their metal dull in the grey, rain-soaked light. Everywhere was scrubbed and stung with the smell of bleach, a smell that mixed with that of the bones and was impossible to ignore. Soaked to the skin, Paul shuddered.

Opening the door to a flight of stairs, Morgan turned to him. 'It's up here.' He hesitated. 'As I said, it's not much...'

Brushing past him, Paul began to climb the stairs. He glanced back at Morgan who was hesitating still, dripping rain from the hem of his trench coat. For a moment Paul saw him in cap and puttees and he smiled slightly. 'There's no time like the present, Sergeant.'

At the top of the stairs Paul found himself in a room that was empty apart from a mattress covered in blue and white striped ticking, a large, brown stain at its head. Above it was a window that was too high to see from, a grill of wire mesh covering it. Pictures had been torn from a magazine and stuck to the wall above the fireplace: a fat baby in a tin bath advertising *Pears Soap* and a soldier with a girl on his knee. The smell of bones and bleach was overlaid with mustiness. Behind him a floorboard creaked and Paul turned round.

'It's been empty for a while,' Morgan said. Awkwardly he added, 'There's a kitchen, and another smaller room...'

Paul took off his coat and folded it on to the floor. 'You should rent it out.'

'Maybe.'

'But then you wouldn't be able to show me around.'

'No. That's what I thought.'

'So you've been thinking about it?'

'A bit.' He glanced over his shoulder as though expecting someone else to walk in. Distractedly he repeated, 'A bit.'

Paul stepped towards him. Touching his arm he said, 'You're soaking.'

'So are you.'

'Do you want to get out of those wet things?'

'Do you?'

Paul looked towards the mattress. 'Do you have any blankets?'

Morgan reached out and cupped his face. Surprised by his tenderness, Paul stood very still. Morgan's long fingers were dry and hard; as he pressed his palm to his cheek Paul could feel its calluses and he remembered the weight of it, pressing his head down into the mud of no-man's-land. He closed his eyes. The memory was vivid and he laughed shortly, appalled to find that he was crying.

Softly Morgan said, 'Hush now. It's all right.' Still holding Paul's face he wiped the tears away with a careful sweep of his thumb. 'You're all right now. Safe.' Morgan pulled him into his arms. He rocked him, stroking his hair, repeating over and over the same quiet words. At last he whispered, 'Lie

146

down. I'll hold you. I'll make it all right. Lie down.'

Wiping away snot and tears with his hand, Paul gasped for breath. Morgan kissed him, a soft, dry kiss. His hand cupped Paul's face again and he kissed him more forcefully until Paul responded.

Morgan led him to the mattress and they lay down. He pulled Paul into his arms, his hand slipping beneath his clothes to rest over Paul's heart. 'There,' Morgan said. 'Almost calm.'

Paul closed his eyes, his head on Morgan's chest rising and falling as he breathed. For a while they stayed like that and he imagined he would sleep listening to the sounds of the other man's body, as though he was a shell pressed against his ear. He thought of the nightmares he wouldn't have, the memories drowned out by the thud of his heart.

'I remember the first time I saw you.'

Paul opened his eyes, startled from drowsing.

Quietly Morgan went on, 'I wasn't afraid until then. I couldn't stand that you might be killed.' He shuddered, holding him still closer. 'It was all I thought about, how terrible it would be to lose you.'

The rain pounded on the roof. A drop of water appeared on the ceiling and began a steady beat to the floor. The room grew darker and cold seeped from the damp mattress. Warmed by Morgan's body, Paul began to drift into sleep again, finding himself at sea. There was no land on the horizon. Both England and France were far away. Waves crashed the decks, soaking him. The ship rose from the high sea again and again, riding the storm.

Patrick watched Paul sleep, half sleeping too, going in and out of dreams of ditches and trenches and stone-cold cellars where dead men lounged nonchalantly against green-moss walls. He saw Very lights dazzle the dark sky and illuminate the ragged stumps of trees, and he focused on the rain dripping from the ceiling so that he wouldn't see more. Beneath Paul's body his arm went to sleep. The rain stopped. Watery winter sun slanted through the high window and he closed his eyes against it.

147

They must have slept for an hour or more. Paul murmured, frowning as he looked up at him. 'What time is it?'

'Three o'clock.'

'Oh Christ!' He struggled to stand up, going at once to his coat on the floor. Searching through its pockets he took out his cigarettes. Patrick watched from the mattress, saw that his hands trembled as he attempted to strike a match. He got up, took the matches from him, and lit one.

'I had to be somewhere.' Paul laughed bleakly, accepting the light. 'It's too late now.' Glancing at him he said, 'Did you sleep?'

'A little.'

He looked down at the cigarette. 'I'm sorry. Crying like that...I'm sorry.'

'It's all right.'

'Feeling sorry for myself ...'

'It doesn't matter.'

He held out the open cigarette case. 'Sorry, I should have offered you one.'

'No, thanks.'

'I smoke too much.' Bowing his head he said, 'I'm really sorry. I shouldn't have come here. When I saw you at that dance...Anyway. I'm an idiot.'

'No. No you're not.'

'I have to go.'

'Paul...' He'd never used his name before. For the first time in his life he felt himself blush.

Gently Paul said, 'I'm married, Patrick. My wife is pregnant.'

'Then why did you come here?'

'I don't know.' Patrick looked at him and laughed painfully. 'I was thinking about you, the last patrol we went on, before ...' He exhaled a long breath of cigarette smoke. 'Before all that other business. I suppose I thought seeing you again would put it all in perspective.'

'No other reason?'

He laughed again, looking away.

Quickly Patrick said, 'I don't want anything from you. Just to see you from time to time...We could meet here. I could make it nicer.'

'Fix the leaky roof?' Paul smiled. 'I've been fucked in worse places.'

'It's not just about that.'

Paul looked down at the cigarette. After a while he said, 'When I first saw you...In France when we first met …' He hesitated then went on quickly, 'I tried not to think about you, to look at you, even. I just wanted you safely out of my sight.'

'I think about you all the time.'

Paul tossed his cigarette stub into the fireplace. 'And I went to that pub wondering if you really would be there; half hoping you wouldn't be … then you walked in.' He laughed shortly. 'I'm still getting over the shock.'

Attempting to smile Patrick said, 'I'm not so shocking.'

'You are to me.'

He forced a laugh. 'Why?'

Paul gazed at him. 'Because you make me feel like a fey little queer when you look at me? I don't know.'

'I don't mean to make you feel like that.'

'It's all right. I am a fey little queer.'

Patrick stepped towards him. 'Paul, let me see you. It's safe here – no one will suspect anything.' He tried to make his voice lighter. 'Who would suspect two old comrades meeting up from time to time?'

'To re-live the past?'

'No! It's finished, all that. I just want you. Since I first saw you …'

Paul put his coat on, glancing at him as he fastened the buttons. 'I really have to go.'

'Next Sunday, I'll be here. I'll be here all day.'

'Wednesday evening would be better. About seven o'clock?' Paul pulled on a pair of gloves. 'Is that all right?'

'Yes.'

Paul smiled. Briskly he said, 'Good. I won't cry and you can fuck me as much as you want. I'll look forward to it.'

'Paul …'

About to go downstairs Paul turned. 'It's what you want, isn't it?'

Patrick wondered if he was blushing again. 'You want it too.'

'Of course. I'm up for anything. Seven o'clock, Wednesday. Don't worry if I'm late.'

Chapter Seventeen

In the park, Hetty and Mick took shelter from the rain in the bandstand.

Breathless and laughing Hetty said, 'Look at us! Two drowned rats.'

Mick frowned at her. 'You're soaking. I don't want you to catch cold.'

'I'm all right. Besides, what can we do? We'll just have to wait here until it stops.'

'I'm sorry. I shouldn't have suggested going out.'

'It wasn't raining when we set off.'

'All the same.'

She smiled. 'Did you watch the bands play here?'

Lighting a cigarette he said, 'Sometimes. I came here once when I was on leave. I remember the band was playing *Keep The Home Fires Burning* as a girl handed me a white feather.'

'Silly cow.'

He laughed, looking down at the cigarette. 'I think it must have been a swan's feather. It was huge.'

'I hated the girls who did that. Our Albert was given one and he was only sixteen.'

Clamping the cigarette between his lips Mick wheeled himself to the edge of the bandstand. Looking out over the park he said, 'Do you think it rains more than it used to?' He glanced at her over his shoulder. 'In France I used to think that the whole country would be washed away. I had a Sergeant who believed the bombardments caused it to rain ... I forget what his theory was now. Mad as a hare. I had him sent home, poor bugger. Sorry.' He smiled slightly. 'Pardon my French.'

Hetty smiled back, thinking of Patrick and trying to see the likeness between him and this frail, dark-eyed man. Their similarity seemed insubstantial to her. She thought of Patrick's silences, his unpredictable moods, and her familiar disappointment in him made her sigh.

'What are you thinking about?'

Hetty shook her head. 'Nothing.'

'I'm sorry I've kept you out so long. As soon as it lets up we can go home.'

'I don't mind being here with you.'

'No? It's cold, isn't it? It's cold and wet and the wind sounds as though it's going to blow the roof off and you're stranded with a cripple whose chair will probably sink into the mud as soon as we leave here.'

'There's a path.'

He snorted. 'Well, that's all right then.'

Laughing, she said, 'You sound like Patrick when you get cross.'

'I sound like him all the time.'

'No you don't. You sound posh all the time. Patrick sometimes forgets to.'

'Posh eh? My father used to tell us we sounded like …' He stopped and looked away.

'Like what?'

'Nothing. It doesn't matter. He was a pig of a man.'

'That's a hard thing to say. He must have loved you.'

'I wonder why people say that?' He wheeled himself back to the centre of the bandstand, turning the chair round to look at her. 'Why do they presume such a thing? Probably because their own fathers and mothers love them. My father was a drunk who beat us with a leather belt. I don't think love was important to him.'

'Wasn't he proud of you?'

'Should he have been?'

'Of course! My father's proud of you and he hardly knows you.'

'Is he proud of Patrick, as well?'

'Patrick wasn't a major.'

'No. Patrick just did all the hard work.'

152

'I suppose for the whole of the war you just sat around giving orders?'

'I suppose I did.' He smiled at her. 'And then they had the temerity to drop a great big shell on the nice cosy dugout I'd set up for myself. Unbelievable.'

'Is that how it happened?'

'It? You mean this?' He looked down at himself. After a moment he laughed. 'I remember a second lieutenant finding me. He was covered in mud, from head to toe, but his face was so pale he looked like a ghost. He asked me if I was dead so I asked him if he was dead and he said no, he didn't think so. He wandered off then. I wanted to believe he'd gone to fetch help but he didn't come back. Two stretcher-bearers dug me out a couple of hours later.'

'How could he leave you like that?'

'He *was* dead, I think. In a way.'

'You lay all that time?'

'My legs were only broken … it wasn't as if … well, you know. All that came later.' He smiled. 'Anyway. Now you know. You're the only one who does.'

'Except Patrick '

'Pat's never asked.' The rain stopped. Throwing his cigarette down he said, 'Let's go home.'

Back outside the house Mick said, 'Come in and get warm before you go.'

'I should get back, really.'

'Do you have to?'

She hesitated, thinking of the dull Sunday afternoon stretching ahead of her, her mother asleep behind the *News of the World* and her father retreated to bed. She wondered if Patrick was in the house and glanced towards its dark windows.

Mick laughed slightly. 'I bought a cake. *Pat* bought a cake, actually. But it's cake, all the same. I was hoping you would share it with me.'

'What kind of cake?'

'I'm not sure, to be honest.' He smiled slowly. 'Your favourite?'

'Well, if it's my favourite.'

The cake was ginger, dry and crumbly, the kind of shop-bought cake her mother treated with contempt. Watching her eat it at the kitchen table Mick said, 'Perhaps it was the only cake left in the whole shop.'

She frowned at the half-eaten slice on her plate. 'Now you've made me feel sorry for it.'

He laughed. 'Then you shouldn't have such a soft heart.'

'I haven't really.'

'No? I think you have.'

She sipped her tea. Placing her cup down on the saucer she said, 'There's a young couple moved in a few doors down from us. Really young they are – well, she is. They only got married a few weeks ago and she's pregnant – showing – you know.' Hetty sighed. 'I asked her when the baby was due.'

Mick exhaled softly, 'Oh.'

'I know. I don't know what came over me to be so nasty…'

'Don't worry, Hetty. She's newlywed, she'll be walking around with her head in the clouds no matter what anyone says to her.'

'Harris, they call them. He's odd-looking, the husband.'

He gazed at her. 'Is he? I heard that girls swoon when they see him.'

'He's too thin. And he has a glass eye.'

Mick laughed. 'That is quite horrible, isn't it? Poor thing.' Still smiling at her he said, 'So, he isn't beautiful?'

'That's a funny word to use about a man.'

'His brother was beautiful. Now, if you'd seen Robbie Harris you would have swooned. All the girls did.'

'I don't swoon.'

'No. You're too sensible. Robbie and I were invited to a ball, once. Both brand new first lieutenants, fresh from the front, Christmas 1914. We were glamorous in those days – Rob was, anyway. He was fighting the girls off with a stick.'

'I bet you were, too.'

'Oh, I just stood close to him, basked in his glory.' He lit a cigarette, shaking the match out slowly. 'He wrote to me when

154

he heard I was wounded. Didn't stop writing until he was killed.' He laughed shortly. 'And it wasn't as though I was swamped with letters from Patrick. I think the nurses thought I hadn't anyone in the world apart from Rob Harris.'

'I would have written to you, if I'd known.'

'Then it's a shame we didn't know each other. I could have put your picture by my bed and all the other men would've been jealous of me.'

She laughed, embarrassed, looking down at the cake crumbs on her plate. 'They'd wonder why you didn't have someone prettier.'

The front door slammed. From the hallway Patrick called, 'It's me.'

Mick rolled his eyes. 'Who else?' He looked at her. 'Before he comes in, tell me you'll come and see me next Sunday?'

Standing in the kitchen doorway Patrick smiled at her broadly. 'Hetty! I didn't think you'd still be here.'

'Well she is.'

'You've had some cake. Good.'

Sharply Mick said, 'The cake was awful.'

'Was it, Hetty?'

'Are you drunk?'

'Am I? What do you think?'

Mick glared at him. 'Perhaps you should go and lie down.'

'No, I'm all right. I'll walk Hetty home; it's nasty out there. Are you ready, Hetty?'

'There's no need.'

Patrick grinned at her. 'Now, are you sure?'

'I'm sure.' She edged past him but he followed her into the hallway.

'Have you had a nice afternoon, Hetty?'

'Yes, thanks.' About to go, she said, 'Goodbye, Mr Morgan. Tell Mick I'll see him on Sunday.'

Patrick closed the door and returned to the kitchen.

'I'm *Mr Morgan* now and you are *Mick*. Now, what does that tell us?'

Mick sighed. 'Do you want to tell me what's happened?'

Patrick sat opposite him and hacked off a piece of cake.

Through a mouthful of dry crumbs he said, 'You tell me what's happened.'

'I wouldn't like to guess.'

Patrick laughed, spraying ginger cake. 'You usually do.'

'You went to the pub. You drank too much then went to the toilets behind the Parish Church and buggered some poor, furtive bastard who's now trying to hide his shame from his wife and children. There. How accurate was that?' He pushed himself away from the table and manoeuvred his chair to the door. 'I'll be in my room.'

Alone, Patrick sat down. He could still feel Paul's weight across his arm, still smell and taste him. He thought of the hole in the ceiling and the mattress's damp stink. Tomorrow he would start on the job of making the room presentable. He smiled to himself. For the first time in his life he felt truly happy.

Into the darkness Paul said quietly, 'Margot, would you like me to fetch you a glass of water?'

'I'm all right.'

'You're crying.' He touched her shoulder and she jerked away from him.

'Go to sleep.'

'I can't. Not when you're upset like this.'

She sat up suddenly, pulling the covers away from him and clasping them to her chest. Through her tears she said angrily, 'You still stink of beer. Breathing beer all over me. How could you get drunk like that?'

'I wasn't drunk.'

'Well, Daddy thought you were! He could smell it, too. And you lit a cigarette in front of him when you know he hates it!'

'And I put it out again, as soon as he asked.'

'I've never seen him so angry … I thought he was going to hit you.'

Paul laughed despite himself. 'So did I.'

'It's not funny. Why couldn't you just be on time? Why did you have to go to a pub and get drunk? You're just making him hate you.' Tears ran down her face and he sat up and put his arm around her shoulders. She shrugged him off. 'He hates you and now he thinks you're a drunk as well.'

'I'll go and see him tomorrow, after school. I'll tell him …'

'What? What will you tell him?'

'I don't know. That I'll never do it again?'

Wiping her eyes she said, 'He wants you to come to church with me on Sundays.'

'No, Margot.'

'Why not?'

'I'd feel like a hypocrite.'

'That's just a fancy word for saying you can't be bothered.'

He lay down again, groping for his cigarette case and matches on the bedside table. As he lit one he thought of Patrick Morgan refusing to chain smoke like him. He thought it almost pointless to take or leave cigarettes like that. Closing his eyes he inhaled deeply, picturing Morgan's face as he kissed him.

'Paul?' Hesitantly she said, 'If you came to church with me it would make things easier. It would show Daddy that you respect him.'

Daniel had seemed calm. He had stood up when he walked into the room, seeming to assess his breathlessness and his still soaking clothes as proof only of his stupidity. Then he had caught the smell of brown ale on his breath and the colour left his face.

'You've been drinking,' he'd said, and his voice had quaked with anger. 'What kind of a man are you?'

Paul felt Margot's hand close tentatively around his. After a while she said, 'Would it be hypocritical to sing a few hymns and close your eyes during prayers?'

He got up. Shrugging on his dressing gown he said, 'I'm going to make a cup of tea. Would you like one?'

'No.' Pulling the covers over her she turned her back on him.

Downstairs, waiting for the kettle to boil he smoked another cigarette and thought about Morgan, just as he had thought of

157

him all afternoon. All afternoon he'd been aroused by thoughts of him, even as Daniel ranted and Margot wept. He thought of Wednesday and smiled in anticipation.

Chapter Eighteen

April, 1920
Forgive me, Father. It's been six months since my last confession ...

Patrick sighed. He could begin with small sins and work up or he could begin and end with Paul. He glanced towards the confessional box and the few waiting penitents. In the aisle the younger priest genuflected and walked quickly from the church. At least he wouldn't be hearing his confession. He smiled, imagining the boy's jug ears burning crimson.

Paul had laughed at him. 'You'll be on your knees flogging yourself from now until Christmas. Are you sure you've thought this through?'

'No one gets flogged.'

'Pity. Well, do what you have to. It seems pretty pointless to me.' He frowned.'Unless you don't intend to fuck me again.'

'Don't call it fucking.'

'Patrick, the priest will say go and sin no more or whatever it is they say. If you won't take any notice of him why bother unless you want to end it?'

'Of course I don't want to end it! I love you, for Christ's sake!'

Paul had sighed, covering his face with his hands. The sheet had gathered at his waist, exposing his chest, and Patrick had reached out, circling his nipple with the edge of his thumbnail. Paul lowered his hands. 'Will you keep going back to confession, week after week? Turn me into a sin you need absolution from?'

Patrick had kissed his mouth gently. 'No. You're not a sin.'

'A sinner, though.'

'No!' Exasperated, he'd held Paul's face between his hands and forced him to meet his eyes. 'You're the best person I know. Have known. Ever.'

Paul had grasped his wrists to lift his hands away. 'Ever and ever, cross your heart? How many people have you known, Patrick?'

'Armies of them.'

Paul gazed at him intently. 'Tell me again.'

'What? That I love you? You know I do.'

'No …' He'd laughed a little. 'I know you *love* me.' At last he'd added softly, 'I love you, too.'

The narrow door to the confessional opened. Realising he was next in line Patrick got up and walked out into the spring sunshine.

The day after their meeting in the Castle & Anchor, Patrick had fixed the leak in the shop roof and thrown the old mattress away. He had taken the brittle, yellowing posters down and painted the walls the colour of milky Camp coffee. From Ellen Avenue he had brought his parents' feather bed and covered it with a Paisley silk shawl. The chimney was swept. Every Wednesday afternoon, after Hetty had gone home, he would light the fire and lie down on the bed to wait, his fingers worrying the shawl's silky tassels as he watched the shadows lengthen on the ceiling. Paul always arrived on time. After three months of Wednesdays his heart still raced when he heard his light, quick steps on the stairs.

Walking back now to the shop through the Wednesday market, Patrick stopped at the sweet stall. Remembering that his lover had a sweet tooth, he bought half a pound of chocolate caramels.

Paul said, 'What are you giggling at, Wilson?'

'Nothing, sir.'

It was the end of the school day, the boys noisily jostling one another to get out of the classroom as quickly as possible. Stepping in front of Wilson, Paul held out his hand. 'Show me.'

'It's nothing, sir. Honestly.'

Paul snatched the folded piece of paper from his hand. Looking at it he crumpled it and threw it in the waste paper basket beside his desk. 'You can go.'

'I didn't draw it, sir.'

'Get out of my sight.'

The boy dodged past Adam who smiled at Paul from the classroom door. 'What was all that about?'

'Do you want to see? It's not a very good likeness, but I think the huge, dead, staring eye will give you a clue who it's suppose to be.'

'Oh. Well, we can all expect that kind of thing. Best to rise above it.' Stepping inside the classroom he closed the door behind him. 'So, how are things? Are they behaving themselves, apart from that? There's nothing you're concerned about?' He laughed, embarrassed. 'No advice needed?'

'There is one thing you can tell me – how do you get through the day without a very stiff drink?'

Adam sighed. 'Look, Paul. As head of the English department the headmaster's asked me to have a word with you.'

Paul glanced at him while packing exercise books into his briefcase. Adam smiled awkwardly. 'He told me that he passed your class the other day and had to come in.'

'Yes, he did. I had no idea he could shout so loudly.'

'Apparently he had to, because of the noise your class was making. He told me you'd lost control.'

Paul looked down at the briefcase: twenty essays on *The Merchant of Venice* to be marked. Shylock's pound of flesh seemed nothing; it would be easy to survive such a wound. He felt Adam's hand light on his arm. 'Yes, he's right. I lost control of the little bastards.'

'And it wasn't just that lesson, was it?'

'Adam, what has the head told you to tell me?'

He coloured. 'That I'm to keep an eye on you.'

'Nice choice of words. Anything else?'

'Paul …' Sighing, he said, 'I know you're not happy.'

'Do I have to be happy? Are any of the old duffers in the staff room happy? There's not much sign of life in there, let alone happiness.'

'All I'm saying is perhaps you need to think about what you really want to do. Teaching is a calling, after all.'

'And no one called me, eh?' Snapping the briefcase closed he made to pass.

Adam caught his arm. 'I miss you, you know.' Awkward still he repeated, 'I miss you.'

Paul avoided his gaze. 'I have to think about Margot. And it's not as if we never meet.'

'Three, four times a month if I'm lucky? She should let you out more.'

'She's my wife, not my bloody jailer.' He fought down his irratation, desperate to get out of the school gates so he could have a cigarette. Two cigarettes, one quick after the other. He felt for the case in his pocket, rubbing his thumb over the smooth patch his fingers had worn in the silver.

'Adam, I have to go.'

'Right, of course. I'd walk home with you, but I have work to do.'

Paul touched his arm as he brushed past. 'Goodnight, Adam.'

Lighting a cigarette as soon as he got outside the gates and the possible sight of the head, Paul hesitated, imagining going back inside the school and finding Adam. Adam's new Head of English office was tiny but it had a lock on the door and a window with a thick, dark blind. The fucking could be over in a matter of minutes, the holding and reassuring would take half an hour or less. It would save having to tell more lies to Margot; it would save an evening in Adam's bed, listening to talk of timetables and staff room gossip. For a little while it would save him from the constant guilt. He drew deeply on the cigarette, thinking about throwing it down to the ground and returning to the dank atmosphere of the school. He thought about Patrick, of being held in the warm, quiet peace of their room, and the cigarettes he could smoke without any guilt at all. He glanced at the barred windows of the school and walked away.

Hetty swept the shop floor, thinking of Mick. Tonight, as she did most Wednesdays and Sundays, she would tell her mother she was going to the picture house with Elsie and walk instead to Ellen Avenue, letting herself in with the Chinese lion's key and calling his name into the gloom. He would come out from his room, smiling his dazzling smile and she would have such an urge to kiss him it was indecent. He would take off his glasses, folding them into his pocket, and push his fingers through his unruly hair as though he was transforming himself into someone else for her. He would say her name gently, as though surprised that she should have kept her promise and turned up to see him again, as if she could stay away. He was all she thought about; he made weighing sausages and scrubbing bloody trays and standing on her feet all day bearable, because at the end of it all she could go and see him and he would smile as if she was the most beautiful girl he'd ever seen. In his room she was always aware of his bed behind them, so conscious of it her skin tingled. She wondered if there was something wrong with her to want him so badly.

Sweeping up the bits of mince and sawdust she looked up as Patrick walked through from the back of the shop and turned the sign on the door to 'closed'.

'There. They're too late for pork pies now.'

'We've sold out anyway.'

'Have we? Good.' He smiled absently over his shoulder as he opened the till and began counting the takings. 'You can go now, Hetty. I've left some ham and bread in the pantry for Mick's supper. There's an egg custard, too, if he wants it.'

She carried the dustpan outside to the yard. From the shop she could hear Patrick humming under his breath. She frowned, picking up the tune at last – *The Boy I Love*. It played in her head as she fetched her coat and walked home.

The baby had kicked and punched all day. Kicked and punched and danced on her bladder so that it seemed she had

163

spent most of the afternoon watching spiders dart from the corners of the outside lavatory. Sitting in the kitchen, her hands fumbling with knit one, purl one, Margot watched the clock on the dresser, waiting for Paul.

Her mother had spent the morning trying to teach her to knit, just as she had tried at the beginning of the war. Then there had been a misshapen balaclava her mother had unpicked and now there was this half-finished bootie, trailing grubbily from its needle. Paul would ignore it unless she said something and then he would kiss her and say it didn't matter. Nothing mattered to Paul, the price of food, the rise in their rent, the unrelenting contempt her father held him in – nothing. She sighed, looking down at the knitting and pulling at it in a desperate attempt to give it shape.

Paul came in through the back door and kissed the top of her head. She caught his scent of outside and cigarettes as he placed his briefcase on the floor beside her. He went into the pantry, coming out with the tin of biscuits. Beginning to eat his way through them, he frowned at her. 'What are you doing?'

'Mummy's teaching me to knit.'

'You haven't forgotten I'm going out tonight?'

'I don't usually forget, do I?' She looked up at him. There were shadows under his eyes, contrasting darkly against the pallor of his skin. During his nightmares last night he had cried out so loudly the neighbours had hammered on the wall. Laying the knitting down she reached out and squeezed his hand. 'I don't mind you seeing your friend. He should come here, one evening, and then you wouldn't have to go out in the cold. I could meet him … is he married? He could bring his wife.'

'He's not married.' Paul drew his hand away from hers. 'I'll make a start on supper, shall I?'

Outside the discreetly anonymous door at the back of the shop, Paul glanced up and down the alley before taking out his key and turning it in the lock. He locked the door behind him quickly and walked through the yard. Inside, he ran up the stairs. As always, he felt like a criminal.

Patrick was smoking on the bed, his left hand trailing to the floor, his fingers twisting at the dull colours of the rag-rug. As Paul walked in he turned slowly to smile at him and Paul's insides softened with the familiar mixture of love and lust. His beauty was astonishing. It always made him smile.

'Hello, *sir.*'

Paul knelt beside him and kissed his mouth. 'Sergeant.'

Touching his face Patrick brushed his thumb gently beneath his good eye. 'You're all right?'

'Are you?'

'I am now.' He made room on the bed and they lay side by side, passing the cigarette between them until it was finished. Eventually Patrick said, 'I was thinking just now, I don't know when your birthday is.'

Paul laughed. 'Why? Are you planning a party?' He stood up. As he took off his jacket he said, 'Your birthday's in June. I remember you were sent a cake and you shared it amongst the men.'

The men had sprawled in the long French grass, their faces lifted to the hot sun as they licked cake crumbs from their fingers. He had approached them, curious about their laughter, jealous of it. Wanting to be included, all he had done was kill the atmosphere as effectively as if he'd thrown a grenade amongst them. Patrick had scrambled to his feet and brushed the unseemly crumbs from his tunic. The sun behind his head had created a halo for him.

Tugging at his tie Paul said, 'Why do you want to know when my birthday is?'

'Because I don't know and I feel I should. There are all kinds of things I don't know about you.'

Paul began unbuttoning his shirt. 'All right. My birthday's in October. I'll be twenty-four. I hate tripe and suet puddings but other than that I'll eat anything. What else? Oh yes. Wednesday is my favourite day of the week.'

'That's funny. Wednesday is my favourite, too.' After a while Patrick said, 'You haven't told me anything yet.'

Paul thought of all the things he might tell him: that he had

165

made a better soldier than he had thought he would, or that he was terrified of being blind again. He could confess that he was afraid he would make a bad father, or that every day when he went into school he was sure he would be sacked. He could tell him about Jenkins, of course, although Patrick knew all about that. When he'd first started visiting him in this room he'd imagined he would find the courage to talk about what he'd done, but the time he spent with him had become too precious to be ruined by the past.

Aware of Patrick waiting for a reply he said, 'My earliest memory is watching my grandfather planting roses in our garden. He died when I was twelve and I still miss him. When I'm gardening I imagine he's there with me.' He smiled. 'There you are – I like gardening. You didn't know that.'

He finished undressing and lay down beside Patrick. Taking his hand Patrick said carefully, 'When did you realise you were different?'

'Different? Is that what we should call it?' Paul smiled at him. 'I can't remember. I always knew, I think. What about you?'

Patrick was silent for a long time. At last he squeezed Paul's hand tightly. 'There was a man my father called a nancy-boy in the shop where he bought our school uniforms. He was so arch, you know? Flapping and mincing about.' He laughed shortly. 'I was fifteen and I knew I wasn't anything like that. I wasn't like him and I wasn't like Mick. I didn't seem to fit at all.'

Standing up Patrick began to undress. 'I used to tell myself that I'd change, get married, eventually, putting the idea off until some time in the future when everything would be all right. I even went to a prostitute, once.' He smiled at Paul over his shoulder. 'Seeking a cure, I suppose. I didn't think much about marriage after that.' He took off his shirt and tossed it down. 'Then I saw you. I saw you and I thought – he's like me, a queer who's not a flapping, mincing nancy-boy.'

Naked, he knelt beside Paul, his hand going to cup his face. 'Tell me about the first man you went with.' His eyes were dark and unreadable and Paul frowned, grasping his wrist to

166

lift his hand away. Patrick said softly, 'What was he like?'

Paul got up and fetched his cigarettes from his jacket. Lighting one he heard himself say calmly, 'He was my French teacher. He buggered me on the floor of his study. He didn't bother to undress me. He didn't try to make it easy. He just fucked me. Afterwards he couldn't look me in the eye. I speak French well, though, my French is pretty good.'

Patrick gazed at him from the bed. 'I'd like to kill him.'

'The Germans saved you the bother.'

'I wanted there to be someone who did undress you, who was tender and careful.'

Paul thought about Adam, that first time when they had undressed each other. Adam's eyes had never left his as though he was afraid he was about to be stopped. Paul drew heavily on the cigarette. Looking at Patrick he said, 'There was one boy. He was the same age as me, nineteen, a Second Lieutenant, like me. We'd both been gassed. The hospital where we were sent was by the sea. We walked through sand dunes, far away where we wouldn't be found. It was July and he was pale as winter. We had to be careful with each other because everything hurt so much – the sunshine, the grass, even the salt in the air. I think we both just wanted to be comforted by someone neither of us had to talk to.'

He tossed his cigarette into the fire and lay down on the bed again. Rolling on his side Patrick pulled him into his arms and held him tightly.

Jenkins's teeth were chattering and he was crying and wouldn't stop and Paul pushed him back against the ladder scaling the side of the trench. All the others had climbed it and were crawling towards the German line. But Jenkins went on shaking and crying and Paul held his face between his hands, forcing him to meet his eyes.

He started and grabbed at the sheets to stop himself falling. He felt Patrick's arms around him, hugging him more tightly. 'I'm here, it's all right.'

'How long have I slept?'

'Not long.' Patrick was silent for a while. At last he said,

'I'm sorry about earlier. I had no right to ask you those things.' He got up and lit the candles on the mantelpiece. In the soft light his honey-coloured skin became flawless. Paul couldn't see the moles on his back, or the raised, white scar that disfigured his thigh and was a permanent reminder of the Somme. He watched the shadow of Patrick's body, his muscular arms and shoulders, fold into the corner of the room, the candles flickering in the draught he caused. He thought of how Patrick was the only person in the world who knew how wicked he was and yet he didn't seem to mind.

He said, 'I wish we hadn't met in France.'

Patrick climbed back into bed. He reached for Paul's hand. 'We wouldn't have met at all if it hadn't been for the war.' He looked at him. 'Unless you'd walked in the shop and suddenly fancied a bit of rough.'

'I think I probably would have been too scared.'

Patrick laughed. He began to kiss Paul and his mouth moved down his body until his lips closed around his semi-erect cock.

Every Wednesday evening after he'd kissed Patrick goodbye, Paul went to Parkwood to bathe. George frowned as he ushered him through to the warmth of Parkwood's kitchen. 'Are you all right? You look exhausted.'

'I'm fine.'

George peered at him anxiously. 'You look awful. Such dark rings under your eyes … are you sleeping?'

Paul went to stand in front of the fire. On the mantelpiece his own face looked out at him from his wedding picture. Avoiding Margot's eyes he glanced at George. 'Don't look so worried, Dad, I'm all right.'

Pouring him a measure of Scotch George handed him the glass. 'Sit down. Drink this while I run the bath.'

The French master had been called Mr Rouse; his fingernails had been too long and his breath had smelt of peppermints. One Friday afternoon he'd kept him back after the class. 'Have you fallen out with the other boys, Harris?'

In the bath, Paul winced at the memory. How could the man not know that masters weren't supposed to notice such things? It had been one of the few occasions he remembered blushing.

Rouse blushed, too. 'I only ask because you always seem to be on your own. It seems quite hard on you.' He laughed, embarrassed. 'Is there anything I can do to help?'

Paul gazed at him, his colour returning to normal. 'No, thank you, sir.'

Hurriedly, Rouse said, 'You know, your French is very good. I have some books in my room that may help you progress even further, if you're interested? If you're at a loose end you could come and have a look at them.'

Paul remembered how the man's voice had quavered a little, how he had cleared his throat and looked away to the window and the fourth form playing cricket on the school field. He heard the thwack of the ball on the bat and the applause as the batsman was caught out. Rouse breathed heavily, waiting.

'What time should I come, sir?'

Paul submerged himself in the water, counting seconds as he concentrated on not breathing. He wouldn't think about the scratch of those long fingernails, or the sweet shop taste of his breath. He wouldn't remember that afterwards the man had wept with shame, or that Jenkins had caught him coming out of his rooms. Jenkins had grabbed his arms, pinning him against the wall.

'Extra tuition, Harris?'

'Let go.'

Jenkins wrinkled his nose. 'What's that smell?' He made a show of disgust. 'Harris, you *stink* of old queer! You disgusting, filthy little pervert. I think we should get you cleaned up, don't you?'

Two of Jenkins's friends appeared from the shadows. Jenkins smirked at them. Pushing Paul ahead of him he said, 'Let's go.'

He remembered that when they stripped him he imagined he actually did stink and a part of him felt that this was one

169

punishment at least that he deserved. The bath water had been freezing; the other two had held him down as Jenkins took a toilet brush to his genitals. He'd been sore for days, imagining everyone could smell the stink of bleach every time he undressed for bed. Jenkins made sure all the boys in their dormitory knew what he'd done. The rumours spread around the school. He'd contemplated suicide.

Paul broke to the surface, gasping for air. The water was becoming cold and he got out of the bath and dressed. Catching sight of his reflection in the steamed-up mirror he turned away quickly, hating the sight of himself.

Chapter Nineteen

The liver was arranged on a tray, sprigs of bright parsley tucked between its folds, blood tinging the tight green curls. Liver was cheaper than chops or ham. Standing outside the butcher's shop window, Margot thought of the few coins she had left in her purse. She watched a bluebottle crawl across the snout of the model pig. If the fly landed on the liver she would buy something else. The fly took off and flew out of sight. Margot sighed. They would have liver for supper, just as the doctor ordered.

The shop was empty and she walked up to the counter decisively, already taking out her purse. The butcher smiled. 'What can I get you?'

'Half a pound of liver, please.'

He went on smiling at her. At last he said, 'It's Mrs Harris, isn't it? Lieutenant Harris and I were in the same regiment. I remember seeing you at that dance at New Year. Are you well?'

'Yes, thank you.' She looked down at her purse again, disconcerted by his steady gaze. 'Half a pound of liver, please.'

As he weighed the liver he glanced over his shoulder. 'Would you like anything else?' He placed the small, neatly wrapped parcel on the counter in front of her. 'Some bacon to go with the liver, or a nice chop, perhaps?'

She fumbled for coins. 'No, thank you. How much is that?'

'Free to new customers.'

'Free?'

He smiled. 'Free.'

She put her purse back in her handbag, thinking of what

171

she could buy with the money saved. Glancing at him she said, 'Thank you.'

'My pleasure.'

She remembered Robbie saying, 'I had a letter from Paul this morning, about a piglet. Apparently his men chased the creature round an orchard, butchered it and then roasted it on a spit. He drew pigs in the margins, all curly tails and snouts.' He'd laughed. 'The letter was all about nothing, really. You'd think he was at a Boy Scout camp.'

Walking home from town, Margot remembered that Robbie said, 'I never thought he'd make much of a soldier. At school he was always such a fearful little thing. Odd, really, how he's turned out.'

Not really interested she'd asked, 'And how has he turned out?'

Robbie was silent for a while. At last he said, 'Have you heard of Stoics, Margot? Nothing mattered to them, everything was accepted as it was, as though they'd risen above human feeling and emotion and nothing could touch them. Insane, really, if you think about it, but that's how Paul is. Doesn't complain, doesn't question. The perfect junior officer.'

She laughed. 'I think you mean he's brave.'

'It's a kind of bravery, I suppose.' He'd sighed, squeezing her hand. 'I suppose I thought he was more intelligent than to accept it all without doubt.'

At home Margot slipped the liver on to a plate. She touched it gently, thinking of the piglet Paul's men had caught in an orchard in France and imagined its insides slopping on to the grass. The handsome butcher had probably played a big part in the slaughter.

She went upstairs and lay down on their bed. Taking Paul's pillow she held it to her, inhaling the faint smell of him. The baby had been still for a while and she pressed her hand against her side. She felt a tightly bunched fist push against her palm and was reassured. Robbie's baby would be strong like him; she imagined a bold little boy, nothing like Paul – she couldn't imagine he would be anything like Paul.

172

Closing her eyes she thought of Robbie walking through the graveyard, remembering how she would watch him from her bedroom window, willing him to stop and look back. He never did. He kissed her goodbye cheerfully, called her his sweet girl and didn't look back, making her wonder if he thought about her at all when she wasn't with him. She tried to imagine his body beside her each night, his cries waking her instead of Paul's, but all she could see was his back as he walked away. Soon she would forget what he sounded like and only photographs would bring back his face. Softly she said his name, letting it go into the silence.

From the classroom doorway Adam bawled, 'Quiet! You will all be quiet this instant! Ramsey – sit down at once, boy!'

Ramsey sat. The banging of desk lids stopped and all the boys looked straight ahead, their backs straight as their faces. Adam stepped forward and a few in the front row flinched.

'Mr Harris,' Adam said. 'Would you wait for me outside, please?'

In the corridor Paul leaned against the pea-green wall, the noise still ringing in his ears. It had started quietly at first, soft thuds that could almost be ignored; then Ramsey had stood up and begun to conduct his orchestra of desk lids and the boy's flaying arms had brought the level of noise to a deafening climax. They couldn't hear his feeble requests for them to stop and he knew they would've ignored him even if they had. For those few minutes he was back in boarding school, singled out for special punishment. As the noise became louder it was all he could do to stop himself crying.

Coming out of the class room Adam said, 'Go and have a cigarette.'

'No. I'll go back and face them.'

Adam stopped him by placing a hand firmly on his chest. 'Go and have a cigarette. You're white as a sheet. They shouldn't see you like this.'

'Will you tell the head?'

'I won't have to, Paul. I think the whole school heard.' He sighed. 'Look, have a walk around the yard, calm yourself

173

down, then come and see me in my office. We'll talk.'

'What about them?'

'Leave me to deal with them.' He touched his arm. 'Go on, off you go.'

From the dugout doorway Jenkins said, 'Davies is weeping again.'

Paul looked up from his supper of cold, tinned stew. Unwinding the scarf that covered much of his head and face, Jenkins sat down opposite him. 'Do you ever feel like weeping, Harris?'

A shell exploded. Earth fell from the ceiling on to the table and Paul pushed his plate away. Standing up he said, 'I'll go and speak to him.'

'It won't do any good. Besides, why shouldn't he have a good old blub?'

'I don't want the men seeing him like that.'

'Then off you go and talk to him. I'm sure the poor mite couldn't feel any worse anyway.'

'What do you mean by that?'

'He's scared of you, Harris! Absolutely terrified you'll tear him off a strip for some minor infringement! Maybe you're best leaving him to Sergeant Morgan, now I come to think about it.'

'Morgan?'

'Didn't I say? Morgan's taking care of him. It's quite sweet to see, really, the big man sitting so quietly with the boy. Morgan had one of the men make him a cup of tea. Plenty of sugar, no doubt.'

'Why didn't you bring him in here? He shouldn't be bothering the men. For God's sake, they have enough to put up with!'

'What's really the matter, Harris? Scared you've got a rival for Morgan's affections?' Jenkins laughed. He sat back in his chair and lit a cigarette, flicking the spent match on to the shiny gristle left on Paul's supper plate. 'There's something about the Sergeant, isn't there? Cut above. I don't wonder you can't keep your eyes off him.'

'Why don't you go to hell!'

'Now, I could be trite and say we're all already *in* hell.' He gazed at Paul. 'I had a quiet word with Davies. You know, the boy's so innocent he hardly knew the meaning of the word *pervert.*'

In the schoolyard, Paul drew heavily on the cigarette. He remembered that he couldn't bring himself to stay in the dugout with Jenkins and had gone out into the trench. The men were dark shapes huddled against the sandbags; he could smell the stew they were spooning into their mouths, a stink like over-boiled bones. That morning he had inspected their feet and Corporal Taylor had joked that he was like Christ, about to wash the feet of the disciples. Further along the trench Morgan crouched beside Davies, watching as the boy sipped from an enamel mug. He caught his eye and for a moment they'd stared at each other.

In the school playground Paul closed his eyes, sucking smoke deep into his lungs. The cigarette was finished, burnt almost to his fingers. In a few minutes the bell would ring and hundreds of boys would swarm outside, making him want to find somewhere to hide. Tossing the cigarette down he turned and walked back inside the school.

Adam said, 'Sit down, Paul.' He smiled too brightly. 'Feeling better?'

'I'm fine.' He sat down, aware of Adam watching him from the other side of his desk. Attempting to smile back at him he said, 'I've stopped shaking, anyway.'

'That's good. Right, I've given the whole class detention and the headmaster will cane Ramsey tomorrow. The boy will also apologise to you in person and in writing.'

'That should prove embarrassing.'

'I don't care who's embarrassed. We're trying to instil discipline. Besides, he deserves to be embarrassed.'

'Do I?'

Taking off his glasses Adam pushed the heels of his hands into his eyes. 'I've made myself hoarse shouting at those boys.

175

I don't think I've been so angry in my life. All I could think about was that this is my fault. I should have realised you weren't ready for this.'

'I am ready, most of the time.'

'You should see yourself, Paul. You look worse now than when you first came home. And you *are* still shaking.' Frowning he said, 'Perhaps you should take a day or two off.'

'No. Things will be better tomorrow. I can't put off facing them.'

'I hate seeing you like this. Listen, why don't you come and see me tonight? We'll talk some more.' He stood up and walked around the desk. Holding the door open for him he said, 'Seven o'clock?'

In Adam's bed Paul thought about Second Lieutenant Davies. In October 1918 a sniper had shot him in the head. His had been a quick, painless death – a second's carelessness and then nothing. He had written to the boy's parents and said that their son had always been brave. Reading over his shoulder Jenkins had laughed.

Adam propped himself up on his elbow. 'Do you want to tell me what happened today?'

Paul closed his eyes, remembering how helpless he had felt as the first thuds of desk lids broke the unnatural quiet of the class, increasing in speed until the noise grew louder and louder. All the boys had looked at him, all of them smirking. He wondered if it would have been worse if one of them had looked ashamed. At last he said, 'It was a prank, that's all. Do we have to make so much of it?'

'Yes, if it's the only way I can get you to come and see me.'

'So am I here for a fucking or a bollocking, then?'

'Don't talk like that. God, you're a crude little sod, sometimes.' He sighed. 'You were an officer, Paul. Why can't you cope with a few thirteen-year-olds?'

'I don't know. Maybe because the school hasn't issued me with a tin hat and a machine gun.'

Adam was silent for a while. At last he said quickly, 'The

head wants to give you your notice. I've persuaded him to give you another chance.'

'Thanks'

'For Christ's sake try and sound a bit more grateful.'

'I am. Really.' He managed to smile at him, although the shame of almost losing his job had his heart racing.

Adam laughed bleakly. 'Do you want to *show* me how grateful you are?'

Paul closed his eyes as Adam pushed him on to his stomach and entered him roughly. He wondered when they had stopped making love, when Adam had given up on tenderness for this quick, angry fucking. Adam called out triumphantly and the bedstead rattled against the wall like the clatter of desk lids.

Chapter Twenty

Mick said, 'I hate Sundays. I've always hated Sundays, the way they drag. Patrick looks forward to them, he had quite a spring in his step this morning. Of course, it's his day of *rest*, whereas I rest every day.'

Hetty looked up from the book she'd been reading to him. 'I knew you weren't listening. Do you want to hear how it ends?'

'Not really.' Throwing his cigarette stub into the fire he said, 'Do you ever see your new neighbour? You know that young girl – Mrs Harris. Has she had the baby yet?'

'I see her sometimes, and no, she hasn't had the baby yet. She came in the shop. Patrick gave her free liver.'

Mick raised his eyebrows. 'Did he?'

Hetty sighed. Closing the book she said, 'I think he took a fancy to her. I suppose she is pretty. And it's not as if she'll be a good customer – poor as mice, her and that husband. All make-do-and-mend. She peered into her purse as though it was a big, black, scary hole.'

Mick laughed but his eyes remained questioning. 'Do you see much of her husband?'

She frowned at him. 'Why?'

'I knew his brother, I told you.'

'I did hear one thing about him. Mrs Shipley who lives next door to them told Mam how he makes such a row in the night she has to bang on the wall with her shoe, says he sounds like he's back fighting the war single-handed. She says her Fred is ready to go round there and throttle him, one eye or not.'

Mick lit another cigarette. 'What did *her Fred* do during the war? Don't tell me. Reserved occupation.'

'He was too old to be called up.'

'Lucky him.'

'It can't be easy being woken night after night.'

'No. It's not easy.' He stared into the fire, his mouth set in a thin, angry line. After a while he said, 'It must be hard on the boy's wife.'

'I suppose so.'

'You suppose so? Can't you imagine how frightening it must be for her? For God's sake, can't you empathise even a little?'

Returning his angry gaze Hetty said, 'Maybe I just think she's lucky to have a husband and a baby on the way.'

'Even a husband whose screams wake the neighbours? Will any husband do, Hetty?'

'Not any, no.'

He flicked cigarette ash at the hearth. Without looking at her he said, 'I'm tired. Perhaps you'd better go home.'

'I thought you wanted to go for a walk in the park?'

'I hate that park, it's full of bloody women who can't keep their little brats from staring.' He looked at her at last. 'I think you should go, now. Thank you for coming to see me.'

'I don't want to go.'

'No? Do you want to read me another chapter of that terrible book? Or we could play cards. There's such a lot to keep you here, isn't there?'

'There's you.'

'Me?' He manoeuvred his chair back, turning it round to face the window. Staring out over the garden he said, 'You shouldn't let me keep you, Hetty.'

'Why not?'

He looked at her. At last he said, 'Because I think I'm in love with you. I *am* in love with you – and that's terrible because what business do I have falling in love? A great bloody useless lump like me?' Turning back to the garden he said, 'I thought your company would be enough. It isn't. It's too bloody painful.'

'What if I was in love with you?'

'Are you?' He frowned.

'Yes.'

'But what's the point in that? I'll never be any good for you … and people look at me and think … they think …'

'I don't care what they think.'

'I do! They think I don't have normal feelings, and if I do …' His face twisted into an angry smile. Bitterly he said, 'Well, no one likes to think about it, do they?'

She crouched beside him. 'I do love you. I have for ages now.'

He gazed at her. 'You love me?' He searched her face, his eyes intense. Cupping her cheek with his hand he said, 'I can't have you love me, Hetty.'

She kissed him, gently at first, until she felt his resistance give. He groaned softly, his hand going to the back of her head and his fingers knotting in her hair as his tongue searched out hers. As he pulled her closer to him the arm of the wheelchair pressed against her and she drew away. She laughed a little, frustrated. 'I can't get close enough.'

He pressed his hand against her cheek. 'Maybe you should go.'

'Do you really want me to?'

'No. But if you stay …' Desperately he said, 'I just want to hold you so badly.'

'I know. I want that, too.'

'I don't want you to do anything you might regret.'

'I won't.'

'If we just hold each other, that's all.'

She nodded, impatient with desire. 'That's all.'

He laughed as if he couldn't believe the passion in her eyes. Softly he said, 'Help me on to the bed.'

Margot watched Paul shave at the kitchen sink. Earlier, he had taken his eye out and cleaned the socket while the eye watched from a glass of water. The eye didn't produce tears and throughout the day he would drop water into it to prevent the socket from becoming dry. Usually he did all this in private but this morning it seemed he had forgotten she was there.

The *Sunday Post* was spread out on the table in front of her.

She had been pretending to read the same article for the last ten minutes. Turning the page she said, 'You promise you won't be late?'

He glanced at her, razor poised. There was a line of soap on its blade and he rinsed it off. 'I promise.'

'Because you know what Daddy's like. And it is his birthday.' After a moment she said cautiously, 'You'll make an effort, won't you?'

Looking in the mirror he'd propped up on the window ledge, he dragged the razor across his cheek.

'I know you don't want to go, Paul.'

He smoothed back his hair with both hands. Catching her reflected gaze he said, 'I'll be there, don't worry.' He shrugged his jacket on. 'Are you sure you don't want me to walk you to church?'

'I'm sure. Go and see your friend, have a nice time.'

After he'd gone Margot went into the front parlour and lifted the lace curtain away from the window to watch him walk towards the High Street. Letting the curtain fall, she thought of thin French actresses and looked down at her own mountainous body in despair.

Paul walked to the Red Lion pub where he had promised to meet Patrick. There was a group of young lads on the corner of Tanner Street and he felt his heart beat quicken. He wished often he didn't look so obviously like a frail little queer. He tried to walk a little taller and resisted quickening his step as he passed the youths. Not one of them looked twice at him and he wanted to laugh at his paranoia but it was too depressing. He thought of the boys at school and wondered what they had in store for him next. He knew he was completely at their mercy, just as he had been at Jenkins's.

Last night he'd dreamt of Jenkins again and woke in a sweat to find Margot standing over him, her hair dishevelled from sleep and her eyes wide with fright. 'You were swearing!' She gazed at him in disbelief that he could use such terrible words. 'And who's Jenkins?'

'No one.' He held out his hand to her. 'No one, come back

181

to bed.'

No one. Paul lit a cigarette as he turned the corner on to Skinner Street. If only.

Jenkins crouched beside him and sang softly, 'The boy I love is up in the gallery, the boy I love is …'

Paul had been asleep on his bunk. Startled, he'd sat up, fumbling in his haste to fasten his tunic buttons. He searched his pockets for a cigarette, appalled to see that his hands were shaking as he struck a match.

Jenkins laughed. 'Lord, you're uncivil! Aren't you going to offer me one of those? Isn't that the done thing?'

As Paul made to get up, Jenkins placed a hand on his chest, pushing him down again. 'Hawkins asked me this morning if I knew what was wrong with you. Said you'd been behaving strangely. I wonder if he knows just how strange you are. Perhaps I should have a quiet word with him, put him in the picture.'

As if on cue, Hawkins came in. He frowned from Jenkins to Paul. 'Harris, have you told him yet?'

Paul scrambled out of his bunk, trying to avoid brushing against Jenkins who, as usual, stood too close to him. Straightening his tunic he said, 'No, sir, not yet.'

Hawkins grunted. 'All right, I'll do the honours.' He looked at Jenkins. 'You and Harris and twenty of the men are going on a little raiding party. Top brass want us to catch a Fritz prisoner.' He grinned at Paul. 'They imagine we can find out a few of their secrets, eh, Harris?'

'Yes, sir.'

To Jenkins he said, 'I wouldn't normally send the two of you but I think you can learn from Harris's experience. So mind you take notes, Jenkins – you'll be doing it on your own next time.' Hawkins sat down at the table. 'Be a good chap and go and tell Johnson to fetch me a cup of tea, would you, Jenkins?'

When he'd gone, Hawkins looked at Paul. 'Do you think he'll manage?'

'I don't know, sir.'

Hawkins frowned at him. 'I'm worried about you. I hope

you're not coming down with something.'

'No sir, I'm fine.'

'Fine! You always say you're fine, thank God!' He sighed. 'I'm sorry I've had to foist Jenkins on you, Paul. But he has to start pulling his weight some time.' After a moment he laughed. 'The bugger went very white, didn't he?'

Crossing the High Street close to Patrick's shop, Paul remembered just how white Jenkins had gone. He had wanted to feel gratified but instead he had felt sick at the thought of having to rely on him if anything went wrong. The only comfort was knowing that Patrick would be with him. Later that night as they prepared for the raid, he'd caught Jenkins watching him as he cleaned his pistol.

'Morgan's going on the raid.' Jenkins grabbed his arm, forcing him to turn to look at him. 'If Morgan's going you don't need me – you can tell Hawkins you don't need me!'

Jenkins's face was twisted with fear and anger. Unable to cope with his fear as well as his own Paul shook off his grasp and turned back to his gun.

'Did you hear me, Harris? Tell Hawkins you'll do it on your own – you and bloody Morgan!'

'He won't listen to me.'

'He will! You're his blue-eyed bloody boy! He will listen!'

Paul stared at him. He felt as though he was seeing him properly for the first time in his life. He had only ever looked at him obliquely and always with a creeping sense of his own cowardice for not facing up to him. He saw how ordinary he was, rather plain and pasty-faced beneath his veneer of arrogance. For a moment he felt sorry for him. 'Listen, you'll be all right. It's really not as bad as you think it's going to be, once you're out there. Just stay close to Morgan and me – '

Jenkins had laughed so harshly he sounded like a mad man.

Paul stopped along the alley that led to the Red Lion. He leaned against the coal-blackened wall and breathed in deeply in an effort to manage the panic rising inside him. In St Stevens, when he'd allowed himself to remember that raid, a nurse had found him curled into a ball on the floor of the common room, fellow patients gazing at him with mute acceptance. A doctor was fetched; there was the usual carefully suppressed exasperation with him when despite their coaxing he couldn't speak, although he'd wanted to tell them that the guilt felt like a terrified animal trapped inside him. If he didn't stay still enough to keep it contained its panic would kill him. Eventually they had carried him to bed. An injection was administrated.

He pushed himself away from the wall and steadied himself. Taking another deep breath he walked inside the pub.

In The Red Lion Patrick looked around for a familiar face and was relieved not to find any. Tucked away in one of the back alleys that ran off the High Street, the Lion was used mainly by the market traders and its Sunday afternoon trade was quiet. Two men stood at the bar; in the far corner a middle-aged couple nursed two halves of stout. From a room above the pub he could hear scales being practised on the piano, the same flat notes repeated over and over, jarring the pub's sullen silence. At the bar the barmaid smiled at Paul as she handed him their drinks. Patrick watched her curiously and tried to work out if the interest she showed in Paul was merely professional friendliness or something more appreciative. The way others looked at Paul had always preoccupied him; whenever they were in public together his jealousy made sure he was never quite at ease.

Paul sat down. He set the two pints of beer on the table and immediately lit a cigarette. He placed the open case between them. 'I'm pleased you came.'

Patrick took a long drink. Wiping his mouth he said. 'Did you think I wouldn't?'

'I wasn't sure. I thought you might be wary.'

'Wary!' He laughed dismissively. 'Those two at the bar. Are they queer, do you think?'

'I doubt it.'

'So why should they think we are?'

'They might think I am.'

'Of course they don't.' He frowned. 'Don't say things like that. You're just like any other man.'

184

'Am I?'

Patrick looked away. The woman with the stout was rummaging in a large handbag and he watched her, wondering what might appear. A handkerchief. She blew her nose noisily. The man sitting next to her sighed.

Patrick took one of Paul's cigarettes, a cheaper brand than the one he smoked. He picked up the silver case, touched by the irony of something so expensive containing such rubbish. Turning the case over he read the inscription on the back, squinting at the ornately curling script.

Paul said, 'My father gave it to me for my twenty-first.'

He read the inscription aloud. '"To Paul with my fondest wishes and love."' Weighing it in his hand he looked at him. 'Your father?'

'You don't believe me?'

He placed the case down gently. 'Yes. I'm sorry, I believe you.'

Paul trailed his finger through the condensation on the side of his glass. Without lifting his gaze he asked, 'How's Mick?'

'All right. He's with his girl, Hetty.'

'Does he know who you're with?'

'No!'

Paul frowned at him thoughtfully. After a moment he said, 'You're lying. You do it so badly I can tell. He knows you're with me.'

'He doesn't know anything about you!'

'He was great friends with Robbie, did you know that? They served together at the beginning of the war. I think he confided in him.' After a moment he said, 'Rob could hardly ever bring himself to confide in me. At school he avoided me like the plague. Didn't want to be tarred with the same brush.' He smiled at Patrick, only to look down at his pint again. 'I couldn't blame him, really.'

'He should have looked out for you – if I'd been your brother – '

'He did – once or twice, when I was getting my head kicked in.'

'Christ!' Patrick shook his head. 'I would have made sure

no one even touched you!'

'What does Mick say about you seeing me?'

Patrick considered lying to him again but found himself saying, 'He says what you'd expect him to. He thinks you've corrupted me, of course.' He sighed in exasperation. 'I don't take any notice! I don't care what anyone thinks.'

The piano practice stopped and Paul glanced up. 'Every good boy deserves favour.'

'What?'

'It's a scale, the first letter of each word represents a note, e, g, b, d, f.'

'You play piano as well as all your other talents?'

'Very badly.'

Patrick smiled at him, holding his gaze for so long that Paul looked away, glancing quickly at the two men at the bar. 'Perhaps this wasn't a good idea.'

'You wanted to come here.'

'I like pubs. And I don't have any other drinking partners. Besides, I feel cooped up in the house, in school, in your little room. I needed a change.'

Paul became silent, drinking steadily and smoking with his usual fixed concentration. In their room Patrick welcomed his quietness, it felt calming and easy knowing they would talk only if they wanted to. But today his silence had an edge to it, as though there was something preoccupying him that he didn't feel he could share. Patrick shifted uncomfortably. There were times when he felt he would never know Paul properly just because of the difference in their class; he suspected that Paul behaved differently around the men he'd shared the officers' mess with and that different Paul was outgoing and talkative. He imagined if he had been a doctor's son rather than a butcher's Paul wouldn't be so silent.

Determined to make him understand that he wasn't just a thick, taciturn butcher, Patrick cleared his throat. 'Is there something wrong, Paul?'

Paul jerked his head up to frown at him. 'Why do you ask?'

'You're quiet.' He laughed awkwardly. '*Quieter*.'

'So? You're all right with that, aren't you?'

'Yes – '

'For Christ's sake, Patrick, don't you start too! Why does everyone feel that I should be talking all the time? What is there to say, anyway? Bloody words – they don't make the slightest bit of difference to anything!'

'All right. I'm sorry.' He looked so agitated that Patrick had the urge to take his hand. Instead he said gently, 'Do you want another drink?'

Paul shook his head. 'No. I have to go. I have to go and *talk* to my father-in-law over lunch. Talking proves that you're a good sort, apparently.' Exhaling cigarette smoke he said, 'I'm sorry. I shouldn't lose my temper with you – you don't deserve it.'

Patrick smiled. 'Is that you losing your temper, then? Blink and you miss it?'

'Pathetic, isn't it?'

'A bit. We should have a ride out up on to the moors – you could practise having a good shout at some sheep.'

'Is that all I'm fit for?'

'No! It was a joke – are you feeling sorry for yourself now?'

Paul drained the dregs of his beer and stood up. He touched his brow above his glass eye as though straightening an imaginary patch. It was a habitual, reflexive gesture that Patrick guessed he was hardly aware of performing, and as ever he felt soft with pity. He picked up the cigarette case and handed it to him, discreetly brushing his fingers. 'I'll see you on Wednesday.'

Paul nodded.

Patrick watched him walk out, wishing that he could leave with him and that they could walk through the streets without any dirty-minded bastard suspecting anything. But they had to be careful, Paul was insistent on the amount of care they took. 'Look at me,' he'd once said to him, 'and imagine what men like Thompson would think if they saw us walking down the street together.'

He knew Paul was right. Despite what he'd said earlier he knew it was a risk just sitting together in this pub. Patrick glared at the backs of the two men at the bar. Suddenly he hated everyone as much as they must surely hate him.

Chapter Twenty One

Walking through the cemetery from church her father asked, 'Have you thought of any names for the baby?'

'Grace, if it's a girl.'

'That's nice, I like that. Grace.' He smiled. 'It's pretty.'

Margot glanced at the stone angel a little further along the path. 'It was Paul's mother's name.'

'Oh.' He laughed emptily. 'What about boys' names?'

Robert, she thought, Robert after his father. She would call him Bobby. Her father looked at her. 'Margot? Did you hear me?'

'We haven't thought about boys' names.'

'No, well, perhaps when you see the baby a name will suggest itself. It's often the way.' He cleared his throat. 'Where is Paul this morning?'

'Seeing a friend. Someone he knew in the army.'

'And what's his name, this friend of his?'

'I can't remember.'

'Really? Haven't you met him?'

'No. He's allowed his own friends, isn't he?'

'Well, they weren't very much in evidence at your wedding. I've never known a groom with so few guests.'

'I think most of them are dead, Daddy.'

He was silenced and she hoped that she had shamed him. As they passed Grace Harris's grave a magpie flew low over the path in front of them, followed swiftly by its mate. Her father laughed a little. 'The male magpie never lets his mate out of his sight, did you know that? They're extremely jealous creatures, magpies.'

She looked at him. 'Are you saying I should never let Paul

out of my sight?'

'That would be rather difficult, wouldn't it?'

'Yes.'

He sighed, stopping to face her. 'Are you happy, Margot? If I thought you were happy then I wouldn't mind him so much.'

'I'm happy.'

'Then why do I never see you smile? Heaven knows the last time I heard you laugh.'

'I'm tired. The baby makes me tired. And sometimes there isn't a lot to smile about, but that's nothing to do with Paul.'

'Then what is it to do with? That dreadful little house?'

'No! It's not dreadful!'

'You're very loyal. I just wish he could do better for you.'

'He works hard.'

They reached the vicarage. From the open kitchen window came the smell of roast beef and the clatter of pots and pans. She turned to her father. 'Please, please don't be horrid to him over lunch.'

He looked surprised. 'Am I horrid? Then I'll try not to be.' He smiled half-heartedly. 'I'll make a special effort on my birthday.'

The Reverend said grace and Paul closed his eyes and bowed his head and said Amen when it was over, and when he looked up Margot smiled at him, pleased. Beneath the table she ran her foot up his shin and he imagined spending the afternoon in bed with her, as they often did on Sundays.

The Reverend said, 'So, Paul, who is this friend of yours Margot has told us about? An army friend, she says?'

He wondered if he should lie, make up a fictional character – a lieutenant he'd known since 1915, a fellow officer he had fought side by side with, through thick and thin. He could have a slight limp from an old wound; he would be easy to construct – a composite of all the second lieutenants he had ever seen killed. Swallowing a mouthful of roast potato he said, 'You probably know him. He owns a shop on the High Street. Patrick Morgan, of Morgan's Butchers?'

190

The Reverend raised his eyebrows. 'A butcher? And he was an officer, was he?'

'No, a sergeant.'

'I didn't think officers and sergeants mixed.'

'Well, we're neither officer nor sergeant, now.'

'Morgan …' Margot's mother frowned thoughtfully. 'Wasn't it the Morgans who were killed in that dreadful accident?'

Paul glanced at her. 'Their car was hit by a coal wagon.'

'That's right! Dreadful, quite dreadful. And their sons were away in France, weren't they? I remember reading about it in the paper. So sad.'

Daniel said, 'If it's the man I'm thinking of he was a rogue. The council wanted to close his shop as a danger to public health – the place was absolutely flyblown. Always seemed to have money, though. Something underhand going on, no doubt.'

Evenly Paul said, 'You don't know that, sir.'

'Common knowledge.'

Paul thought of Patrick's fierce hated of his father and wondered why he was defending him. All the same he said, 'But you don't have any evidence.'

Daniel snorted. 'When a man whose only visible means of support is a disgusting butcher's shop dresses his wife in mink and drives a fancy little car, then I would say the evidence is staring one in the face.'

'Perhaps he inherited money.'

'Don't be naïve, boy.' He looked at Margot. 'I hope you don't shop there. I don't want your and the baby's health risked by tainted meat.'

Margot blushed. 'It's really very clean, now.'

'All the same. Old habits die hard – there are plenty of other butchers on the High Street.'

Paul placed his knife and fork down. Turning to Daniel he said, 'He's a friend. Are you suggesting I shouldn't trust him to sell my wife decent meat?'

'I am, yes.'

'For God's sake!'

191

'Don't dare blaspheme at my table! I know you don't believe in anything beyond your own comfort and convenience, but the rest of us do.'

Iris sighed. 'Oh please, you two. Must you bicker every time you meet?'

'Asking him to show a little respect isn't bickering, Iris.' Daniel frowned at Margot. 'Are you all right?'

'No!' Tears stood in her eyes. 'Why can't you just try to get on! Why can't you just be quiet!' Pushing herself away from the table she ran from the room. Paul got up to follow her but Iris motioned that he should sit down.

'I'll see to her. Finish your meal.' She looked at Daniel. 'Try not to fight.'

As she closed the door behind her Daniel said, 'I have never know my daughter to be so unhappy. She was happy with your brother, but you knew that, didn't you? As soon as I set eyes on you at that wretched party I could see how jealous you were of their happiness. You must have hated Robert. You must have hated him as much as you have contempt for my daughter. You pretend to Margot that you love her but that's all it is, pretence – men like you don't love anyone. You can't!'

Paul laughed, astonished, even as his stomach contracted with fear. 'Men like me?'

'Do you honestly imagine I don't recognise what you are? I'd rather Margot gave the baby up than be married to a creature like you.' Whittaker was staring at him. He leaned across the table, bringing his face up close to Paul's. Exhaling a sharp, sour breath he said, 'When I think of all the decent boys killed …'

Paul looked down at his plate, his fingers going to the glass eye. He thought of the decent men, the ones he could remember, those who had stayed alive long enough to make an impression on him. Then there was Jenkins, of course.

He heard Daniel laugh contemptuously. 'You should look in a mirror before you set foot in my house again. Take a good, hard look at yourself.'

The door opened and Margot's mother came in. To Paul

she said, 'Margot would like you to take her home.'

Paul got up too quickly and swayed dizzily. His legs were shaking and he leaned against the table for a moment. Iris said, 'Are you all right, Paul?'

Daniel snorted. 'He's fine, Iris. Nothing for anyone to worry about any more.'

Paul looked at his father-in-law; he was gazing at him evenly, his eyes still dark with anger. Robbie had admired this man, in his letters he'd called him compassionate. *Nothing gung-ho about the Reverend,* Robbie wrote. *He seems to understand what's going on out there.*

Returning to his meal Daniel said, 'Take Margot home. Make sure you look after her.'

Margot woke from a dream about the baby in which Paul had stood in her father's pulpit and announced to a packed church that the baby wasn't his. He'd only been pretending to be married. He would rejoin the army, he said, the war wasn't over. He had two eyes again.

Lying still on her back she stared at the ceiling, listening to the Sunday silence. Earlier Paul had drawn the curtains against the afternoon sun and now a pale grey light filtered through the thin material. In the corner of the room was the crib Paul had bought from Parkwood. Made from dark oak, it had rockers and a canopy carved with Tudor roses. It was very old, he said. It smelt of empty churches and was too big for their little room. This afternoon she'd told him it was ugly and threw her hairbrush at it. She had wept and hadn't allowed him to comfort her.

Her throat still felt raw from crying. By her side was the crumpled, snotty handkerchief she'd clasped in her fist as she drifted uneasily to sleep. On the bedside table a cup of tea had formed a milky skin; a sandwich curled its corners to reveal a creamy sliver of fatty ham. He'd thought she might be hungry because she had left most of her lunch. She had resolutely ignored this small act of peace-making.

Thinking about the dream Margot remembered that all the faces in the church had been those of strangers and that Paul

193

had been in uniform. She'd thought how handsome he was as she stood at the back of the church. He'd looked straight at her and smiled as he disowned their marriage.

Margot closed his fist around the sodden hanky, afraid that she was about to cry again. Her mother had said it was the baby that made her cry, her body playing rotten tricks. Things would seem so much better when the baby was born. Stroking her hair, hush-hushing her, Iris had told her to be brave.

From the bedroom doorway Paul said, 'May I come in?'

'It's your room, too.'

'I thought you might not want to be disturbed.' He came in and sat at the foot of the bed. Reaching out he set the crib rocking gently. 'I'll take it back to Parkwood. You can choose a new one.'

'We can't afford a new one.'

'I have a little put by. Don't worry about money.'

'How much is a little? It would have to be more than a *little* if I'm not to worry.'

Looking at the crib he said, 'My father will help us.'

'So we have to go running to him, now?'

'Robbie had savings.' He turned to her. 'In his will the money was left to Dad. Now he wants us to have it. Is that running to my father? Or is that claiming what's rightfully yours?'

Ashamed, Margot looked away, unable to meet the pain in his face. Not only had she told him she hated the crib, but that she hated him, that she wished she'd never married him and why did it have to be Robbie who was killed? Her face burned as she remembered and she closed her eyes, trying to keep her tears in check.

Quietly Paul said, 'Don't start crying again, Margot. I don't think I could stand it.'

'I'm sorry. I try not to.'

He lay down beside her on his back and took his cigarettes from his pocket. Lighting one he said, 'Dad thought you might hate the crib. He said he always did – he said it reminded him of something out of a Grimm's fairy tale. My mother liked it, though. She thought it romantic.'

194

Trying not to cry she sniffed, 'Do you think it's romantic?'

'Dad said when I was born he couldn't bear to put me in it. I slept in a drawer by his bed. It had meant a lot to her so he hid it away, out of sight. Is that romantic?'

Hesitantly she said, 'It must have been hard for you, growing up without her.'

'Harder for Rob, I think.' There are photographs of her with Rob. I used to be jealous of him for knowing her. Jealous of him for all kinds of reasons.'

'Such as?'

He smiled slightly. 'He was taller than me.'

'Not very.'

'Enough. Heavier, too. Not such a weed.'

'You're not a weed.' She turned on her side to look at him. Often she felt she could spend hours looking at him; she had decided that his face was perfect, that no other man even came close to his perfection. It seemed wrong, sometimes, that he should be with someone as ordinary as she was. She laid a hand on his chest, wanting him suddenly.

He glanced at her. 'I'm sorry I made you cry.'

'You didn't. It was Daddy's fault. *My* fault. I shouldn't be such a baby.'

He took her hand from his chest and held it at his side and absurdly she felt rejected by this small gesture. Wanting to regain a closeness she felt she had squandered she said, 'I love you.'

He was silent for so long she thought he hadn't heard her; her heart beat faster as she imagined repeating it. At last she said, 'I'd understand if you don't love me, but I love you.'

He turned on his side to look at her. For what seemed a long time he searched her face as though looking for signs that she might not be telling the truth. He pulled her towards him. The baby kicked and she pressed his hand hard against her belly as he kissed her.

Chapter Twenty Two

One Month Later

A double bed had appeared in Mick's room. Hetty stared at it.

Gently Mick said, 'I was tired of sleeping in a child's bed.'

She glanced over her shoulder, almost expecting to see Patrick watching her from the doorway. 'Did Patrick ...' Words failed her. Mick wheeled his chair closer and took her hand.

'I told Patrick the other bed was uncomfortable.'

'So he went and bought this?'

'He didn't have to buy it. The bed was upstairs.' He smiled awkwardly. 'My mother used to call it the guest bed. It was never used.'

'What must he think?' Pulling her hand away from his she stared at him angrily. 'What must he think of me?'

'Why should he think anything?'

'Because of that bed! Doesn't it tell him what to think?'

'I told him the other bed was uncomfortable.'

'So you say! I bet he had a right good laugh.'

'A laugh? Is it funny?'

She looked away from his angry gaze. 'It's humiliating.'

Mick snorted. Manoeuvring his chair around he said, 'For God's sake, sit down. I'm not asking you to test its springs just yet.' He lit a cigarette and wheeled himself towards the open French windows. 'I was thinking we could go out, later. It's a lovely day and there's a band playing in the park.'

'Have you told Patrick about us?'

'No.'

Going to stand in front of him she said, 'Promise me.'

'I promise.' He looked down at his cigarette. 'What do you

take me for?'

'I know how close you are.' She heard Patrick moving about in the room above them and glanced up. 'Maybe he's guessed, anyway.'

'Maybe. Would it really matter? Are you ashamed of us, now?'

'No …' She sighed. 'It was seeing that bed. It's as if you're taking it for granted.'

'It?' He smiled slowly. 'I wouldn't take it for granted, Hetty. I'm far too amazed.'

'Amazed? I'm amazing now, am I?'

'You, *it*. Come here.' He cupped her cheek, drawing her down so that their faces were level. Kissing her he murmured, 'The bed *is* very comfortable …' He kissed her more deeply. 'We could test it, if you wanted.'

'I thought you wanted to go out?'

'We've all afternoon.' His eyes searched hers, smiling. Above them Patrick's footsteps sounded heavily and Mick grinned. 'Lock the door.'

She remembered the first time, how she had helped him on to the narrow single bed before taking off her blouse and camisole and kneeling beside him. As he tentatively touched her breast she kept her eyes fixed on the wall, shy of him now, afraid to glimpse below his waist. She knew that he had unbuttoned his fly, that his hand was moving frantically to bring himself to climax. She heard him cry out and felt his hand fall away from her breast; she lay down and rested her head on his chest, listening to the dramatic thud of his heart and breathing in the soft, musk scent.

After a while he'd said, 'I'm sorry.'

She looked up at him. His eyes were closed and he'd covered his face with his forearm. Reaching up she took his hand. 'We were both scared, I think.'

He made a noise like a laugh. '*Scared*. I'm still shaking.' Lowering his arm to look at her he said, 'That was horrible, wasn't it? For you, I mean. I'm sorry.'

'It's all right.'

'Let me hold you.' He moved on to his side so that they faced each other, their noses almost touching. Pressing his hand against her cheek he said, 'Your breasts are beautiful. I knew they would be. *You're* beautiful, my beautiful, sweet girl. How did I live without you?' He kissed her. 'I love you.' After a while he said hesitantly, 'It really wasn't that you felt sorry for me, was it?'

'No!' She frowned at him and he touched her mouth as if to silence any further protest, smiling in relief.

Lying in his arms now, in the new big bed, Hetty kissed his chest. 'You're so handsome, you know? The most handsome man I've ever seen.'

He laughed. 'What brought that on?'

'I've always thought so.'

'Have you? Astonishing.' He rested his hand lightly on her head. 'Hetty, on my desk there's a letter addressed to me. Would you fetch it?'

She got up, padding naked across the room, aware of his eyes on her. Smiling to herself she picked an envelope up from the desk and turned to him. 'Is this it?'

'Yes.' He held his hand out. 'Now come back to bed. I want to read it to you.'

She weighed the letter speculatively in her hand. 'It feels important.'

'It is. Now come here.'

As she climbed into bed again he sat up and reached for his glasses from the table. Hooking the frames around his ears he cleared his throat and for a moment he looked embarrassed. 'I've been keeping something from you.'

Anxiously she said, 'Oh? What?'

'It's nothing to worry about. It's foolish, really. Well, not foolish, exactly … I've been writing …'

'Writing? Who to?'

'No, not letters. Poetry.' He coloured. 'I've been writing poetry. I sent some poems away to a magazine.'

'Oh …' She smiled at him uncertainly, relief mixing with surprise. 'And they've written back to you?'

'Yes. They've written back to me.' He glanced at her from the letter. 'Several times. They wanted to see more, so I sent more.' After a long pause he laughed. 'They're talking about publishing a volume, a *slim* volume, but a volume, nevertheless.'

'Of your poems?'

'Yes.'

'Well ... that's good. Lovely ...'

'They're going to pay me, Hetty. I've actually earned some money!'

'Well done. I'm really pleased.'

Taking off his glasses he looked at her. 'Well, I think it's exciting, anyway.'

'So do I!'

'Then you might act as though you do.'

'I'm surprised! You never mentioned anything, not even that you wrote.'

'I wanted to keep it to myself ... if I'd failed ...'

'Failed?'

'If no one had wanted them ... anyway, now I've told you. Now you know. I write. It keeps me sane when you're not here.'

'What do you write about?'

'The war.'

'Oh.'

'I tried to write about other things but it was all terrible, sub-Wordsworth stuff. And it's all I know, isn't it? War. And butchering, I suppose. Not too many good poems in a pig's innards, though.'

'But there are in men's?'

'Yes.' He gazed at her. 'You think I shouldn't exploit it? I'll write about how lovely the spring flowers are, shall I? Not upset anyone.'

'Are your poems upsetting?'

He was silent, reaching for his cigarettes and lighting one. Hetty watched him until he met her eye. At last he said, 'I didn't write them to upset people. I know you lost your brother ...' After a while he said, 'I wrote things as I remembered

199

them.'

Hetty lay down. She tried to imagine him writing, settling himself at the desk with paper and pens and realised she didn't even know what his handwriting looked like. She imagined poets as dishevelled and eccentric, their desks littered with papers. Mick's desk was almost bare. She imagined he kept its drawers locked.

'I knew you liked to read, but writing poetry ...'

'It's quite common, really. Lots of men scribbled away – the trenches were chock-a-block with poets.'

'Did you write then?'

'I've always written.'

She thought of the poetry she learnt in school, lines learnt by rote that left her feeling hollow with boredom. She remembered the empty hours staring at the strange formation of words on paper, listening to the drone of her teacher's voice, the beat of his ruler on his desk as he kept time. Agitated by the recollection she got up suddenly and began to dress.

Mick said, 'Don't you want to hear what the letter says?'

'It says they want your poems, doesn't it?'

He tossed the letter down on the bed. 'That just about sums it up, yes.'

'Do you want to go out?' She buttoned her skirt. 'I think it's a good idea. The fresh air will do you good.'

She felt his eyes on her as she finished dressing. At last he said, 'I thought you'd be excited. Pleased, at least.'

'I am. I'm pleased for you.'

'It's the most exciting thing that's ever happened to me.'

She laughed without thinking. 'Is it?'

'Apart from you.'

Turning to him she said, 'Do you want to wear your suit? If the band's playing everyone will be out in their Sunday best.'

'Hetty, don't be like this.'

'Like what?'

'I don't know ... brittle.'

'Brittle? What does that mean? Is that a poet's word?'

'You know what it means.'

'No. I'm not as clever as you.'

'Oh Hetty, you're brighter than anyone I know.'

'Bright! I left school when I was thirteen.'

'So?'

'So? I don't understand poetry, Mick. I don't understand it and it makes me feel stupid. So there. Now *you've* learnt something about me.' Snatching his clothes from the floor she tossed them on the bed. 'Here. Let's get you dressed.'

'Hetty.' He caught her hand, holding it tightly as she tried to pull away. 'Hetty, I haven't changed into someone else since this morning. I still love you. The only thing that's changed is that now perhaps I can be more independent financially. I'll have a little bit more than just my army pension …' Taking her other hand he held them both between his own. 'Do you still love me?'

'I should, shouldn't I?'

'Should?'

Looking away she felt herself blush. 'If I didn't I couldn't do what we do … and you don't just stop loving someone, just like that.'

'Not even if they tell you they write poetry?'

She smiled. 'Not even then. Come on, get dressed up in your suit and let's go and see this band.'

From his bedroom window Patrick watched Hetty push his brother along the street towards the park. In the distance he could hear the brass band playing a marching tune he felt he should know the name of but didn't. The tune reminded him of square-bashing and he drew the curtains in an attempt to muffle the sound. It made no difference and he went to lie on his bed, wondering how he would kill the hours until Mick came home. Looking at the box of Paul's letters by his bed he reached out and trailed his fingers across the ragged tops of the envelopes.

Choosing one at random he switched on his bedside lamp and turned the letter over in his hands. He'd read them all, many times, and recognised this one from the way it had been opened: a ragged tear ran through *A*'s surname, disfiguring the letter *s*. *A* must have been desperate to get to the letter inside; there were greasy fingerprints along the bottom of the envelope, as though he had interrupted his breakfast to open it. Patrick thought of *A* standing in that filthy kitchen, pausing briefly before tearing the envelope almost in half in his haste. Closing his eyes, Patrick tossed the letter down.

He thought of asking Paul about *A* every time he saw him and every time the question wouldn't come. Usually they made love almost at once, Paul slow and sensual, calming him, making him take all the time they had. During this long, sweet process there could be no question of talking.

He could have asked about *A* in the pub, he supposed. Dropped it casually into the conversation between the plink, plink, plinks of the piano. He had thought about it, thought of asking, *Who was best man at your wedding?* He imagined Paul's quizzical look, that smile of his that still brought on the stirring of a hard-on even while making him feel stupid.

Often he told himself that Paul couldn't possibly be seeing this man. He had a wife he seemed to love, and he had himself, enough sex for anyone. More often he believed that Paul did see him and the jealousy kept him awake at night. He would turn on the light then and re-read the letters because oddly they were reassuring. When he wasn't writing about what was going on in France Paul wrote like an adolescent with a crush on his teacher. His words seemed to clamour for *A*'s attention, suggesting to him that *A* could barely summon the interest to write more than a few lines in reply. It made him want to smash the man's face in for his callousness but it also made him believe that the relationship was doomed. He thought about *A* outside the church on Paul's wedding day. He'd looked as though he would rather be a thousand miles away.

Restlessly he got up and went to the window, drawing back the curtains and opening the sash. He leaned out, listening for the band and trying to pick out the tune. Eventually he recognised it: *The Merry, Merry Month of May*. He smiled to himself. With sudden decisiveness he closed the window. He'd follow Mick and Hetty to the park – a normal, Sunday thing to do.

Chapter Twenty Three

Margot's ankles were swollen and her wedding ring cut into her finger. The midwife had told her the baby's head was engaged and she pondered this odd expression as she walked slowly, arm in arm with Paul, along past the cemetery and Parkwood towards the park and the sound of the brass band. She wished she didn't feel so ponderous, like a great seedpod about to burst.

Behind them a voice called, 'Paul! Margot! Wait for us!'

Adam Mason smiled as he walked towards them, a young woman following closely. Breathlessly he said, 'We thought it was you two!'

She had seen Adam only once or twice since the wedding and had hardly spoken more than a dozen words to him since. Now he was smiling at her as though they were the closest of friends. He turned to the girl behind him. 'Emma, you know Paul, don't you, from school? This is his wife, Margot Harris. Emma is one of our French teachers, Margot.'

'Pleased to meet you, Margot.' Emma linked her arm through Adam's. 'It's a lovely day, isn't it? Adam and I thought it was perfect weather for a stroll in the park.'

The girl was slight as a boy, neat in a grey two-piece and a matching hat. Her skirt skimmed her calves fashionably and Margot noted that her shoes and handbag matched and that she wore the slightest suggestion of lipstick. She looked severe and clever at once and she felt huge beside her. Self-consciously she moved even closer to Paul as though he might shield her from the girl's condescending smile.

Paul said, 'We're going to the park, too, if you'd like to join us.'

'But we're slow.' Margot laughed awkwardly. 'You'd have to drag your feet...'

The girl said, 'Oh, we don't mind, do we, Adam?'

'Of course not. It will give us more time to enjoy the air.'

Paul stopped to light a cigarette, allowing Margot and Emma Hargreaves to walk a little further ahead of them. He smiled at Adam who looked away sheepishly. 'So, what's this about, then?'

'It isn't about anything. She lives in one of those bleak boarding houses on Jesmond Terrace. I felt sorry for her spending every weekend alone, she's homesick.'

'You're not courting, then?'

'No!'

Paul smiled at Adam's look of horror. Because he was so easy to tease he said, 'She's a lovely girl. You could do a lot worse – should I be thinking about buying Margot a new hat?'

'What?'

'For your wedding.'

'Do you think that's funny? Is that your idea of a joke?'

'No – I only thought ...'

Adam shook his head angrily. 'You think I'd get married? You really think I could be as immoral and faithless as you are?'

There was such venom in his voice Paul stepped back. Adam was glaring at him. 'I'm sorry,' Paul said. 'I didn't mean to upset you.'

'*Upset me?* You think you still have the power to upset me? You don't know anything about me! So, I'll tell you some home truths, shall I? I'd never marry! I wouldn't treat women as you do – I wouldn't be so bloody cruel!' There was a thread of spittle hanging from Adam's mouth and he wiped it away with the back of his hand, his eyes blazing. 'You know – *you're* the joke! You're the one who can't decide whether he's fish or bloody fowl! You should grow up and realise you can't have all the sweets in the fucking sweet shop!' All at once he turned away and ran to catch up with the two women.

Hetty parked Mick's chair at the end of the last row of deck chairs. 'Here will have to do.'

'Here's fine. Sit down and stop fussing.'

'I'm not fussing.' She sat down gingerly, never fully trusting of folding chairs. 'It would've been nice to get closer to the bandstand, that's all.'

A family of children turned to stare at Mick. Hetty poked her tongue out at them then said loudly, 'There should be places reserved for veterans. Veterans should get special treatment.'

'Be quiet!' Mick glared at her. With quiet intensity he hissed, 'Don't call me a veteran. You make me sound like some decrepit old soldier.'

A man in front hushed them and Mick stared at him angrily. As he turned away Mick tapped him on the shoulder. 'Are we bothering you?'

'What?'

'I know you heard me because you've got extra sensitive hearing, but I'll ask again: are we bothering you?'

'Yes, so shove off.'

'Say that again.'

The man laughed. 'Shove off, you bloody freak, you're frightening the kids.' He turned away and Hetty watched anxiously as the colour drained from Mick's face.

She touched his hand. 'Ignore him, he's ignorant.'

Mick leaned forward in his chair and hooked the man around the throat with his right arm, dragging him backwards. The man's deck chair collapsed and he gasped in shock as Mick hauled him up by the neck, bringing his face close to his own. 'What did you call me?'

The man's children began to cry. Pulling uselessly at his arm, Hetty said, 'Mick, please, let him go!'

'Major, can I help, at all?' Paul Harris squatted down beside Mick's chair, placing a hand on his free arm. 'Sir, perhaps you should let him go, he's going a funny colour.'

Mick snorted, releasing his grip. The man stumbled to his feet, rubbing at his throat and glaring at Hetty. 'You should keep him under lock and key – he's a bloody maniac!'

Standing up straight Paul Harris said to the man, 'Perhaps

you should take yourself off to the hole you crawled out of while you still can.' To Mick he said gently, 'Are you all right, sir?'

Mick didn't look at Paul but stared after the man's retreating back. Curtly he said, 'There's nothing wrong with me. You can go now.'

Hetty laughed, embarrassed by his rudeness. Over Mick's head she smiled apologetically, only for Mick to turn on her. 'Don't you dare humour me! Take me home.'

'Yes, all right.' She sighed. 'I'll take you home.' As she pushed Mick's chair past Paul she mouthed, 'Thank you.'

He smiled and she noticed how frail he looked. She glanced back at him. He was lighting a cigarette, watching them.

Emma said, 'Well! That was horrible.'

Margot looked at Paul anxiously. 'Are you all right?'

'Yes,' Adam said. 'You shouldn't get involved with people like that.'

Angrily Paul said, 'Didn't you hear? He called him a freak! I couldn't just sit here.'

Emma laughed. 'He seemed to be handling it quite well on his own.'

Paul looked at her in disgust. To Adam he said, 'And what do you mean, people like that? He was a major during the war.'

Under his breath Adam said, 'But the war's over now.'

'I'm sorry?' Paul frowned at him. 'Maybe you should speak up.'

'I said the war's over now. We should all start behaving like civilised human beings.'

'Really? Well, if men who've lost both legs fighting for *civilised human beings* weren't called freaks perhaps we might.' He turned to Margot. 'I think we should go home.'

He was walking too quickly and Margot stopped trying to keep pace and said, 'Paul, slow down.'

He stopped. Still angry he said, 'Sorry. Are you all right?'

'Are you?' Concerned by his paleness she said, 'You look ill.'

'I always look ill.'

'Should we stop at your father's house? We could catch our breath and have a cup of tea.'

'I'd rather go straight home.'

'I just thought – '

'Dad only worries. He'll guess something's happened and start worrying.'

They were walking along the path leading to the park's main gate. Ahead of them Margot saw the girl from the butcher's shop pushing the major's wheelchair. The girl stopped and seemed to re-arrange the blanket covering what was left of his legs. Margot shuddered involuntarily and Paul turned to her. 'I'd like to introduce you.'

'Oh, Paul.' She frowned. 'I don't know …'

'Come on.' Holding her hand firmly he led her towards them.

Paul said, 'Major, I'd like you to meet my wife, Margot.'

The man glanced up. Sullenly he said, 'Mrs Harris. How do you do?'

'I'm fine, thank you.'

The girl smiled too brightly. 'Well, the baby must be almost due, is it?'

'Hetty! For God's sake don't start embarrassing her again.'

Margot blushed. 'No, it's all right. Yes, due next week.'

'I hope it goes well for you.' He looked at her. 'I wish you luck.'

Hetty smiled awkwardly. To the Major she said, 'Come on, then, you. Let's get you home before you cause any more trouble.'

Almost at the park gates Patrick had changed his mind about going to see the band. They had started to play *Tipperary* and he imagined the soft, sentimental faces of the crowd and their maudlin voices as they sang along. He would feel like punching them until they stopped.

The tune followed him down the lane of Victorian villas that backed on to the park. When he came to the last of these houses, the oldest and grandest, he stood looking up at its blank windows. Paul had been born in one of its rooms that overlooked the cemetery. He thought of him working in the garden and remembered the letters. He'd written about the garden often, with each new season remembering what was about to come into its own, the words so poignant that sometimes he found he couldn't read on. He would picture Paul then in tin hat and great coat, caked in mud or soaked with rain, shivering and blowing on his hands as he lined the men up for inspection.

There was a gate in the garden wall and Patrick pushed against it, expecting it to be bolted. It creaked open, the swollen wood catching on the ground. Pushing harder, Patrick saw that the gate led on to a kitchen garden, neglected and overgrown and screened from the rest of the garden by a copper hedge and tall trees. Glancing over his shoulder Patrick edged through the narrow opening.

He stood on the threshold and looked around. In a cleared space was the remains of a bonfire and he walked towards it, turning over the ashes with the side of his foot until a smell of autumn hung incongruously on the late spring air. A robin hopped closer; it seemed expectant. He smiled to himself. The bird probably missed the harvest of worms and insects Paul disturbed as he worked. He closed his eyes, breathing in the scents of his garden. He missed him with a sweet longing that was every bit as sentimental as *Tipperary*.

Watching Paul inspect the men's feet, Thompson had said softly, 'Ever fancy it?'

Patrick had made himself smile. Looking down at the stub of cigarette burning between his fingers he laughed. 'You're a dirty-minded bastard, Bill. If I didn't know better I'd say you were bloody obsessed with him.'

For once the weather had been warm and dry, the sun beat down on their heads, the stink of sweat only partly camouflaged by the smoke from their cigarettes. They leant against the sandbag wall, feeling the drying sand shift and give against their weight. A bird sang, a short, surprising burst of noise. Paul crouched to examine another foot. Thompson said, 'He's a good lad for all that he's a fucking shirt-lifter, a sight better than the other lazy bastards.'

Patrick said, 'He's too soft on the men.'

'Aye, well.' Thompson crumbled what little remained of his cigarette between his fingers and pushed himself away from the sandbags. 'Unlike you and me, Patrick lad, he feels sorry for the poor buggers.'

It was true he'd felt little for anyone except Paul. Men were killed and were replaced. He had stopped crossing himself whenever he saw a corpse. When the earth released a bloated body to bob in a flooded shell-hole, when he saw the remains of men and horses scattered along straight, poplar-lined lanes, he only thanked God that it wasn't him, that he was still alive to keep Paul safe.

There was a noise and the robin flew into the hedge. A few yards away a youthful-looking middle-aged man in shirtsleeves stared at him.

'You're trespassing.' The man's voice was exactly like Paul's. Stepping towards Patrick he said evenly, 'If you're looking for work I've nothing for you.'

'Are you Doctor Harris?'

Paul's father frowned. 'Yes.'

'I'm a friend of your son's.'

'Paul? He isn't here. He doesn't live here any more.' He came closer, obviously curious. Patrick was surprised by how young he was, forty-five at most, his hair still thick and dark like Paul's, his eyes the same startling green. He smiled Paul's smile. 'Were you in the army with my son?'

'Yes.' Patrick looked away, unsure of what to do next. The doctor was slight like Paul and he felt big and clumsy beside him, a man easily mistaken for a casual labourer. The robin hopped down from the hedge and he watched it, feeling the weight of the other man's gaze.

Gently, as though he was a child, Doctor Harris said, 'Won't you tell me your name?'

'Jenkins.' Patrick looked at him. 'Anthony Jenkins.'

He nodded, although he didn't seem to recognise the name. Suddenly he said, 'Look, come into the house and have a cup of tea. I was doing a spot of gardening but frankly I hate it, you'd be doing me a favour by dragging me away.' He turned towards the house. 'I have a fruit cake that's begging to be eaten.'

He was shown into the kitchen, a huge, cluttered room, neglected and dingy. Newspapers fanned out on the floor beside an armchair and a half-empty bottle of whisky and a sticky-looking tumbler stood on the hearth. On the mantelpiece was a framed photograph of Paul and his brother. Patrick picked it up, smiling at the artful, back-to-back pose.

He heard George laugh. 'That's Paul's brother in the picture with him – I suppose you guessed. Two peas in a pod, Rob and Paul, everyone said so.' Taking the picture from him he replaced it on the mantelpiece. Without emotion he said, 'My eldest son was killed in an accident.' Turning away he said briskly, 'Tea. Tea and cake. Please, sit down, make yourself at home.'

Patrick sat on the armchair, trying not to look around too obviously. He would have liked to explore the whole house and imagined walking from room to room, opening cupboards and drawers, searching for sides of Paul he suspected he kept hidden. Already he'd realised that the ordered, elegant home he'd imagined Paul growing up in was nowhere near the reality, and that his father was nothing like the old, fussing man he'd pieced together from the little Paul had told him. He smiled to himself, searching his pockets for his cigarettes. He hadn't expected George to be fanciable.

'You smoke, too? Why do all you young men smoke?' Doctor Harris sighed. 'No, don't answer that. I know.' Setting a tray of tea on a side table he said, 'Paul smokes like a chimney. I never see him without a cigarette these days.'

'How is he?'

'Oh, you know.' Sitting down in the chair opposite he said, 'I suppose you know he was wounded? That he lost an eye?'

Patrick nodded.

'He copes all right with that. His nerves are terribly bad, though.' He glanced at him. 'I suppose that's something else you'd know all about, Anthony?'

Patrick smiled. 'My nerves are pretty bad, too.'

211

'Sometimes I look at Paul and wonder if perhaps they should have kept him in hospital even longer.' He laughed lightly. 'I'm sorry, you didn't come here to listen to my worries.'

'I'm sure he appreciates your concern.'

'Oh, he doesn't! He thinks I fuss. Least said soonest mended, that's Paul. If you ask Paul everything's *fine*. Even when it obviously isn't.'

He poured the tea and handed him a cup and a plate of dark, moist cake. 'Did you know Paul was married at Christmas?'

'Married?'

'He obviously doesn't write to you?'

Patrick sipped his tea. Placing the cup in its chipped saucer he said, 'No, we lost touch after he was wounded.'

'Were you over there long?'

'Three years.' Patrick stood up. 'May I use your bathroom, Doctor Harris?'

Patrick stood in the bedroom he'd decided was Paul's. The bed had been stripped to its mattress; the wardrobe doors hung open revealing only a few coat hangers; dust had settled on the wooden floor and dulled the colours of the Persian rug. He sat down on the bed and stared towards the sash window. A horse chestnut tree grew close to the house, blocking the sunlight and tapping its heavy, candle-like blossoms against the glass. Beside him was a pillow and he picked it up and hugged it to his body. He closed his eyes, breathing deeply to catch Paul's scent, remembering.

They had waited in position for almost an hour before dawn, sinking into soft mud with the weight of equipment on their backs. The porridge in Patrick's belly had become an anchor, holding him fast to the earth. He imagined standing up, as he must in a few minutes, imagined that it would be a slow, unwieldy business, graceless and panicked. In truth he knew he'd be first to his feet when the signal came, that he'd run faster than anyone – a devil, Thompson called him, swept on the gales of hell. He closed his eyes, more scared than ever.

He crossed himself.

Paul crawled on his belly towards him, slowly making his way down the line, whispering encouragement and stopping occasionally to check on individual men. He stopped for a little while with Cooper. Patrick was certain he was praying with the boy, and knew it would be a short, sensible Anglican prayer. Paul squeezed Cooper's shoulder as though murmuring a final benediction. He moved towards him and Patrick held his breath.

'Sergeant Morgan ...' For a moment they pressed themselves further into the mud as a machine gun opened fire. When it ended he felt Paul's hand on his shoulder. 'All right, Sergeant?'

'Sir.'

'The cooks are bringing hot tea down the line. Shouldn't be long now.'

'The tea or the off, sir?'

'Both.'

'Good luck, Lieutenant Harris.'

Paul smiled at him. 'I'll see you in the German trenches, Sergeant.'

He remembered that Cooper bled to death in his arms, his blood soaking his tunic so that later he would pick off the dry crust, noticing how it cracked into crazy-paving patterns beneath his busy fingers. Cooper's blood stayed beneath his fingernails for days, and sometimes he imagined it was pigs' blood, that he hadn't been clean since the slaughtering in the shop's yard. He remembered that in the German trench Paul had used his pistol to shoot the machine gunner and that he seemed not to notice the blood and brains that splashed his face. Worse than the noise and confusion, worse than Cooper's bloody, silent death, was his fear for Paul, the terror of having two lives to lose instead of one.

From the bedroom doorway Paul's father said, 'Have you seen enough?' Patrick looked at him blankly, he had forgotten where he was for a moment, and the doctor said coldly, 'You knew Paul well, didn't you? Is it still going on?'

'I'm sorry.' Patrick stood up, the pillow falling at his feet.

213

'I should go …'

Doctor Harris stood aside, allowing him through the door. As Patrick brushed past him he said, 'Leave my son alone. He's married now. His wife's expecting their child. Leave them be.'

Without looking back Patrick ran down the stairs and out of the house.

Mick said, 'Where the fuck have you been?'

'Is it any of your fucking business?'

'Well, I know where you haven't been. I know you haven't been buggering that vile little queer. I know that much at least.'

Patrick sighed. 'Mick, just keep your disgusting mouth to yourself.'

'Do you want to know how I know?' Wheeling his chair close to him, Mick smiled slyly. 'You do. I can see it. Desperate to know. Well, I saw him. Him and that sweet little wife of his. She looks about ready to drop. Funny, he doesn't look capable of screwing a woman, let alone getting one up the stick.'

Patrick turned away from him. 'How was Hetty? What did she think of the new bed?' Lighting the gas beneath the kettle he glanced at him. 'I hope you're careful – it's surprising who's capable of getting a woman up the stick.'

'And it's surprising who isn't! Christ! Who would have thought that a brother of mine – '

Patrick laughed. Grasping the sides of the wheelchair he brought his face up close. 'Who'd have thought it, eh, Mick? A brother of yours! Jesus – the great Major Morgan has a fucking fairy for a brother! It's just not on, is it?'

'You make me sick.'

Patrick straightened up. 'I make myself sick.'

'Then stop! There are women who'd give their eye-teeth to be with you.'

'I know. I'm gorgeous. They make great big eyes at me in the shop.' Rolling his eyes in impersonation he smiled bitterly. 'And you know what? They make me sick, as well. In fact if I think too hard about them I actually vomit.'

He began to make tea. As it brewed he buttered slices of bread, then went to the pantry for ham and pork pies. 'Are you hungry? I thought we'd have a Sunday tea, a proper Sunday tea like Mam used to make. I've made a blancmange, there're tinned pears, too.'

'Did you know his wife's expecting a baby?'

Patrick placed the plate of bread on the table. 'Yes, I know.'

'And doesn't that concern you at all?'

'No.'

'For pity's sake, Pat! Have you seen that poor girl lately?'

Patrick turned to face him. 'What do you imagine is going to happen, Mick? That he'll leave her? That we'll set up home together and humiliate her by walking down the street holding hands? He sees me for a couple of hours a week, the rest of the time he's with her.'

'It's still adultery, Patrick. And what if you're caught together? You'll both go to prison.'

'They won't catch us together.'

'People talk ...'

'Talk!' Scornfully he said, 'I don't give them anything to talk about, Mick. You do, though. They talk about you and Hetty. Perhaps you should care more about her reputation than mine.' He poured out the tea. 'Come and sit at the table, have a ham sandwich.'

Mick ate in silence and from time to time Patrick studied him. It must have been seeing Paul's wife that triggered this righteous anger. For a moment he felt sorry for the girl, a feeling immediately taken over by his jealousy of her.

Pushing his plate away Mick lit a cigarette. 'I made a fool of myself today. Someone called me a freak so I tried to throttle him.'

'How is that making a fool of yourself?'

'Oh for Christ's sake – look at me, Pat! Picking a fight when I'm stuck in this bloody thing? I just made a show of myself. A fucking freak show.' He bowed his head, turning a box of matches over and over on the table. Softly he said, 'Do you remember when Dad burnt all my notebooks? Everything I'd ever written thrown on the fire, page by page. He made me watch, remember? My nose all bloody from the beating he'd given me. I felt like a freak, then. A freak for writing and a freak for not standing up to him.'

'We were sixteen, Mick. Don't you remember how frightening he was?'

'I felt so angry. So angry and all I did was stand there because I was so bloody scared of him. I never wanted to feel so helpless again. But now, here I am. Worse than helpless.' He laughed bleakly, stubbing out the cigarette. 'Do you know what the worst of it was? Your little *friend* Harris had to step in to save me, made me realise what an arse I was making of myself.' He glanced at Patrick. 'Quite commanding in his way. I could almost understand what you see in him.'

'What? In a whey-faced little pansy?'

'Well, he does look like he needs a bloody good dinner inside him. Is he ill? He looks ill.'

'He's fine.'

'Just so long as you can bugger him, eh?'

Patrick stood up and began clearing the table. Catching his arm Mick said, 'You'll be careful, you and him, won't you? Promise me you'll be careful.'

'I promise.'

He nodded. Releasing his arm Mick said, 'Leave this now. Let's go out for a drink. I feel like getting pissed.'

Chapter Twenty Four

Hetty watched her mother wrap the matinee jacket and bootees she'd crocheted. 'There,' Annie said. 'That's neat enough, isn't it? You'll take it round to her later, won't you? Doesn't harm to be neighbourly.'

Hetty sighed. Reluctantly she said, 'Yes, all right. But you should take it, it's your hard work.'

'She'd rather have someone her own age to talk to. I wouldn't know what to say to someone like her.'

'She's not royalty, Mam. Her dad's only a vicar.'

'All the same.' Annie looked at her. 'The Major told me you're going to see him this evening?'

'Yes.'

'That's nice, he gets tired of being on his own.' She smoothed the brown paper she'd used to parcel the baby's clothes. 'He seems to like you – it was *Hetty this* and *Hetty that* when I was giving him his dinner.'

Cautiously Hetty said, 'You like Mick, don't you?'

'The Major? He's a gentleman.' Annie picked up the parcel and put it on the dresser. 'Set the table for us, pet. Your dad will be home for his tea soon.'

In her bedroom Hetty lay down on the bed. She remembered the first and last piece of advice her mother had ever given her. It had coincided with her first period: '*Never lie down with a man until you're married.*' She'd learnt more from dirty jokes amongst the girls at the sugar factory. She thought of Milly Jackson, weeping in the factory yard because the lad she had gone with had been killed at Ypres. Over and over she'd stressed that she'd only done it with him once. Only once and now he was dead and she was expecting. The small band of women gathered round her tut-tutted in commiseration, not so much for the death of her lover, more for the fact she'd been so unlucky. *Once!* Behind the weeping girl's back the women smirked at each other.

She had lain down with Mick three times. After the second time they made love she had forced herself to look properly at his legs. The stumps looked as though they had been patched over with ragged scraps of flesh, each placed haphazardly on top of the other, the healed skin forming a mass of protective scars. She had touched his left thigh gently, just above where his leg had been amputated, watching his face. He had only smiled his extraordinary smile.

She knew why her mother didn't guess what was going on between them. To Annie he was a neutered man, one whose potential for getting a girl into trouble had been taken away along with his legs. Besides, no normal girl would want to *lie down* with a cripple. But when they were together his wheelchair was forgotten, although she knew that if it hadn't been for the chair she wouldn't have climbed into his bed until they were married. She closed her eyes, appalled all over again at the wanton way she behaved when she was with him and the excuses she made to herself. Nothing was normal, the war had seen to that, so she slept with Mick because she wanted him, because the opportunity was there and no one suspected enough to call her a slut. And because she loved him, of course. She opened her eyes, listening to her mother's bangs and clatters from the kitchen. She loved him, and that wasn't an excuse, it was a reason.

Margot Harris smiled over the little jacket and held up each bootie in turn to admire it. She smiled as she folded the garments back into their paper and reminded Hetty once again to thank her mother for her kindness.

'Would you like a cup of tea?' Margot began to get up but her movements were awkward and Hetty stood up quickly.

'I'll make it.'

'Oh, don't bother. I hate tea these days, I don't think we

even have any milk, anyway.'

'Would you like a glass of water?'

'I'd like a cigarette but I've none left. I'm desperate for Paul to come home just so I can smoke his.'

'You smoke?'

'Awful, isn't it? I don't think Paul minds.' She glanced around the untidy kitchen. 'He doesn't mind anything, really.'

Hetty sat down again. After an awkward silence she said, 'It was good of Paul to help us on Sunday.'

'Your friend didn't think so.'

'Mick was upset, I'm sorry he was so rude.'

Margot laughed oddly. 'I didn't want him to step in like he did. I wanted someone else to do it. But it seems he *has* to take responsibility for everything.' She creased her face suddenly, pressing her hand to her side. 'Ouch. Little monkey's never still.'

'Are you all right?'

'I think so.' She smiled. 'Don't look so worried.'

'Do you want me to stay until your husband gets home?'

'There's no need. I've got days to go yet.' Shyly she added, 'But stay, if you like, I don't have many visitors. I'm sorry I can't offer you any tea.'

'That's all right.' Nodding at Margot's bulging waist she said, 'Do you think it's a boy or a girl?'

'A boy, he kicks so hard. Here.' Taking Hetty's hand she pressed it against her body. Hetty felt a balled fist punch at her and she laughed, meeting Margot's gaze.

'You must be excited now it's so near.'

'Yes, I suppose I am. Paul is.'

'He looked so proud of you on Sunday.'

'Did he?' She looked down, picking at a snagged thread in the tablecloth. 'Well, I'm proud of him.' Looking up she asked, 'Have you known your friend long?'

'Mick? Not long, really.'

'I remember him at that dance at New Year, he looked so striking in his dinner jacket.'

'Mick likes expensive clothes. I think he misses his uniform.'

'I think Paul does, too.' Margot opened the paper and drew the baby's jacket towards her. Her fingers worried the lacy stitches around the jacket's hem. 'What's Mick's brother like? Paul sees quite a lot of him.'

'Patrick?' Hetty paused, not sure how she might describe him. She realised that despite working for him for almost a year she barely knew Patrick Morgan. Besides, since getting to know Mick she took no notice of Patrick, he seemed like a poor imitation in comparison.

Margot looked up at her. 'Patrick, yes. Tell me what he's like.'

Hetty was surprised by the sharpness in her tone; it was as though she was desperate to know. Disconcerted, Hetty said, 'We don't speak very much. He's quiet. He keeps himself to himself.'

Margot nodded and seemed to accepted this poor description. At last she said flatly, 'He seems nice, anyway. Kind. A nice, kind man.'

The back door opened and Hetty looked up as Paul Harris walked in. He smiled in surprise. 'Hello, there.'

'Paul, this is Hetty, we met on Sunday in the park.'

'Yes, of course. How are you, Hetty?' He kissed his wife's cheek. 'Hello, sweetheart.'

Margot gave him such a shameless look of love that Hetty glanced away, embarrassed. Making an excuse she left.

Paul said, 'I promised I'd go for a drink with Patrick tonight, but if you like I'll stay here with you.'

'If you promised you should go.' She was frying bacon. 'You shouldn't break promises.'

'Not a promise, exactly. And I worry about you … look, why don't I walk you to your mother's? You can spend the evening with her and I'll come and collect you on my way home.'

'I'd rather be on my own – I'd know if the baby was coming tonight. In that book I borrowed from your father it says a woman knows instinctively …' She blushed. After a moment she said, 'Go, you know you always enjoy it.'

Paul laughed strangely and she frowned at him. 'You do, don't you?' When he didn't answer she prompted, 'You do enjoy seeing him, don't you?'

'For God's sake, Margot!' He gazed at her angrily. 'If you don't want me to go I won't, it doesn't matter.' He lit a cigarette, his movements quick and impatient. Exhaling smoke he said harshly, 'You should go to your mother's, stop me worrying.'

She set a plate of bacon and eggs in front of him. 'All right, I'll go to Mummy's. If you're going to make such a fuss I'll go.'

'It will be a change for you.'

'Will it? A change to listen to her telling me how disappointed she is in me?'

He rested his cigarette on the ashtray as he began to eat, ready to smoke between each mouthful. 'Your mother's not that bad.'

She sat down. After a moment he pushed his half-eaten meal away and lit a fresh cigarette from the butt of the last. Wearily he said, 'Stay here, if you want, I'll only be gone an hour, two at most.'

'Aren't you going to finish your supper?'

'I'm not hungry.' He got up. 'If you don't mind I'll go now.'

Chapter Twenty Five

Paul got up from Patrick's bed. He was thirsty, a raging thirst that often came after sex and was made worse by supper's cheap, salty bacon. Naked, he went into the tiny room on the other side of the hall with its sink and single cold tap. Waiting for the water to run icy cold, he held on to the edge of the sink. Drops splashed his body, cooling him, and he stuck his face under the tap, swallowing greedily.

Patrick watched him from the doorway. Wiping his mouth with the back of his hand, Paul brushed past him into the bedroom and lay down on the bed.

Carefully Patrick said, 'Paul? Come on, you know I hate it when you're like this.'

'Like what? Too thoroughly fucked to talk to you? Just give me a minute.'

On the bedside table his own face looked out at him from a silver picture frame and Paul turned away to avoid its gaze. The photographer who'd taken the picture owned a magpie, tame as a canary, which had watched him from a perch behind the camera and talked in the high-pitched, grating voice of an effeminate inquisitor. The bird was a prop, showing off its metallic tail feathers in dull pictures of mothers and babies, soldiers and sweethearts. In France, in a photographer's studio, there existed a picture of himself and this bird, man and magpie holding the other's gaze as though spellbound. He hadn't wanted that picture, he'd remembered that birds were unlucky, and had bought only the one of him alone to send home. Keen to keep the magpie photograph, the photographer said it would be displayed in his window and titled *English Officer with Pica*.

The mattress dipped as Patrick lay down and Paul tensed in case he should touch him. Patrick liked to hold him after sex, manhandling him roughly until he was comfortable, his body giving off too much heat and scent. Moving away from him he said, 'I have to go soon.'

'You've only just got here! You can't go.'

'I daren't leave Margot for long. She could have the baby at any time.' He lit a cigarette. 'I'll smoke this and then I'll go.'

Patrick sat up. Taking the cigarette from Paul he crushed it out between his fingers and tossed it on the floor. 'We haven't finished yet.'

'Yes, Patrick, we have.' He reached for his cigarettes again but Patrick caught his wrist, pinning his hand above his head.

'No, *Lieutenant*, we haven't.' He kissed him, forcing his tongue deep into his mouth. Still holding his hand above his head, he reached down with his other hand and grasped Paul's cock. He pulled his face away. 'You know how quickly I can make you hard again.'

'Patrick, please. Let me go.'

Patrick smiled slowly. 'You could always fight me off. Try it.' He gazed into Paul's face. 'You're not putting up much of a fight, Lieutenant Harris. Now I think that's because you don't want to go anywhere.'

Paul grasped his hair, jerking his head back. 'I said let me go.'

Patrick smiled. 'Hair pulling, that's a girl's game, isn't it?'

Digging his fingernails into Patrick's scalp Paul pulled his head back even further. Patrick released him, only to move quickly to kneel astride his body. With a hand on each of Paul's shoulders he kissed his mouth lightly. 'All right, if you're going to be in this mood I give in. You win.'

He lay down and lit two cigarettes. Passing one to Paul he said, 'Thanks for helping Mick the other day.'

Paul laughed shortly. 'We both made total fools of ourselves.' He thought of the way Adam had sneered at him, remembering that he had given him the same look the first time he'd seen him in uniform, as though he couldn't quite believe he would do something so brainlessly patriotic as join the army. 'Christ,' he'd said. 'All you need is to grow a moustache and you'll look like every other idiot in the country.'

On the High Street below the window a tram rattled by. The bed creaked as Patrick rolled on to his side to look at him.

'You and Mick would get on, if you met properly, you have things in common.'

'Like what?'

'You were both good soldiers.'

'He might have been.'

'He was. And so were you.'

'And so were you.' Paul got up and began to dress. Buttoning his shirt, he said, 'The three of us, good, brave and true. We all had a topping time.'

Patrick laughed. 'Do you remember when we came across that demolished shrine? You should have seen Bill Thompson's face when you flung the Virgin's head into the sky. He was so shocked. I don't know what shocked him most – that it was sacrilegious or that you were so angry. We'd never seen you angry before – poor little Collier almost burst into tears.' Patrick gazed at him. 'It rained so heavily that day. I just wanted to get you away somewhere dry and quiet and calm you down. Somewhere away from that bloody smirking Jenkins.'

The mention of Jenkins's name made Paul's heart race. Trying not to think about him, he fixed on the memory of that day, how they had been marching all afternoon in the rain before they came across the shell-blasted shrine to the Virgin. He had been at the head of the platoon and had stopped to make sure no one was lagging too far behind. Rain dripped from his helmet and the waterproof cape he wore; he was blinded by rain, made invisible by it. On either side of the road the poplar trees were no more than a grey colour wash, the fields beyond a flood plain. Hunched against the downpour the men filed past him. He'd called out encouragement and sounded like a parody of himself; the little reserve of strength he had left had dwindled almost to nothing. Jenkins had been with the platoon a month. A month had been all the time he'd needed to demolish him.

Draping his tie around his up-turned collar he saw that his hands were trembling cigarette ash to the floor. He felt Patrick's eyes on him.

Patrick smiled. 'Come back to bed? It's early yet.'

'I have to get back.'

'Oh, for Christ's sake!' Patrick sprang from the bed and crossed the room. Holding him at arms' length he frowned. 'Have I done something wrong?'

'No.'

'Then what is it?'

'Nothing! All right?' Paul shrugged him off. 'Don't talk about the past, that's all. I don't want to talk about it.'

'I'm sorry. It's just that sometimes I think it's the only thing we have in common.'

'We're queer, isn't that enough to have in common?'

'No! That's like saying – I don't know – two men have lots in common because they're on a sinking ship together … I want more than that …'

Paul stepped past him but Patrick caught his hand. He led him back to the bed and made him sit down. Sitting beside him he took his other hand and held them on his lap. After a while he cleared his throat nervously. 'I have a confession to make. I went with someone. A man I picked up.'

Paul sighed, wanting only to get away. Patiently he said, 'Patrick, you don't have to tell me – and don't feel guilty. I understand.'

'Don't you want me to be faithful?'

'How can I ask that of you?'

'I want you to. And I want you to be faithful to me, I don't want there to be any other men.'

'There aren't.'

'Is that the truth?' Searching Paul's face he said, 'The man I picked up had a picture of you by his bed. He kept a box of your letters from France beside it.'

Paul drew his hands away from Patrick's. He tried to picture Patrick and Adam in bed in that squalid room and found himself wondering how the fastidious Patrick had brought himself to lie down on Adam's sheets. He imagined the disgust that Patrick would have struggled to conceal once the sex was over. Feeling weary suddenly he lay down on the bed and pressed his hands into his eyes.

After a while, aware of Patrick watching him, he laughed bleakly. 'So, you slept with Adam. Well, ours is a small world, I suppose. Was it any good? He can lack imagination in bed, I find.' He lowered his hands to look at him. 'Although usually I forgive him – he tries so hard to be *good*.'

'You still see him.' Patrick sounded incredulous.

'Do you?'

'No!' Patrick stood up. 'No, for Christ's sake! It was once, months ago, before you and I started meeting here. Are you still going to his house? How often? Do you love him?'

'It's none of your business, Patrick.'

'Yes it is! Of course it is! I love you!' Standing up he said, 'Do you love him more than you love me?'

Wearily Paul said, 'Look, I have to go – I promised Margot – '

'Promise me you won't see him again.'

'I promise.'

'I don't believe you.'

'Then what can I say, Patrick?' Exasperated suddenly he said, 'Anyway, what does it matter?'

'It matters to me! Does he know about us?'

'No.'

'Should I tell him?'

'Oh for god's sake, Patrick. Listen, Adam's just Adam, I've known him for years.' He almost added that there was nothing between them any more because since Sunday it seemed true.

Patrick slumped down on the bed. He held his head in his hands and looked so defeated that Paul knelt in front of him. He touched his knee. 'Patrick? Come on, you knew I wasn't a blushing virgin.'

'Were there many before me?

'A few – '

'A few?'

'Yes. I told you.'

Patrick met his gaze. 'Davies?'

'What?'

'Second Lieutenant Davies, the poor little sod who could never take his eyes off you. Did you seduce him?'

'*Seduce* him?' Paul stared at him in astonishment. 'For Christ's sake, Patrick – you make it sound as though it was a fucking debutantes' ball! Were we buggering each other between bombardments? Did I *miss* something?'

Patrick bowed his head again. 'I'm sorry. It was just a stupid rumour. I never believed it, not really.'

'Not *really*? Do you honestly think so badly of me? You know what things were like over there – you know what the boy was like …' He felt sick suddenly. He remembered how Davies always seemed about to cry, how he'd wanted to offer his usual hollow encouragement only to be repelled by his snivelling. Eventually he found he was unable to even look at him, afraid that the boy's weakness might break his own puny resolve. He knew that Davies watched his every move. Ironically he'd believed he'd hated him. Agitated he got up and walked across the room, only to turn to face Patrick again. 'What was said?'

'That you and he … it was rubbish, everyone knew it was a lie – I shouldn't have said anything, it was only because I felt so jealous – '

'What was said!'

Patrick hesitated. Avoiding his gaze he said quickly, 'That you were found together, in your bunk. It was nonsense, of course it was. Jenkins was a liar – no one believed what Jenkins said.'

Jenkins. Afraid his legs would buckle he leaned against the wall. Patrick got up and stood a few feet from him. Cautiously he said, 'Paul? Are you all right?'

Paul wanted to say yes, that there was nothing to worry about, that he could push Jenkins from his mind if he really tried hard enough, but the words wouldn't come. Jenkins was suddenly alive and in their room. Wanting to run, instead he felt Patrick pull him into his arms as though he thought he was

227

going to fall.

At first the pains made her smile. At last something was happening and Margot paced round and round the kitchen table, occasionally using a chair to support herself through a contraction. She looked at the clock. Soon Paul would be home and he could ask their next-door neighbour to fetch the midwife. Excited and afraid at once, she stopped pacing to double up against a stronger pain. Her waters broke.

Margot stared at the stain spreading over the floor, truly scared now. She remembered what she'd discovered in the book on pregnancy and knew that she needed help. Between pains, she slowly made her way next door.

'Mam!' The child who answered her knock stared at her as he shouted for his mother. Supporting herself against the doorframe, Margot tried to smile at him. From the kitchen came the smell of steak and kidney pie and a woman wiping her hands on an apron. The woman frowned. 'What's up?'

'I think my labour's started.'

The child giggled, covering his mouth with his hand, and the woman clipped him round the head. Taking her arm she said, 'Come on, love, let's get you home. You'll be all right, I'll look after you.' She turned to the boy. 'Run round to Miss Rowe's, tell her to come straight away. You hear? Straight away.'

Helping her up the stairs her neighbour said, 'Where's that lad of yours?'

Margot gasped for breath, lowering herself painfully on to the bed. Finally able to speak she said, 'He should be here soon.'

'Do you want me to send Alfie to look for him when he's fetched the midwife?'

Another pain came and she clenched her body against it. As it passed she said, 'He'll be here … I'm sorry, I've forgotten your name.'

'Moira.' She smiled. 'Do you think that daft husband of mine has had the sense to turn the gas off on that pie?'

'I'm so sorry to be a nuisance.'

Moria laughed. 'Don't you worry about it!' Closing her eyes tight Margot felt the other woman's arm around her, helping her up the bed. 'Don't hold your breath, love, try and breathe, it'll soon be all over.'

Patrick led Paul to the bed and made him lie down. Kneeling on the floor he said, 'I thought you were going to faint. Are you all right?' When Paul didn't answer he said helplessly, 'Maybe have a sleep, eh? You'll feel better.' Paul closed his eyes and Patrick sat back on his heels, ready to watch over him on his knees all night as a penance for his jealousy, and for being such a fool as to mention that little bastard's name.

He remembered how Jenkins had whispered, 'I can't do this, Harris. I can't.'

They had just started out on a raid. Patrick saw Paul signal for him to stop and motion that he and the other men should stay where they were. Half way across no-man's-land, Patrick tried to ignore the whispering going on between Paul and Jenkins and concentrate on the sequence of events he and Paul had planned that would give them the best chance of surviving the night. Jenkins had sat with them and Paul had patiently tried to explain each stage to him. He wouldn't listen. It was as if he didn't believe he would actually be made to do any of it. Patrick could see Paul despairing; he knew as well as he did that if they didn't work together it was more likely that one of them would be killed.

Even before they set out Patrick knew the venture was doomed. The men could see Jenkins working himself up into a state before they'd even left the trench and it made them jittery to imagine that an officer might bugger their chances. Sensing their disquiet, Paul had talked to the men individually, knowing each one well enough to personalise the reassurance. To him he had said only, 'Is there anything you feel we need to discuss again before we go, Sergeant?' He had shaken his head. He had known Paul wouldn't reassure him: they were in this together as equals.

Paul climbed the ladder over the top of the trench, followed by the men and then Patrick himself. Jenkins's fear radiated from him like a bad smell; when his turn came he froze on the first rung. After a moment Paul scrambled back down into the trench.

Patrick heard Jenkins's frantic whispering and crawled back. He peered down to see what was going on. In the darkness Paul's face was white but his hand held his pistol to Jenkins's temple steadily. Snivelling, Jenkins climbed the ladder.

In no-man's-land between the trenches, Collier turned to look at him and Patrick tried to reassure him with just a movement of his eyes. Pressing his body into the ground with an idea of muffling the terrible noise his heart was making, he saw that the rest of the men were still and silent as the ground itself. He thought of the bodies left after a battle and felt his flesh crawl as though the worms had made an early start on him. He began to pray, picturing the crucifix that was safe beneath his uniform.

Paul and Jenkins began moving towards him and Paul signalled that they should move on again. Again Patrick began to visualise the plan. He saw himself cutting the German wire and moving closer and closer towards their trench. He pictured the layout of the land they were crawling through and knew that in a few yards it would begin to slope. To their left was a shell hole marked by rusted wire and the ragged scraps of cloth that clung to the barbs. On windy days the cloth would flap like birds desperate to escape a trap and the eye was deceived into believing that there really was something alive in the waste the shells had made. Now, though, the air was still and the only movement he could see was that of the dark outline of the man ahead of him.

After a few feet he sensed something was wrong and looked back. Jenkins had stopped crawling. Once again Paul signalled that he and the others should stop, and once again he heard the same, frantic whispering. Patrick decided he would rather know what was going on than wait helplessly. He shuffled back until he found himself next to Paul.

With his mouth close to Patrick's ear Paul whispered, 'I can't get him to move!'

'What do you want to do?'

Before Paul could answer Jenkins was on his feet. In a half crouch he ran back towards their line.

The sniper's shot was too low. It hit Jenkins in the shoulder, knocking him off his feet and into the shell hole. Paul stared after him. After a moment he dropped his head to the ground, banging his forehead against the frozen mud and Patrick was scared he was about to lose his nerve, too. But at last he looked up. 'They'll know we're out here now. You and the men go back. I'll get Jenkins.'

'I'll help you, sir.'

Paul held his gaze and Patrick began to worry that he would insist on the order. At last, to his relief, he nodded. 'All right. Send the others back first.'

Kneeling beside Paul, Patrick kissed his head lightly. He remembered how Jenkins used to hum *The Boy I Love* under his breath whenever Paul was in earshot and how Paul would pretend not to hear although Patrick could see his body tense as well as Jenkins could. Often he thought about killing him, how, with a carefully planned accident, he could spare Paul his torment. His thoughts became elaborate fantasies in which Jenkins's death was replayed over and over. He told himself that one more death in the scheme of things wouldn't matter and, despite his creeping doubts, that fantasies didn't matter at all.

When he'd given the order for the others to return to their trench, Patrick had crawled back to the shell hole. He'd wondered at his heart's capacity to go on beating at such a pace and couldn't imagine it ever recovering to a normal beat. When the single shot sounded he thought for a moment that he was hit and he'd rolled into the shell hole, afraid of the pain to come. He'd found himself next to Jenkins's body. He remembered crossing himself cursorily, a habit he had thought he'd forgotten. He felt he should have said a prayer but he knew there was no point. Already the mud had begun to claim Jenkins; he might have been dead for centuries.

Paul placed his pistol back in its holster and looked at him as though challenging him to speak. He kept silent. After a moment, Paul leaned across the body and closed Jenkins's eyes.

Hetty slowed her usual fast walk as she neared home. She turned, hearing footsteps hurry behind her and saw the midwife and Alfie Simms. The little boy grinned at her. 'We're helping Mrs Harris have her baby.'

The midwife laughed. 'That's enough, Alfie. Mrs Harris won't want the whole world to know.'

Surprised, Hetty said, 'I was only with her a couple of hours ago.'

They had reached Margot's open door. The midwife said, 'Come in, if you're her friend, then this young man's Mammy can get back to her family.'

Reluctantly Hetty said, 'I don't want to get in the way.'

The woman laughed, already climbing the stairs. 'Don't worry pet, I'll let you know if you do.'

Margot had stopped asking for Paul and had begun to cry for her mother. Feeling useless Hetty said, 'It's all right. She'll be here soon.'

Heaving herself up the bed, her chin pressing hard on to her chest, Margot clutched Hetty's hand. She grunted, a deep, animal-like noise, her face red and sweaty with effort. The midwife smiled, looking up from between her splayed knees. 'Oh, you're a good brave girl! You'll have your baby in your arms in no time.'

'Oh God!' Margot cried. 'Oh God help me …'

All at once the bloodied baby was laid across Margot's belly, arms and legs flaying, screaming outrage at being forced out into the cold. Hetty laughed in astonishment and the midwife caught her eye and grinned with relief.

Paul got up. Beside the bed, Patrick scrambled to his feet but Paul ignored him and went into the kitchen. He splashed cold water on his face. His eyes were sore and he took out his false eye and held it under the running tap. Replacing it, he

232

remembered how he had woken in a field hospital with bandages around his face and how he had panicked because, for a moment, he'd believed he was back in school and this blindness was some new trick of Jenkins's. Then he'd remembered that a shell had exploded as he and Sergeant Morgan were returning from the aborted raid and that suddenly he was covering his eyes with his hands and wouldn't allow anyone to prise them away. He'd remembered too that Jenkins was dead and that the relief he'd felt when his tormentor's body slumped against his had immediately become something else he had to keep at bay along with fear and cowardice and grief. It would be best to keep silent, he decided; there would be less chance of a breach in his defences.

Patrick said carefully, 'Paul? Are you going to be all right?'

Paul could see how frightened Patrick was; Patrick knew as well as he did that Jenkins had wrecked everything. Because there were no words to help he simply kissed him. 'I should go,' he said. 'Margot will be worried.'

The midwife hesitated at the front door. 'You'll stay with her until that husband of hers shows his face?'

'Yes.'

The woman sighed. 'The buggers like to keep out of the way until it's all over. They don't like to hear their wives suffering. It makes them feel guilty.'

Closing the door behind her Hetty looked up the stairs. She had left Margot dozing, the baby swaddled and asleep in the great ugly cot. The midwife had said to make her a cup of tea and so she went into the kitchen to put the kettle on, wondering if Paul Harris had thought to buy milk before he disappeared. She glanced at the clock on the dresser. It was only eleven o'clock. She'd been sure it was later.

She heard the front door open and went out into the hallway. Paul Harris frowned at her. 'Where's my wife?' There was panic in his voice and he looked past her into the kitchen. 'What's happened?'

'She had the baby – '

He was running up the stairs at once.

His eyes were swollen and he looked like he had been crying. Half asleep, Margot reached out and touched his face as he knelt beside the bed. He really was the most beautiful man, even when he cried. She wondered why he'd cried but it seemed not to matter now that he was here. She felt euphoric with relief and laughed, but it was a weak little noise and she felt it should have been louder. Paul smiled at her, fresh tears in his eyes that she wiped away. 'It's a boy.' Her voice was hoarse and too quiet so she repeated, 'A boy. I think we should call him Robert.'

Chapter Twenty Six

Hetty watched from behind the French windows as Patrick thrust the spade into the heavy clay of the flower bed, burying it deeply and with such force she wondered at the effortless way he lifted it out again. His sleeves were rolled up past his elbows, his muscles bulging with the effort of the work. The rose bush he was digging out trembled, scattering white petals at his feet. She thought of confetti and smiled to herself. Patrick stopped to wipe his brow with the back of his hand and caught her eye. He gazed at her coldly.

Mick said, 'Quite a specimen, isn't he?'

Startled, she turned round. Taking off his glasses Mick folded them in their case and looked out of the window at his brother. 'Pat's always turned heads. I've seen him walk down the High Street and half a dozen women have stopped to look at him go by.' After a while he turned to her. 'You know I'm afraid to tell him, don't you.'

'You'll have to tell him soon.'

They watched Patrick take off his shirt, unbuttoning it slowly as though he was aware of their eyes on him. The shirt was dropped to the lawn where it lay crumpled in the long grass. He stretched, arching his neck so that the curve of his throat was exposed to the sun. There were sweat patches on his vest; a crucifix nestled in his chest hair, too delicate a thing for such a broad, powerful man. Hetty turned away too quickly. Beside her Mick bowed his head, closing his eyes as though the sunlight hurt.

'I think I should go,' Hetty said. He nodded and she crouched beside his chair, covering his hand with hers. 'You'll tell him today, won't you, before we go to Mam's?'

235

'Yes.'

She kissed his cheek, imagining that Patrick had become the watcher.

Patrick washed his hands at the kitchen sink, lathering the soap and scrubbing the mud from beneath his fingernails. Soil always made him feel unclean; he hated the creatures that crawled through it, the worms recoiling from the cold of the spade, the fat slugs contracting to hide their underbellies. He had come across a dead blackbird, maggots gleaming beneath its body. His nostrils flared in disgust as he remembered. Behind him Mick said, 'You've caught the sun on your shoulders, you should rub on calamine lotion, stop it getting sore.'

'I'm all right.' He scooped up handfuls of water to wash the sweat from his face. Groping for the towel he asked, 'Has Hetty gone?'

'Yes.'

He threw the towel down. 'What do you want to eat?'

'I'm not hungry. Sit down, I'll make us a cup of tea.'

'I'll do it. It takes you three times as long.'

'You've left your shirt in the garden.'

'It was hot out there.'

Mick lit a cigarette. Looking down at it he said, 'I've asked Hetty to marry me. She said yes.'

'Really? Well, well, brave little woman! Good for her.' He pulled out a chair and sat down, turning Mick's box of matches over and over on the table in front of him. Sensing Mick's anxiety he glanced at his brother. 'It's all right, Mick. I won't hang around getting in the way. You can have the house, you and Hetty.'

'It's your house, too, we thought we could divide it, you could have the upstairs – '

'I don't think so, Mick.'

'You could live above the shop.'

Thinking how cold and lifeless those rooms were without Paul in them Patrick laughed bleakly.

Mick said, 'I love her, Patrick. If it wasn't for her, well … I can't believe she's taken me on.'

'Oh, you're a handsome bastard, Mick, I'm sure that has something to do with it.'

He looked down at the box of matches, thinking of Paul and the first time he'd taken him to the rooms above the shop. He remembered the effort he had to make to stop himself calling him sir and how gauche he had felt, huge and clumsy beside this slight, gorgeous man who talked and carried himself like an officer. Yesterday afternoon, as Paul stood in the shop for what Patrick knew would be the last time, he had almost looked like any young father who lived along the terraced streets, a beautiful, frail impersonation of one of those exhausted men. Only his voice had kept its officer's authority.

Patrick said, 'Paul's wife had the baby. A boy.' He laughed emptily. 'He was with her, I didn't keep him from his duty.' After a moment he said, 'He's going away. To university. He came to see me after I closed the shop yesterday. He told me then.'

Paul had refused to go upstairs to their room. Standing in the shop he had said, 'It's not for a few months, the new term doesn't start until October, but I've decided to give up teaching and move back with Dad. Margot will be more comfortable there.' On a rush of breath he went on, 'It's best I go away, Patrick, best I'm on my own. I'm no good to anyone. You understand, don't you? It's for the best.'

He had wanted to kneel at his feet and beg him not to go. He pictured himself doing just that and knew that Paul would be dismayed, and that they would end up in their room making love because retreating into the mindlessness of sex would be so much easier than such an embarrassing scene. But he knew they would lie together afterwards and the familiar emptiness would creep back and Paul would still leave, as he always did: too quickly and silently as if he felt words might encourage him.

Mick said gently, 'Patrick?' He wheeled his chair closer to him and touched his arm. 'Will you be my best man?'

Patrick said, 'I would have taken care of you, you know that, don't you? No matter what.'

Hetty's mother had set the table in the parlour. Sardine sandwiches, scones and a pink blancmange for afters were all laid out on the best lace cloth she had spent the morning starching. A vase of Sweet William stood next to Albert's photograph on the mantelpiece, their scent spiking the parlour's fusty, unused air. Beside the flowers the candle's flame was a pale ghost in the sunlight.

Wheeling himself into the little room Mick said, 'You shouldn't have gone to so much trouble, Annie.'

'No trouble, Major. It's just a bit of tea.'

'You must call me Mick.'

Her father laughed awkwardly. 'Aye, mother, you're not on parade now.'

Giving him a withering look Annie said, 'Hetty, you can help me in the kitchen.'

As Hetty edged past Mick's chair he squeezed her hand. She smiled at him nervously, wishing her mother had served the tea in the kitchen, as she would've for any other young man she brought home. Tea had been days in the planning, furniture had been moved to accommodate the wheelchair, her father ordered to be on his best behaviour, scrubbed, shaved and sober. Catching her father's eye she realised he was as nervous as she was, and she smiled at him.

In the kitchen Annie was brisk. 'Set the tray with the best cups, see that you don't use the chipped one, mind, the Major won't drink from a chipped cup.'

Hetty sighed. 'He wouldn't mind, Mam. You don't have to put on a show for him.'

'Don't I? Why not? You know – he might have been Albert's commanding officer. What would we do if *he* came to tea, eh? You'd want everything right then.'

'He wasn't Albert's commanding officer.'

'No, but if he *had* been.' She sat down suddenly, her face flushed. 'I'm just saying if he *had* been.'

Hetty squatted at her side. 'It's all right, Mam, don't get upset ...'

'I got a letter from his captain, you know? Saying what a

good lad Albert was. I used to imagine him coming here in person, handing over Albert's few bits and bobs. Daft, really. He probably hardly knew who Albert was.'

Hetty found her eyes straying to the photo of Albert her mother kept on the dresser. He had been her mother's favourite, but she hadn't minded – she had her father, after all. The plain, no nonsense boy in the photograph gazed back at her and she looked away quickly, not wanting to believe any more than her mother did that he was dead.

Straightening up she said, 'Shall I make the tea?'

'I'll do it. You can put a few of those biscuits out. We'll show the Major a nice spread.'

Mick ate three sandwiches and two scones, her mother constantly pressing him to eat more. As she filled his teacup for the third time he cleared his throat, smiling at her. 'Mr Roberts, Mrs Roberts.' Reaching across the table he took Hetty's hand. 'I've asked Hetty to marry me and she said yes.'

As though relieved it was finally out in the open Joe said quickly, 'Well! Married, eh? I'm very happy for you both. We both are, aren't we love?'

Hetty looked at her mother. She swallowed hard, tasting the vinegary sardines again. 'Mam?'

Annie turned to Mick. 'Do you love her?'

'Yes.'

'She won't be your skivvy, you know. You'll have to treat her well.'

'I know, I will.'

Annie turned to her husband. 'Get that bottle of sherry out, Joe. We'll have a bit of a toast.'

In his room Patrick spread Paul's letters over the eiderdown and arranged them into date order. Starting with the earliest he read each one again. He knew them all by heart, the familiar descriptions of men and landscapes, endearments and questions and jokes he didn't get. Paul had drawn in the margins, recognisable caricatures of Thompson and Cooper and Hawkins, but there was nothing of him, he didn't even mention his name. They hardly knew each other then, of course.

Patrick tossed the last letter down. It described a ruined church and each time he read it he stood again on its stone flagged-floor and looked up at the wooden sculpture of Christ still nailed to his cross. Paul wrote how the nail through his feet had fallen away, the agony preserved in the perfect round of the nail-hole. He had inserted his finger into the hole, felt the splintered wood, the soft pad of sawdust. The wood had smelt so bitter he could taste it.

Patrick's fingers went to his own crucifix and traced its raised outline through his shirt. He remembered how Paul had once rubbed its figure of Christ between his fingers, his expression as curious as a heathen's; after a moment he'd smiled, eyebrows raised as though Patrick had told him he believed that fairies lived in the bottom of the garden.

He tied the letters together, resisting the urge to keep one back to hide between the last pages of his mother's bible. Those last, all at once colourful pages, depicted the map of the World of the Patriarchs, the Travels of the Apostles and Paul's Missionary Journeys. As a child he would trace the red lines promising himself that one day he would follow the maps from Ur through Damascus to Beer-sheba, from Jerusalem to Antioch. Even as a child he knew he would welcome the heat of the sun on his face and the feel of dry sand beneath his feet and that he wouldn't miss the mud and rain and cold of Europe a bit. After Mick's wedding he would go to Palestine; he would find a dark-eyed, olive-skinned boy who loved him and wouldn't feel ashamed.

Taking the letters, Patrick left the house and walked towards the rows of terraces that ran from the High Street. In an alley he stopped, scanning the line of wooden gates that led into the backyards of the little houses. He guessed which gate he wanted from its peeling paint and pushed it open cautiously. At once he knew he'd guessed correctly. The yard he found himself in was obviously neglected: there was no woman in this house to scrub the back step or whitewash the walls. Beneath his feet the cobbles were slimy with moss and he remembered almost losing his footing on that night months earlier when he had followed *A* into this house.

For a moment he waited just inside the gate, as ready to turn back as he had been since leaving home, but then the back door of the house opened. *A* stood in his shirtsleeves frowning at him fearfully. He was holding on to the door as though ready to close it quickly and slip the inside bolt, barricading himself against past indiscretions. Patrick noticed that the hairs on *A*'s forearms had raised as if he had seen a ghost. He stepped forward cautiously, aware that sometimes he could appear frightening.

'Hello.' Patrick smiled awkwardly. 'Hello again.'

'You shouldn't be here.' The man's voice broke and he cleared his throat, glancing nervously over his shoulder into the dark interior of the kitchen. Turning to him he said, 'Not here.'

Patrick took another step forward, conscious of the slipperiness of the ground. 'Do you have someone with you?'

'No. It's just – '

'I won't keep you.' He thought how odd the expression was, as though he could hold him against his will. He remembered the skinniness of *A*'s body beneath his own, how he'd felt he would crush the life out of him, how he was frail compared to Paul, who only appeared breakable. *A*'s fright was genuine and so he said carefully, 'I won't stay. I just wanted to return these.' He held out the letters and saw them now only as a poor excuse. He thought of Paul writing them and his heart felt like a stone suspended in mud.

Adam took a step back and opened the door wider. 'Come in. Quickly.'

He made a pot of tea. He said, 'I'm sorry I don't have any sugar.'

The kitchen smelt of dirty dishcloths; a pair of longjohns and a vest hung grey as corpses from a clothes-horse in front of a banked-down fire. School exercise books were stacked in piles on the floor, one of them open and straddling the arm of the only easy chair. Patrick sat at the kitchen table. He cleared a toast-crumbed plate to one side and set the letters down. He pushed them away a little, hoping they could be ignored.

Adam glanced at them only to turn away to rummage in a cupboard. 'I have biscuits,' he said. 'If you'd care for one.' Sitting down opposite Patrick he placed a plate of shortbread between them and smiled too brightly. 'I'm afraid they may be a bit soft. It's the damp. The house is damp. The doctor says it doesn't help my asthma.' He hesitated. Glancing at the letters again he said, 'Asthma kept me out of the war.' He smiled bitterly as though remembering some humiliation. 'Unfit for active service – almost any activity at all, in fact.' For the first time he met Patrick's gaze directly. Behind the thin lenses of his spectacles his eyes were hard and brightly defensive. Patrick held his gaze, knowing exactly what a recruiting sergeant would have made of this man; he thought of the scathing remarks he may or may not have spared him.

Adam poured the tea and Patrick saw that his hands shook a little as he handed him his cup and laughed nervously. 'You know, I don't know your name.'

'Patrick.'

'Adam.' After a moment he said, 'That what's the *A* stands for. Adam. He – the person who wrote those letters – he couldn't write my name, obviously. Well – it's *obviously* if you've read them, I suppose. Have you read them?'

'I'm sorry.'

'Oh, don't be. Really, don't be! I don't even know why I kept them. He would have been amazed that I didn't simply burn the lot.'

'Why didn't you?'

'I forgot about them, to be honest.'

As if he knew how blatant his lie was he took off his glasses and polished the lenses on a corner of his shirt. He wasn't wearing a collar and his sleeves were rolled up past his elbows as though he was about to do heavy work. His fingers were ink-stained, the nails bitten to the quick. Patrick thought of Paul taking one of those childish-looking hands and pressing its palm to his mouth. He would have just arrived here, still stinking of the long journey home, the rattle of the train still in his head, fear as dogged as a shadow at his heels. He would toss his kit bag down and pull Adam into his arms and they would cling together wordlessly. Or at least Paul would be silent; there were so few words in him he could barely imagine his greeting. Adam might dare to speak. Adam would have a mouthful of words for Paul to suppress.

Patrick picked up a biscuit and took a careful bite, expecting staleness. But the shortcake was sweet and buttery; he finished it in a couple of mouthfuls and washed it down with hot, strong tea. He felt comforted, as though he hadn't realised how hungry he'd been.

Sharply Adam said, 'Why did you bring the letters back?'

'They're yours.'

'But you wanted them.'

'They were on my conscience.'

Adam laughed shortly. Disconcerted, Patrick looked down at his teacup. He thought of the boy who wrote the letters, a sweeter, more optimistic Paul than the man he knew. He looked up at Adam, wanting to guess from his expression how much he still loved Paul, his need to know as irresistible as the urge to worry a rotten tooth.

Adam suffered his gaze only for a moment. He stood up abruptly. 'We'll go upstairs. That's what you came for. All I can say is I'm glad you had the excuse.'

Patrick followed him up the stairs. He felt outsized, his feet too big for the narrow treads, the threadbare carpet disintegrating with each heavy step; the house seemed to shrink so that he felt he would have to bow his head as he walked through the bedroom door. He remembered how Adam's bed had seemed small as a child's and imagined it buckling beneath his weight. On the landing he stopped, his hand still grasping the stair rail; the walls were closing in on him. He saw Paul in the shell hole calmly closing Jenkins's eyes; there was blood on his fingers where they had brushed against the wound in the side of the man's head. He had wiped the blood on his tunic, casually, as though it were dust from a bookshelf. There was a fine spray of blood on his face. This had seemed ordinary, too.

Patrick sat down on the top stair. He held his head in his hands and part of him was aware of how melodramatic he must look to the frail, wary man waiting in the bedroom doorway. He told himself that in a moment he would clamber to his feet and behave in a way that was as close to what was expected of him as he could manage. He would make love to *A* and it would be Paul's body he was breaking into, fucking him with all his heart and strength that he might weaken him enough to be comforted. It was terrible how brave Paul was; by rights such brittle self-containment should have been easy to break.

Paul had said, 'I love you, Patrick.' He said the words instead of goodbye, standing in the shop doorway before leaving to walk in the direction of Parkwood and his wife and child.

Adam sat down beside him, keeping still and silent so that eventually Patrick felt himself leaning against him, felt the other man's arm rest lightly around his shoulders. He smelt of coal fires. He remembered how sweet he tasted when he'd kissed him. Patrick closed his eyes; his breathing became steadier. After a while Adam took his hand and led him to the bedroom.

THE END

Paper Moon

Prologue

Soho, January 1939

The robe the man had given her to change into was dark blue silk, printed with storks and Japanese gardens and tiny bridges on which pigtailed men crossed shimmering streams. The silk felt cold and slippery against her bare skin, and she shivered as though snakes slithered over her flesh. She raised her hands and lifted her hair free to fall around her shoulders.

From behind the camera, the man who had introduced himself only as Jason held up a hand as if to silence her. She hadn't thought to speak – the idea that he thought she might surprised her, because she was scared and cold and her teeth were chattering. The camera flashed and Jason lowered his hand. She blushed darkly.

'Well done.' His voice was posh and effeminate, and she remembered what was said about certain types of Englishmen. 'Now,' he said, 'take off the robe.'

There was a café across the road from the studio in Percy Street, off London's Tottenham Court Road. It was the place where Jason had first introduced himself and told her she had good bones for the camera, as though the camera was a beast in need of feeding. The tables were covered in oilcloths in red checks and steam hissed from a tea urn on the counter. Bath buns sweated beneath a glass dome smudged with an intricate pattern of fingerprints. Men sat at the other tables, hunched possessively over fried bread and bacon and eggs that ruptured and spilled yellow yolks over the thick white plates. Nina looked away, remembering she was hungry.

At the counter, her companion pointed at the buns. She

heard him laugh and looked up. In the studio he had seemed serious, not given to friendliness; he had barely spoken to her at all, only watched as Jason took photo after photo. Behind the café's counter the woman lifted the glass dome and dropped two buns onto a plate, obviously charmed.

He carried the tray of tea and buns to her table and sat down opposite her. His face was serious again. He took cigarettes from his pocket and offered her the open packet. When she shook her head he frowned.

'You don't smoke?'

'It makes me sick.'

'You get over that.' He went on frowning at her, shaking out the match he used to light his own cigarette. 'If you want to be an actress you should smoke. Smoking gives you something to do with your hands.'

He poured the tea, pushing a cup towards her along with the plate of buns. 'Come on, now, eat up.' He imitated her Irish accent so accurately she blushed, bowing her head to hide it. She heard him laugh and forced herself to meet his eye, intending to give him a fierce gaze. But he was smiling at her and once again she was struck by how beautiful he was, like the colour plate of Gabriel in her Children's Illustrated Bible.

She said, 'He takes your picture, too, doesn't he?'

He nodded. 'And afterwards I come here for sticky buns.'

'To feel normal again.'

He gazed at her. Holding out his hand he said, 'Bobby Harris, pleased to meet you.'

His hand was cold and dry in hers. Letting go, she said, 'Nina Tate.'

'Tell me your real name.'

She looked down, stirred sugar into her tea. At last she said, 'Patricia O'Neil.' She met his gaze, daring him to laugh. He only nodded. Taking one of the buns he bit into it and discreetly licked the sugar crystals from his lips.

'Nina, would you like to go to the pictures after this?'

He was eighteen, only months older than her. He was posh, like Jason, but not like him, because she guessed that the photographer had trained himself to talk as he did, whereas

Bobby had been born to it. In the dark warmth of the cinema she studied his profile as the lights from the screen alternately shadowed and illuminated his face. There was a perfect symmetry to his features; his hair was thick and dark, falling over his forehead so that from time to time he pushed it away from his eyes that were green as a cat's. His nose had been broken – there was a small bump on its bridge where it had mended, and she stared at it, wondering how anyone could have hurt him, until he caught her eye and smiled. She looked away. On the screen Fred Astaire danced his impossible steps and sang, '*If you're blue and you don't know where to go to, why don't you go where Harlem flits ...*' Bobby leaned towards her, his mouth close to her ear. Softly and in tune he sang, '*Putting on the Ritz,*' and a shiver ran down her spine.

He lived in a room above Jason's studio. They lay on his bed, fully clothed, side by side like effigies on a tomb, his hand closed loosely over hers. An oil lamp cast shadows but left the corners of the room in darkness so that she couldn't see the things he might possess. The bed was big enough to leave a decent space between them – she could sleep without touching him, she could pretend to be innocent, even though he had seen her naked. But that had been an odd kind of nakedness; she hadn't given anything away. Daring herself to look at him, she turned her head on the fat, feather pillows. He'd lit a cigarette, releasing tremulous rings of smoke into the dull yellow light. The silence between them made her feel safe and lazy, as though she need never talk again.

As the smoke rings flattened against the ceiling she imagined he could hear her heart beating. She wondered if he guessed she loved him, although she had only realised it a moment ago, recognising what Jason must've seen – that they were the same, a matching pair like the Dresden shepherd and shepherdess on Father Mitchell's mantelpiece. It seemed immoral to love someone because they looked like you, and she thought of the orphanage nuns who had told her that only the soul was important, although in their pictures Christ was always exquisite, even in agony.

He turned on his side and edged closer so that their noses

almost touched. He said, 'I'm learning to fly,' and at once she imagined wings sprouting from his narrow shoulders, heavy, immaculate wings, white as doves. He was Gabriel, after all, grounded for a time. She smiled and he touched her mouth with his fingers. 'It's true.'

He was silent again, staring at the ceiling where it seemed the smoke rings had left indelible marks like halos. She believed she would sleep – her limbs felt weighted to the bed. She would dream of smoke and flying. His hand squeezed hers.

He said, 'I'd like to make love to you, but it won't mean anything. I don't want you to love me, or think I might love you. Loyalty is what matters.'

She felt as she had when she'd allowed the Japanese robe to slip from her shoulders, a catch-your-breath mixture of fear and excitement that came from knowing she was as wicked as the nuns said she was. She wasn't disappointed that he disregarded love – she suspected men did, at first. She wondered about loyalty, deciding it was safe. He looked at her. He seemed very young and all at once she felt powerful. She smiled, hiding it with her hand.

'You're shocked,' he said.

She stopped herself smiling and arranged her face into a suitable expression of seriousness. Lowering her hand from her mouth she said, 'It won't mean anything?'

'Except that I think you're lovely.' He seemed to think the word inadequate because he frowned. 'Beautiful. Is that enough?' He gazed into her face before closing his eyes and pressing his mouth to hers.

She became his girl. He bought her copies of the latest Paris fashions made by refugees in back-street tailor shops. He bought her gloves and high-heeled shoes and sweet, sexy hats with polka-dot veils or flighty feathers. He taught her how to speak as he did and to smoke; he taught her how to hold her head up and sway her hips when she walked so that men smiled after her and whistled. In Jason's photographs around that time she looked as if she was keeping a secret, although

Jason guessed she was in love and told her to keep it to herself, that it showed in her eyes and ruined his composition. She guessed that he was jealous, newly sophisticated enough to know that Jason loved Bobby, too.

That summer in Hyde Park they watched workmen dig trenches, cover from the bombs no one could imagine falling. The smell of the cold, disturbed soil reminded her of graveyards and she shuddered, slipping her arm around Bobby's waist and leaning close to him. His blue RAF tunic was rough against her face; she traced her fingers over the wings on his chest and pictured him flying in his comical little plane: Bobby the pilot, her delicate, fine-boned boy. He seemed invented for the air, for light and space and speed; the drudgery of the trench diggers would break him in two.

He said, 'Jason took his last photograph of me today.' He didn't look at her but went on gazing at the men waist deep in the earth. 'He doesn't know yet. He thinks we'll go on as we were.'

His cap shaded his eyes and he bowed his head to light a cigarette, shielding the match with cupped hands. She wondered how anyone could imagine they could go on as they were when Bobby was so changed. After Jason took his photographs he'd discarded the ordinarily beautiful clothes he'd arrived in for the extraordinary transformation of his uniform. He'd adjusted his cap and straightened his tie in front of Jason's wall of mirrors, mirrors they'd used to check other dressing-up costumes. There was no irony in his pose; he didn't smile to include her in this new, elaborate joke. She'd watched his reflection, seeing at last the way he saw himself: serious, intent on the future and a war that couldn't come fast enough. Soon he would look at her and not see the same person but someone he'd known ages ago, a shadow from his childhood.

The workmen climbed from their trench. Clay clung to their boots and smeared their faces where they had wiped sweat from their brows. They looked like creatures of the earth, as weighted to it as she was. Only Bobby could escape.

Chapter One

Soho, April 1946

Standing behind his father's wheelchair, Hugh Morgan scanned the crowded room, looking for the blonde he'd noticed earlier. A moment ago she'd been flirting with Henry, his father's editor, whose cheeks had flushed the same shade of red as the girl's dress. She had laughed suddenly, flashing her teeth and reminding him of the shark in *Mac the Knife*.

Hugh lit a cigarette and blew smoke into air already thick with tobacco fumes. He'd noticed that the girl used a cigarette holder and that her dress clung to the curve of her backside and plunged between her breasts. He imagined he'd seen the dimple of her belly button through the sheer fabric, realising with dismay that he must have been staring. It seemed as though he had forgotten how to look at women.

Hugh had arrived in London that morning. His ship had docked in Portsmouth the day before and he was now, officially, a civilian. The London train had been full of service men and women, all looking like misplaced persons, grey-faced and anxious, as though the prospect of facing those left behind at the start of the war filled them with dread. What would they say to them? *The bed's too soft*. The line from one of his father's poems had come back to him as the train rattled through the English countryside. Beside him, an RAF sergeant had fallen asleep, his Brylcreemed head almost resting on Hugh's shoulder, his body a heavy, warm weight against his arm. The WREN opposite had smiled in sympathy and he'd realised that women in uniform would never call him sir again. He'd felt liberated, dislodging the still sleeping airman to lean across the carriage and light the girl's cigarette. It had been an uncharacteristic move; all at once he'd found himself too shy to strike up the kind of conversation that might have led to an end to his months of celibacy. He'd spoken to the WREN as though he was still her superior officer. Henry would've had a better chance of getting her knickers off.

Hugh sighed, and gave up looking for the girl in the red dress. She had probably left, bored by his father's middle-aged, bookish friends and the awe-struck fans that turned up to his poetry readings. All Hugh's life his father had been famous, or as famous as poets could be. A crippled veteran of the Somme, turned war poet, Mick Morgan had struck a chord with the British public. A Kipling for the modern age, *The Times* had called him in its latest review, a great populist. Hugh knew that the article would have angered Mick: the last thing his father wanted to be was popular.

The girl in the red dress appeared again. Twisting round in his wheelchair to look at him, Mick said, 'Her name's Nina Tate. She's a model.'

'What's she doing here?'

Without irony his father said, 'She loves my work. She had a dog-eared copy of Dawn Song she wanted me to sign.' Watching the girl he said, 'You should introduce yourself, Hugh. Tell her I wrote *Homecoming* for you – you'll be irresistible.'

'I'd say I'm not her type.'

'How do you know that? For God's sake, boy, if I were your age …'

'Weren't you married when you were my age?' Hugh frowned at him, pretending he didn't know. 'Anyway, why don't you go and talk to her? As the writer of *Homecoming* you've got a head start on me.'

'I've already invited her to dinner. You can come too, if you like.'

They watched the girl together. A blonde ringlet had escaped from her chignon, bobbing against her long, white neck, and she tucked it behind her ear. Her fingernails were painted scarlet. Hugh imagined their scrape across his back, feeling the stirring of desires too long suppressed.

A week earlier, a few days before Bobby left London, Nina had told him she was going to the book launch. He'd laughed shortly. 'What's he writing about now? Don't tell me – the pity of war, *again*. More books should be burnt – I was with Adolf on that one.'

Bobby was walking her home from her job as sales assistant in Antoinette Modes. She knew he had spent the day alone in her room and that boredom had soured his mood. Only a week since his release from hospital, he still waited for the cover of darkness before braving the streets. She'd sighed, searching out his hand from his pocket and holding it gently, as though the burns that disfigured it were still raw and painful. After only a few steps he stopped and lit a cigarette, an excuse to draw his hand away. The match flared, illuminating the taut, immobile mask skin grafts had made of his face, and he held her gaze, his eyes challenging her to look away. He would often test her like this, always alert for expressions that might betray her.

He shook the match out, tossing it into the overgrown garden of a bombed house. Bitterly he said, 'Do you have to go?'

'Not if you don't want me to.'

He sighed. 'Go, buy a pile of his books – we'll have a bonfire.'

She'd laughed despite herself and he'd smiled, reaching out to touch her face before drawing his hand away quickly. 'Be careful of Michael Morgan, he's a womaniser.'

Sitting opposite Morgan now in an Italian restaurant, Nina began to eat the spaghetti the waiter had set in front of her. The pasta was over-cooked, the sauce too thin, sweet with the taste of English ketchup. The bread grew staler in its raffia basket as the poet, his son and his minder ate their meals without comment. They were all used to worse, and the taste could be washed away with the sour red wine, but suddenly she was tired of terrible food and she pushed her plate away and fished in her bag for her cigarettes. Mick Morgan leaned across the table with his lighter.

'Would you like something else?' he asked.

Henry Vickers said, 'They used to do v...v...very g...g...good ice cream here, before the w...w...war.'

Sitting beside her, Morgan's son pushed his own, cleared, plate away. 'You brought me here as a child, do you remember, Henry? Chocolate ice cream in a tall glass and two long spoons. I believed you when you said they wouldn't serve grown-ups ice cream.'

'I didn't think I was such a g...g...good liar.' He smiled at him lovingly. 'I thought you were humouring me.'

'No.' Hugh caught Nina's eye and laughed as though embarrassed.

Nina got up. Smiling at Henry to lessen his discomfort she said, 'Would you excuse me? I have to powder my nose.'

In the ladies' toilets, the sole concession to a powder room was the cracked mirror above the sink. Taking a lipstick from her bag she unscrewed it, then paused. There was no need to put on more – it was simply an automatic response to a mirror, but it helped, sometimes, to look harder than she actually was. She applied it quickly, pressing her lips together to even out the stain. Her reflection smiled back at her, glossy and seductive. Turning away, she went back into the dim, red light of the restaurant.

'She's lovely, isn't she?'

Hugh sighed. 'Dad, just stop. I'm tired, I could sleep for a month – I'm not interested in her.'

'Then why come with us tonight? Henry can manage quite well on his own.'

Hugh looked at Henry's empty chair. 'I hurt him, didn't I? I didn't mean to. I suppose I'm out of practice when it comes to dealing with men like him.'

'Oh? I thought the navy was stuffed with queers. I would've thought you'd get plenty of *practice*.' More harshly he added, 'Anyway, Henry loves you like a father. Maybe if he had been your father you wouldn't be so bloody ...' He seemed lost for words and Hugh looked at him.

Levelly he said, 'You haven't asked me how Mum is.'

257

'How is she?'

'Fine.'

Wanting a drink, Hugh turned towards the bar. The same bunches of dusty wax grapes and vine leaves hung from the walls, looking less exotic now than when he was a child and ice cream was on the menu. They sat on the same plush-covered banquettes he remembered itching against his short-trousered legs and the same posters of Pisa and Rome curled their corners from the walls as red candles cascaded wax down the sides of wine bottles. Only one thing had changed – the man who had been proprietor then, who had pinched his cheek and smiled his rapid, incomprehensible endearments, had been interned on the Isle of Man. He'd died there, so Henry told him. Hugh sighed, trying unsuccessfully to feel anything but exhausted.

Failing to catch the waiter's eye he turned to his father. 'Do you want a Scotch?'

'No, I've had enough.'

As Henry came back Hugh said too heartily, 'You'll join me, Henry, won't you?'

'Will I? In what?' Henry and Mick exchanged a wry look. Irritated, Hugh turned away.

Nina Tate sat down beside him. She touched his arm briefly and at once turned her attention on his father. 'Would you mind if your son and I go dancing?'

Hugh laughed, astonished. 'Shouldn't you ask me first?'

He felt her foot brush against his ankle; she had taken her shoe off and her silk-stockinged toes worked their way beneath his trouser leg. To Mick she said, 'Thank you for this evening.'

On the street outside the restaurant Hugh said, 'I'm not a very good dancer.'

The girl linked her arm through his. 'Come on,' she said. 'I'll teach you how to jive.'

On the Empire's dance floor, Nina rested her head against Hugh Morgan's shoulder. The lights had been dimmed for the last, slow dance, the spinning glitter ball casting its shards of light at the dancers' feet. From the stage the singer crooned, *'I'll be seeing you, in all those old familiar places ...'* Nina closed her eyes, remembering that this was one of Bobby's favourite songs, that one September evening in 1940 she'd noticed him leave a dance as the band began on its opening bars. Outside a bright, full moon hung low in a troubled sky, and she'd watched him gaze at the racing clouds as the music played on without them. Years later he told her that fear would charge at him out of the blue, a huge monster of a feeling that left him feeling flattened and useless. That night he'd turned to her and smiled, his eyes dark with exhaustion. 'Sad songs,' he said. 'Shouldn't be allowed.'

In the Empire the singer drew breath for the last verse. Soon the lights would come up and she would be revealed, smudged and dishevelled in the merciless brightness designed to discourage lingering. She couldn't allow Hugh Morgan to see her like that and so she stepped away from him, smiling fleetingly at his questioning face. Opening her bag she took out the cloakroom ticket and held it up in explanation. 'Shall we avoid the queue?'

'May I see you home?'

As the hat-girl handed them their coats, Nina glanced at Hugh. Thinking about Bobby had made her feel as vulnerable as he was – as though she wasn't wearing knickers and everyone could see through the flimsy fabric of her dress. She put her coat on quickly, bowing her head to fasten its buttons. When she looked up again he was watching her, a good-looking, wholesome man, certain of sex. In the dance hall, she'd noticed other women casting sly glances over the shoulders of less glamorous men, their eyes lingering on his face. Nina could tell what they were thinking from their smiles: too handsome. Such good looks were almost preposterous.

She turned up her astrakhan collar. 'It's only a short walk,' she said. 'Not far.'

*　　　　*　　　　*

Hugh Morgan was tall as well as handsome, broad and muscular as a navvy, his skin tanned. She'd always imagined sailors as small and lithe. She supposed she'd seen too many films in which agile boys climbed the rigging of sailing ships, quick as monkeys. But the navy didn't have sails any more, just the industrial metal of battleships. In the newsreels the ships were vast and slow and looked invincible. Lieutenant Hugh Morgan would be at home on such a deck.

In her bed he slept on his back, a sheet gathered at his groin. On his left arm, close to his shoulder, a Chinese dragon roared fire, its eyes bulging malice, its tail twisting to a devil's point. He'd smiled as she'd traced her finger over it. 'I was drunk. I wanted an anchor.'

'Too dull.' She drew her hand away, sitting back on her heels.

He'd reached up to cup her face in his palm. After a moment he asked, 'Why did you come to Dad's party?'

'I wanted to meet him. Ever since I first read his poetry –'

He laughed, shutting her up. Fumbling on the bedside table for his cigarettes, he'd glanced at her. 'Have you read the new book?'

'Of course.'

'I haven't. Not a single line.'

Still sleeping on his back he snored, a noise that broke into garbled speech. She sat up, taking care not to wake him, and shrugged on the silk robe with its pattern of Japanese gardens. In the corner of her bed-sit she set the kettle on the single gas ring and stood over it, ready to turn off the heat as soon as its whistle sounded. Above the sink her window looked out over the huddled rooftops of slums, the crooked line broken where bombs had dropped. She could see the dome of St Paul's in the near distance, so unaffected by the surrounding destruction that there was talk of divine intervention. Such talk made her feel weary. She rubbed at a sticky spot on the glass; a few days ago she'd removed the strips of tape a previous tenant had criss-crossed over the pane, the process a chore rather than the ritualistic celebration of the war's end she'd imagined it would be. In the end, there had seemed nothing to celebrate.

For the whole of VE Day she had stayed in her room. Below her window crowds sang and cheered and she imagined strangers embracing on the street. Later a fight had broken out, American voices cursing like film gangsters, a lone police whistle sounding frantic, foolishly impotent. There was a noise like a gunshot, a car backfiring or a firework kept safe for the duration, exploding for the victors. All the same, in the morning she'd expected to see a body sprawled on the pavement, blood thick as tar in the gutter. She'd kept the blackout curtain closed tight, keeping the revelry at bay, and thought about Bobby enduring yet another operation on his hands. She hoped that the streets around the hospital were quiet, that someone would explain to him when he woke from the anaesthetic what all the fuss was about. After an operation he was confused and anxious and she'd wished desperately to be at his bedside, at the same time guiltily relieved that she wasn't.

The kettle whistled shrilly and the stranger in her bed garbled a command from his sleep. Turning off the gas, she stayed very still, watching to make sure he slept on. At last, reassured, she made weak, black tea, sweetening it with the last of her sugar ration before taking *Dawn Song* from her bag. Curling up in the room's only armchair she began to read.

Chapter Two

Nina was singing *Paper Moon*. Spot-lit on a stage, she appeared small and vulnerable as a child refugee, a cardboard suitcase at her feet, a luggage label pinned to her chest. The song's jaunty words became fainter and her voice was thin as paper ashes floating up towards the theatre's vaulted ceiling. Way back in the stalls, a Gestapo officer sitting either side of him, Bobby strained to hear the final note. He knew that when she stopped singing he would be shot and he couldn't wait for the song to end and the sadistic, teasing suspense to be over. His tongue felt huge in his mouth, his lips ballooned to ten times their size. He couldn't speak; the fire had destroyed his voice.

A hand seized his shoulder, shaking him, and he opened his eyes. Standing beside his bed, his half-brother Mark smiled shyly. 'Bobby? Are you all right? You were shouting …' As though embarrassed by his nosiness he asked, 'Who's Nina?'

Still scared from the dream Bobby said too harshly, 'What are you doing here?'

'You left the door open … I heard you calling out. Sorry, I didn't mean to disturb you.'

The boy looked so dejected that Bobby forced himself to smile. 'It's all right. You startled me, that's all.'

'Sorry. I'll go, if you want.'

Bobby sat up. He'd fallen asleep fully clothed and he caught sight of himself in the wardrobe mirror. His hair stuck up messily and dark sweat stains spread beneath his arms. The jaunty words of *Paper Moon* rang in his head; he could still smell the leather of the Gestapo men's coats. Sweat trickled down his back. Imagining he stank, he began to unbutton his shirt.

From the corner of his eye he saw Mark glance away quickly. Remembering the boy's shyness, Bobby paused. Mark had never been sent away to school, never shared a bedroom, let alone a dormitory. It was possible he'd never seen a naked body. He buttoned his shirt again.

'Have you been to school today?'

'Just this minute escaped.' Mark blushed, obviously aware that he sounded too eager to be with him. At sixteen, blond and blue-eyed, he was taking after his father rather than their mother. Already Mark was taller than he was, thickset, strong; he smiled often, sweet, innocent smiles. There were times when Bobby felt so self-conscious around him his skin crawled.

Bobby looked up from putting on his shoes. 'Mum will be wondering where you've got to, won't she?'

'She knows I'm here.'

'Does your father know?' Bobby found himself anxiously counting seconds. He knew the longer Mark was silent the angrier his stepfather must have been over this visit. He counted a slow ten before he stood up, shrugging on his jacket to hide the worst of his sweat-stained shirt and shoving his cigarettes into its pocket. Mark shifted from one foot to the other; he seemed to radiate childish awkwardness. Briskly Bobby said, 'Come on. I'll make you a cup of tea.'

Bobby had been four years old when his mother remarried. He remembered his grandfather crouching in front of him, holding his hands as he told him he couldn't live with him any more. He was to be a good boy for his mother and her new husband, the man who called him a cry baby when he hid behind her skirt. He hadn't been a cry baby until then but his stepfather liked labels and for a while at least this was his.

Sitting at the kitchen table, Mark said, 'I'm sorry about your grandfather. He was a nice man.'

Bobby took the tea caddie from the shelf above the stove. The tin had a relief of long-robed Chinese men who followed each other round and round its sides. His fingers searched out

263

each figure, feeling the contours of their heads, their individual pigtails, remembering the once bright, exotic blues and reds and greens of their robes. The caddie was old, its colours almost worn away. He set it down gently.

Hesitantly Mark said, 'Mum wanted to go to the funeral, but they had a row about it.'

'A row?' He raised his eyebrows, holding his gaze until Mark looked away.

'Well, you know – not a row, exactly.'

'He raised his voice and she backed down.'

Mark blushed again, although the colour had barely faded since the last time. 'I would've gone with you, if it hadn't been for school.'

At the funeral that morning the church had been half-empty; Bobby had had the front pew to himself. Afterwards, when the coffin had been lowered into the family grave, he'd stood about, at a loss to know what to do next, until someone had taken his arm and wordlessly led him back to the house. A funeral lunch had been laid on, slivers of spam sandwiches and a cake that tasted of ashes and must have used too many of someone's coupons. He hadn't discovered which of his grandfather's patients had taken the trouble because no one stayed long enough to be asked. He was relieved when they'd gone; their embarrassment around him was excruciating.

Spooning tea into the pot Bobby said, 'He's left me this house. Should I sell it, do you think?'

'Do you want to?' Mark looked appalled and Bobby laughed.

'Would it be so terrible?'

'Yes! I couldn't imagine not being able to come here. Besides – you'd miss the garden.'

'It's overgrown now. A jungle.'

'I'll help you with it! I could do all the hard work – you just tell me what to do.'

'I can still garden, Mark.'

'Yes, of course. Sorry.'

Bobby smiled. Sitting down opposite him, he ducked his head to look into his downcast face. 'Just because I look like a petrified gargoyle ...'

Mark met his gaze. 'Not to me. Anyway, after a while ...'

Unable to help himself, Bobby prompted, 'After a while?'

'You get used to it.'

Bobby sat back. He took his cigarettes from his pocket, turning the packet over and over on the table slowly and deliberately, knowing he was drawing his half-brother's attention to his hands. The fire that had melted his face into its lop-sided leer had made a claw of his left hand, although it retained just enough movement to make it serviceable. His right hand had got off lightly in comparison, although its scars were horror-film shocking. Perhaps he could make a living playing monsters, the same, raw-faced monster over and over until everyone was bored to death of it.

Lighting a cigarette he said, 'You wanted to know who Nina is. She's a girl I know in London. I was dreaming about her when you woke me.'

Mark grinned, attempting to tease him. 'A girl? I bet she's a peach, is she?'

'A peach? Nina's too skinny for peachiness. Nina's ...' He frowned, wondering how he might describe her. At last he said, 'Nina's all angles and shadows.'

'Oh.' Mark looked blank. 'Is she foreign?'

'No. Why?'

'Her name.'

'Stage name. She's really called Doris or Ethel or something.' He stood up. 'Shall we have toast with this tea? I'm starving.'

When Mark had gone, Bobby cleared the dining room of the funeral's cake-crumbed plates and washed the teacups that had piled up in the sink. He dried them, twisting a tea towel inside each one to rub away the stains, noticing that almost every plate and cup he had inherited was cracked or crazed or chipped. He looked around the kitchen, seeing for the first time the cobwebs in the corners trapping the dust that filmed every surface, the mould stealthily sowing its black spoors across the ceiling. Newspapers were piled by his grandfather's chair, some of them months old, thin, wartime newspapers

265

with brisk, morale-boosting headlines. The latest was the one he'd hidden behind on the train coming home, his grandfather's unexpected death causing him to leave Nina sooner than he'd intended, and much sooner than he felt ready to. All the same, it crossed his mind that she seemed relieved to see him go, that despite her assurances that he was welcome to sleep on her floor she hadn't really expected him to take her at her word. The trouble was he had nowhere else to go. Nowhere, at least, that he felt safe.

He sat down in the threadbare armchair that exhaled his grandfather's scent of Wright's soap and whisky. On the mantelpiece opposite stood a photograph of his father and beside it one of himself. They were both in uniform, his father in the khaki of an army officer, the dull colour lending itself more naturally to the sepia print. The air force blue of his own uniform appeared only as a flat grey, the wings on his chest hardly standing out at all. They looked like the same person, his grandfather said, same person, different war. He'd said the unfairness of it made him want to howl with rage.

Bobby got up. His damaged fingers fumbled but at last he managed to take the photograph of himself from its frame. Without looking at it, he tore it in two. There were too many photographs of that face, they were everywhere, if you knew where to look. At least he could take control of this one. Squatting in front of the hearth, he crumpled the two pieces and threw them into the cold grate before setting about the careful business of lighting a fire.

At the door of Jason's flat, Nina hesitated. Taking her compact from her handbag she peered into its mirror and smiled experimentally. The look she was aiming for was one of restrained sympathy. She mustn't look too upset, Davey had said. He'd smiled, sad and resigned. 'I try to act as though he'll be up and about tomorrow.'

Nina sighed, snapping the compact shut. She glanced back towards the three flights of stairs she'd climbed. A baby screamed from one of the other flats. Its pram had blocked the hallway, one of the rusty wheel spokes almost snagging her stockings as she edged past it so that she'd cursed softly at the idea of such a calamity.

The door to Jason's flat swung open suddenly and Davey threw out his arms to her. 'Nina! My darling girl!' He kissed her cheeks, pausing to whisper in her ear, 'He's in a difficult mood. Never mind, least said and all that.' Standing back he smiled, 'Come in, come in. We've been on pins all day looking out for you.'

Nina followed him into the main room of the flat, a large, square space that always reminded her of a stage. Windows looked out on to plane trees growing close to the building, their half-bare branches like a painted backdrop. Centre-stage was Jason's chaise-longue.

Davey said, 'Look who's here!'

'Nina.' Reclining on the couch, Jason struggled to sit up, the magazine he'd been reading tumbling to the floor, revealing a pre-war centre spread of Chanel evening dresses. He held his hand out to her. 'Nina, my waif and stray.'

'Sit down, Nina.' Davey stood behind a chair, turning it a little more towards Jason. 'Sit down here, nice and close so he can see you.' More loudly he said, 'Nina's wearing dark blue today. A nice little two piece with a nipped waist. Not too utility.' He smiled at her. 'Now, you'll have a cup of tea, won't you?'

As Nina sat down Jason leaned towards her. Jerking his head at Davey's retreating back he said, 'I'm not blind, not yet.' He gazed at her, searching her face. At last he said, 'I can still see you, little waif.'

His skin had shrunk over his face, grey and thin as a workhouse blanket, revealing the outline of skull bones. It seemed, though, that he had made an effort for her. He had shaved and slicked back his hair, and there was a dark gold cravat tied at his throat and tucked beneath his navy silk dressing gown. He smelt of cologne, which masked a little the sour taint of his breath. Beside him on a low table was a vase of white lilies and he reached out, stroking a still closed bud.

'Bobby sent them,' he said. 'Davey says they're funeral flowers. He just stuck them in a vase – none of his usual

267

fussing.' Still looking at the flowers he said, 'They are funereal. Bobby's joke, I suspect.' After a moment he looked at her. 'There was a note with them, saying he was going home. Has he gone?'

'A few days ago.'

Jason snorted. 'He'll come back – his home's here, with his friends. That family of his!' He shook his head in disgust. 'They don't care a flying fuck about him.' Nina smiled and he caught her eye and laughed a little. There were tears in his eyes. 'He won't hide forever, not my Bobby.'

She remembered that Bobby had told her trees and high walls surrounded his grandfather's house. 'It's like the Beast's house,' he'd said. 'Secretive.' They had been sitting in a café close to King's Cross. Even in their shadowy corner people stared at him, the mixture of horror and pity on their faces barely disguising their curiosity. She'd found herself staring back until they looked away. Sensing her agitation, Bobby had reached out and covered her hand with his own, squeezing her fingers until she faced him again.

Jason slumped back on the couch. As though the effort of greeting her had exhausted him he said weakly, 'You're looking even thinner. I'm no one to talk, but all the same, I hope you're not pining too much for him, I know how dreadful that can be.'

'I'm not pining.'

'No? That's hard to believe. Although a little bird told me you've been seen with someone fabulous.'

Nina laughed, thinking of Hugh Morgan. 'What else did your spies say about him?'

'It's true, then? They said he looked too straight. But then the information one gets largely depends on one's sources. Anyway, it's none of my business.' Pointing to a photograph album on the floor between them he said, 'I've been compiling a few memories.'

Nina picked the album up. It was heavy, bound in dark leather, its pages thick and serrated. Her heart began to pound as she wondered which photographs Jason had decided to commit to such an album. She glanced at him.

'Go on,' he said, 'The first one is so beautiful. If it wasn't for Davey I'd have it hanging above the fire-place.'

Her fingers hovered above the flimsy paper covering the first picture. She could just make out the white of the plaster Ionic columns from the studio on Percy Street. 'Are they all of him?'

'There are some that were taken when he was very young, before you met. Some you haven't seen.'

She closed the album and placed it on the floor again. 'He is fabulous, the man your friends saw me with. He was an officer in the navy. He has a tattoo.' She traced a circle on her arm. 'An extraordinary tattoo, just here.'

'He sounds like a natural. Could he get it up for the camera as well, do you think?'

Davey kicked the kitchen door open. He set down the tray he was carrying and turned to them. 'There. Did I give you long enough to talk? Have you had time to look at all the lovely pictures, Nina?' Picking the album up, he smiled too brightly and tapped the cover. 'Some of his best work in here. The lighting effects are quite marvellous. Works of art, even if they are all of the same subject. But then, Monet had his water lilies, Turner his sunsets and Jason had that boy's cock.'

Reaching out, Jason snatched the album from him. He looked down at it on his lap. 'It's right we should remember him as he was.'

Davey shook his head, exasperated. Turning to her he said, 'You know he wouldn't see him, don't you? Told me to turn him away because he couldn't bear to see his poor face all burnt away. He sent those flowers because I had to tell him Mr Sensitive here was too ill for visitors.' To Jason he added, 'Not that he seemed that upset. Hard to tell though, there's not much expression left.'

Nina sighed. She sat forward and took Jason's hand. 'It's not as bad as you imagine.'

Quietly Jason said, 'I should've seen him. I should have faced up to it.'

Davey snorted. Taking the album from him he said, 'I should burn this. It's so hard to get enough coal, it could be put to some good use.'

Jason looked at her. 'I've willed the photographs to you, Nina. When I'm dead they're yours.'

'And there are boxes and boxes, darling. Not just this album, not just the tasteful portraits, but all the *arty* pictures, too.'

Nina stood up. If she stayed she would be compelled to look through the album and each picture would be a reminder of what she'd lost. Forcing herself to smile she said, 'You're tired, I should go.'

As Davey showed her to the door, Jason called, 'My solicitor will have the pictures delivered to you. Promise me you'll keep them safe?'

Nina hesitated. She imagined the boxes of photographs piled up in her room. They should be burnt; it would be better for everyone. Turning to Jason she smiled. 'You'll keep them safe for a long time yet.'

Chapter Three

Hugh Morgan was standing outside Nina's flat when she returned home. He was holding Cathy, her neighbour's baby, jogging her up and down and singing *Run Rabbit, Run*, as her neighbour searched her handbag. They all turned to her as she reached the landing, Cathy wide-eyed and drooling on Hugh's shoulder. Hugh smiled, shifting the baby from one arm to the other. 'This lady can't find her purse.'

Nina sighed. 'How much do you need, Irene?'

The woman looked at her. Belligerently she said, 'I've run out of milk.'

Nina took a half-crown from her own purse. 'Here. You can pay me back next week.'

Without meeting Nina's eye, the woman pocketed the money before taking the baby from Hugh's arms and walking downstairs.

Nina took her keys from her bag. Her surprise at seeing him had turned to irritation, a feeling made worse by Irene's fecklessness. She had wanted to be alone, to change out of her too dressy, putting-on-a-front suit and wash away the smell of Jason's sickroom from her skin. Instead, here was this smiling, artless man, waiting expectantly. Behind the locked door of her flat, her room was neat and orderly; she wouldn't have it disturbed. On impulse she dropped the keys discreetly back into her bag.

'It's such a lovely day,' she said. 'We could go for a walk.'

'I thought a picnic, actually.' He grinned, suddenly pulling a banana from each of his jacket pockets and pointing them at her in a gunslinger's pose.

Astonished, she laughed. 'Where on earth did you find

them?'

He tapped the side of his nose with one of the fruits. 'Ask no questions. Now, I saw a park along the road. We'll go there.'

They sat on a bench overlooking the park duck pond where a pair of swans swam side by side. Nina smiled to herself, remembering a costume Bobby had made for her from lace and organza and soft white feathers saved from a moulting boa. They'd enacted their own version of Swan Lake and the lovely, flighty costume hadn't stayed on very long. She remembered the ticklish feel of the feathers against her skin, how one of them had caught in Bobby's hair. Unseen by the camera she had brushed it away, moved by tenderness for him as she faked her cinematic climax.

Watching the seamless glide of the birds, she finished her banana, peeling back the skin monkey-fashion. From the corner of her eye she saw that Hugh Morgan was watching her. After a moment he said, 'I never cared much for bananas as a child. Absence makes the heart grow fonder, I suppose.'

Thinking of Bobby she nodded, placing the yellow-black skin beside her on the bench. 'Were they very expensive?'

'Arm and a leg.' He smiled at her. 'And I had to queue for ages. Still, I had a sudden fancy that just had to be indulged.'

She looked at him properly for the first time since she'd seen him outside her flat. In daylight he looked younger than she remembered, less condescendingly arrogant. He wore dark wool slacks with a sailor's flare and a white, roll-neck Arran sweater that complimented his square jaw. Earlier he'd taken off his short, double-breasted jacket and it lay folded beside him, its brass buttons glinting in the sunlight. His aura of wholesomeness was stronger than ever. She remembered the tattoo on his arm; it seemed incongruous now.

He said, 'I'm sorry about the other night. I don't usually fall asleep like that.'

'What do you usually do?'

He laughed, as though shocked by her question. 'Go back to my ship, I suppose – not that it happened often.'

Surprisingly he blushed. 'It's not true – that old lie about a girl in every port.'

'That's a pity.'

He met her gaze. 'Is it? Who for?'

She stood up. 'Your father's reading this afternoon in a bookshop in Kensington. I'd like to hear him.'

He frowned incredulously. 'You are joking?'

She began walking towards the park gates. Glancing back she saw him get up, tossing the limp banana skins into the bushes behind the bench, before picking up his jacket and following her.

The last time Hugh had attended one of his father's readings a woman had cornered him, her face flushed, her eyes bright with what he could only think of now as sexual excitement. 'Your father,' she told him breathlessly, 'is a genius. A true …' She'd caught her breath, her hand fluttering at her throat as she sighed, 'Genius.' She had smelt of a heady, musk perfume; when she touched his arm some of her excitement transferred itself to him, even though he'd found the evening dull, his father as predictable as ever. It was the smell of her, he supposed, the passion in that breathless voice, that made him take her hand and lead her outside to Henry's conveniently parked car. Only afterwards, as she rearranged her clothes, after he'd buttoned his flies and offered her the consolation of a cigarette, did he allow himself to acknowledge that it was his father, and not himself, who had inspired such passion. The knowledge depressed him but was only to be expected. All that adulation for the great poet had to be channelled somewhere.

Standing at the back of the crowded bookshop now, Hugh stole a sideways glance at Nina. Her heavy blonde hair was coiled in a net snood studded with black polka-dots. Her expression was intent as she concentrated on the poetry. From time to time she smiled slightly, or nodded as though at some profound understanding. He had an urge to heckle his father, to catcall and jeer. It would be the ultimate test of her loyalty, a test he felt sure she would fail.

He remembered her naked in his arms, her sweet, small breasts, the hollowness of her belly. She'd shaved her legs and beneath her arms, but between her legs, too, so that there was a definite shaping of her pubic hair that had shocked him. Later, alone, imagining that careful, deliberate shaving, he'd become as aroused as when he'd been with her. He'd been planning on never seeing her again, had marked her down as another of his father's conquests by proxy, despising himself for his compliance. But the memory of that shocking triangle of dark blonde hair had him bathing and dressing carefully, had him standing in line for bananas: the only excuse he could think of to visit her again. Listening to the rhythmic rise and fall of his father's voice, watching her hang on his every cadence, he silently cursed himself as a fool.

The last poem was read. There was a pause, a moment his father always timed perfectly before removing his glasses and closing his book and wheeling his chair ever so slightly backwards as though the resounding applause took him by surprise. Hugh stopped himself applauding – he could be one part Philistine, at least. Nina grinned at him, the most natural, spontaneous look she'd given him since they'd met. She didn't seem to notice his churlishness. He exhaled, hating the edge in his voice as he said, 'Do you want to speak to him?'

'Don't you?' She laughed. 'Were you just going to sneak away without even saying hello?'

He snorted, covering his irritation by lighting a cigarette. As he shook the match out he said, 'I don't want to get caught up here. I know how these affairs can drag on.'

'We won't stay long, I promise.' She held his gaze and for a moment the noise and bustle around them receded. He imagined taking her hand and leading her out on to the street, hailing a taxi to take them back to her room. He couldn't remember wanting anyone so badly and her reasons for wanting him had become totally irrelevant. Nothing mattered except the urgency to get her alone.

He took her hand tightly in his. 'We're going,' he said. 'Right now.'

*   *   *

She whispered, 'Are you all right?'

Hugh stared into the blackout darkness of her room. Beneath him the bed sagged and his feet were hard against the metal frame so that he imagined deep indentations in his soles. From the anxiety in her voice he guessed that he'd been calling out from his nightmare and he wondered what she'd heard. The dream was still fresh; he could still see the slicks of oil burning on a millpond Atlantic. The men were still drowning: Jackson, Barker, Wilson with his face all black from the explosion. A slow motion newsreel with the sound distorted, it played in his head most nights lately. He closed his eyes, aware of her watching him.

'I'm hungry,' he said.

She got up and shrugged on a brightly printed dressing gown. 'I'll make you a sandwich.'

He watched her as she went to the sink and filled the kettle, as she lit the gas beneath it and took bread and what looked like a tin of sardines from a cupboard. She worked efficiently, rolling back the tin lid with its key, emptying the oily-smelling fish into a bowl and mashing the flesh before spreading it onto dry bread. The sandwich was sliced corner to corner and placed on a plate. The kettle boiled. Licking her fingers, she made tea, looking up to smile at him as she poured a tiny amount of tinned milk into two cups.

He frowned at her as she set a cup of tea on the bedside table and handed him the plate. 'Aren't you having anything to eat?'

Climbing back into bed she said, 'Later.'

'Share this with me.'

She hesitated a moment before tearing off a corner of sandwich and popping it into her mouth. Swallowing, she said, 'I mashed up the bones. They're good for you.'

'So I hear.'

'It's all I have, I'm sorry.'

'It's all right – I'm used to weevil-infested ship biscuit.'

She smiled and he felt his heart soften towards her. Her hair had fallen around her shoulders and he reached out to hook a thick strand behind her ear. 'Vinegar, that's what we

275

need. Sardines are always helped along by a splash of vinegar.'

He bit into the sandwich, anticipating the disconcerting grittiness of bones, and reached for the tea to wash it down.

Nina lay back on the pillows and said, 'I hope we didn't offend your father, leaving like that.'

'He didn't even notice we were there.'

'He smiled at me.'

'He smiles at every pretty girl.' He glanced at her. 'We didn't offend him.'

Looking up at him from the pillows, she seemed to be studying his face, frowning as though he was some particularly odd exhibit in a museum. Hugh sipped his tea, pretending to be unperturbed.

'You don't like your father, do you?'

'Nooo ...'

She propped her head up on her elbow. He noticed how her hair fell in a straight, shiny blonde curtain and resisted the urged to comb his fingers through it, aware suddenly that touching her had become a compulsion. At last she asked, 'Why don't you like him?'

'I don't know!' He laughed uncomfortably. 'He's vain. It's hard to like someone with such a gigantic opinion of himself.'

'Do you love him?'

He closed his eyes, resting his head back against the bed frame. He didn't want to think about Mick; in truth he hardly ever thought about him. Occasionally a too-well-read fellow officer would discover he was his son and ask idiotic questions as though he was an expert on poetry. He was usually rude to these men. Rudeness shut poetry lovers up, he'd found.

Nina was still watching him, allowing his silence to go on. Her coolness intrigued him – most women he knew couldn't allow such gaps in conversation. He looked at her. 'Do you love your parents?'

'I don't have any.'

'I'm sorry.'

'Why?'

'Because you're alone in the world, I suppose.'

276

'I'm not alone.' She turned away from him and he realised he'd offended her. He touched her head.

'Sorry, I'm tactless.'

Ducking away from his touch she said sharply, 'We have a friend in common.' Glancing at him, she went on, 'Bobby Harris.'

'Bob?' Astonished, he frowned at her. Just to make sure they were talking about the same person he said, 'Flight Lieutenant Bobby Harris? Same age as me, slight, dark, skinny?' It was an inadequate description, but his surprise robbed him of words. He remembered Bobby as a sixteen-year-old boy, the last time he'd seen him; even then he defied description. Mick, succinct for once, had called him unnaturally beautiful, making it sound like a flaw, but as far as Hugh had been concerned the only unnatural thing about Bobby was his self-possession. Even as a small child Bobby had seemed grown up.

Nina sat on the edge of the bed and drew the robe around her tightly. He could see the sharpness of her shoulder blades through the material, the bumps of her spine. It dawned on him that she would be just Bobby's type: thin and chic, as far removed from run-of-the-mill women as he imagined Bob was from run-of-the-mill men. It would be impossible for Bobby not to know such a woman.

She had her back to him still. A rush of jealousy made him grasp her arm, forcing her to face him. She met his gaze defiantly, jerking herself free.

He expected her to say something. When she didn't he made himself say, 'How is he, our mutual friend?'

'Didn't you hear what happened to him?'

'Dad told me.' He exhaled sharply, knowing he sounded cold. Often he'd tried to picture Bobby's disfigured face, only to find it impossible to imagine. More gently he said, 'Is he coping?'

'I don't know.' Responding to his tone, her expression became softer. 'He's gone home.' She laughed painfully. 'Hiding away. He's pretending he's the star of a fairy tale, I think.'

'Sounds like Bobby.'

Bitterly she said, 'It's a stupid act. He should be here, among his friends.'

It was the second time she'd called Bobby a friend. Surprised by the fierceness of his jealousy, he tossed the bedcovers aside and got up.

Nina said, 'You're angry. When I telephoned him this morning he said you would be if I told you.'

He pulled on his trousers. Harshly he said, 'So why tell me?'

She stood up and went to the sink, filling a glass with water and taking a long drink. She kept her back to him, her hand gripping the tap, her body taut. He imagined touching her, how she would jerk away from him, a feral cat that had allowed herself to be petted for just as long as it suited her. She was Bobby's girl, all right. Bobby would find her endlessly entertaining.

Nina set the glass down. Her trip-wire tautness gave and she slumped a little. Wearily she said, 'His grandfather died.'

She looked at him, seeming to gauge his reaction to this news, but he'd hardly known the old man.

Nina said, 'I know you were good friends from the way he spoke about you.'

Hugh snorted. 'I haven't seen him for years. I'm surprised he even remembers me.'

'Of course he does!' She became animated. 'He asked how you were, what you were doing now, what kind of war you had, everything! He seemed so sad that you'd lost touch.' She hesitated, clutching the dressing gown together at her chest, as though now was the time to protect her modesty. After a moment she said cautiously, 'It would be so nice if you wrote to him'.

He laughed.

'Why is that funny?' Her voice rose a little. 'He needs friends. Nice, ordinary people around him …' She had the grace to look embarrassed. Hugh gazed at her, smiling angrily.

'Well, that's me – nice and ordinary. Boring? I bet that word came up in your conversation.' He shook his head. 'Bob

Harris doesn't need people around him. He never gave a stuff about anyone.'

He'd finished dressing. Fetching his jacket from the chair in the corner of the bare little room, he shrugged it on. He turned to her. 'I'll say goodbye, I think.'

'Please write to him.'

He patted his pockets for his wallet, putting on an act of ignoring her that even Bobby Harris would have been proud of. Glancing at her he said, 'Listen, I'd rather you kept away from my father. He may seem worldly, but he's a bloody poet, after all. Please don't make an idiot of him, too.'

She paled, clutching the robe around her more tightly. She seemed more beautiful than ever, almost translucent, and anger mixed with the stirring of desire. If he stayed any longer he would take her again, roughly, making sure he hurt her, a fast, furious fucking that would banish Bobby from his head. Instead, he walked out, knowing he wouldn't rid himself of Bobby's disrupting ghost all day.

Chapter Four

Bobby stood at his bedroom window watching the steady trickle of worshippers walk along the road and into Thorp's graveyard that surrounded St Anne's church. They walked up the main path in groups of twos and threes, dressed almost identically in dark, sensible utility coats. Even the women's hats were drab and colourless, their shoes clumpy, lace-up brogues, their ankles thick in lisle stockings. Thorp women lacked any sense of style – they had no flair. He smiled to himself; the men weren't much better. Difficult to believe that Mick Morgan had been born and bred here.

He remembered the first time he'd met Morgan and how impressed he'd been by the poet's raffish, easy-going charm, how his wheelchair somehow added to his charisma. Mick Morgan had even smelled delicious, a rich, warm expensive smell of cigar and sandalwood and something he couldn't place, books, he'd supposed, the scent of an intellectual.

He sighed, closing his eyes against this memory, wishing Nina had not telephoned and stirred up so much of the past with her excitable talk of renewing friendships. He had tried to sound coolly interested, asking after Hugh as he would ask after any old friend. Except he had never had any friends like Hugh, no one he had loved so much. Nina didn't understand that such friendships, once broken, couldn't be mended.

He went downstairs. In the kitchen he lit the gas under the kettle, sliced the stale bread for toast, then went into the larder. He sniffed at the inch or so of milk left in the bottle. The cold weather had kept it from turning and at least there was a scraping of plum jam in the jar, although he had finished the last of his butter ration, allowing himself only the most miserly amount each day. Despite his frugality, he would have to shop soon.

Tea and toast made, he sat down in his grandfather's armchair and lit his first cigarette – another small luxury that had to be rationed if he wasn't to be forever walking out to Clark's, the tobacconist's, and running the gauntlet of stares and comments. Clark's daughter blushed scarlet whenever she had to serve him, leaving his change on the counter rather than risk touching his damaged hands. Once, she had even dodged into the back of the shop when she'd noticed him in the queue, leaving him waiting when his turn came until, shame-faced, the old man himself had shuffled out to serve him. Clark avoided his eye, too, unable to bring himself to behave normally.

Since he'd left hospital, most people behaved like Clark; some even adopted a different tone of voice when they talked to him. Some became too jolly, pretending they really hadn't noticed that he looked like a monster, and if they had were totally at ease with it and much too nice to react in any way. Others became off-hand: he was offensive and shouldn't be out and about embarrassing them. He did his best to oblige these latter types, going out as little as possible and having as much as he could delivered to the house. The telephone in the hall had become his true ally, until today.

Nina's voice on the phone had been excited, but there had also been a cautious edge to her tone so that straight away he'd guessed that she'd climbed into bed with Hugh within hours of their meeting. Jealous, he'd begun to speculate on the kind of man Hugh had grown into. He'd be tall, of course, he was always tall, and his shoulders would be broad, his body tapering to a slim waist. He would be tanned; he remembered how easily the sun took to him, lightening the fine hairs on his arms to gold.

He remembered the last summer they had spent together, when they'd swum naked in the sea, leaving their clothes on the tiny, deserted cove they'd found near Robin Hood's Bay. In the freezing water he'd been content to stay in the shallows, watching Hugh swim further and further away with the strong,

281

sure strokes of an athlete. He swam so far that fear knotted his guts and he'd swum out of his depth to search for him. Hugh had surfaced suddenly, so close their noses had almost brushed, his hair dark and sleek as sealskin as he'd grinned through his breathlessness. Bobby pretended not to be angry, trying not to show how scared he'd been. Later, on the beach, the salt had dried on Hugh's golden skin, a delicate, white etching.

Bobby drew on his cigarette, trying not to think about Hugh. He concentrated on the cigarette, wishing they'd invent an endless smoke, one that never burnt down to his petrified fingers but went on and on. He'd never have the bother of fumbling with matches that leapt like crickets from his grasp or suffer the indignity of failing to spark a lighter. He would sit in this chair and smoke and smoke and he wouldn't bother about food; he'd even ignore the nagging voice in his head that insisted he should do something. The voice was slowly becoming hysterical as days went by without him even bothering to dress. Dressing was as much of a chore as striking a bloody match; there were too many buttons, and laces, and ties. Too much bloody effort.

Before he'd left London even Nina had asked him what he would do. He'd forced his face into its best-practised smile.

'I've got an interview to be a solicitors' clerk.'

Her eyes widened. 'Really?'

He couldn't be bothered to go on teasing her. 'Nina, of course I bloody haven't. They'd be too afraid I'd scare their customers off.'

They'd been waiting for the Darlington train at King's Cross. Close by a group of American airmen jostled each other good-naturedly. Each seemed too young to have seen wartime service, too fresh, somehow. One of them caught Nina's eye and smiled broadly, only to notice him and look away, that generous American mouth turning down with a mixture of concern and revulsion. He'd felt that he should step away from her and pretend that they weren't together. Nina always enjoyed a flirtation and his presence beside her was spoiling the fun. He saw the American lean close to a comrade and speak quietly. They both glanced at him, the others too, and at once their mood became sober.

On the train, he'd pulled down the window, leaning out to kiss her goodbye. Remembering Morgan's launch party, which she seemed intent on crashing, he said, 'Mick Morgan is very charming. Don't let him sweep you off your feet.'

She laughed. 'He won't talk to me!'

Bobby gazed at her, amazed that she could still be so innocent. He'd wanted to ask her again not to go to the damn party, but he also wanted news of Morgan, to know for certain that he'd aged and had not stayed the glamorous, charming man he remembered. He knew he could rely on Nina to report back accurately, hoping she would inform him of someone old and pathetic, someone who'd grown into his lechery.

Instead, of course, she'd informed him of Hugh.

Bobby stubbed his cigarette out. He drank the lukewarm tea and ate the rubbery toast and forced himself to wash and dry and put away the plate and cup, knife and teaspoon. He concentrated on making his hands behave, promising himself another cigarette once he had swept the kitchen floor, once he had rinsed through the shirts and underwear he'd left soaking overnight in the scullery sink. He wouldn't think about Hugh, that sleek head breaking the sea's surface, that smile that was his alone for that one, perfect moment.

Irene said, 'I never hit it off with sailors. I prefer the army, myself.'

Nina bowed her head to kiss Cathy's hair. She had just bathed her, using a tiny amount of her own shampoo, and her dark curls had sprung to life. Clean and sweet smelling, she was a different baby from the screaming, red-faced child she'd taken from Irene's arms an hour ago. Nina wrapped the thin towel around her more snugly, gently combing her fingers through her hair to dry it, while a nappy, vest and nightdress aired by Irene's fire. Blue Bunny dangled by his ears from Cathy's mouth, her gums working on him mercilessly, saliva darkening the threadbare plush. Nina squeezed the toy's tired body but his squeak had long ago given up. 'Bunnies don't squeak, anyway,' Bobby had said. 'Only in their death throes.'

He'd been holding Joan, explaining dreadful, bunny facts in a smiling voice. Joan had smiled back at him, a star-shaped, podgy hand gently slapping at his mouth, and he'd kissed her, brushing his nose against hers. 'Poor Blue Bunny.' He'd smiled. 'Silenced by love.'

'She likes him.' Irene stood over her, jerking her head at the stuffed toy.

Reaching for Cathy's clothes, Nina lay the baby across her knee and dressed her. 'Have you warmed her milk?'

'I'll take her. You can get home now.'

'It's all right, I'll stay 'til she's asleep.'

'If you want. Looks like you won't separate madam from the rabbit, anyway, not while she's awake.'

Nina looked up at her. 'It was Joan's.'

Irene nodded. 'Do you want a cup of tea?'

With Cathy finally asleep in her cot, Irene took a half bottle of rum from the curtained cupboard under the sink and poured a dash into Nina's tea. She lit a cigarette and casually placed the open packet beside Nina's cup, then sat down in the other worn-out easy chair so that they faced each other, legs stretched in front of the dying fire. Drawing deeply on the cigarette, Irene rested her head back against the yellowing antimacassar before exhaling a long, exhausted breath. 'So,' she said. 'Is the sailor coming back?'

'No.'

'Gone back to his ship, has he?'

Quickly Nina said, 'Joan used to like rusk when she was teething. Those really hard rusks you can thread a ribbon through and hang around their necks. I'll buy some, if I see any.'

Irene sipped at her own rum-doctored tea. Pensively she said, 'I thought he was a Yank coming up the stairs, he had their easy way about him.' She smiled and began to sing *Run Rabbit, Run* under her breath. Glancing at Nina she said, 'Never mind. Plenty more fish in the sea.' She grinned. '*On* the sea. Sod them, anyway. Bastards.'

Nina looked across at the photograph on the mantelpiece of

an army corporal, a jug-eared boy of about twenty, his cap tilted a little too far. Following the direction of her gaze Irene said, 'He was all right. When I told him about Cathy he said, "It's all right girl, I'll marry you no matter what me old Ma says."' She laughed. After a while she added, 'I get his widow's pension, anyway.'

Nina had lived next door to Irene for over a year and sometimes felt ashamed to think they were friends only through Irene's persistence. On the day she'd moved in Irene had watched from her own doorway as the landlord pocketed her first month's rent and handed her the key. As soon as he'd gone, Irene had walked over, two bottles of stout dangling from her fingers, new-born Cathy curled against her shoulder. She'd grinned at her, lifting the bottles a little so that they clinked hospitably. 'How about a housewarming?'

Nina had spent the rest of the day with Irene, wondering if she would have allowed her to stay if it hadn't been for the baby and her own, masochistic, urges.

Wistfully, Irene said, 'That sailor was very good looking.'

Nina snorted, remembering Hugh Morgan's jealous anger when she'd mentioned Bobby. She wondered how she could have been bothered with such a predictable man. He had been a distraction, she supposed, a balm to take away the sting of Bobby's leaving. Such unimaginative men usually helped in the wasteland Bobby left.

Nina said, 'I telephoned Bobby. He sends his love.'

'He doesn't need a housekeeper, does he?' Irene smiled. 'Maybe we should both just show up on his doorstep. One look at Cathy and he wouldn't be able to turn us away.'

'People used to think Joan was his, the way he was with her.'

Irene was silenced for a while. Eventually she said, 'Why don't you go and see him?'

'He wants to be on his own.'

'Do you want to be on your own? You must do, otherwise you wouldn't have let sailor boy walk away.'

'Don't you think sailor boy has a will of his own?'

'I won't bother answering that.' Irene reached beside her

chair for the bottle of rum and held it out to her.

Nina shook her head. 'He wasn't my type, anyway.' Remembering the last poem his father had read the evening she'd met him, Nina found herself smiling. 'Do you know the poem *Homecoming*, by Michael Morgan?'

Irene yawned, covering her mouth only at the last moment. Dully she said, 'I only know that one about the dead soldier. We had to learn it at school – I think it'll be stuck in my head forever – *Birds sing now in sapling woods …*'

'*Homecoming* is about Hugh. Wouldn't that be marvellous – to have a poem written for you? A whole book of them dedicated to you?' Nina sat forward in her chair, her cup grasped in both hands. Only when she caught Irene's amused eye did she realise how animated she'd become. She sat back. 'I'll let you borrow the book, if you like.'

'And when have I time to sit about reading poetry?'

Nina sipped her tea, tasting only the Christmas warmth of rum, wondering if sailors were still given a rum ration. For the whole of the war Hugh Morgan had served on destroyers, escorting the Atlantic convoys. He had told her so in a sentence, summing up his naval career. She'd asked him why he'd joined the navy when his father had been so famously connected to the army and he'd laughed. Looking up at her from lighting a cigarette, he'd suddenly cupped her cheek in his hand, sweeping his thumb beneath her eye, his own eyes passionate. 'I love the sea,' he said. After a moment he let his hand fall away. 'Besides, I was scared of being stuck in a trench.'

Remembering, Nina touched her face where he'd touched her. His fingers had been hard and dry, his gentleness belying their strength. He'd held her gaze, frowning as though puzzled by her. She'd known he wouldn't allow himself to puzzle very long, he'd already convinced himself of the kind of girl she was. But just for a moment she'd felt herself soften towards him and wished that she hadn't taken him straight to bed, but had behaved herself. She'd even imagined their courtship, conventionally chaste before their walk down the aisle. Bobby would give her away, he always said he would.

Nina set her cup down on the floor and stood up. About to lift Blue Bunny from Cathy's cot she paused to tuck the blanket more securely around the sleeping child. She remembered that the hard rusks Joan liked were called Toothy Pegs and she turned to Irene to tell her. Irene was asleep, snoring softly. After a moment's hesitation she left Blue Bunny snug beside Cathy and tiptoed from the room.

Chapter Five

Hugh said, 'I've decided to go home.'

Mick frowned up at him from *The Times* editorial. 'Home? So where's home, these days?' His frown intensified. 'Not Thorp, surely?'

'For a little while, yes.'

'Thorp? Seriously? You'd really go back there?' Mick snorted. He folded the newspaper, tossed it down to the floor, and took off his glasses. Hugh felt himself under scrutiny, just as he had as a child when his school reports failed to meet his father's expectations. Brazening it out for as long as he could, at last he got up and went to the window.

Looking out on to the quiet street he said, 'I've been in touch with an old school friend. He can get me a job in his bank.'

'A bank?' Mick managed to sound amused and angry at the same time and Hugh spun round to face him.

'Yes. A bank. Right up my street, wouldn't you say?'

'I say you'll be bored out of your head within a week! Tell me again why you left the Navy, Hugh. So you could clock-watch your life away counting shop-keepers' pennies?'

Hugh turned back to the window, clenching his fingers into fists so that his nails dug into his palms. Beyond his father's neat square of garden a young woman pushed a baby in a shiny-bodied pram. The child sat upright, harnessed by leather reins that at once reminded him of parachute straps. He thought of Bobby Harris, wondering if he'd been shot down over land or sea, trying to get an idea of how scared he might have been. It was hard to imagine Bobby scared, almost impossible. Frowning, he turned to Mick, 'That girl, Nina, did

288

she tell you she knows Bobby Harris?'

'No, she didn't, but I can't say I'm surprised. I'd say she was trouble from the little I saw of her and like attracts like. Harris was bound to go to the bad.'

'You liked him well enough once.'

'I tolerated him because he was your friend. I always had my reservations.'

Hugh couldn't be bothered to argue, although he knew that Mick had loved Bobby almost as much as Bobby had worshipped Mick. He had been jealous of their relationship, suspecting that Bobby was the son Mick had wished for. Inevitably Bobby had done or said something that had hurt Mick badly enough for his father to never want to see him again. Bitterly he wondered if he'd ever be allowed to know what that something was.

Mick said, 'That girl – I hope you were careful.' When Hugh didn't answer, Mick sighed. 'Perhaps you should see a clap doctor.'

'Why? Because she knows Harris? Why do you have to talk like that? Honestly, I try to have a sensible conversation–'

'A sensible conversation?' Mick laughed as though astonished. 'You come here, wittering on about wasting your life in some bloody bank and you call that sensible? For God's sake, boy! You're a fit, able-bodied man! Why you left the Navy beats me. Do you think I'd have left the army if I hadn't been wounded? Jesus Christ – I wouldn't have gone near a civilian outfit if it hadn't been for this bloody thing!' He banged the arms of his wheelchair, gazing at him angrily. 'You should stop looking so sorry for yourself. You're still in one bloody piece, after all!'

Mick manoeuvred his chair to his desk and opened a drawer. Taking out his chequebook he wrote out a cheque and thrust it at him. 'Here. Take yourself off somewhere for a few weeks, away from me, away from everyone. Take some time to think about what you want to do with the rest of your life.'

'I don't need your money.'

'Yes, you do, otherwise you wouldn't be talking about taking on some dead end job.' Mick went on holding out the cheque. Calmer, he said, 'Take the money. Go to Cornwall, you always loved it there. Hire a boat, do whatever you sailors do.' He smiled slightly. 'You were always better at sea than on land.'

'I'm going home, Dad. I just want to go home.'

Mick looked down at the cheque. After a moment he folded it and tossed it down on to the desk where it stood out amongst the neat piles of paper and sharpened pencils he used to write with. At last he said, 'Sometimes home is the worst place.' He looked up at him. 'After I was wounded I longed to go home, and when finally I got there it felt like a prison.'

Stubbornly Hugh said, 'It was different for you.' He sat down on the couch, the only piece of furniture, other than the desk and a small dining table, in the room. His father had always lived with the minimum of things – furniture got in the way of the wheelchair – and the leather couch was pushed hard against the wall, bought as a concession to the few visitors Mick allowed inside his home. The flat was the ground floor of a Georgian house, its tall windows casting oblongs of sunlight on to the polished wood floor. There were no carpets to slow the chair's progress and Hugh winced at the noise he made whenever he took a step. Even when he tried to tread softly his shoes squeaked and squealed on floorboards grown used to the glide of wheels.

The couch was dusty and Hugh traced patterns on its arm, avoiding his father's eye. He knew Mick was watching him. He lit a cigarette and after a while Mick took an ashtray from his desk. Wheeling himself toward him, he held it out. 'I don't want ash on my floor. Henry will tell me off.'

Hugh took the ashtray. 'I thought he'd be here. He told me he was visiting you this afternoon.'

'Is that why you came, because you thought Henry would stop me making too much fuss about your news?' Mick was smiling in an attempt to make the peace that only made Hugh feel as though he was being patronised. When he remained silent, his father sighed. 'I am expecting Henry. Why don't you stay and have supper with us? I'll go and make a start in the kitchen.'

When Mick had gone, Hugh gazed at the pattern of figure eights he'd drawn on the leather, almost as appalled at the thought of working in a bank as his father was, afraid that leaving the Navy was the worst decision he'd ever made. At the time he'd thought he'd had enough of the sea, of his bleakly dangerous and comfortless life. For months at the end of the war he could think only of the luxuries of land, dreaming of safety, of warmth and stillness, hating the treacherous blackness of the North Atlantic. Now though, sleeping in Henry's spare room and wandering the blitzed city like an awe-struck tourist, he felt as if he was nearing the end of a too-long leave. As though his body clock was set to some natural span ashore, he felt himself mentally preparing to go back to his ship. Even meeting Nina had added to this feeling. After all, she was the kind of girl shore leave could be frittered away with, a good time, dinner-and-dancing girl, one you could leave sleeping in a rumpled bed and give only a fleeting, smiling thought to on the way back to base.

Hugh stubbed his cigarette out in the ashtray. He tried to ignore the hopeless, empty feeling he had whenever he thought about Nina. As soon as he'd found himself on the street outside her wretched bedsit he'd realised he didn't care if she'd slept with Bobby Harris a thousand times or never. All that mattered was having her to himself from that moment on.

He thought about her slim, supple body beneath his, her practised, patient responses to his own, too-urgent needs, and tried to ease his sense of loss by telling himself that this was only a sexual attraction, one that would have spent itself as quickly as sugar on a fire. She wouldn't have made a wife. Hugh covered his face with his hands and groaned softly. Who needed a wife, anyway?

There was a gentle tap on the sitting room door and Hugh looked up to see Henry. 'May I come in?'

Before Hugh could speak, Mick called from the kitchen, 'Henry – help yourself to a Scotch. And pour one for my son – see if we can't put a smile on his face.'

Crossing the room towards the dining table and the bottles and glasses arranged on it, Henry glanced at him. 'Would you

291

like a drink, Hugh?'

'Yes. Thanks.'

'What have you been up to today?'

'Nothing much.'

Henry handed him his drink and sat down on the other end of the couch, setting his own drink on the floor as he searched his jacket pockets, finally producing his cigarette case. He held it out and Hugh took one, knowing that Henry's cigarettes were the best he'd ever tasted. Turkish, his father once told him – as if he didn't know – then laughed one of his rare, dirty laughs. Accepting Henry's light, Hugh noticed that the other man's hands trembled slightly and that tobacco had stained his fingers sulphurous yellow. He smelt of some subtle, spicy cologne and Hugh found himself inhaling deeply to catch his scent. At once he sat back, appalled at himself. Unintentionally he caught Henry's eye.

Dryly Henry said, 'It's all right, Hugh. You're not my type.'

Hugh felt himself blush. He sipped his drink, the sweet cigarette burning untasted between his fingers. After a while he managed to glance at him. Henry was gazing straight ahead towards the window and the darkening street, a thoughtful, serious man, wiry and strong enough to heave Mick's chair up and down and around all the various obstacles London could put in their way. Though a few years younger than his father, he'd fought for three years during the Great War. Mick's poetry had helped Henry come to terms with his own experiences, or so he'd written in the foreword of *Dawn Song*.

In an effort to make the atmosphere less frosty, Hugh said awkwardly, 'I was telling Dad – I'll be leaving for home in a couple of days.'

'P…p…perhaps that's for the best.' Henry looked at him. 'You're rather at a loss here, aren't you?'

Hugh drew on his cigarette. Exhaling, he said, 'Thanks for putting up with me.'

'Any time.' Henry turned towards the door as Mick came in. At once his expression softened. 'Mick, I think we should take Hugh out this evening if he's not going to be st..staying

292

much longer.'

'Would you like that, Hugh?'

Hugh shrugged. He felt all of sixteen, just as sullen as he'd ever been. He thought of Bobby Harris, who never let the grown-ups see him behave so badly, and surprised himself by deciding he would visit him.

Chapter Six

Standing in front of the hall mirror, Bobby wrapped a scarf around his throat, pulling it up a little so that the soft wool covered the lower half of his face. Satisfied, he put on his coat, his fingers struggling with the buttons. He turned its collar up, hiding a little more of his injuries. Finally, he forced his hands into leather gloves and stood back from the mirror. If he wore a hat he would look like the illustration of H G Wells's invisible man. But he didn't own a hat, had no intention of ever buying one. Hats made him look like a spiv.

He went into the kitchen and checked once again that the back door to the garden was locked. In the drawing room he checked the French doors, and then, as an afterthought, dragged an armchair in front of them. Lately, boys from the terraces beyond the park had begun climbing over the wall and throwing stones at his windows. The first time they ventured into the garden he'd gone to the front door, intending to chase them away, but his nerve had failed at the last minute. As he stepped back inside, one of them spotted him and their mocking shouts and laughter had followed him into the house. A stone hit the door, causing his heart to race. For what seemed like an age he'd stood in the hallway, hardly daring to breathe until the silence convinced him they had gone. Since then they returned most days and he hid himself away behind closed curtains, despising himself for his cowardice as his heart leapt at every sudden noise.

He locked the door behind him, nervousness making his fingers clumsier, and walked past the cemetery and along Oxhill Avenue towards Thorp High Street. If he had to go out, he would go out properly and not restrict himself to the corner shop. He would go to Robinson's, Thorp's only department store, and browse around the menswear department, perhaps even choose a new tie or some shirts. He needed socks and underwear and handkerchiefs; he would like some bath salts, the kind his grandfather bought that filled the bathroom with the green fragrance of pine. Most of all, he had a craving for chocolate, something dark and so sweet it would smother the metallic taste of anxiety that was constantly with him and that cigarettes could only subdue for a while.

A cold wind stung his face. His eyes watered, rheumy as an old man's, and he wiped them impatiently. In the cemetery men were cutting the grass between the graves and he thought about his overgrown garden. If it didn't look quite so neglected perhaps those boys wouldn't think to trespass: he was sure they didn't bother his respectable, industriously tidy neighbours. Or perhaps it was just his presence in the house that drew them, the little bastards deliberately setting out to bait the beast.

On the corner of the High Street the matinee crowd streamed out of the Odeon Cinema. Bobby stopped, bowing his head and pretending to search his pockets for the cigarettes he didn't have, rather than become caught up in the scrum. The cinema displayed posters for forthcoming films on its walls and he studied the face of Laurence Olivier, determined and aloof beneath his *Henry V* helmet. He'd liked him better in *Wuthering Heights*, a film he'd watched with Nina, her head light on his shoulder, her arm hugging his as the actor glowered from the screen. As the film ended she'd turned to him, her eyes bright as a Hollywood starlet's in the darkness. 'You're more handsome than he is.' Remembering, Bobby smiled to himself and touched the glass protecting Olivier's image.

At Robinson's, breathless from his long walk, Bobby took the lift to the menswear department on the third floor. There seemed to be no other customers but him; a bored-looking assistant lounged against one of the mahogany and glass display cabinets. The smell of wood polish and new cloth hung heavy in air that seemed unchanged in years. Too warm, he began to sweat in his muffling scarf and coat.

Reluctantly, he unwound the scarf from his face and removed his gloves, shoving them into his coat pocket. At once he realised that in his anxiety he'd left his wallet at home, along with his coupons and ration book, picturing them exactly where he'd left them – safe behind the clock on the kitchen mantelpiece. He'd had a pointless journey, all his effort wasted. He almost wept in despair.

The shop assistant walked towards him, stopping a few feet short. 'May I help you, sir?'

Bobby looked away at once, fixing his gaze on a display of silk ties in dull, schoolmaster colours. 'Not at the moment, thank you.'

'Then please, feel free to look around. But may I remind sir that the shop will be closing in around five minutes.'

Forcing himself to look at the assistant Bobby said, 'You're open until seven.'

'No, sir. We close at five-thirty.'

'But this shop has always stayed open until seven!'

'Perhaps in your day, sir.'

'In my day?' Bobby stared at him. He looked about fifteen, weedy and anaemic, as though this subdued electric light was all he was ever exposed to. Stepping towards him Bobby said, 'How old do you think I am?'

The assistant shifted uncomfortably. Bobby repeated the question. Sullenly the boy said, 'I don't know.'

'I'm twenty-five.' He stepped closer. 'Twenty-five.'

'We're still closing in a minute, sir.'

'You said five minutes.'

'Yes, sir.'

'So what can I buy in five minutes.'

'Sir …?

'What?' Bobby heard his voice rising. Unable to stop himself he went on more loudly, 'What can I buy? One of those ties, perhaps?' He walked over to the display. Picking one up he let it slither through his fingers to the floor. He picked up another and another, dropping each one so that they coiled in pools at his feet.

Behind him a voice said, 'Bobby, stop that now.'

He swung round. His mother gazed at him, the calmness in her voice betrayed by the panic in her eyes. His two half-sisters stood beside her, stiff with embarrassment. Stepping forward she crouched down beside the boy and helped him gather up the ties. 'There,' she smiled. 'It's just as well you keep your floor so clean. No harm done. All the same, I'm sorry.'

'Sorry?' Bobby's voice was shrill with anger. 'What are you apologising for? Has this *anything* to do with you?'

The boy's pale face flushed. To Bobby's mother he said, 'The shop's about to close, madam.'

'Is that all you can say – the shop's closing? For Christ's sake – I thought the customer came first! Have you never heard of service?'

A bell sounded and the boy looked towards the clock above the lifts. Rather desperately he said, 'There's the closing bell now.'

'Fuck the bloody bell!'

'Bobby, please!' His mother took his arm. More softly she said, 'Let's go home, eh?'

He shook her off. 'You go home. This is none of your business.'

'Of course it is.' Beneath her pinkish face powder her cheeks were dark with embarrassment. She smiled at the assistant. 'I'm so sorry. My son hasn't been himself lately.'

Bobby stared at her, wanting to scream with rage at this fantastic lie. Almost in tears he shouted, 'What the hell would you know about it?'

'Mummy, let's just go ...' Kate, the older of his sisters, pulled at her mother's arm. 'Please let's go.'

'I can't leave your brother like this!' To him she said, 'Darling, why don't we all get a taxi back to Parkwood and I'll come in with you and see you settled ...'

The bell sounded again. The boy was at the lift, holding the doors open. Bobby felt his heart racing, the stuffiness of the shop closing in on him. He had to get out quickly if only to catch his breath, but panic kept him rooted to the spot. He stared at his mother. To his horror he began to cry, the sobs constricting his throat so that he gasped for air.

Stepping quickly towards him, she took his arm. Quietly she said, 'It's all right. We'll walk slowly down the stairs together – it's so hot and close in those lifts, isn't it? We can take our time, can't we? We can take our time, just you and me.'

Sitting in the armchair in Parkwood's kitchen, Bobby watched his mother make tea. Margot Redpath was forty-five, her soft, round figure held rigorously in check by corsets, her plumpness keeping her skin smooth and unlined so that she could easily pass for forty. Her glossy dark hair was pinned up in much the same style captured in the photographs on the day she married his father. That marriage had lasted only two years before she was widowed. It seemed to Bobby that she didn't much mourn her husband, he was barely mentioned, his grave never visited and when she remarried he became an official taboo. He would have been re-named Redpath, just as she was, if it hadn't been for his grandfather's horrified stand.

As Margot poured boiling water into the teapot Bobby said, 'You don't have to stay, Mum.'

She looked up at him. 'Oh, Bobby! Don't be silly. I'll stay until you're feeling better.'

He looked down at his hands, wishing he had a cigarette to occupy them. Haltingly he said, 'I'm sorry, about earlier. I'm an idiot, behaving like that.'

'It's understandable.'

'No, it's not. I didn't have any money, you know? I'd forgotten it. I went all that way ... stupid. I'm so stupid.'

She went into the pantry. Coming out again she said, 'You don't have any milk, or any food that I can see. Make a list of things you need. In the morning Mark can run some errands for you.'

'I can manage. Really, I can. It's just today was a bad day.' He met her eye. She was gazing at him fondly and he imagined flinging himself into her arms. But years ago he had decided it would be best to do without her completely, unable any longer to cope with the absent-minded, piecemeal affection she doled out to him. Once he'd stopped trying to compete for her attention it hardly seemed necessary to speak to her any more.

Carefully his mother said, 'Bobby? Darling, I wish you'd let us help you.'

'Us?'

She handed him a cup of tea. 'Yes, us, your stepfather and me.'

'He wouldn't help me.' He looked at her. 'I bet you won't even tell him you've been here.'

'Of course I will! He's not a monster, Bobby. He cares for you, in his own way.'

He laughed bleakly. 'Does he? Maybe his lawyer could use that in mitigation when he finally kills me.'

'Oh Bobby, don't talk like that! Such dramatising! He only ever disciplined you. You vexed him so, you know you did.' She sighed. 'You know you're like him, in a way. You're both so stubborn.'

'How can I be like him? He's not my father!'

'Bobby, quiet now, don't start getting excited again. Right, I should go. Don't forget to make that shopping list. Have a little think about what you want – some treats, perhaps.'

She hesitated, as though she expected him to protest at her leaving. When he didn't speak, she turned away and picked up her coat and handbag from the chair where she'd left them. She glanced at him, giving him another chance to ask her to be a mother to him. He avoided her gaze, stubbornly silent.

At last she said, 'Good night, Bobby. In the morning ask Mark to mow the lawn – it's such a big job, your father used to spend hours looking after it.'

Despite his resolve he said, 'Did he?'

'He loved the garden, you know that.'

'No, I didn't know.'

Pulling on her gloves she said, 'Make Mark useful – he's more than willing.'

'What else did he like?'

'Sorry, darling?'

'My father. What else did he like?'

'Paul?' She frowned. 'Oh, I don't know. It was such a long time ago.'

Bobby followed her to the front door. Unable to contain his curiosity he blurted, 'Do I take after him?'

For a moment he thought she was seriously considering his question. He watched her, surprised by how much he wanted her to tell him even the smallest detail. At last she said, 'Your father was a very kind man. I remember he was kind. Poor Paul. We were both so young. Babies, really.' For the briefest moment she hesitated before kissing him on the cheek. 'I'll send Mark over in the morning.' Patting his arm, she turned and walked away.

Mark mowed the lawn and raked the grass into a haphazard haystack. He uprooted a sycamore sapling that had seeded itself in the border and dug over the weedy vegetable plot, burying the rotten, yellow stalks of last year's Brussels sprouts. Against Bobby's wishes he took a ladder from the garage and propped it against the largest chestnut tree. Holding on to the ladder to steady it as best he could, Bobby watched, terrified, as Mark climbed up and sawed off the branches that grew too close to the house.

Safely down, Mark wiped sweat from his forehead with the back of his forearm, the saw dangling from his other hand. He'd rolled up the sleeves of his checked shirt, inadvertently showing off muscled arms, and undone the top few buttons, exposing blond chest hair. Bobby grinned at him, relief that he hadn't come to any harm mixed with surprise that Mark, when not dressed in his school uniform, appeared to be grown up.

'Never climb up there again, do you hear me? You'll give me a heart attack.'

Mark laughed. 'It was safe enough.' He looked up into the half-bare canopy. 'It needs felling, really.'

'Felling? You're a lumberjack now, are you?'

His brother was serious suddenly. 'All the trees should be cut down. They're growing too close to the house, damaging the foundations.'

300

'I like the trees.'

'Look.' Mark pointed to a crack appearing in the side of the house. 'What do you think is causing that?'

'Bomb damage?'

'Be serious, Bob! Thorp wasn't bombed – well, not much anyway. And not round here.'

'No? You should've let me know – I could have arranged something.' Briskly he said, 'Right, it's lunchtime. Come on in, I'll make you a sandwich.'

'I didn't go shopping for you only so you could feed me.'

'Don't you think you've earned a cheese sandwich?' The urge to reach out and ruffle his hair was strong but he had an idea that Mark would be repelled by his touch. There was still an awkwardness between them, an uneasy atmosphere he wanted to put down to the number of years they'd spent apart rather than his own shyness with other men. The fact that Mark had once hero-worshipped him made this shyness worse. He remembered the first time he'd visited Thorp in his uniform, how Mark and his friends had crowded round him, all of them excited by the glamour of *the few*. Remembering Churchill's rhetoric he smiled bitterly.

Mark touched his arm. 'Bob? Are you all right?'

He began to walk towards the house. 'Come in and wash your hands.'

Sitting at the kitchen table Mark swallowed a mouthful of bread and cheese. He cleared his throat before saying, 'We're doing that play at school, the one by Michael Morgan – *Theory of Angels*. Damn silly title. I've got the part of Captain Teddy Palmer.' He looked down, dabbing up crumbs from his plate with the tip of his finger. After a while he said, 'Pretty daunting really, it being the lead an' all. Mum told me you played the same part when your school staged it.'

Standing up, Bobby cleared away the plates to the sink. 'Do you want a cup of tea?'

'No, thanks.' He seemed to draw breath, as though working up courage. Quickly he said, 'I thought you might help me with my lines.'

Bobby turned the tap on and held a plate under the running water. His gaze fixed on his hand, the ugliness of the healed, shrunken flesh, the weals and ridges and raw discoloration. Sometimes, on waking, his hands took him by surprise. In that too brief time between sleep and full consciousness he forgot the horror of them and his life was just as it had been. He was even fit to play Captain Teddy Palmer. He turned the tap off hard, aware of Mark watching him, waiting for his response.

'You don't need me to help you with your lines. I don't think I'd have the time, anyway.'

'Oh.' Mark looked nonplussed. 'All right. Well, it was just an idea.'

'And I'm just telling you. I can't help.'

'Fine.'

Too sharply Bobby said, 'Don't sulk.'

'I'm not! I'm sorry I've upset you.'

'You haven't upset me! And don't be sorry. For God's sake, why do you keep apologising to me? Tiptoeing round me all the time! Do you know how much it grates on my nerves?'

'I'm sorry ...'

'There you go again! If you can't behave normally around me then don't bother coming here. I'm not some pathetic bloody creature you have to treat with kid gloves!'

'I know that! I only thought ...'

'Don't think. Just go. I don't want to hear about your trivial bloody school play.'

Mark stood up, knocking his chair over in his haste. Without a word he righted the chair and walked out.

For a while Bobby stood at the sink. His legs were shaking, a horrible echo of his first bouts of stage fright. He could feel again the stiff coarseness of the Captain's khaki uniform, remembering how he'd sweated in it beneath the hot lights of his school stage.

Morgan had written *Theory of Angels* to commemorate the dead of the first war and Captain Teddy Palmer was the lead role. Bobby had never expected to be given the part, but that Easter, when his mother suggested it would be easier on everyone if he stayed at boarding school for the holiday, he'd practised the lines in the empty dorm until he was word perfect. At the auditions he surprised the teachers, knowing that until the moment he walked on to the stage he'd always been invisible. That night he'd written to Hugh and told him he'd won the starring role, but it was Mick Morgan who had written back to him saying he would come and see the play. *'Friends should support each other,'* Morgan wrote. He had read that letter over and over, smiling in disbelief at Morgan's choice of words. On the final evening of the play's three-day run Mick Morgan took his place in the front row, accompanied by another man. He'd been too nervous to wonder who this stranger was.

He found out at the party afterwards. Pushing Morgan's wheelchair towards him Henry Vickers gushed, 'You were w...w...wonderful, young man! Absolutely marvellous! W...w...wasn't he just as you imagined Palmer, Mick?'

'Just.' Morgan smiled at Bobby. 'You were very good, Bob. Excellent, in fact.'

'Thank you, sir.' Still high on performance adrenaline, Bobby thrust his hand out towards Vickers. 'Bobby Harris, sir. Pleased to meet you.'

Morgan laughed. 'I'm sorry – I should have introduced you. Henry is my agent in London, Bob. Henry, this is Bobby Harris, one of Hugh's friends.'

Vickers shook his hand and Bobby felt how slick with sweat it was, saw that his eyes were so bright he wondered if the man was feverish. Bobby drew his hand away and wiped it discreetly as the headmaster approached them. The head beamed, puffed with pride at having such a distinguished visitor at the school. Because Mick Morgan was only there because of him, Bobby had stopped being the boy whose name he couldn't remember to become his favourite pupil.

'Mr Morgan – we're honoured to have you here. I hope you enjoyed our humble production of your great play!'

'Not so humble, Headmaster. Not with such a star, eh?' Morgan winked at him and he'd bowed his head, smiling. As the Headmaster monopolised his famous guest, Vickers took his arm and led him to one side.

303

'W...w...w...would you like to be a professional actor, Bobby?'

'I don't know, sir. Perhaps.'

'You're very g...g...good.' He drew breath as though trying to control his stammer. 'Come to supper with Mr Morgan and me this evening. Would you like that?'

'I don't know if I'd be allowed to, sir.'

'Oh, I think Mr Morgan can arrange it for the st...st...star of the show.' He smiled, his eyes shiny, searching his face. Bobby had gazed back, feeling daring and grown up.

Putting on Captain Palmer's voice he'd said, 'There's quite a good hotel in town that serves decent food, The King's Arms.'

'Mr Morgan and I are staying there! We'll go now, shall we? I think it's t...t...time we rescued Mr Morgan from your headmaster.'

Remembering, Bobby closed his eyes. That night, amongst the horse brasses and oak beams of the hotel's dining room, the two adult men had flattered and teased him over Brown Windsor soup and roast beef. They'd allowed him a glass of red wine, then another, exchanging an amused look as a complicit waiter topped up his glass again and again. Vickers hardly took his eyes off him and Morgan would smile at his friend indulgently as Vickers plied him with questions about how he saw the character of Palmer, how he had come to play the role so well. He'd been Morgan's showpiece, his little protégé to be exhibited. Morgan might as well have pinned a label on him.

In Parkwood's kitchen, Bobby sank down in the armchair. After several attempts he lit a cigarette, drawing the calming smoke deep into his lungs. Even so, he still saw Henry Vickers' face and smelt the red-wine taint of his breath.

Vickers groaned, 'Oh you're so sweet, so sweet ... Beautiful ...'

The hotel bedroom was lit by a full moon shining through a gap in the curtains. He'd watched Vickers' shadow on the wall as he'd undressed, feeling drunk for the first time in his life, too disorientated by the speed of events to move. Somehow he was naked; there were cool sheets beneath his belly. Naked too, Vickers sat beside him on the bed and placed his hand gently on the small of his back.

'It's not your first time, is it? Boys like you … so knowing. Born knowing …'

His head felt heavy, his thoughts sluggish from the effect of the wine. He knew that he should make some kind of protest but a deferential voice in his head told him he shouldn't offend this friend of Mick Morgan's. Besides, the room was spinning, he couldn't move, too afraid of throwing up all over the hotel bed. He wondered why he'd undressed; it had seemed funny at the time, part of the naughtiness of being away from school for a night without permission. Vickers had promised to make it all right with his housemaster, giggling with him as they'd stumbled up the stairs. In a room on the ground floor, Mick Morgan had retired to bed. When they'd passed his door Vickers had pressed a finger to his lips, smiling as though to make him believe Morgan had no part in the conspiracy.

Lying down beside him, Vickers pulled him into his arms so that they lay face to face. Vickers was breathing heavily. Hoarsely, seemingly in control of his stammer, he whispered, 'You're tense. Try and relax. It's nothing you haven't done before. Many times, eh?' Stroking his hair back from his face he repeated, 'Many times. I expect you experiment all the time, all the younger boys in love with you …You'll have your cherry pick of them …' He groaned softly. 'You're beautiful, beautiful. I didn't believe him when Mick said how astonishing you were.'

Lying rigid on his side, he felt Vickers' erection against his belly and attempted to pull away from him. 'I think I may be sick.'

Vickers held him more tightly. 'You drank too much. We should've been more careful of you.' He kissed his mouth, his lips closed, his eyes focused on his, as they had been most of the night. 'You're g…g…going to be sweet to me, aren't you? Sweet and still and g…g…good? I don't like rough boys. But you're not rough, I can see that. As soon as I saw you I knew that you'd be good.'

Later, going over and over that night in his head, he'd tried to understand why he didn't push him away, why he lay rigid as a corpse and allowed Vickers to arrange his legs, to shove pillows beneath his groin so that his body was angled in the best position. All he knew was that he kept his eyes closed, hoping that this frightening humiliation would stop, his voice lost somewhere deep inside him. Vickers went on, interpreting his silence as acceptance. He tore inside him, overcoming Bobby's resistance with a force that made Vickers curse with satisfaction. Bobby remembered that the agony of it had taken his breath away, keeping him silent.

The sheets had smelt of harsh soap and the bed had banged against the wall, a pounding din that was the fitting accompaniment to the terrible, shaming pain. He had grasped handfuls of the sheets, trying to keep his body still to stop the rhythmic friction. He had an erection, he would come, and he was too shocked and horrified by this to think straight. Perhaps his body's disgusting response was the reason he hadn't struggled; he had felt too vile and worthless, a nothing, a hole to be used. But he had known he was worthless all his life, just not like this. Not as filthy and dirty as this.

Vickers, who had looked so slight, was a dead weight on top of him; the man grunted like an animal, his fleshy lips close to his ear, like a pig rooting in muck. Bobby knew that he was hurt, that he could never be the same again, but now Vickers slipped out of him, soft, spent. Breathless on his back, he reached for Bobby's hand and squeezed it. 'Good boy,' he said. His voice became puzzled. 'You really weren't a virgin, were you?'

In Parkwood's kitchen Bobby's cigarette had burnt down to his fingers and he stubbed it out. He thought of Vickers' smile, how it had vanished in slow motion as he realised what he'd done. Vickers had covered his mouth with his hand, muffling his words as he groaned, 'Oh Christ. Why didn't you say something? You led me to believe …'

Bobby had sat up then. The room had spun and spun. He didn't have time to make it to the sink in the corner of the room but threw up all over the floor.

In the kitchen, Bobby lit another cigarette. He used to wonder how Mick Morgan had found out what Vickers had done to him, whether he could smell it on him at breakfast, or whether his metamorphosis was so complete that it would have been blindingly obvious to anyone.

In the hotel's bleak little lounge Morgan had gazed at him for some time. Behind his wheelchair a mounted stag's head watched with startled eyes and Bobby remembered keeping his own eyes fixed on it, unable to look at the man in front of him. At last Morgan said, 'You're never to go near my son again, do you hear?'

He'd frowned, unable to understand what Hugh had to do with it. Morgan went on looking at him, his expression unreadable, so that when he finally did understand he'd imagined there was a chance of changing his mind.

'Sir, you can't mean that.'

'Yes, I can. Now, I want you to promise – you won't write to Hugh and you'll return his letters unopened. During the holidays in Thorp you'll stay well away from my house and won't try to contact him at all. Is that clearly understood?'

'Hugh's my best friend –' Bobby felt his eyes fill with tears. The horror of the previous night was still raw, but it also felt distant, the details hazy as if it had happened to someone else. He had an idea that if he could only convince Mick Morgan he was the same person who had played Captain Palmer everything would be back to normal. Stepping towards him he said, 'Sir, I haven't done anything, truly. Honestly – whatever you think …'

Morgan wheeled his chair backwards a little, reclaiming the distance between them. 'Bobby, I'm not going to argue. I know what kind of boy you are and it's a pity and I feel sorry for you and for your future, I know how difficult life is for men with such a perversion. Now, will you promise me you won't see Hugh again?'

'No!'

'All right. Then I must tell him what happened here last night. He has to know about you, for his own protection.'

'Know what about me?' Frightened, he struggled to keep his tears in check. 'Nothing happened! I swear to you.'

'Don't lie to me! Why can't you people behave? Why do you have to lie and make excuses for yourselves? Isn't it enough your own lives are ruined without attempting to ruin everyone else?'

'I don't …I haven't …' He wiped the tears from his face with his fingers, too confused and ashamed to think clearly. 'Please, please don't tell Hugh.'

'Then you must promise. You won't see him again, ever. You must make me your most solemn promise, and I'll make my promise to you that I won't breathe a word of this to anyone. You promise?'

Bobby nodded, unable to speak for the effort of suppressing his tears.

A little more gently Morgan said, 'Will you be all right? I've had the hotel order a taxi to take you back to school. There's a note here saying it was my fault you were kept out after curfew.' He held out an envelope. Impatiently he said, 'Take it. You don't want to be in any more trouble.'

In Parkwood Bobby covered his face with his hands, all the shame he'd felt then as terrible as ever. He remembered how much he wanted to make himself invisible as he waited for the taxi, how he'd slunk in the corner furthest away from the curious looks of the receptionist. He'd stunk, a grown man's filthy stink of vomit and cigarettes and sex.

He lit another cigarette, catching sight of his father's picture on the mantelpiece. Lieutenant Paul Harris wore a uniform exactly like Palmer's. Reaching for the photo he studied his features carefully. Everyone used to say how alike they were and he knew that it was one of the reasons his stepfather hated him: he was a living, breathing reminder of his mother's shotgun wedding that had ended so ignominiously and made such titillating gossip for his stepfather's new neighbours. Redpath just couldn't seem to get over the scandal and the frequent beatings he gave him were always treated as an opportunity to remind him of his bad

308

blood.

He traced his fingers over the photo. His father was photogenic – Jason would've adored him. Bobby could understand why his stepfather would despise such a man.

Bobby placed the photograph down on his knee. For a long time he gazed at his father's face. For the first time in his life he missed him so badly; it was like a new, surprising grief and he drew breath at the sudden, extraordinary depth of pain. Holding the photograph to his chest, he bowed his head and wept.

Chapter Seven

Each Thursday afternoon Nina was left in sole charge of Antoinette Modes. From one-thirty to closing time at six she would be lucky if she saw two or three customers and it would be an achievement if she actually sold anything. The shop used to specialise in evening wear, clinging bias-cut satin dresses in dark jewel colours, the softest kid shoes and long, buttoned gloves that could be dyed to match. Tiny evening bags were displayed in a square glass display case in the centre of the shop floor, each bag heavy with jet beads or embroidered with bright, exotic flowers and fantastical birds of paradise. Antoinette Mode bags had been famous amongst a certain London crowd, the badge of a risqué sense of style.

The glass case displayed only black leather gloves nowadays. The slinky dresses had long ago been replaced on the racks by A-line, knee-length skirts and functional jackets, their cloth cut to suit the dictates of rationing. There were even slacks hanging where the tea-dance dresses used to be displayed. Nina trailed her fingers along the row of trousers in navy blue or grey worsted cloth. She suited trousers – when she wore them she felt she could become someone else, someone quick and practical and self-reliant, the kind of girl who assembled engines or drove ambulances or flew Hurricanes or Spitfires across country to whichever base they were needed. Bobby had told her about such girl-pilots and at first she hadn't believed him. When he'd assured her such women really did exist her jealousy had been intense. She wondered how long it could be before he would fall in love with such a dashing creature. She had felt soft and useless and out of step because the war frightened her more than it seemed to frighten anyone else.

Nina went to stand behind the shop counter. The clock above the door showed ten to six, although it felt much later. Mid afternoon she had wondered how she would get through the rest of the day, the dead hours stretching ahead of her, a test of endurance. By five o'clock she allowed herself to think of the small pleasures of home, and now, at almost the end of the day, she could tell herself that perhaps the job wasn't too bad, she'd got through the day after all.

She sighed, tired, longing for a hot bath; she hoped the bus would be on time and that she wouldn't have to stand. She pictured walking up the stairs to her flat and letting herself in, finding it as it should be: everything in its place, exactly where she'd left it. There would be none of Bobby's possessions cluttering her space – no suitcase that was too big to be hidden away, no suits and shirts and ties hanging from her picture rail because there was so little room in her wardrobe. The camp bed he'd slept on had been returned to her downstairs neighbour, it was no longer an obstacle to bang her shins against. Even the scent of him had faded away; she wouldn't be dismayed by the sleepy stuffiness that told her he had spent the day in bed. Bobby still smelt of hospitals and sickness; when he undressed for bed she had found the sight of his pale, too-skinny body repellent.

She went to the door and locked it, turning the sign to Closed. Walking back through the shop she caught sight of herself in the full-length mirror and stopped. She looked at her reflection critically, turning sideways and pressing her splayed hands against her belly. It was flat, almost hollow; her hips bones protruded a little and her breasts were too small. Her body didn't give away the fact that it had nurtured a child. She thought of Hugh Morgan, bowing his mouth to her nipple as his hand moved between her legs. He had no idea of her past and didn't care. Unlike Bobby, she could disappoint him and it wouldn't matter.

She had taken the afternoon off work the day Bobby was finally released from the last convalescent home. The day before she'd managed to buy a single pork chop and she remembered the cold, satisfying weight of it in its greased paper wrapper as she carried it home and her sense of achievement at being able to feed him properly. She'd served it with a potato and mild, white cabbage, dressing the meat with its sticky juices from the frying pan. The fat was browned and melting, the flesh tender when she'd pressed a fork against it. Her mouth had watered. She'd taken a piece of bread and mopped up the residue from the pan, eating it greedily and furtively as Bobby sat down at her table.

As she set the plate in front of him he'd said, 'Aren't you eating?'

'I ate earlier.' She sat opposite him. She had wanted him to be astonished and grateful but he had only frowned, his hands hesitant over the knife and fork.

'Nina, I'm not very hungry. Why don't you have this?'

She'd laughed, wanting to hide her hurt and anger from him. 'I've eaten! Besides, it's for you. I bought it for you.'

His hands were still over the cutlery. After a moment he met her gaze across the table. 'I'm sorry, but I'd rather you didn't watch me eat.'

She had got up at once. She tried to busy herself making tea, rigidly keeping her back to him, her ears straining to hear the clatter of his knife and fork against the plate. There was only the ordinary quiet of her flat. At last he got up. She tensed, unable to turn to face him. Not for the first time since they'd met, she wished him miles away.

Softly he said, 'Nina, I'm sorry. Sit down, please. Talk to me.'

She looked at the tea caddy in her hand. 'Eat your supper.'

She heard him take a step towards her and forced herself not to cringe, standing up straighter as she spooned tea from the caddy. 'Sit down, Bobby. Don't let your meal go cold.'

'Sod the bloody meal!'

She pressed the heels of her hands into her eyes, forcing out tears. She laughed brokenly. 'You do know I had to sleep with the butcher to get that chop?'

'Don't say things like that.'

'It was a joke.'

312

He fumbled to light a cigarette. 'Shall I go? I could find a hotel.'

'I want you here.'

It wasn't really a lie. For weeks she'd anticipated looking after him. She would nurse him back to full health; she would help him face the world again; she would be a comfort and a support, full of empathy and understanding. She had expected what little awkwardness there was at the start to be easily overcome. Impatience hadn't figured in her plan.

'Eat your supper, Bobby. Please don't waste it.'

He sat down meekly and began the slow process of cutting up food and putting it in his mouth. He chewed as though the meat was leather, all the time keeping his head bowed over the plate. She watched him despite what he'd said; his hair seemed thinner, cut too short, the brutal cut emphasising the way his ears stuck out a little too far. In the dim light from the standard lamp his disfigured face was as expressionless as a Greek tragedy mask, his eyes dull. He wasn't beautiful any more and his ugliness felt like a betrayal.

In the shop, Nina turned away from the mirror. This was her evening for telephoning Bobby and she wondered if she would tell him that Hugh had been jealous and angry just as he'd predicted. She remembered Bobby's silence when she had first mentioned Hugh's name so that for a moment she'd thought the line had gone dead. When at last he spoke it was in his officer's voice, the one she imagined him using when dismissing a subordinate.

The telephone was kept in the little office at the back of the shop. A respectful space was cleared for it on the scarred and tea-ringed desk. Large and black, most of the time the phone kept a dignified silence, its rare, surprisingly shrill ring causing her heart to leap in panic. In the whole of her life the telephone had brought only bad news.

Sitting down at the desk, Nina lifted the receiver and dialled Bobby's number. The receiver was heavy, the warm smell of Bakelite a reminder of phone calls from senior RAF officers. Their news had been delivered in the quick, apologetic tones of authority as she listened dumbly at the end of a crackling, sympathy-distorting line.

She held the receiver hard against her ear, listening to the persistent impertinence of the ring tone and imagining the hallway in Bobby's house where he'd told her the phone was kept. He'd told her he sat on the stairs to talk to her, and she pictured him casually holding the telephone in his lap, its cord snaking across the floor. She listened and was about to hang up when Bobby finally answered.

Chapter Eight

Nina said, 'I dreamt about Joan last night.'

Her voice was so quiet Bobby had to press the receiver hard against his ear. From her tone he sensed that she was smiling, the kind of smile that wobbled on the edge of tears. He heard her draw breath and his hand closed tight around the receiver, willing her not to cry. His other hand twisted the telephone cord, worrying it into knots as he avoided his reflection in the hall mirror that showed his own eyes red from crying. When he spoke he knew his voice would be hoarse. He closed his eyes, listening to Nina quietly pull herself together.

At last she said, 'Do you remember that little outfit Jason bought her? The one with the sky-blue pixie hood?' Her voice was too bright. After a moment she said cautiously, 'Bobby? Are you still there?'

'Yes.' His voice broke and he cleared his throat. 'Yes. I'm here.'

'In my dream the hood was too small for her. She'd grown …' There was another silence and then, 'We went out shopping for a new one to replace it but I lost her. You were there. You helped me search. We were in the Army & Navy store. In the haberdashery department. I was sure you'd find her!'

'Nina, it was just a dream –'

'I know. It was so vivid, though. And you were in uniform, still. There was a baby-sick stain on your shoulder.'

He had woven the telephone cord through his fingers tightly and weals appeared on the skin. As she described more of the dream he carried the phone over to the stairs and sat down on the fourth step, his feet firmly on the hall floor. Her dream was full of sound and colour and the frantic, muddled logic of the dreamer. He knew that in the dream his face and hands were still intact because such a miracle was possible in dreams. But the miracle she most wanted couldn't be realised. Even in Nina's dreams the dead couldn't be brought back to life.

She drew breath. 'Bobby?'

'I'm listening, sweetheart.'

'Do you remember that song you used to sing to her?'

There were lots of songs. He flexed his fingers as much as he could and watched the cat cradle of phone wire expand. In his ear her voice was cautious.

'Bobby?'

'Which song, Nina?'

'*Paper Moon*.'

He closed his eyes tight, fresh tears welling behind them. He remembered Joan laughing as he sang and bounced her on his knee in time with the sad, jaunty words. Trying to keep the tears from his voice he said softly, 'Paper moon, cardboard sea…'

'Your voice sounds different.'

'No, I don't think so.'

'You've been crying!' He could hear the awe in her voice

'No. Nina, don't cry, please.'

Her sobs became muffled and he imagined her pressing her handkerchief to her mouth and nose, one of those tiny squares of off-white Irish linen with the deep edges of scratchy lace. The handkerchief would smell of her perfume and face powder, a sweet, erotic scent. He listened to the sniffling sounds she made and rhythmically bumped the side of his head against the wall.

'I'm sorry,' she said at last.

'Don't be.'

She laughed painfully. 'You sound awful!'

'I might have a cold.'

'You haven't been … upset?'

'No. I haven't been upset.'

'Would you tell me if you had?'

316

'Depends.' He made himself smile, knowing she would hear it in his voice. 'I made a fool of myself in a shop yesterday. A child of a shop assistant mistook me for an old man so I threw a display of ties on the floor.'

'Oh, Bobby, you didn't!'

She sounded so appalled that he laughed. 'There's worse – my mother caught me in the act and insisted on taking me home.' Remembering, he felt again the humiliation, although at the time he had felt only rage and frustration and self-pity. He unwound the wire from his hand and stared down at the fresh red marks. He realised that selfishly he had brought the conversation round to himself. It hadn't been his intention. In his mind's eye he could see her shoving the lacy hanky into her sleeve and sitting up straighter as she assumed the posture of sympathetic listener.

Carefully he said, 'I remember the blue pixie hood. She looked so sweet in it.'

'It made her eyes look even bluer.'

'I told Jason blue was for boys. I'd never seen him look more scornful.'

'Very scornful, then.' After a moment she said, 'Sometimes I think the pain will never get better.' She laughed slightly. 'And sometimes I forget altogether. Isn't that terrible? Though it's not really forgetting, it's just –'

'Getting on with your life.'

'Maybe.' She sighed. 'Maybe.'

He was hopeless with other people's pain, even hers. Even the most carefully chosen words sounded glib to him so that often he couldn't bring himself to say anything and all he could do was hold her. She would rest her head against his chest and allow him to stroke her hair and they would end up in bed, their lovemaking taking on a frantic energy as if all their pain and grief could be excised by an orgasm.

Quietly she said, 'Are you still there Bobby?'

'Yes.'

'You have been crying, haven't you?'

He laughed, impatiently swatting tears from his eyes. 'I'm all right, really.'

'It wasn't my fault, was it?'

'No! Of course not.' He thought of Joan. When he had sung all he could remember of *Paper Moon* she would say, 'Daddy sing again.' Sometimes he wouldn't, sometimes he was tired and had had enough. He closed his eyes again, he forced himself to be brightly chatty. 'So, how is Jason? Did you go and see him in the end?'

'Yes. He sends his love.' Carefully she said, 'I remembered you to Hugh Morgan.'

He swallowed hard to suppress his tears. At last he managed, 'Did you?'

'You were right – he was angry.'

Bobby leaned against the wall. Since answering the phone the evening had grown darker and he shivered, cold suddenly. At his back the stairs ascended into the gloom; at his feet the dim light from the porch cast the long shadow of the hatstand across the floor, its almost-human shape folding into the corner. It seemed all Parkwood's ghosts had gathered to watch him: the whole, nearly extinct Harris tribe. Without thinking he said quickly, 'Nina, I miss you so much.'

'And I miss you too –'

'Do you? Shall I come home?'

When she hesitated he laughed, a shaming, defeated noise. 'Home! Where's that anyway? I thought it was here.'

'And isn't it?'

He couldn't answer; his throat was constricting with the effort of not crying. Gently Nina said, 'Bobby, is there anyone there with you?'

He laughed brokenly. 'I've scared them all away.'

'Oh Bobby, don't say that.'

There was a note of impatience in her voice and he remembered how much she hated him – any man – to show weakness, to be too hotly dramatic. After a moment he managed to sit up straight and ask the ultimate cool question. 'So, tell me what happened with Hugh.'

'Nothing much.' After a moment's hesitation she said, 'You should have told me you'd fallen out with him so badly.'

'It was a long time ago.'

'You must have really hurt him.'

'Of course! Because that's what I do, isn't it? Go around hurting people I care for.'

'You should have told me. He was so angry.'

'But I told you he would be, my darling.' He could hear the campness in his voice and despised himself for it. Making an effort to be calmer he said, 'Nina – didn't it occur to you that he was just jealous? I don't know why you wanted to mention me –'

'Because I thought it would be nice for you to hear from an old friend! Is that so bad?'

'No.' He sighed. 'It's not so bad.'

She must have heard the resignation in his voice because she said, 'I won't see him again.'

'No?'

'He has no imagination.'

Bobby laughed, remembering how Hugh would enter into the spirit of the games he invented only when he had satisfied himself that they were proper boys' games. If he had to dress as a cowboy or an Indian or a redcoat soldier there had to be enough hunting and killing. Knives had to be stolen from the kitchen, along with matches for bonfires and broom handles for makeshift bayonets. Hugh would camouflage his face with mud, even allow him to smudge Indian war-paint stripes across his cheeks, although he drew the line at feathered headdresses. Hugh was fastidious, even as a small child.

Curious suddenly Bobby asked, 'Is he handsome?'

'Cartoon handsome.'

'Did he ask after me?'

'I told you, he was angry.'

'But did he …' He trailed off, not knowing how to form the question without giving himself away. At last he said, 'He doesn't have very much to be angry about.'

'No, probably not.' Her tone had changed and he knew she was ready to wind down the conversation and to hang up, duty done.

Too quickly he said, 'How's work? How's Irene and Cathy?'

'Fine.' She laughed bleakly. 'Irene envies you, your escape from London, it's so depressing here. Everyone you see looks so sick and tired –'

'You could escape, too, if you wanted.'

'Could I? How?'

He forced a smile although his heart was hammering and his hand tightened around the phone. 'You could come here. For a visit.'

He hadn't meant to ask her; if he'd thought about it he knew he would never have summoned the courage. Listening to her silence he thought about pretending he was joking, that of course she wouldn't want to travel two hundred miles north just to see him. Instead, to his surprise, he remained silent too, realising how much he wanted to see her.

At last Nina said, 'Would you really want me to?'

'Why not?' He made his voice light. 'It would be fun, wouldn't it? I could show you all Thorp's interesting sights.'

'Does it have many?'

'No.' When she laughed he said, 'There's not so much of the war about up here, not so many memories. Will you come?'

He pictured her expression, the one she used when she wanted to let him down gently, one that was all too familiar since he was burnt. As he was about to give up hope she said, 'I suppose I'm owed a few days holiday.'

He closed his eyes in relief. 'Come this weekend. I'll send you the money for a first-class ticket.'

Chapter Nine

As she stood on the platform at King's Cross Nina thought about Cathy and wished she had kissed her goodbye. But the baby had been crying most of the night, she'd heard her through the wall, and she knew that she would be exhausted. When she'd gone to say goodbye to Irene she'd only stood over Cathy's cot, watching her sleep for a while. Laid on her back, her hands were clenched in fists above her head, her left cheek shiny and red so that Nina knew it would be hot and tight as a drum. Joan had suffered with teething, too.

Bobby had said, 'She's beautiful. Like you.'

It was a few days after Joan's birth, and he stood at the foot of her hospital bed, cradling Joan in his arms, the white cellular blanket like a cloud against the blue of his uniform. He looked up from studying her baby's face. 'You know I'll take care of you both, don't you?'

She'd struggled to sit up, still sore and aching from her long labour. Her once small breasts were hard and so tender she dreaded the greedy clamp of her daughter's gums. Even now milk leaked from her, staining through the complicated seams and fastening of her maternity bra and sensible nightdress. Her hair hung in greasy rat-tails; she stank of blood and milk. As usual, Bobby looked immaculate and smelt as if he intended to make love to someone that afternoon. She remembered holding out her arms for her daughter, angry with him suddenly. She'd hardly heard what he'd said, hardly understood, too taken up with the anger she felt towards him in those days. A few months earlier he had held her hands as he told her that her husband was dead. He had seen his Spitfire shot down. He was convinced he hadn't suffered. He had held

321

her as she'd wept and his body had been stiff and awkward because her marriage had made them strangers for a while.

Her train pulled into the station and she walked along the platform, looking into carriages until she found one with a vacant seat. On board, she stowed her bag away and sat down. Opposite, a woman cradled a toddler on her knee, a protective hand shielding his head as he slept. Nina smiled at her, wishing she'd chosen another carriage.

As the train began to pull away, there was a commotion on the platform as a man sprinted through the crowds. He called out to the porter, only to push past him and pull open the door of Nina's carriage. Inside, he slammed it shut with a noise that woke the sleeping child. The child's mother glared at him.

'Sorry.' He was panting, his chest heaving. 'Nearly missed it …'

Nina longed for a newspaper to hide behind. As Hugh Morgan finally sat down next to the woman and crying child, she looked out of the window quickly, buying time to compose herself. All the same, she felt his eyes on her and could sense his astonishment.

After a few moments he said, 'Hello.' She turned to face him and he smiled awkwardly. 'Small world.'

The child's crying stopped. He seemed to sleep again and with her free hand his mother took a book from her handbag on the seat beside her and began to read. Hugh glanced at the woman, then sat forward, closing the gap separating him from Nina.

'I almost missed the train,' he said conversationally.

Nina sat further back in her seat.

'I slept in. Can you believe it? I've never over-slept in my life. Henry asked me only the other day if I needed an alarm clock, I said no. Never needed one until now.'

He was dishevelled; it was obvious he'd dressed quickly and hadn't had time to shave. He would suit a beard, she thought, and immediately reprimanded herself. Hugh Morgan could grow a beard long enough to strangle himself with for all she cared.

Taking out his cigarettes he offered her the open packet.

When she shook her head he shrugged, lighting one himself. Shaking out the match he sat back in his seat again and exhaled a long plume of smoke down his nose. It was obvious he was trying to think of something else to say. Looking up from her book, the woman next to him met Nina's eye and smiled archly before lowering her gaze back to the page.

Nina stared out of the window her hands folded in her lap, her feet primly together. She was thankful she'd worn her green two piece; its skirt was the longest she had, the tweed material thick and concealing. Her cream blouse was buttoned to her throat, and she'd put her hair up beneath the suit's matching felt hat with its single, dull feather.

From the corner of her eye she saw Hugh rest his head back and close his eyes. She hoped he would sleep, or at least pretend to, easing the embarrassment between them that was causing such an atmosphere in the carriage. She looked at him furtively, remembering his mouth on hers. Although everything else about his technique had been quick and hard and frantic, surprisingly his kisses had been long and luxurious, as though he savoured the taste of her. His kisses had taken her back to her adolescence, the sweet, heavy petting in the back row of the Roxy picture house in the days before Bobby. Bobby had introduced her to more sophisticated pleasures; with Bobby there had always been beds, unless he had invented reasons to do without them.

Hugh Morgan began to snore quietly. Relieved, Nina gazed out of the window, watching the narrow back gardens and red brick houses of the suburbs speed past. Much of the city was one huge bombsite, filthy with the brick dust and debris from collapsing buildings. Everywhere boards had gone up around craters in the earth where shops or homes or offices had stood. Yesterday she'd seen a street closed, Danger, Unexploded Bomb signs being unloaded from the back of an army truck. It would be easy to imagine the war wasn't over, that the world was even bleaker now than it had been in 1939. As the train picked up speed she began to relax a little, glad to be leaving London behind.

*   *   *

Hugh woke with a start. Disorientated, he grasped the edge of his seat to stop himself falling, realising that it was only the jolt of waking, that he wasn't plunging into a black, freezing sea. He glanced around the carriage. Nina still sat diagonally opposite him, still watching the countryside recede; all the other passengers had gone. He rested his head back, his heart still pounding, and allowed himself to look at her, careful to keep his eyes half-closed so that she might think he was still sleeping.

Earlier, when he'd settled himself in his seat and saw her sitting there, he'd felt the kind of excitement he could only remember from being a child at Christmas, a kind of joyousness rising from the pit of his stomach. He'd given himself away of course; his foolish smile must have stretched from one ear to the other. She had only gazed at him coldly, losing none of her perfect composure.

The train jolted over points and Hugh opened his eyes fully, no longer caring if Nina noticed that he was awake or not. He wanted her to speak; even ordinary, empty small talk would be better than this pointed, painful silence. He sighed, remembering again what an arse he'd made of himself last time they were together.

'You keep sighing, Hugh.'

He looked at her sharply. Flustered, he said, 'I'm sorry. I didn't realise.'

'Pretend we're strangers.'

'Sorry?'

'You can tell strangers on trains all your worries and then get off at your station and never have to face them again.'

'Face what – the stranger or the worry?' He smiled. 'I don't think I have any worries, not real ones, anyway.'

'Lucky you.'

She returned her gaze to the window, giving him the feeling that he'd inadvertently snubbed her, although her expression was so maddeningly inscrutable he had an idea she might be laughing at him. He sighed again, only to catch himself, and Nina smiled at her reflection in the grubby glass.

Too stiffly he said, 'Do you have any worries?'

324

She looked at him. 'Only one, at the moment.'

'Shall I pretend to be your stranger?'

For a while she held his gaze, only to look down at her hands. He noticed for the first time there was a wedding ring on her finger, she twisted it around before looking up at him again. 'Are you going to Thorp?'

'Yes. Are you?'

'Bobby's invited me to stay with him.'

'Oh.'

Lightly she said, 'It's a holiday. He's going to show me around –'

Hugh laughed. 'That won't take long. There's not much to Thorp.'

'So why are you going back?'

He looked away, catching sight of the pale ghost of his own reflection in the window. At sea he would sometimes dream of Thorp, that his ship had sailed right up the Tees to that point where the river broadened accommodatingly behind Thorp High Street. Anchor dropped, gangplank lowered, he would shoulder his kit bag and disembark on home ground like a rescued Robinson Crusoe. His ship would disappear. Awake, he could never decide if the dream was good or bad.

Nina said gently, 'Hugh?' He glanced at her and she smiled as though concerned. 'You go miles away, sometimes.'

'Sorry.'

'It's all right, I understand.'

He smiled, politely accepting her belief – the belief of most civilians – that she had any understanding at all. He thought of Bob Harris, wondering if she claimed the same understanding of his sudden, spiritual absences, and a hot prickle of jealousy made him look away. He felt his smile curdle and he took out his cigarettes, self-consciously aware of her watching him.

He offered her the open packet and she leaned forward to accept the cigarette he'd pulled out a little. He caught the scent of her perfume and remembered that he had tasted its bitter, chemical sting on the skin between her breasts, that it failed to mask the real, sweat-and-honey smell of her. Remembering, he found himself becoming aroused, hating his body's unruly, schoolboy responsiveness. He turned back to the window and saw that his mouth had set into a hard, angry line.

From the corner of his eye he saw Nina take a small book from the handbag on her knee. He recognised the bold black lettering on its dull khaki cover and knew that the book was *Dawn Song*. He glanced at her and she caught his eye and smiled almost apologetically.

'It fits in my bag easily.'

'Light verse?'

She laughed, looking down at the open book and smoothing her fingers across the pages. He couldn't bear the thought that she was about to start reading the poems in his presence and he reached out and took the book from her.

He said, 'You know them by heart, don't you?'

'Some of them.' She met his gaze coolly, as though he was an unpredictable child she needed to assess before taking action. '*Homecoming* is the most memorable, the way the lines scan –'

'He tells people he wrote it for me. He didn't. He just likes everyone to think he's a good, family man.' He looked down at the book, hating the smooth dry feel of it, the ostentatious arrogance of the embossed title. Placing it on the seat beside him he said, 'I don't recognise anyone in his poems, not me, not my mother, no one.'

She exhaled smoke down her nose and turned to look out of the window. After a moment she said, 'Bobby hates his poetry, too.'

Jealousy made his voice harsh as he said, 'You know – that only makes me like him less. Odd, that, don't you think?'

She picked a stray strand of tobacco from her tongue, a delicate, sexy gesture. 'It's not so odd, really. Most men dislike Bobby.' She held his gaze, reinforcing his idea that she only mentioned Bobby to provoke him. Evenly she said, 'Women adore him, of course. I've seen all kinds of women make terrible fools of themselves over Flight Lieutenant Bobby Harris.'

She stressed his name and rank as though it was a joke and the bitterness in her voice seemed to sting the close, over-used air of the carriage. He watched her draw on the cigarette and exhale a long-held breath of smoke. Unable to help himself he said, 'You sound as though you hate him, too.'

'Hate? I didn't mention hate. No one hates Bobby. He doesn't allow them to get close enough.' She seemed to consider, then, 'Unless you hate him?'

He looked down at the book beside him. Picking it up he held it out to her. 'Here. Read if you want to.' She ignored the book. At last, feeling foolish, he put it down.

The train raced along tracks cut between fields that sprouted green with shoots of plants he couldn't name, or were grazed by black and white cows, the same utilitarian animal repeated over and over. He wished he could sleep again but the atmosphere was too charged for that now; he shifted uncomfortably, wanting to break the silence but unable to think of a single thing to say that was safe and ordinary and didn't involve bloody Bobby Harris.

He saw her turn the wedding ring on her finger and blurted, 'I didn't know you'd been married.'

'Why should you?' She looked up from her hands. 'He was a fighter pilot, he was killed in 1940.'

'I'm sorry.'

She folded her hands in her lap; he noticed that she kept her feet together on the floor, her back ramrod straight. After a moment she said, 'We had a baby, Joan, but he didn't live to see her. She died, too, of measles. She was three.'

Hugh felt himself blush. To his astonished dismay tears came to his eyes and he looked out of the window before she could notice. Trying to keep control of his voice he said, 'That's terrible. I'm so sorry.' He wiped his eyes surreptitiously with his fingers. 'I'm truly sorry.'

'Are you crying, Hugh?'

'No!' He laughed brokenly. 'No –'

She got up and sat beside him. Taking his hand between hers she frowned at him. 'Hugh?'

He managed to meet her gaze. 'You must think I'm a fool.'

'No.'

'I wish you'd told me before.'

She drew her hand away but remained so close beside him their thighs touched. At last she said, 'I wanted you too much.'

'You still could have had me.'

'It wouldn't have been the same.'

'And now that you have told me?'

'I don't know. You're terribly handsome. I like handsome men. It's very shallow of me.' She smiled. 'Are you flattered?'

He touched her face, gently forcing her to hold his gaze. Once again he was astonished by how lovely she was. Unable to believe she could see anything in anyone as ordinary as himself he said, 'I don't want you to flatter me, Nina. I just want to see you again, to get to know you –'

She drew away from his touch. 'I'd like that, too.'

'But?'

'You'll be in Thorp, I'll be in London.'

Quickly he said, 'Let me take you to dinner while you are in Thorp – maybe I can be persuaded to go back to London with you –'

'You'd change your plans for me?'

'It's not much of a plan. I may even have cold feet already.'

'Hugh,' she sighed, drawing out his name in a way that thrilled him. 'Hugh, you know I'm staying with Bobby. If I see you I won't keep it secret from him.'

He made himself smile. 'Of course. Everything above board. May the best man win and all that.'

She got up and went to sit in her original seat. 'You can't believe Bobby and I are just friends, can you?'

'If that's the truth.'

She laughed, stubbing out her cigarette in the ashtray between the seats.

Carefully he said, 'I was going to see him, once I'd got settled. I was going to ask him how he felt about you. What do you think he would say?'

'Truth?'

He tried to keep his voice light. 'Well, I would hate it if you lied to me.'

She hesitated. As if coming to a decision, she said quickly,

'When he was first in hospital I thought we'd be married when he was well again. Then, as the weeks and months went by, I knew it would never happen. The Bobby I'd loved was burnt away.' She looked at him steadily. 'So, if you asked him how he felt about me he'd say I'm a shallow girl, as I said.'

'Did he ask you to marry him?'

'Not then. Not in so many words.'

'But if he had you would've said no because of his face?'

'Yes.'

Hugh realised he'd been hunched forward in his seat, concentrating on her. Now he slumped back, crushing out his own cigarette to avoid her gaze. She was looking at him defiantly, as though she had just confessed to murder and was waiting to be scornful of his horror. In truth he was unsure how to react. If he was honest with himself he knew that he was pleased, but all the same he felt pity for Bob. The poor sod probably held out some hope. After all, it would be difficult to give up on a girl like Nina.

After a moment she said, 'You probably think I'm a heartless bitch.'

He winced. 'I don't think that.'

'Well I am.'

'Nina … it's not your fault if you didn't love him …' He hesitated. 'Did you love him?'

There was a long pause. Dramatic effect, he thought, until he saw she was frowning as though giving his question serious consideration. At last she said, 'He didn't love me, ever. Then, when he needed me, I couldn't bear to be near him. I let him down, but sometimes I feel it was more a kind of revenge. Isn't that wicked? Is it hypocritical to say that we're even friends?' She looked down at her hands, twisting her wedding ring. 'He was Joan's father, not biologically, but in every way that mattered. He loved her. She's the bond between us.'

His jealousy came back, bitter as ever. He pictured Bobby Harris holding Nina's child in his arms and the baby lent him maturity: he was a grown-up and not the irresponsible Brylcreem Boy he'd imagined. He realised how badly he wanted Bobby to be the caricature RAF officer, cocksure and

329

promiscuous and unforgivably careless. Such a man wouldn't love Nina or bring up another man's child. But Nina's Bobby was far more complicated – there was so much guilt and pity and regret, there was so much history between them. It was impossible to believe they were merely friends.

Too sharply he asked, 'Is he meeting you off the train?'

'Yes. I told him not to – he's so nervous in public – but he insisted.'

'What shall I do? Shake his hand or make sure he doesn't see me?'

She gazed at him coolly. 'You must do what you think best. But there's no reason to avoid him.' Impatiently she said, 'Won't you say hello? He'd be so pleased to see you.'

'I wouldn't be, if I were him. I'd want you to myself.' Deciding it might be better to be blasé for a change, to take a more active role in this odd game of hers, he smiled. 'Of course I'll say hello. I'm quite looking forward to seeing him again.'

She looked surprised and relieved at once. On a rush of breath she said, 'Try not to look too shocked when you see him.'

His smile disappeared, his puny bravado flattened by a disconcerting mix of pity and anxiety that he wouldn't be able to respond well enough when he and Bobby finally came face to face. Bobby would have the upper hand, no doubt used to the clumsy reactions of others. He would be shown up in front of Nina. He imagined Bobby smirking, his face made even more grotesque, and he sighed.

Nina said, 'Bobby's very sweet, really, once you get past all the brittleness.'

'We were friends, once, remember? I know what he's like.'

She nodded, quick to appease him now she had what she wanted. Both of them knew, of course, that he had no idea what Bobby was like. She had described him as brittle and he could only guess what she meant, but it didn't seem like a description that fitted the Bobby he'd known.

The train slowed and stopped at a station. The carriage door opened and three soldiers climbed aboard, stowing their kit

330

bags in the overhead lockers and taking up too much space with their boots and elbows and khaki-sweat stink. He noticed Nina sit further back in her seat, her eyes fixed on the window as if to avoid catching anyone's eye. Inevitably the three men glanced at her, only to perform cartoon-like double takes. Perhaps they thought she was a film star. Even in that dull, matronly suit she might be Betty Grable in disguise.

Hugh picked up his father's book of poetry and discreetly held it out to her. When she took it he caught her eye and smiled conspiratorially. She didn't respond, only sat back in her seat again, making herself small and inconspicuous, hiding behind the book's pages and foiling his attempt to claim her as his in front of their new fellow passengers.

Chapter Ten

The black Morris Minor had stood in the garage since his grandfather's death. For a few days after the funeral Bobby had forgotten all about it, only to remember with a start of anxiety. Apart from the house, the car was his most valuable possession; he should take it for a drive and give it a once-over before its tyres went flat or its battery died; he could sell it, perhaps. He had unlocked the big wooden garage doors and opened them fully, as though he intended to drive the car away. Instead, he had stood a few feet from it, unable to bring himself to go any closer. More than his house, more than his furniture or even his clothes, the car belonged to his grandfather so completely it seemed disrespectful to disturb it. He'd stepped closer, smiling as he remembered what a slow, careful driver his grandfather was. Cars were not toys, he'd told him during his first leave when he'd arrived home in the brand new MG Jason had bought for him. His grandfather had never understood his love of speed, of tinkering with engines in the hope of making them go faster.

A few days later he'd gone as far as sitting in the driver's seat, turning the ignition key to listen to the reassuring response of its engine. He hadn't taken off the hand brake or shoved it into reserve gear to back it out into the drive. He had thought that he might wash it, but the car was only dusty, and inside it was as clean as the day it rolled off the production line. It still smelt of new car, hardly used since petrol became scarce even for doctors. Yesterday, in preparation for Nina's visit, he had finally overcome his nervousness and had driven the car around the block. Back in the garage he'd wondered what he'd been afraid of and for the first time since he'd left hospital he felt he'd reclaimed something of his old self.

Waiting in the car outside Thorp Station, Bobby checked his watch again. Her train was due in five minutes. If he got the timing right, he wouldn't have to hang around the platform for a moment longer than necessary. Nina would step off the train and he would greet her and lead her back to the car and it would take a couple of minutes at most. There would be no standing around attracting stares. He should have made use of the car before – the privacy it gave him was liberating.

Bobby wound the window down and lit a cigarette. He had spent the day cleaning the house, concentrating his efforts on the bedroom he'd decided would be hers. The room looked out over the garden, the sash windows folding oblongs of sunshine across the double bed he'd made up with fresh linen and a slippery, satin eiderdown found in a chest. He'd filled a vase with daffodils from the garden and placed them on the dressing table, the tight, green-yellow buds reflecting in the three mirrors and polished wood. Finished, he'd looked around, pleased with his efforts, only to wonder that perhaps she might think he was trying too hard. Neediness could be demonstrated in all kinds of ways, after all. He'd sat down on the bed, anxious suddenly, and caught sight of himself in the dressing table mirrors, ugly in triplicate. Not for the first time that day he'd wondered why she was coming when she really couldn't stand the sight of him.

In the car Bobby exhaled cigarette smoke, hating his nervousness. It was only Nina, after all. Only. He smiled to himself bitterly. Ever since their first naked pose for Jason's camera they had been a secret society of two. No one else had a clue what it felt like to be so ruined, so shocked and thrillingly shocking at the same time. He could feel such tenderness for her he felt his heart would break. Other times he had wanted to escape her, to be ordinary and straight as the men he flew beside; impossible, though, when they recognised how odd he was. Now it was Nina who wanted to escape him, Nina who was tied by sentimental tenderness. He sighed cigarette smoke, wishing once again that they could let each other be.

He got out of the car and turned his coat collar up, an automatic gesture and one that Nina hated. After a moment's hesitation, he folded the collar down again and made himself stand up straighter. He kept his gloves on, even though the evening was mild, and avoided meeting anyone's gaze as he walked into the station. He could be brave in small doses, and most of his courage was spent for today. On the platform, he saw the London train pull in and drew anxiously on the cigarette before stubbing it out underfoot. He would need both hands free to greet her, one steady on her arm as he kissed her cheek, the other reaching for her case. The case would be heavy with her clothes and shoes, the outfits she kept so carefully from one season to the next, altering hem lines and sleeves in an effort to defeat rationing. She would be wearing the green suit, she'd told him, and he remembered how the skirt fishtailed a little at the back and showed off her slim calves. He tried not to think of the rubber bumps of her suspenders felt through the thick material.

The train came to a stop with the familiar squeals and hisses and clanks remembered from a thousand such reunions. At once people pressed forward as porters walked along the platform opening doors. In the press of bodies a man nudged him and he stepped back. He closed his eyes, panic making him feel sick suddenly. He should have waited in the car until the crowd had dispersed.

'Bobby?'

He looked up, his heart racing even faster at the sound of her voice. She frowned at him, concerned, and he made an effort to pull himself together.

'Nina. Hello.' He smiled, kissing the cheek she offered him. When she stood back again he noticed she didn't have a suitcase with her.

She glanced over her shoulder, smiling too brightly. 'I've a surprise for you.'

Hugh said, 'You know it's been ten years since I was last in this house?'

Standing in Parkwood's kitchen, the glass of whisky Bobby

had handed him held against his chest, Hugh Morgan looked around as though he was noticing the damp patch above the window, the grey thread of cobwebs hanging from the light. He smiled awkwardly. 'Ten years. I suppose we should have a lot to talk about.'

Bobby said, 'Sit down, Hugh.'

Hugh ignored him. He went to the fireplace and picked up the photograph of Bobby's father and frowned at it. 'Is this you?'

'Wrong uniform.'

'Of course.' He set the picture down again gently. To Bobby's surprise he blushed. 'Of course,' he repeated. After a moment his hand went to his face, rubbing at the five o'clock shadow that darkened his square jaw and made him look even more like the all-action hero of a comic strip. 'I need a shave,' he said. 'A bath. Hell of a journey, that, I'd almost forgotten.'

'There should be enough hot water when Nina's finished in the bathroom.'

'You think so? You know what women are like.' He lit a cigarette and sat down, looking at him through the smoke screen he exhaled, exactly like his father Mick. 'I could still find a hotel, you know. You don't have to go to all this trouble.'

Bobby sat in the armchair opposite him. 'It's no trouble.'

They could hear Nina moving around upstairs and Hugh glanced at the ceiling, only to look down again quickly as though it was somehow impolite to acknowledge her presence. Flicking cigarette ash into the fire he cleared his throat. 'I was going to stay at the Grand – live it up for a few days.' He laughed slightly. 'Knowing my luck it was probably bombed.'

'No, it's still in one piece.'

'Then I'll stay there, after tonight.'

They sipped their drinks, listening to the knocking and spluttering of the pipes as Nina ran her bath. Bobby noticed how Hugh's eyes continued to stray around the room and he wondered if he realised it hadn't changed at all in those ten years; the table and chairs and rugs and curtains – even the tablecloth – had only become more worn and grubby. When he wasn't glancing around he looked down at his drink, swilling the Scotch against the sides of the glass between taking long, squint-eyed drags on his cigarette.

Used to the cod-polite lengths others went to just to avoid meeting his eye, Bobby watched him, angry that Hugh Morgan behaved just like everybody else. But he had been angry since the moment he saw him at the station. Hugh was taller and broader even than he'd imagined so that he felt puny beside him, shown up as a bag of neurotic bones. Worse, Hugh had not only shaken his hand but had pulled him into his arms, bear-hugging him for all the world to see. How pleased Nina had been, smiling as though she might cry. He'd wanted to leave them both there. His flesh crawled even now as he remembered the embrace.

Hugh said, 'Bob, I'll go, if you want.'

Bobby snorted. Hugh had finally met his gaze but Bobby found he couldn't bear to look back at him and he turned to the fire. Earlier he'd put on more coal and the flames were cheerfully flickering. He took the poker from its stand on the hearth and thrust it into the fire's heart, watching the coals avalanche.

'Bob?'

Bob. He'd forgotten that Hugh could never bring himself to call him Bobby, even as a child. Hunched over the fire he looked up at him, the poker still grasped in his less useless hand.

'She wants you to stay,' Bobby said.

Hugh sighed. 'I don't know about that.' After a moment he added, 'I didn't plan this. I didn't know she'd be on that train.'

Bobby placed the poker back in its stand. 'Coincidence, then, eh? Christ, it's a small world, isn't it?'

Hugh stood up. 'I'll go.'

'Sit down. I don't want her thinking I've driven you away.'

Hugh hesitated, then sat on the edge of the chair, his hands grasped together between his knees, his shoulders hunched. He looked exhausted; for the first time Bobby noticed the dark shadows beneath his eyes. His hair stood up a little where he had pushed his fingers through it, a weary, defeated gesture he remembered from their childhood. Oddly, Hugh Morgan smelt the same as he always had, clean as laundry left to dry in a sunny garden.

Hugh said, 'I was sorry to hear about your grandfather. I remember him looking after me when I had chicken pox; I must have been about eight. He performed this magic trick – produced a penny from behind my ear. Took my mind off the itching.' Hugh smiled as though suddenly remembering. 'You know I used to think he was your father? For quite a while I thought that.' He rested his head against the chair's threadbare back and closed his eyes. 'God I'm tired.'

'I'll show you to your room.' Bobby stood up.

Hugh said, 'There's no hurry, is there? We could at least finish our drinks.' More gently he said, 'It's good to see you, Bob. I know this is awkward but all the same –'

Bobby couldn't sit down again. More than anything he wanted to be on his own. Alone he could perhaps come to terms with the shock of seeing Hugh again; he could think more clearly about what the expression on Nina's face meant when she and Hugh exchanged glances. He knew they were lovers – it was obvious enough – but there seemed to be more than just a mutual attraction between them and he wasn't sure how he felt about this. He did know he couldn't stand the pity in Hugh's voice, the sorrowful look in his eyes as though he'd been told of his impending death. Finishing his drink in one swallow, he set the glass down on the mantelpiece.

'I'm going to bed. Your room's to the left of the bathroom, but feel free to stay up as long as you like – finish the bottle of Scotch, I don't mind. Say goodnight to Nina for me.'

Bobby sat down on his bed and began the fiddling business of untying his shoelaces and taking off his shoes before lying down on his bed. Taking his cigarettes from his pocket he lit one, watching the match burn almost to his fingers before briskly shaking it out. He closed his eyes. He could hear Nina running the bath and he pictured her soaping her breasts with the pink soap he'd bought for her. He thought about her hand moving lower, over her belly and between her legs. His own hand went to his flies only to stop. He wouldn't masturbate, although often it helped him to sleep. Masturbating with Hugh and Nina in the next rooms would make him feel even more of a pervert. He smiled bitterly. Imagine if Hugh walked in on him, thinking it was his room. How much pity he would have for him then! 'You're a sad bastard, Harris,' he said softly. 'It's pity-fucks or wanking from now on, you do know that?' Sweet-faced, ordinary, marry-me virgins wouldn't look at him now.

There had been a sweetheart of a nurse in the first hospital. The farmer who had found him staggering about in his field had later told him she was his cousin. The two of them certainly looked alike, blond and blue-eyed and strong as Aryan gods. The farmer had raced him to the little cottage hospital in his truck, had carried him inside running as though he weighed nothing at all. At the time he couldn't understand his hurry or the panic that dragged at his handsome face. He had tried to tell him to slow down as his head bounced against the man's arm and his feet dangled into space. He had wanted to make a joke and ask where's the fire? Only he found he couldn't speak in anything more than a whisper. The sweetheart nurse told him not to speak and that he should lie still and she would be gentle as she cut off his uniform. He seemed to remember that the pain had started in earnest then. He had tried not to cry because she was so pretty.

Her name was Anne Hill. He thought about her often because she was the kind of girl he had wanted to marry and make pregnant over and over. A lot of girls threw themselves at him because of the uniform he wore but he guessed uniforms didn't impress Anne Hill. And she had been shy, something he hated in himself. She had been kind, but not soppy-kind like Nina, who never could keep the fright and horror from her eyes. That first night in hospital when he'd woken from a dream that red-hot irons were crushing his hands, Nurse Hill had been there at his side, his calm, morphine angel. He suspected he told her that he loved her, cringing whenever he remembered. She couldn't love him back; it was impossible to love someone who cried at the

338

lightest touch and stank like a spit-roasted pig.

Bobby blew smoke rings at his bedroom ceiling. Nina had pulled the plug on her bath and he could hear the water gurgling away. She should have saved it for Hugh to climb into – they were intimate enough, after all. He remembered again how they had looked together at the station, how easy Nina seemed with him. He had to admit they made a handsome pair and that Hugh was a better physical match for her than he was. Hugh was a head taller than Nina, whereas he was more or less the same height. Hugh took her arm or placed a guiding hand on the small of her back as they walked; Hugh smiled at her a lot and was attentive and laughed at her feeblest attempt at a joke.

Bobby tried to remember if he had ever behaved like that with a woman. Of the handful he had slept with he remembered only a kind of strung-out intensity to their courtship, as if each potential fuck truly mattered. He was, in other words, a charmless bastard. Odd how woman had seemed to respond to him so willingly.

He rolled on to his side and stubbed out his cigarette. He could hear Hugh coming up the stairs, the click of the switch as he turned out the landing light, the opening and closing of the bathroom door. He heard him piss, a noise that seemed to go on for ages, a great, long, satisfying piss, his territory well and truly marked. How very manly Hugh Morgan was. Bobby found himself smiling bitterly as the lavatory was finally flushed. Hugh Morgan would never pose nude for pictures for queers to wank over. He closed his eyes, appalled that the truth of what he used to do had come to him so starkly. Usually he was kinder to himself, remembering only the times in Jason's studio when he made love to Nina.

Jason had laughed at him. 'You've fucked her, haven't you? I know, I can tell! Look at you, cock of the walk now you've lost your cherry. Really – what kind of pictures can I take of you now?' He'd waited for an answer as though it wasn't a rhetorical question.

Holding his gaze, Bobby had said, 'You'll have to pay me more. Nina, too.'

Jason laughed. 'All right. But for Christ's sake – don't get her pregnant, I can't use an up-the-stick model. Deal?'

Bobby had turned away from him. Taking off the silk robe he let it crumple at his feet. He allowed Jason a long look at his bare backside, tensing the muscles in his thighs and buttocks. At the same time he thought of Nina, of the way she'd wrapped her legs around his waist as he came, the way she'd moaned and rolled her eyes as though she was in ecstasy. He'd wondered if she was a whore, but what did he know? Whore or not, he had held her face between his hands and kissed her mouth, his spent cock still inside her. She had seemed to like this kissing best. He remembered she had giggled and squirmed beneath him and he realised her eye rolling and moaning was an act, an aping of the grown-ups. For the first time in his life he'd felt child-like and he laughed until she pressed her hand against his mouth.

Years later, when Nina was sometimes mistaken for his wife and Joan for his child, he would wonder why he hadn't married her. There were lots of reasons, the worst being that he was a snob, the best that he was wrong for her, that away from their bed they really didn't get on terribly well. If it hadn't been for Joan he was sure they would be almost strangers to each other by now.

Bobby got up. Now that his guests had retired to bed he could go downstairs again.

Chapter Eleven

Nina couldn't sleep. The bed was too soft and too warm, although she had kicked until the purple quilt covering her feet had slithered to the floor. Trees scraped their branches at the window; an owl hooted; every so often a train would sound in the distance. London was quieter.

She tried to will herself to sleep because she was tired and she didn't want dark bags under her eyes in the morning. Lack of sleep made her jumpy and cross and tomorrow she needed to be calm. Neither Hugh nor Bobby could guess that she wasn't taking this delicate situation in her stride. She sighed, remembering how dismayed Bobby had looked when he saw Hugh, how stiff and awkward he had been around him. She told herself that none of this was her fault. Bobby didn't have to invite Hugh to stay with him; Hugh didn't have to accept. She sat up, punching at the pillows in an effort to make herself comfortable. Outside a cat began howling and she almost wept in despair.

She listened, defeated, trying to make a lullaby of its pathetic cries. But cats sounded like babies crying, sometimes. She tried to put this thought from her mind and stared into the darkness. On the landing outside her door she heard a floorboard creak and she tensed, pulling the covers up to her chin like the grandmother in Little Red Riding Hood.

Nina watched as the door handle was turned with tortuous slowness. As the door opened a crack she quickly turned on her side, drawing her knees to her chest and closing her eyes tight. If she pretended to be fast asleep he – whichever of them it was – would go away.

He came in. He closed the door softly behind him and

moved quite soundlessly toward the bed. She heard him stop breathing and guessed he was holding his breath so that he might hear hers and know if she really was sleeping. He lifted the covers. Climbing in beside her he rested his hand lightly on her hip.'

'Nina?'

Hugh. 'Go back to bed.'

'I can't sleep.' His hand became heavier. 'I just want to hold you.'

'No, you don't.'

He laughed quietly. 'No. You're right.' Propping himself up on his elbow he looked down at her. 'You thought it was him, didn't you?'

'I didn't know.'

'Jesus. So you did half expect him?'

'Go back to bed, Hugh.'

'Would you send him away too? Look at me.'

She sat up and turned on the lamp beside the bed. Hugh blinked as though the dim light hurt his eyes. Coldly she said, 'This is wrong. What if he does come?'

'Then there'll be three in the bed. And the little one said …?' He smiled and reached up to press his palm against her face. 'You're lovely. I can't sleep in the next room knowing you're here.' More softly he said, 'Do you really want me to go?'

'I don't want to hurt him –'

His hand moved to her mouth. 'Then hush. We won't make a sound.'

He used a johnny and when he rolled off her he removed it carefully and dropped it on the floor. She imagined it making a slug-trail on the purple quilt and that Bobby would notice it and know what they'd done. Remembering the daffodils he'd placed in a vase by her bed, the scented soap and the thoughtful way he'd made her bed and laid out towels, she felt her eyes fill with tears. Unable to keep still she tossed the bedcovers aside and sat on the edge of the bed away from the heat of Hugh's body.

After a moment Hugh said gently, 'Would it help if I said I love you?'

She looked at him. 'You don't.'

He held out his hand to her. 'Come here.'

'I'm too hot.'

'Shall I open the window?'

'There's a cat howling outside.' She could hear her voice rising hysterically and she looked at him, not caring if he saw that she was crying. 'We shouldn't have done this.'

'Nina …' He sighed. Moving across the bed he knelt behind her and rested his head lightly on her shoulder. 'Nina, I love you. Right from the moment I saw you at that party.' He kissed her neck and she realised he'd shaved, that he smelled of the soap Bobby had left out for her.

She said, 'You knew I'd sleep with you tonight.'

'Not for certain.' Brushing her hair back from her face he said, 'Do you believe I love you?'

'You don't know me.'

He laughed softly, his mouth against her neck so that she shuddered with pleasure. 'You know what I'd like? To take you away. There's a cottage I know in Cornwall, right by the sea, all you can hear is the waves and the gulls.' He took her cigarettes from the bedside table and lit two at once. Handing her one he lay down and grinned at the ceiling. 'I could really get to *know* you in Cornwall.'

Nina closed her eyes and remembered a pretty, deserted beach with rock pools and sand dunes and the tall, pale grass that could slice unwary fingers. Such insignificant cuts to sting so. Bobby had kissed the tiny wound, drawing her finger into his mouth. They lay side by side and he had taken off his tunic and folded it for a pillow so that her cheeks grazed his wings and she could smell the oil and metal scent of him.

Hugh pulled her into his arms and kissed her head. 'When we're together like this I feel even more sorry for Bob.'

She closed her eyes. Quickly she said, 'He makes my flesh crawl.'

Hugh whistled through his teeth. 'Christ. The poor bastard.' Her head rested on his chest and he put a finger under her chin, tilting her head so that she'd look up at him. 'Do you really feel like that?'

She nodded, unable to speak for the tears choking her throat. Ashamed of herself, she buried her face in Hugh's chest and wept.

Bobby made tea and toast and laid the table in the dining room for three. Upstairs he could hear Nina and Hugh moving from bedroom to bathroom and back again and he found himself hovering at the foot of the stairs, anxiously glancing up. Hugh had left his bedroom door ajar and he'd seen that the bed was just as he'd left it last night when he'd offered to let him stay. The idea of him fucking Nina under his roof was unbearable. He wondered how he could ask them to leave without appearing petty.

He went into the pantry and took marmalade and jam from the shelves, fresh jars bought especially for her. He looked down at them in his hands and wanted to smash them against the wall.

'Bob?'

Bobby pressed himself against the pantry wall, not ready to face Morgan yet. He heard him wander out into the hallway and call his name again. Bobby went into the kitchen and opened and closed the back door. He would pretend he'd been in the garden, he would be nonchalant and leave him to guess whether he knew what had gone on in his own house.

'Good morning.' Bobby smiled as Hugh appeared in the kitchen doorway. 'Did you sleep well?'

'Yes, thanks. You?'

Bobby nodded. 'Go through to the dining room. I'll bring you some tea.'

'It's all right, Bob, we could eat in here.'

He ignored him, decanting jam into a fancy pot he'd found in the dresser. The pot was encrusted with silver daisies and bumblebees, with a hinged lid in the shape of a hive and he realised too late that it was meant for honey. He looked up at Hugh, the spoon dripping strawberry jam on to the table. 'Go and sit down, Hugh, please.'

344

'Should I take anything through?' Hugh smiled at him, eyebrows raised mockingly.

'I can manage, thank you.'

They heard Nina's footsteps on the stairs and both of them turned towards the hall. Hugh laughed, the self-assured, easy laugh of a man who'd spent the night having sex.

'Should I show her to her table?'

'Why don't you piss off, Morgan?'

Hugh gazed at him. After a moment he closed the kitchen door softly and stepped towards him. 'Bob, I don't want to fight with you.'

Bobby felt the familiar symptoms of a panic attack. He placed the spoon down gently and held on to the edge of the table, his head bowed. The sickly smell of the jam caught at the back of his throat and he closed his eyes, waiting for the feeling that his heart was about to burst through his chest to pass.

Carefully Hugh said, 'Are you all right?'

'What the fuck do you think?'

Hugh took his arm. 'Let's get you sat down.' He led him to a chair and made him sit. Crouching in front of him he smiled, his eyes frowning. 'I'll piss off soon, don't worry.' Gently he said, 'Are you sure you're all right?'

'Why? Don't I look the picture of health?' He took a deep breath. 'I'm fine now. Take that bloody look off your face.'

'I was worried you were about to faint, that's all.' Hugh stood up straight. 'Sorry about the bloody look.' His attention seemed caught by something outside. Looking towards the window he said, 'Do you know there's a boy climbing one of your trees?'

Bobby stood up at once and immediately regretted it. He swayed dizzily and Hugh caught his elbow. 'Steady on or you really will pass out on me. It's just some kid messing about –'

Ignoring him, Bobby went out into the garden. Sure it was one of the gang of boys that had been making nuisances of themselves for days, he shouted, 'You're trespassing you little bastard so get down from there before I call the police.'

'It's me, Bobby.'

Mark looked down at him. Sitting astride a thick branch he held a kitten against his chest. He grinned. 'Don't call the police. I'll come quietly, guv', honest.'

Feeling foolish, Bobby said harshly, 'For God's sake, Mark, get down before you break your stupid neck.'

Beside him Hugh Morgan said, 'That isn't your baby brother, is it?'

Bobby glanced at him. 'Yes.'

'Jesus!' He laughed. 'Really? That's what used to be the nuisance brat?'

'He's still the nuisance brat.'

Mark dropped at their feet. Still grinning he held out the kitten. 'Present. He'll keep the mice down.'

Hugh held out his hand to Mark. 'I bet you don't remember me.'

As if seeking approval, Mark glanced at Bobby before putting the kitten down and shaking Hugh's hand. 'I'm sorry, sir. I don't.'

Stiffly Bobby said, 'Mark, this is Hugh Morgan.'

Mark still looked blank. 'Sorry.' He laughed awkwardly. 'Still none the wiser, I'm afraid.'

'Michael Morgan's son,' Bobby said. The kitten was rubbing itself against his legs and he scooped it up before walking back into the house.

Chapter Twelve

Jane Mason watched as the boy on stage dropped to his knees and stretched out his arms away from his sides. He hung his head and closed his eyes and Jane sat further forward, concentrating on the agony in his face and the small, twitching movements in his fingers; she could almost see the barbed wire that was meant to be supporting Captain Palmer's dying body. She smiled, covering her mouth with her copy of the script so the other boys on the stage wouldn't see how pleased she was. She had been proved right: Mark Redpath was a natural. She allowed him to go on kneeling there, keeping up that crucifixion pose for longer than was necessary. He was beautiful and sometimes she liked to watch him suffer.

Jane stood up and clapped her hands twice. 'All right. You can relax now, Redpath, before the stigmata start breaking out.'

The other boys on the stage sniggered and as Mark Redpath scrambled to his feet she saw that he was blushing. Softening her voice she said, 'Well done, all of you, especially you, Redpath. All right. Home. I think we've all had enough for one day.'

Her first world war soldiers became schoolboys again, joking and jostling each other down the steps of the stage. Slinging satchels on their shoulders, they filed out, their heavy footfalls echoing around the school hall. As she gathered her coat and briefcase from a chair, she became aware of someone watching her, and looked up to see Redpath hovering at the hall doors.

As she approached him he held the door open for her. 'Was I really all right, Miss?'

'Fishing, Redpath?'

'No, Miss!' His blush deepened. Quickly he said, 'I wasn't sure, that final scene ...'

'What about it?'

He let go of the door. 'It seems, well, I don't know ... a bit too dramatic?'

Jane smiled to herself. At first she'd worried that he was too modest a boy to carry off Captain Edward Palmer's excesses. Finally, however, his modesty was exactly what had counted in his favour. He brought humility to the role, a trait she'd come to realise it sorely needed.

Buttoning her coat she said briskly, 'It's a very dramatic scene. Palmer's done this terribly noble, selfless thing.'

'I understand that – but perhaps he wouldn't be so, well...'

'Spit it out, Redpath.'

'Showy?'

Jane laughed. 'He's very wordy, I agree. But that's how the part's written. And who are we to argue with the great poet?'

Flatly he said, 'Nobody, Miss.'

'That's right.' She wound her scarf around her neck and pulled her gloves from her pocket. 'Now, I have a home to go to even if you don't.'

He stood aside. As she was about to go he said hurriedly, 'When he was at school my brother played the part in front of Michael Morgan himself.'

Jane paused. Although she was tired and longed to be home, her curiosity got the better of her. 'Did he get to meet him?'

'They already knew each other.' The boy glanced away, obviously embarrassed. Managing to look at her he said, 'He's actually only my half-brother. He's been away, in the RAF. Fighter pilot. He was shot down ...'

She nodded, remembering the gossip she'd heard in the staff room.

'I know he would have been a terribly good Palmer, much better than me –'

'I'm sure you'll be just as good.'

His voice became even more rushed as he said, 'I thought,

since he knew Michael Morgan and everything, I thought – if it's all right with you – that we could ask him to a rehearsal. He might be able to give me some tips –'

She frowned at him. 'I don't think you need any tips, Redpath. Besides, how do you think the other boys would feel about having someone sitting in like that?'

'They wouldn't mind. I asked them …'

'Did you now? Before you asked me? You shouldn't have done that.'

'Sorry, Miss.'

'So your brother knew Michael Morgan?'

'Yes! He used to go to his house and everything.'

'And you don't think he would mind giving up his time to watch you rehearse?'

'No! He's not working …' He trailed off blushing again.

Jane smiled. She liked this boy more each time she spoke to him. 'All right. Ask your brother to sit in one afternoon, if you wish. I don't mind. Now, let's go home. We're finished for today.'

Home for Jane was a small, semi-detached house across the road from Thorp Park gates. The house was newly built when they bought it, its empty rooms smelling of fresh plaster, putty and paint. She remembered standing in its bare, sunny front room and turning around slowly, her arms out-stretched to gain a true measure of her brand new space. There were no lace curtains at the window, no rag-rugs on the floor, and when she'd laughed at this liberating starkness the noise had seemed so indecently loud she'd covered her mouth with her hand. She'd vowed then that she wouldn't clutter her home with the ugly china dogs and Toby jugs, cushions and crocheted doilies that covered every surface of her mother's terraced house. When she'd stopped turning, excited and dizzy, she'd caught Adam watching her from the doorway, his handsome face clouded by the grief that in those days she couldn't begin to fathom. She remembered how quickly he'd subdued her that day, as though she was a drunk confronted by a policeman.

Walking up the tiled path to the house, Jane took her key from her handbag, holding it out like a weapon ready to stab into the lock. As she opened the door she called out loudly, 'It's me.'

She stood in the hallway, listening, uncertain if he was home. Occasionally he would disappear for hours, returning late at night, and she would listen to him creep up the stairs, closing his bedroom door so softly as though terrified of waking her. In the morning he'd have such a look of shame about him his whole body would seem bowed. Remembering, Jane shuddered and caught sight of herself in the hall mirror as she pulled off her gloves. She looked away quickly. Her face was pinched and prissy, condemning. No wonder the boys called her Stony Mason.

In the kitchen, Jane went to the sink to fill the kettle. Through the window she could see Adam on his hands and knees in the scrubby, unproductive patch that was their vegetable garden. He was frowning and his glasses had slipped far down his nose, his hair flopping into his eyes. She watched him, able to appreciate his lean, wiry body, just as she might appreciate a fine sculpture in a museum. His arms were particularly well formed and his hands were strong and expressive even as he reached out to grub up a dandelion. Gentleman's hands, her mother had called them.

Setting the kettle on the stove, Jane lit the gas and sat down to take off her shoes. She kneaded the bunion forming on the side of her foot, absently looking around her. The kitchen was her favourite room, small and square with a tiny table and two chairs pushed against one wall. Taking up most of the wall opposite was a Welsh dresser, the first piece of furniture she had ever bought. Over the six years of her marriage she'd filled it with her finds, Royal Doulton plates, Wedgwood cups and saucers, a Spode server and a tureen in the blue of forget-me-nots. Most of the pieces were seconds, found in flea markets and in the dark, poky junk shops that lined the narrow alleys running off Thorp High Street. The tureen, however, was perfect, part of a discontinued dinner service bought in a sale. She had wanted it for its colour, because some colours had the power to thrill her, those rare colours that brought back snatches of scenes from other lives she'd lived.

Occasionally Adam would examine a new find, holding it up to the light to test the fineness of the porcelain, turning it to read the maker's name. He appreciated expensive things, even those flawed in the small ways that made them affordable. Years ago, she had mistaken this appreciation for interest, but he had only smiled politely at her enthusiastic description of why she thought a cup or plate beautiful. Nowadays she didn't try to explain and, anyway, her finds were becoming rarer. All her spare time and effort was taken up in queues for food. She sighed, remembering that she'd forgotten to shop for supper.

From the back door Adam said, 'You're home.' He looked mildly surprised and she knew that he'd lost track of time in the garden, worrying over the endless problems besetting a headmaster with too few teachers and too many pupils. Since becoming head at the beginning of the war lines had appeared on his face, grey hair at his temples. All the same, he looked younger than his fifty years.

Jane got up and made a pot of tea. Washing his hands at the sink Adam said, 'How was rehearsal? That Redpath boy – he's coping still?'

'Yes.' She stirred the tea, in a hurry for it to brew. She would take her cup upstairs and drink it as she waited for the bath to fill. It was what she always did when she came home, one of her ways of avoiding Adam's school-talk.

Just as she was about to go Adam said quickly, 'So you think Redpath is up to the mark?'

She looked at him. 'Adam, you're not going to interfere in the play, are you?'

'I've more important things to worry about.'

From the kitchen door she said, 'I think there's an egg in the larder. Feel free to have it for your supper.'

In the lounge bar of the Grand Hotel the pianist played *I'll be Seeing You*. Nina glanced around. A couple sat at one of the tables, leaning together so that their foreheads almost touched, the man's hand on the woman's knee. They both laughed, drawing apart suddenly, each mirroring the other with empathic precision. The barman caught her eye. Casting a glance in the lovers' direction he turned back to her and smiled wryly. 'What can I get you, Miss?'

She had taken off her wedding ring and had forgotten to put it back on again. Fingering the place where it should have been she said, 'Gin and tonic, please.'

'If you'd like to sit down I'll bring it over.'

She sat furthest away from the piano, in the corner with the clearest view of the doors. That morning Hugh had moved out of Bobby's house in to the hotel and before he left she'd agreed to meet him here. She hadn't expected Hugh to be late and it occurred to her that he might not come down from his room at all. Despite their lovemaking last night, this morning he'd seemed cool. Over breakfast the atmosphere between Bobby and Hugh had made her heart quicken with anxiety. She had almost expected them to come to blows and guessed that only the presence of Bobby's brother stopped them. She sighed, barely acknowledging the barman who set her drink down gently on a coaster in front of her. It seemed naïve now to have expected Bobby to behave towards Hugh as he had towards her husband Nick.

Bobby had said, 'There's a man I want you to meet.'

He'd been driving, changing down the MG's gears as he took a bend too quickly. Moving up the gears again, he glanced at her. 'He's very sweet. I don't think I've ever met anyone sweeter.'

It was April 1940. She remembered that daffodils were in bloom on the verges, a yellow blur of flowers as Bobby sped along, faster and faster until she thought they might take off. It never occurred to her to be frightened, he was so confident, as though the car was part of him. The top was down, her hair blowing across her face so that she wished she'd worn a scarf, her cheeks chilled by the rush of disorientating air. The sun shone so brightly it hurt her eyes and there was a smell of petrol fumes and new grass. Beside her, in his uniform and officer's cap, Bobby lit a cigarette, hardly taking his eyes from the road. Earlier, as he'd helped her into the low car, he'd smiled and kissed her. Although he'd spent the morning in her bed, she wanted him again, a greedy, urgent want that made her knead his thigh as he drove out of London and along the Kent lanes.

He'd stopped the car. Taking a blanket and picnic hamper from the boot, they walked a little way along a wooded path until they came to a clearing. Primroses grew in thick blue and yellow clumps and daffodils and narcissus bloomed beneath the branches of spindly mountain ash. When the blanket was spread on the earth the layers of dead leaves beneath it made a soft bed. Bobby lay on his side next to her, gently resisting her efforts to draw him closer.

'This man,' he said. 'His name's Nick O'Rourke. He's a Canadian and so homesick he showed me photographs of his *Mom and Dad*.' Bobby picked up a twig, poking it in the ground as he said, 'Mom and Dad, brothers and sisters. A whole tribe of them. They're farmers, in Toronto ...'

Nina pressed her fingers to his mouth but he drew away. Propping himself up on his elbow he said, 'There's something extraordinary about him, something ... generous. He's such a good pilot. Knows all the tricks, I couldn't teach him very much.'

Coldly she said, 'But you think I could?'

Falling on to his back he stared up at the sky. After a while he turned to look at her and the thin branches of the trees cast a pattern of shadows over his face, disguising his expression. Softly he said, 'He's a good person. I feel ashamed, sometimes, when I'm around him, when I remember...'

'We're not ashamed! We should never be ashamed – you said so.'

He fumbled in his pocket for his cigarettes and held the case out to her but she shook her head. After a while, exhaling smoke, he said, 'We drove over to the Rose & Crown yesterday, that little place I told you about the others haven't discovered yet. He told me about his childhood. Like something out of *Huckleberry Finn*.'

He got to his feet suddenly, pacing as though he couldn't keep still. Picking up another stick he snapped it in two, throwing the pieces high into the air. 'He told me that the others think I'm stand-offish. Well, I didn't need him to tell me that. I know what they think of me and it's a sight bloody worse than stand-offish.'

She remembered scrambling to her feet and going to him. She'd slipped her arms around him, pressing her cheek against his back and the reassuring roughness of his tunic. Her hands linked across his chest and she could feel his heart pounding as though he'd been running. She held him tighter, needing him to be calm again, afraid of the mood he was working himself up to. She held her breath; from hard won experience she knew it was best to be as silent as possible.

At last his hands covered hers. Painfully he said, 'I don't care what they think.' He spun round to face her so suddenly she stepped back. 'There's a dance organised at the mess tonight. Come back with me. I want to show you off to them.'

On the other side of the hotel bar the pianist stopped playing only to start after a heartbeat's pause on *Moonlight Becomes You*. Nina sipped her drink, remembering how Bobby had introduced her to Nick, how, with his hand light on the small of her back, Bobby had propelled her towards him, smiling as he said, 'Nick, this is Nina, an old friend. Nina – isn't Nick the most handsome man you ever saw?'

Embarrassed, Nick had laughed. He'd frowned at Bobby before turning to her. 'Bob says you two go way back.'

The mess hall had seemed unusually bright, crowded with airmen and WRAF who danced and flirted enthusiastically under the stark electric lights. There were only a few civilians, all young women, shyly clustering around the edge of the dance floor. From the stage a girl sang *Paper Moon*, her voice sweet and clear and smiling through the sad words. She noticed that the singer couldn't keep her eyes off Bobby, the song's sentiments sung directly at him. Nick had grinned at her. 'Looks like Bob's made a hit with someone.'

Bobby cast her a quick, questioning look. She nodded an almost imperceptible consent as the familiar dull ache settled around her heart. She could stop him, if she could find the courage, she could stop him seducing this one girl, this one night, and he would be amused or angry or both. He would remind her that they were both free to do as they chose.

As she'd watched Bobby walk away to stand closer to the stage Nick said, 'Would you like to dance, Nina?' She remembered he put a particular emphasis on her name, the two syllables rising and falling in his soft, North American accent. When he took her in his arms on the dance floor he seemed shy of her and he held her lightly, as though Bobby had told him she was breakable.

'Nina?'

Hugh Morgan stood over her. Startled, Nina looked up at him and he smiled awkwardly. 'I'm so sorry I'm late. I fell asleep again.'

'It doesn't matter.' She stood up. Glancing towards the courting couple she said, 'Let's go somewhere else, shall we?'

'I don't know if there is anywhere else. I don't think Thorp has a restaurant except the one here in the hotel.'

'There's a pub across the High Street, I passed it as I came here.'

'The Castle & Anchor? It's rough –'

'I don't mind. Anywhere but here.'

Hugh brought her a half-pint of beer as she'd requested and frowned as she sipped at its creamy head.

'Is it all right?'

'Yes. I enjoy beer.'

'Well, good. A cheap date, I like that.'

'You say horrible things.'

He laughed bleakly. For the first time she noticed how weary he looked, how dark the rings were beneath his eyes. There was a gleam of sweat on his forehead and he wiped at it discreetly with his handkerchief. He glanced around the busy pub uncomfortably. She wondered if he'd ever set foot here before. The Castle & Anchor was like the pub close to her London flat that she visited occasionally with Irene: noisy and warm, its air hazy with cigarette smoke, its brown varnished walls decorated with mirrors advertising Beefeater Gin and Guinness. She could relax there, by the coal fire in its ornate

355

grate, she could be one of the girls that Irene collected around her, ordinary and loud and brash – the girl she might have been if not for Bobby.

She said, 'Is the hotel comfortable?'

'It's all right.' He offered her a cigarette and when she declined lit one for himself. 'It's a bit down on its luck, the Grand. I remember it used to be … grander.' Quickly he said, 'It's fine. The bed's fine.' After a moment he asked, 'What did you do today?'

Bobby had said, 'We could go for a drive, if you like. The sea's not far away.'

She hadn't seen the sea for years and he had seemed relieved at her enthusiasm as he said, 'It'll be quiet there, off-season. We'll have the beach to ourselves.'

'Bobby took me to Saltburn.' She met Hugh's gaze. 'We walked along the pier and had fish and chips. Then later we had tea in one of those big hotels along the front.'

He nodded. 'The Queens? The Queens does Bob's kind of teas, all crustless cucumber sandwiches and iced fancies. Does the dining room still have the cherubs on the ceiling? Right up Bob's street, that kind of thing.'

Bobby had smiled at the garishly painted ceiling. 'I'd imagined they would have painted it over by now, that someone would have thought it unseemly during the war.' He'd glanced at her. 'I used to wonder how such fat angels got off the ground with such small wings.'

Hugh said, 'Did you have a nice time at the seaside?'

'Yes.'

'Dad used to take us there – to Saltburn. Me and Bob, and Mum to push Dad's chair. Looking back I can't believe how long-suffering Mum was – I'm only surprised she didn't leave him sooner.'

'Do you ever see her?'

'Not often. She lives in Cornwall. Near that cottage I told you about.'

She sipped her drink, aware of his eyes on her. The silence grew more strained. At the bar a group of men laughed loudly and Hugh glanced over his shoulder towards them. Eventually he said, 'I had a rotten day, if you're interested.'

'I'm sorry.'

He snorted. 'God knows why I'm here. I can't say I wasn't warned.'

'About?'

'Thorp. Coming home.' Taking a long drink from his pint of beer he wiped his mouth with the back of his hand. He seemed to make an effort to lighten his voice. 'Odd that you went to the seaside. I've thought about the sea all day. If I'd known you were going I might have come with you.'

'You would have been welcome to.'

'Of course. All friends together.'

He bowed his head, rolling his cigarette around the rim of the ashtray in the centre of the table. After a while he said, 'I was offered a job today in a bank. If I go to night school and sit exams eventually I could make it all the way up to branch manager. I'll be expected to sit exams. I was an officer, you see – can't get away with just being a lowly clerk the rest of my life.'

'Will you take the job?'

'Maybe. I don't know.' He exhaled heavily. 'Listen, why don't you stay with me at the hotel tonight? Bob wouldn't mind – he's had you to himself all day ...'

'No, Hugh. I'm here to see him.'

'And to hell with me?'

'He doesn't have anyone else.'

'He doesn't need anyone else. Please, Nina.' He began to cough and he pulled out a handkerchief to cover his mouth. His face became pale, the cough racking his body. The film of sweat on his forehead became more obvious and his eyes were brightly feverish. 'I think I may be coming down with something.'

'Do you want to go back to the hotel?'

He nodded. As he got up he leaned on the pub table for a moment before falling in a dead faint to the floor.

Bobby said, 'You were right to bring him here, of course. You couldn't leave him alone.'

He had helped her walk Hugh from the taxi into his house and upstairs. Semi-delirious, Hugh had fought against them but Bobby's strength had surprised her and between them they managed to undress him and put him to bed. Bobby had pressed his hand to Hugh's forehead. He'd looked up at her, concerned. 'I'll call a doctor.'

The doctor had left a few minutes ago and Hugh was sleeping fitfully. In the kitchen Bobby poured her a cup of tea and they sat beside the dying fire. Her hands were still trembling.

'I didn't know what to do. He looked so ill –'

'Doctor Maynard said it's only 'flu. He'll be fine.'

'He fainted!'

Bobby laughed. 'He used to faint when we were children, in infants' assembly. I used to think he only did it to get out of singing hymns.'

'It's not funny.'

'No.' He sighed. 'Poor Hugh. Have you eaten?'

'I'm not hungry.'

'Are you sure? I could make you a sandwich.'

'I'm fine.' Hearing the irritation in her voice she said more calmly, 'I'm sorry. I know you don't want him here.'

'I don't mind, under the circumstances. At least he'll be staying in his own bed.'

She looked away, ashamed. 'I'm sorry about that.'

'I'll get over it

'All the same, I'm sorry. It was unforgivable and you have a right to be upset.'

'I've no right at all.' After a while he said too lightly, 'You never did tell me what you thought of his father. Did the great poet live up to your expectations?'

'He's very charming. Charismatic.' She smiled, remembering how Mick Morgan read his poetry in the bookshop. He had used the book only as a prop and read from memory, word perfect, each inflection and emphasis exact, his attention focused on his audience. She'd noticed how the other women in the shop watched him and guessed they all felt as she did, that he only had eyes for her.

Bobby said, 'I suppose he looks old now, does he?'

'Not really. Early fifties, I'd say. His hair's still very black –'

He snorted. 'He dyes it. He's the vainest man I've ever met.'

'Why do you and Hugh dislike him so much?'

Fumbling to light a cigarette, he glanced at her. 'Hugh dislikes him? Really?'

'You know what fathers and sons are like.'

He drew deeply on his cigarette. At last he said, 'Mark's starring in his school production of *Theory of Angels*. He's Captain Teddy Palmer. He wants me to sit in on a rehearsal and give him a few tips.'

'Why?'

'I played Palmer at school, too. Won a cup for best performance.'

She laughed. 'You never told me that before! So, will you help Mark?'

'I don't know. I doubt it.'

'You should. Why not, anyway? It will be fun.'

'Fun!' He laughed bitterly. 'Fun having a lot of sixteen-year-old boys not know where to look when they meet me?'

'Most people behave well.'

'You think so?'

'Bobby, remember what Doctor Baker said – you have to live your life without worrying about other people. And sometimes you only imagine that others are staring – most of them are too wrapped up in themselves to notice you.'

He became quiet and she fought the urge to say more of the bright, encouraging words she had said so often in the past. She knew that some people did stare at him, but more didn't. Most people were kind: she firmly believed this, but Bobby believed in unkindness. 'He expects the worst from people,' Doctor Baker had told her. 'It will make it worse for him when he leaves here.' The doctor had gone to the window of his study and looked out on the hospital grounds where other men like Bobby sat drinking beer in the sunshine. 'Our expectations of others are usually met, I find,' Baker said. He had laughed suddenly. 'If only I could get Bob to stop taking himself so bloody seriously!'

Gently she said, 'Go to the rehearsal, Bobby. Mark's so proud of you – anyone can see that. Don't let him down.'

He turned from staring at the fire to look at her. 'I should go and see how Hugh is. That doctor said I should keep an eye on him.'

Chapter Thirteen

Hugh was sleeping. He had kicked the blankets away and Bobby covered him again. His hair clung damply to his forehead and his cheeks were flushed, his eyes moving restlessly behind their closed lids. As Bobby stooped over him he mumbled anxiously from his sleep and Bobby touched his arm lightly. 'It's all right, Hugh. You're safe now.' He knew he was dreaming of the sea; earlier as he had helped Nina undress him, he had cried out orders to his men and his voice had been full of the kind of terror he recognised from his own dreams.

He sat down on the chair beside the bed. Already the room smelt of Hugh's sickness although yesterday it had smelt only of dust and old, darkly varnished furniture. The house had five bedrooms in all and two attic rooms. He had hardly set foot in the attics since he was a child and he and Hugh built dens amongst the abandoned metal bed frames once slept in by long-forgotten maids. His school trunk was there, his father's trunk too. Inside the trunks there would be keepsakes his grandfather couldn't bring himself to throw away but couldn't bear to have around. The cup he'd won for playing Palmer was stored in his trunk. Bobby had hidden it away himself before he left for London.

The day he left his grandfather had said, 'Write to me – let me know you're safe, at least.'

'As long as you promise not to tell them where I am.'

'Bobby, please don't do this – your mother will worry so!'

'No she won't!' He had laughed and even to his own ears it sounded forced. He was sixteen; it was the month after the play, after Henry Vickers. He had almost not gone home for the summer at all, had almost boarded the London train from the small station in the village near his school. But he had needed to see his grandfather again, to show his new self to him and be assured that his grandfather still loved him. He'd stayed only one night in Parkwood and his grandfather had watched him with increasing concern. If he'd stayed any longer he might have found him out.

There was a movement from the corner of the bedroom and the kitten Mark had rescued appeared from its hiding place. It sat watching him and he held out his hand until it approached him cautiously. He scooped it up on his knee. The animal purred loudly, bumping its small, bony head against his hand. He thought of the stray cats that stalked the London alleys where the bins of expensive hotels spilled scraps of chicken and cheese rind, shrimp and oyster shells and scraped out jars of caviar. He remembered the homeless men who searched through the waste of such high-class dinners. He had almost been one of them: by the time Jason found him in that Soho café almost all his money was spent.

Sitting in the café he had known that Jason was watching him, had been watching him from the moment he came in with the last of his pennies in his pocket, just enough for a cup of tea. He had taken his cup to a corner table and sat with his back to the man who couldn't seem to take his eyes off him. The intensity of his stare made him feel unclean; his flesh crawled and he hunched further inside his coat, wanting to make himself small and unworthy of notice. He remembered that a feeling like stage fright gripped him, causing his hands to shake a little as he sipped his tea. Looking back it seemed right and proper he should have felt that peculiar kind of nervousness – he performed for Jason; whenever he was with him everything he did was an act.

Jason had sat down opposite him. He didn't speak but after a while ducked his head to look into his downcast face. He smiled slowly. 'Hello, you look hungry.'

Bobby had turned away to the café's window. Outside rain had begun to fall, a heavy summer downpour that sent rubbish scuttling along the gutter in a fast-moving stream. He watched the rain run down the grimy glass, willing the man to go away. Instead he heard him strike a match and smelt his cigarette smoke. He made himself turn to him, and put on his best Captain Palmer voice.

'I'd prefer it if you sat somewhere else.'

The man laughed. 'Really? Would you really *prefer* it?' His voice was soft and cultured, as though he'd spent time working on it and expunging any betraying accent he once had. He was blandly handsome, his complexion pink and well scrubbed and closely shaved. He took off his trilby hat and placed it on the chair beside him before smoothing back his red hair. Ash from his cigarette fell to the table and he brushed it to the floor with the side of his hand, smiling apologetically. Bobby caught a whiff of cologne, subtle and expensive as the diamond ring he wore on his little finger.

Calling out to the man behind the café's counter he said, 'Pedro – egg and chips for the young man here, if you don't mind.' He looked at him 'Bacon, sausage?' He nodded as though Bobby had ordered the meal himself. 'Excellent choice.' Raising his voice again he said, 'The full works, Pedro, please. Fried bread, too.'

Holding out his cigarette case he said, 'Do you smoke?'

'No. And please, I don't want anything to eat.'

'Yes you do! Christ – you look starving! What's your name?'

Bobby kept silent and eventually the man said, 'Listen – whatever your mother told you about never talking to strange men, forget it. Tell me your name – I won't steal it from you.'

Bobby looked down at his cup. 'Bob.'

'Bob? Oh well, it's a start.' He sat back in his chair, frowning as he studied him. 'Have you run away from home, Bob?' Gently he said, 'Do you have somewhere decent to stay?'

'Please leave me alone.'

A plate of food was set in front of him. Although he was hungry Bobby ignored it. Finishing his tea he stood up.

'Where are you going?' The man grabbed his hand and held it tightly. Appalled, Bobby tried to pull away but the man only laughed. 'Don't look so horrified! Look, sit down and eat your dinner. You don't want to offend Pedro, do you? He's not a bad cook, really.'

'I don't want your charity!'

'Oh, it's not charity. More an investment, I'd say.' He was still holding his hand, his grip tightening. Not knowing what else to do Bobby sat down and the man released him. 'There, that's a good boy. Now, eat up. You look like you might pass out from hunger.'

In Hugh's bedroom the kitten turned in circles on Bobby's lap, kneading his thighs with its claws unsheathed so he felt their pinpricks through his trousers. After a while it settled down to sleep. In the bed, Hugh rolled on to his back and flung his arm out so that his fingers almost brushed Bobby's knee.

Jason had watched him eat and Bobby remembered the satisfaction he seemed to take from his watching. Despite his hunger the food became a trial he had to get through, each mouthful a lump of gristle to be swallowed quickly. All the time he kept his head bowed, studiously avoiding the man's gaze.

When he'd almost finished the meal, the man said, 'I'm Jason, by the way.'

He ignored him, pushing his plate away. Bacon rind curled in a pool of hardening egg yolk and the chips he couldn't bring himself to go on eating took on the filthy, waxy appearance of food tossed into the gutter. The little he had eaten sat like a stone in his stomach and he felt disgusted at himself. He was afraid of what this man – Jason – would want in return. He remembered the tenacity of his grip, the greedy look in his eyes as he watched him. He remembered Henry Vickers and his breath against his ear. As always the memory panicked him and he found himself saying hotly, 'I'm not a queer!' He felt his face burn, hating the way his voice had risen like an angry child's. Jason laughed as though astonished.

'No? Well, all right. I wasn't sure. Although you are a very beautiful boy.' He gazed at him, a different, cooler look and Bobby felt he was looking for faults he could rectify. At last he said, 'I'm a photographer.' Taking a business card from his pocket he shoved it across the table. 'I'd very much like to take your photograph. I will pay you, of course. I'll pay you quite a lot, actually.'

Hugh mumbled in his sleep. Opening his eyes he looked directly at Bobby. He frowned. 'Bob?' In groggy, dreamer's disbelief he said, 'It *is* you.'

'Yes.' Bobby touched his still outstretched hand. 'It's all right, go to sleep.'

In the café a group of men had come in, labourers who had been digging up the road a little further along. Rain had soaked their donkey jackets and they left muddy footprints from the door to the café's counter. They smelt of tar and coal braziers; they filled the place with their smell and bulky bodies and the man turned his cool gaze on them, as though they were a tableau to be lit. Keeping his eyes on the men Jason said, 'Come to my studio.' He looked at him. 'No strings. I just want to take your picture.'

Remembering, Bobby closed his eyes and rested his head against the chair's high back. He remembered how scared he'd been at the idea of being penniless in London, but more scared of going home to another of his stepfather's beatings. That morning he'd gone from hotel to hotel, asking for a job in the kitchens, the only job he thought himself even half-capable of. He had been met with hostility or amused contempt. There was no work to be had, and besides, he didn't look like a dishwasher: he was a posh little public schoolboy, soft and useless.

After Jason had left him alone in the café he'd picked up his card and read it carefully, turning it over in case there should be any more clues on its back. The card was thick, its edge sharply serrated, its print boldly stark. *Jason Hargreaves: Photographer*. Hargreaves seemed to him a safe, ordinary name. He traced his finger over the indent the name made on the card and read again the address typed in smaller print in the left hand corner. His studio was only a few doors away. He looked out of the window; the rain had stopped. He would go there, he decided, he would be paid to have his picture taken. After everything that had happened to him such payment seemed inevitable. He remembered that on his way out he caught sight of himself in the mirror behind the counter and thought how terrified he looked.

There was a tap on the bedroom door and he opened his eyes to see Nina standing in a pool of dim yellow light from the hallway. She whispered, 'How is he?'

Bobby got up and went to her. Just as quietly he said, 'He's sleeping. I'll sit with him tonight.'

'I should – I feel responsible for him being here.'

'No, you look tired. Go to bed.'

She smiled tearfully. 'I'm sorry – it's a mess, isn't it? I didn't mean to hurt you.'

He drew her into his arms and held her, careful not to hug her as tightly as he wanted to. He kissed her cheek and stepped back. 'Good night, Nina.'

'Good night.' She pressed her fingers to her lips then touched them to his mouth and he had the urge to stop being so carefully polite, to grab her and kiss her properly, his body hard against hers, his hands clutching her head so that she couldn't escape him. She would give in to him of course, out of pity and for the sake of old times, but she would be repelled, too, hating the feel of his claws and his thin, bloodless lips. She would probably squeeze her eyes shut and think of Hugh.

He turned away from her and closed the bedroom door behind him.

In the morning Nina went into the kitchen to find Bobby's brother making tea. He smiled shyly. Glancing towards the window he said, 'Bobby's in the garden. I was just about to take him a cup of tea. Would you like one?'

She went to the window and watched as Bobby walked across the lawn and sat down on a bench that encircled the base of a horse chestnut tree. He hunched forward, his hands grasped between his knees, and the tree's white, candle-like blossoms scattered petals on the breeze to catch in his hair. As though he sensed he was watched he looked up and she smiled, holding up her hand in greeting.

Beside her Mark said, '*Would* you like a cup of tea?'

'Oh – yes, thank you.' She smiled at him. 'Do you come here every morning?'

'Most mornings.' He turned away and busied himself pouring the tea. 'Do you want to take this out to him?'

Mark had made toast, too, and she carried it out on a tray, the tea spilling a little into the saucers. She sat down with the tray between them. 'Breakfast is served, m'lud.'

He looked towards the kitchen window. 'Is Mark being tactful?'

'I think so.' She followed his gaze. 'He's sweet.'

Still looking at the house, Bobby said, 'Hugh seems more settled, I think.'

'Good.'

'How do you like my garden?'

She looked around. The garden was very much as he'd described it: as though the trees had been planted to protect the house from prying. The chestnut tree they sat beneath was in the centre of a large lawn; other trees screened the house from the road. She imagined that whoever had planted them had no idea for the future other than this need for privacy, no thought given to how tall the trees would grow or how they would shade the house so that its rooms would be cold and gloomy even in the summer. The house itself seemed cowed by the trees, an impression heightened by its neglect. Guttering and a drainpipe had come away from the wall beside the kitchen window and a green stain was spreading where rainwater ran down unchecked. Following her gaze Bobby laughed despairingly.

'The place is crumbling. I keep expecting to come across Miss Haversham holed up in one of the bedrooms. Perhaps I should sell it.'

'And go back to London?'

'No. No, I don't think so.' He lit a cigarette as Mark walked towards them. Tossing the match down he said, 'Are you going, Mark? I don't want you late for school because of me.'

Nina said, 'I hear you're the star of your school play.'

He blushed.

She looked at Bobby. 'You are going to help Mark with the part, aren't you?'

Mark asked. 'Will you, Bob?'

'Of course he will!'

Mark grinned. 'I'll let Mrs Mason know.'

Bobby sighed. 'Go on. Get off to school.'

Watching his brother walk away he said, 'You shouldn't have told him I'd do it. He doesn't need me interfering.'

'It's just a school play, Bobby, that's all.' She stood up. 'I'll go and check on Hugh.'

Hugh lay in bed watching the shadows the trees made on the wall and ceiling. Every part of him ached as though he'd been tossed about in a dinghy on rough seas. Too weak to move, his head felt thick and full of the dreams that had troubled him all night. He thought of Bob sitting patiently at his bedside, how sometimes he thought he was merely part of his dreams only to wake fully and know that he was truly there, accepting the strangeness of it only to incorporate him into his dreams again. Sometimes Bobby was a child, at other times a grown man, his face as it should be. In other dreams his scars were worse than they really were and he became afraid of this silent, watchful man at his bedside. Hugh closed his eyes, worrying about what he may have called out from his sleep.

When he'd met Bob on Thorp Station he had found himself overcome with emotion. He wondered now if it was the start of this illness that had made him feel so susceptible to pity. He had felt it on the train when Nina had told him about her child's death: it was as though he'd been stripped of a layer of skin that had once insulated him from the grief and suffering of others. He had felt raw and emotional but also fervent, like one of his father's Catholic saints that had just been shown Christ's wounds. And so, as soon as he saw Bob on the platform, he had pulled him into his arms and hugged him. He had felt him stiffen with embarrassment until his damaged hands gently patted his shoulder and he stepped back. 'Hugh,' Bobby had said. 'How are you?' His voice was coolly polite.

Worse, beneath the coolness was a note of contempt so that he'd felt large and foolish and loathed his own clumsiness.

The bedroom window was open a crack, enough to allow in a breeze scented with horse-chestnut blossom. The tree's shadow made different patterns on the ceiling. He rested his hands flat on the eiderdown and felt the spine of a feather through the satiny material. He worked at it until gradually it broke through and the feather curled into his fist.

Hugh remembered the first time he had visited this house, ordered by his father to call for the silent little boy who sat next to him in Miss Gray's infant class. He had stood outside the house he knew Bobby went to after school, intimidated by its size and forbidding grandeur. He'd expected it to be grand inside, too, nothing like the boxy, dull little bungalow built to accommodate his father's wheelchair. Plucking up his courage, he'd rung the doorbell, believing a butler would answer. Instead, Bobby had opened the door and looked at him with a surprise he quickly covered up. He didn't remember him speaking, only that he turned away at once and led him through the untidy, cold and damp hall of his grandfather's house. His cheeks were striped with war paint and he wore a Red Indian's headdress made of card and braid and feathers. The gold and red feathers bobbed and shimmered as he walked ahead of him, their colours bright and intense in the brown varnish décor. As he followed him Hugh noticed a smell he couldn't place. Later, he recognised the smell as that of a house left to its own devices.

Bobby had built a wigwam in the overgrown garden. He led him inside and sat cross-legged on the ground. 'We should be blood brothers,' he'd said. Hugh had only nodded, mesmerised by the war paint and the feathers and the complicated construction of branches and canvas and blankets that made up their hiding place. He suspected that Bobby was allowed to do exactly as he pleased, as free from adults as Peter Pan, so he wasn't surprised when Bobby took a pin from his headdress and grasped his wrist. 'Hold out your finger. Are you scared?'

He'd shaken his head and with a quick sharp jab Bobby

pricked his fingertip. A bright jewel of blood appeared. Bobby raised his eyes to look at him. Still grasping his wrist he said, 'Now you.' He held out the pin stained with his own blood. Hugh's hands shook as he took it and Bobby watched him intensely as though afraid he would fail the test. He remembered squeezing his eyes shut as he stabbed the soft pad of Bobby's finger and the feel of their blood mixing as Bobby pressed their wounds together. When he opened his eyes Bobby had said, 'There. We're brothers. You can come here whenever you like.'

In his hot hand the feather from the eiderdown had become ragged. Hugh let it drift to the floor, remembering how later that afternoon Bobby had taken a feather from his headdress and handed it to him as he'd left. All at once Bobby had become the shy little boy he was at school rather than the confident Indian brave he'd been all day. 'Will you come back?'

Hugh remembered being surprised that he thought there could be any doubt. The world Bobby created was far more exciting than anything he had ever experienced. He touched his face where Bobby had smeared two broad, red lines: the war paint he would have to scrub away before his mother saw him. Suddenly the thought of returning to his neat and tidy home and his neat and tidy mother was more than he could bear. Fiercely he'd said, 'Of course I'll come back! We're brothers, aren't we?'

From the bedroom door Nina said, 'How are you feeling?'

He turned to look at her. The floral print dress she wore was shapelessly demure, its collar fastened with a pearl button, its skirt modestly covering her knees. Most curiously of all she wore flat, sensible shoes and her hair was pulled back into a severe bun so that it seemed to him she was trying to transform herself into the kind of girl his mother would approve of. He held his hand out to her and she came to stand at the foot of his bed.

He let his hand fall to the bed redundantly. 'Aren't you going to come any closer?'

'Can I get you anything?'

'Aspirin?'

'Yes, of course. I'll go and see if Bobby has any. Anything else?'

'Some company would be nice.'

'You should rest.'

'I am resting.' He began to cough and struggled to sit up. She watched as though trying to decide whether to make a move to help him.

When he stopped coughing she said, 'Do you think you need the doctor again?'

'Again?' He wiped cold sweat from his face and fell back on the hot, crumpled pillows. Frowning at her he croaked, 'Did a doctor come here last night?'

'Yes. He didn't stay very long – he was annoyed with Bobby for calling him out. Only 'flu, he said. Bobby told him that people die of only 'flu.'

'Very cheering.' He gazed at her. 'I'm sorry I spoilt your evening.'

'You couldn't help it. I'll go and fetch you that aspirin.'

As she was about to go he said, 'Will you sit with me when you come back?'

She hesitated in the doorway. 'We'll see.'

Bobby had come in from the garden and was washing the breakfast dishes.

'How's the patient? I've just remembered Maynard left a prescription for him.' He began to dry his hands. 'I'll go to the chemist now.'

'I'll go.' She smiled too brightly. 'I'd like a walk out and I don't suppose it's far, is it?'

Bobby frowned at her. 'No, it's not far.' After a moment he said, 'What's wrong, Nina?'

She laughed. 'Nothing! I just want some fresh air, that's all!'

'Are you sure?'

'Yes. You shouldn't have to run around after him when it's my fault he's here.'

'It's no one's fault.'

371

Sighing she said, 'He wants some company. You know how hopeless I am around a sick bed …'

'He's not so ill, you know.'

'I know.' She glanced away, embarrassed by his concern. Making an effort to sound cheerful she said, 'Now – give me the directions to this chemist's.'

Chapter Fourteen

In the school hall Jane climbed up on to the stage. She stood with her hands on her hips looking down at the group of boys sitting hunched around the cardboard brazier.

'You lot! You're supposed to be hungry, cold, terrified. You're in a trench and you're being shelled – you're not at a tea party! Try and look worried, at least!' She sighed, realising she couldn't get what she wanted from them today. 'All right. Let's stop for this afternoon.'

As the boys scrambled to their feet, she felt a presence at the back of the hall and glanced up. Adam smiled his encouraging headmaster's smile. He began to walk towards the stage and she smiled back at him, professionally.

'Headmaster. Come to check up on us?'

'I have.' His smiled broadened, his attention focusing on Mark. 'Redpath! That was an excellent speech you made just now. Every word clear as a bell!'

'Thank you, sir.' The boy blushed and once again Jane wondered how someone who was so forceful on stage could be so shy off it.

Gently she said, 'Off you go, all of you. See you tomorrow afternoon.'

Mark stepped towards her. Flustered he said, 'Miss, about my brother, is it still all right?'

'Have you asked him, then?'

'Yes, he'll do it.'

'Well fine, he can come tomorrow, if he wishes.'

When the boys had gone Adam stepped up on to the stage and wordlessly helped her to rearrange it for the morning. He glanced at her as he straightened a row of chairs for the

373

teachers who sat on the stage during assembly. 'Redpath is excellent. I had no idea. I thought he was rather a mousy child, in manner, at least.'

Jane kept her eyes on the chair she was moving. 'He's very handsome though. Just as Captain Palmer should be. Do you think the play was intended to be homoerotic?'

She sensed him stiffen. He took off his glasses and polished them briskly on the corner of his handkerchief. Hooking the metal frames over his ears he said, 'I always thought the character of Palmer was completely wrong, totally over-written. The men I knew who fought in the Great War were nothing like him. They were much more …' He frowned, as though trying to think of the right word. At last he said, 'Much more silent, I suppose.'

'Silence doesn't go down well in plays.' Moving a chair she said, 'Redpath wants his brother to sit in on a rehearsal. Apparently he played Palmer in front of Michael Morgan.'

'Did he indeed? God help him – Morgan is a nasty piece of work.'

Astonished she said, 'I didn't know you knew him.'

He stepped back, examining the rows of chairs for straightness, infuriating her with his familiar, deliberate pauses. At last he turned to her almost as if he'd forgotten she was there. Absently he said, 'We're the same age, Morgan and I. We lived in the same town for years. I knew him, of course I did.' He moved a chair a fraction to his right. 'I knew Morgan's brother, too.' Looking at the chairs again he said, 'His brother was the most beautiful man I've ever laid eyes on.' He turned to her, holding her gaze, acknowledging the taboo she had broken so that she felt like a child who had pretended to be too knowing.

Awkwardly she asked, 'What happened to him?'

'He moved away. Abroad.' He exhaled sharply. 'Right. All ship-shape again, ready for tomorrow. It's a shame we don't have a drama room big enough for rehearsals, but there we are – never enough money, never enough space.' Turning to her he said, 'Shall we walk home together?'

She nodded and he smiled briefly. 'I'd forgotten what a

good teacher you are, Jane. I was impressed with what I saw today.'

'Thanks.' She sounded so grudging that he laughed.

'Let's go home. I'll even cook supper.'

She remembered taking Adam home to meet her mother for the first time, how nervous she had been. She had bought a new outfit for the occasion, the kind of girlish, impractical clothes her mother liked to see her in. Her pale, summery frock, still stinking of dress-shop newness, stuck to her back in the stuffy train carriage as they travelled from Thorp to Durham, and the silly, jaunty little hat she'd bought to match seemed to wilt on her head like a just-picked dandelion. She had even worn white lace gloves. Used to seeing her in sensible, schoolmarm suits, when Adam called for her at her bed-sit he'd masked his astonishment with a smile. 'You look very nice,' he said, only to frown. 'Your mother's not expecting other guests, is she?' Adam didn't have much idea about mothers, especially not hers.

Because it was July and hot, her mother had set out a table on the scrubby piece of lawn in the back garden. On the uneven, not quite dried out ground, their chairs tilted and sank a little, making her feel even less sure than she normally did of what could and could not be trusted. Almost holding her breath she had watched her mother's reaction to Adam, wanting her to see what she saw in him, his steadiness and kindness, the fact that he was, at heart, a nice man. She didn't want her to notice how much older than her he was. She didn't want her to notice the way he fussed over small things, or that he could be cutting, accurately poking holes in the pretensions of others. In this, at least, her mother would have been an easy target. In her mother's parlour, surrounded by knick-knacks made of Whitley Bay shells and watched over by a picture of the king and queen and the little princesses, she had caught Adam looking around with a straight-faced interest that hadn't deceived her. Luckily the weather had been too warm to stay inside the house for long.

They had left Adam sitting alone in the garden while in the

375

dark little kitchen she helped her mother arrange a tray with fruit cake and ham sandwiches. Her mother had paused, lifting the net curtain to look out of the window at Adam. Smiling in approval she said, 'Such lovely manners! And his hands are so clean! Your father never could get his hands as clean as that.'

Cautiously she'd asked, 'You like him, then?'

'Of course! I couldn't be happier.' She managed to drag her gaze away from Adam to look at her. 'I'd given you up as an old maid.'

Adam had seen her as an old maid, a spinster to be rescued from the shelf. She knew that before they met he had made a calculated decision to marry, weighing up the pros and cons. But he had to find the right girl, one who would be so grateful to be saved from spinsterhood that the conformity of being a Mrs would be enough. As soon as they met he seemed to recognise that she wasn't a woman who took a fierce pride in being alone; she wasn't the type who was undaunted by men and scornful of women who seemed to need them so badly. He guessed that she was a woman who took to being single as though it was a debilitating illness, that she would become frailer and more frightened with each year alone.

Eating the supper of spam and boiled potatoes Adam had prepared, Jane glanced at her husband surreptitiously. His book was propped up against the teapot as he ate, its pages held back by the salt cellar. He frowned as he turned the page quickly; even this necessary interruption was an irritation.

'Good book?'

'Not bad.'

'But you can't put it down?'

Closing the pages on a bookmark he said, 'I'm being rude, sorry.'

'It's just something you do. I don't mind.'

'All the same.' He touched the book's cover as though he couldn't bear to be kept from it and she expected him to start reading again when he'd judged a decent interval had passed. Instead he surprised her by pushing it further away. Placing his knife and fork down on his cleared plate he said, 'Redpath's brother – I heard he was badly injured during the war, burnt

376

…?'

'Yes, I heard that, too. Lots of gossip doing the rounds.' She looked at him, challenging him to deny he didn't know as much as she did. He only nodded, impervious as ever.

'I knew his family – his father's family. Long time ago now – they're all dead. Just the boy left.' He cleared his throat, shifting slightly as though embarrassed he had brought the subject up. He smiled a little. 'Most of my generation is dead, the men, at least. I feel like a freak, sometimes, not only not dead but also unscathed. I suppose the men who were left out of this last war will feel the same, once it sinks in a bit.' After a moment he said, 'That play you're rehearsing – I never could stand its preaching. The first time I saw it – made myself see it – I wanted to smash Morgan's teeth in. I couldn't believe he could write such rubbish! Captain Palmer, for example …' Taking off his glasses he pinched the bridge of his nose, something she only saw him do when he was particularly upset. Eventually he said, 'I don't know. Perhaps Palmers did exist. Maybe Morgan based him on himself – arrogant, stupid and cruel.'

'There's more to Palmer than that –'

He looked at her sharply, a different, harder looking man without his glasses. Frowning he said, 'He leads his men to almost certain death, and quite cheerfully.'

'Bravely.'

'Oh, he was brave, all right. And that excuses everything, doesn't it? If they'd all stopped being bloody brave …' He exhaled, hooking his glasses around his ears. 'Sorry. It's just that I can't see the merit in what Morgan does, the way he rubs our noses in the pity of it.'

She was about to get up and clear the table when he said, 'Do you think Redpath's brother will come to the rehearsal?'

'I doubt it.'

He seemed about to say something only to think better of it. She felt bitter suddenly, the vicious urge to make him give himself away irresistible. Keeping her voice light she asked, 'Do you want me to let you know if he does turn up so you can introduce yourself?'

377

He held her gaze, a glimmer of contempt in his eyes. At last he said, 'I don't think he'd be interested in meeting me.' He stood up. 'If you don't mind I have work to do.'

When he'd gone she sat for a while at the table, remembering how optimistic she had felt when Adam proposed to her, imagining that living as man and wife without any of the complications of romantic love would be easy, comfortable even. Pragmatic and sensible, Adam had called it, and took the plush box from his jacket pocket, opening it to reveal an engagement ring; its chip of diamond winked as it caught the light. He had looked from the ring to her, smiling apologetically and her heart had softened with something like love for this kind, modest man. Now she wondered if he'd been apologising not for the smallness of the diamond but his uselessness as a potential husband.

They married one Saturday in late August and honeymooned in Scarborough. Their hotel room had a view of the sea and the crowded beach, a picture-postcard view complete with fat ladies with sunburnt skin and weedy husbands who rolled their trousers to their death-white knees and dangled toddlers at the sea's edge. Later, when the families had trailed away and deck chairs flapped their candy-striped canvas wistfully towards the sea, she'd got up from their bed, believing him to be asleep. She stood in the window, wishing herself far away, on one of the slow, grey ships on the distant horizon. The lace of her brand new negligee scratched at her breasts where it clung in a deep, revealing V, and still smelt of the perfume she had chosen with such care. The negligee was cut on the bias, a heavy, pale ivory satin, luminous as fresh water pearls, the most beautiful thing she had ever owned. It made her feel huge and clumsy. She put her hands to its lacy front and imagined tearing it in two.

From the bed Adam had said, 'I'm sorry.'

His voice had been quiet. He'd sounded young and frightened and despite herself she turned to him. Earlier he had taken off his glasses, folding them on the bedside table as though their removal was a necessary prelude to what he was supposed to do next. His face had looked changed without them, vulnerable, so that she had kissed his cheek. Remembering, she shuddered, turning away from him as a breeze from the open window raised goose pimples on her bare arms.

'Jane?'

She heard the scrabbling on the glass-topped table as he reached for his spectacles. The bed creaked and she knew that he had got up and was standing stiff and still as she was, working himself up to approaching her. Her skin bristled in appalled anticipation of his touch and she stepped closer to the window, staring down at the pavement where a gull attacked a discarded ice cream cone.

'Jane, I'm so sorry. I thought …' He trailed off, only to start again. 'I thought if I tried …'

He was standing only a step away now and she cringed, aware suddenly that the light from the window would make the ivory satin almost transparent, that she might just as well be naked. She rushed past him. Her coat still lay across the chair where she'd carelessly tossed it earlier and she put it on quickly, wrapping it around her, her arms crossed over her chest. She gazed at him. In his pyjamas he looked foolish, vulnerable even. There was a smudge of her lipstick on his cheek, her silly, pink, humiliating mark.

Trying not to cry she said, 'What did you mean, when you said you couldn't …' She closed her eyes and tears ran down her cheeks.

'Don't cry. Oh Christ, Jane … I'm sorry!'

She flicked the tears away impatiently. 'What did you mean? Couldn't tonight? Couldn't here? Couldn't with me?'

Helplessly he said, 'Perhaps if you come back to bed –'

'So you can *try* again?'

He slumped on the bed and covered his face with his hands. After a while he let them drop and hunched forward, his long fingers dangling between his knees. Dully he said, 'I thought that because I love you … because I love you it would be different. But it doesn't work like that – I suppose I knew, deep down. But I still love you. I respect you.'

'But you don't want to …' She couldn't bring herself to

say it, just stood with her coat pulled around her, the ludicrous night-dress hanging limply below its hem. Unable to say or do anything, she went on standing, waiting for him to do or say something that would make it all right.

At last he said, 'Perhaps if we give it time.'

Outside a gull screeched and he took off his glasses again and pinched the bridge of his nose. 'Let's get dressed,' he said. 'We can have a drink in the bar.'

Jane cleared the table and washed and dried the supper pots. Placing the knives and forks back in their drawer she wondered when she had stopped imagining that they were still giving it time, that there might still be a chance of their marriage being consummated. She supposed it was the day they had moved into this house, a few weeks after their wedding. Upstairs she'd found he'd set up a single bed in the spare bedroom along with his desk and his books and an armchair from the house he'd lived in as a bachelor. There had been no discussion; neither of them had mentioned that they had slept in separate rooms when they met at breakfast the next morning. Neither of them had mentioned it since.

She sighed, closing the cutlery drawer softly. She had work to do, too, a programme to design for *Theory of Angels*. There should be a picture of a soldier on the front cover, a beautiful boy in an officer's cap, his eyes dead, his lips parted a little as though about to speak. She smiled to herself bitterly. Adam knew this picture intimately – they both did, although he thought he kept it hidden in his family bible, a nice, ironic touch. On the back of the photograph of this beautiful boy a round, childish hand had written *To Adam, with my dearest love forever*. One day she would take the boy's picture from between the pages of Luke's gospel and place it in a frame on Adam's desk. Their separate beds would have to be discussed then.

Taking out her pencils and sketchpad, she sat down and began to draw until, in quick, fluid lines, the boy soldier appeared on the paper.

Chapter Fifteen

Hugh had been in bed for some days, becoming more bored as he recovered. Aware of his boredom, Bobby had offered to play chess with him. Downstairs, Nina had begun to prepare supper and after a while the smell of frying onion drifted up the stairs to Hugh's bedroom. He was about to move his knight, his fingers loose around the horse's head, when he put it down and fell back against his pillows. 'I can't be bothered, Bob.'

'Do you want to sleep?'

'No. I don't think I want to do anything. I don't think it's 'flu. I think it's bloody exhaustion. War sickness.' He smiled at him wearily. 'Or peace sickness, maybe.'

'You miss being told what to do.'

'Exactly!' He began to cough and Bobby helped him to sit up, plumping the pillows behind him. As he lay down again he said, 'I was sure of myself in the navy. Now ...' He laughed, coughing at the same time. 'Now I don't seem to know my arse from my elbow. I mean – a bank! Can you see me working in a bloody bank?'

Bobby thought how exhausted he looked. He'd been afraid the cough was something else and he'd called the doctor again. 'Pneumonia?' Doctor Maynard had been dismissive. 'No. A bad cold – burning the candle at both ends, I shouldn't wonder. Don't call me again for God's sake. How are you, anyway? Settling in all right?' Bobby had nodded and the doctor had looked relieved. 'Good show.' Patting his arm he'd added, 'Well done, anyway.'

Bobby smiled at the memory; he still wondered what he'd done well.

Hugh said cautiously, 'I suppose you miss flying, Bob?'

'Sometimes. *All* the time.'

'Could you, still, do you think? Fly, I mean?'

Bobby began gathering the chess pieces into their box. Each had its own plush nest shaped to fit the piece exactly. The set was Victorian, the same set his grandfather had taught him to play on, setting up the ivory pieces on their board on the kitchen table. George would tell him how well his father played, how he invariably won. Bobby invariably lost, and felt he disappointed his grandfather in not having Paul's aptitude for the game. He knew he didn't have his father's brains or charm just from the stories his grandfather told. He had his looks, that was all, a peculiarly mixed blessing that anyway had gone up in flames one bright morning in 1944.

Sensing Hugh waiting for an answer, Bobby said, 'I wonder what Nina's cooking.'

'Is she a good cook?'

'If I say yes will it have an impact on any future decision?'

Hugh laughed. 'Probably.'

'Nina is a good cook. The nuns taught her, she told me. Perfect mashed potato on pain of a beating from Sister Mary.' He looked up at Hugh as he pressed the last chess piece into place. 'She does a particularly good Irish stew.'

'What more could a man want?' After a moment he said, 'Listen, Bob – if you still love her – if you think there's still a chance the two of you, well, you know … I'll bugger off out of your way.'

Bobby folded the chessboard and placed it on top of the pieces. He thought how easy it had been to become friends with Hugh again, that he was as uncomplicated as he had ever been. Over the last few days he had begun to understand how much he'd missed him. Hugh belonged to a time before Vickers, before Jason and his pictures. When he was with him none of that might have happened. All the same, when he thought of Hugh and Nina together he felt sick with jealousy. Hugh was too much like Nick and from the moment he'd introduced her to that easy, good-looking man he'd regretted it, couldn't believe what a fool he'd been. He had wanted a sweet, ordinary girl who didn't know about his past, a girl his fellow officers would accept as the right sort. Knowing Nina put him even further outside their charmed circle. But from the moment he saw Nick lead Nina on to the dance floor all his reasons for wanting to let her go had suddenly seemed idiotic, snobbish and vile. It hadn't even worked – the others still thought he was an oddity.

Hugh said gently, 'Bob?'

Bobby looked at him. Dully he said, 'Nina's not interested in me. She loved Nick, her husband.'

'Did you know him?'

'Yes.' He remembered the first time he saw Nick unfolding himself from the cockpit of a Spitfire, how when he'd jumped down he'd caught his eye and held up his hand in a casual salute. 'Hi – it's Harris, isn't it? You weren't in the mess last night when I arrived – the others told me all about you.'

He remembered a sinking feeling in his guts as he'd wondered what his fellow officers had said about him.

Hugh said, 'What was Nick like?'

Bobby exhaled sharply, remembering Nick's voice over his radio, its terror as he realised he'd been hit. Aware of Hugh looking at him, he said, 'He was good-looking, kind. Good company. The best pilot I knew. I liked him.' After a moment he said, 'His plane was shot down over the Channel. Because I knew Nina they asked me to break the news to her.'

He remembered how Nina had stared at him in disbelief. Her pregnancy had just started to show and she'd spread her hands over the small bump as though to protect it. 'This is your fault,' she told him. 'All of this is your fault.'

Bobby stood up, too agitated by jealousy to keep still. 'I should let you rest.'

As Bobby reached the door Hugh said, 'I'm sorry to be a nuisance, Bob.'

'Try and sleep. Perhaps later you'll feel like eating.'

In the kitchen Nina said, 'How is he?'

'He's all right. He needs to rest, that's all.' He sat down and watched as she rolled out pastry. Flour was spread over the table and there was a dusting of it on her cheek. From the gas ring came a rich smell of braising meat. Beside her sat a spring cabbage, its dark green leaves splattered with mud as though it had just been picked from the garden. She caught him looking at it and grinned.

'I was passing those allotments behind the cemetery. I called out good morning to a man digging and he gave me that cabbage! Wasn't that kind of him?'

'Very. And all you said was good morning?' He raised his eyebrows.

'Well, we chatted a little.'

'I bet you did. I bet he couldn't believe his luck.'

'It wasn't like that! He was old – seventy at least. He was very sweet.' She began to ladle the meat into a pie dish. 'He said he knew you. Knew *of* you. He said how sorry everyone was about your grandfather and everything.'

He snorted. 'And everything.'

Ignoring him Nina said, 'He knew your father. Said what a lovely man he was, apparently they used to swap gardening tips.' She glanced at him slyly. 'He said what a terrible tragedy it had all been. Of course, I had to pretend to know what he was talking about, since I'd told him you and I were such good friends.'

Bobby lit a cigarette. Standing up to fetch an ashtray he caught a glimpse of his father's photograph on the mantelpiece. He picked it up and held it out to her. 'That's him. He killed himself when I was two. He was shell-shocked during the first war and never got over it. That was my grandfather's excuse, anyway.'

She looked from the photograph to him. 'Excuse?'

'He left his wife and baby alone and near penniless. Granddad had to give him a good reason to do such a thing – saints have to have bloody good reasons for being selfish.'

'Not selfish, surely? He couldn't have been in his right mind –'

'All the same – he had a responsibility. I could never have done what he did, no matter what.'

She set the photograph down gently. 'You look like him.'

'I did.' He remembered how he had looked even more like him in Captain Palmer's uniform and inevitably the memory led to Henry Vickers. He made an effort not to remember but the shame and humiliation was suddenly as fresh as it had been that night. Unable to keep still he paced the room, wanting to kick out at something. He turned on Nina, his impotent rage fuelled by jealousy.

'How could you have brought Morgan here? How could you do that? Do you have any idea what it felt like to hear him screwing you in the next room, to have to face you both the next morning? Did you have to rub my fucking nose in it like that?'

Her face paled. Her hand went to her throat and this familiar expression of vulnerability almost made him relent but his anger was too fierce. He felt consumed by pain and frustration and he reached across the table and grasped her wrist. 'Do you imagine Morgan cares about you? Someone who would fuck him as soon as look at him? Why do you have to behave so cheaply?'

She pulled away from his grasp. Coldly she said, 'You know why. We're both cheap! Cheap and nasty and used. It doesn't matter who we *fuck*.'

She gazed at him with the same hatred in her eyes he'd seen the day he told her of Nick's death. He felt all his anger drain away, leaving him empty of any feeling other than shame.

She laid the pastry on top of the meat and began to crimp its edges between her thumb and forefinger. After a while she said, 'It's steak and kidney. I thought it might tempt Hugh. It might even tempt you.'

He sat down. He knew she was used to his sudden flashes of temper, his vile tongue, he knew she made allowances for him. She had told him once that she would forgive him anything because of what he'd suffered. But that had been in the early days of his recovery when they both believed they had a future together. She might have said anything to him then, her pity was so great. Now she hardly said much at all, and she almost certainly wouldn't forgive such an outburst.

385

Still avoiding her eye he said, 'I'm sorry Nina.'

'It's all right. We don't have to say sorry to each other, do we?' Her voice was curt; he knew she wouldn't discuss it any more.

Awkwardly he said, 'The pie smells good.'

'Well, it's our combined meat ration, so it should. We'll have to live on cabbage soup for the rest of the week.'

He watched her as she opened the oven door, letting a blast of heat escape that he instinctively drew back from. A strand of her hair fell down and she hooked it back behind her ear with quick impatience. Her face was still pale, her expression still angry and closed against him. Without make-up or lipstick, with the dusting of flour on her cheek, she still looked extraordinarily beautiful. He remembered how Jason used to light her face from below so that her cheekbones looked even more sculptured, her lips even fuller: swollen ready for sex, Jason had said once. Jason had been studying her freshly developed photograph, and it was a throwaway remark made without his usual sly glance to see if Bobby had risen to his goading. By then there had been many pictures of Nina. He was used to seeing her through the camera's distorted eye. He was used to everything Jason did or asked them to do, was immune to how cheap he had become.

The pie was shoved into the oven and Nina straightened up. She looked at him. 'I was going to tell you later, after supper, but you might as well know now. When you were upstairs with Hugh a telegram came for me. It's from Davey. Jason died last night.' She seemed to watch for his reaction and he lowered his eyes to his cigarette unable to behave as she wanted him to. He heard her sigh in exasperation.

'He's asked me to the funeral,' she said. 'He's invited you, too.'

'I can't go.'

'You mean you don't want to.'

'Yes.' He looked at her. 'That as well.'

'Can't and won't? You sound like a spoilt child! You should go, it's the least you should do!'

'The least? You mean there's something else I should do?

What? Put up with Davey's snide remarks? All his queer friends whispering behind my back about what a shame it is I can't be their pin-up any more?'

'Jason was good to us –' She stopped herself from going on, aware of how ashamed he was of their mutual past. 'Anyway. He's dead and Davey wants us at the funeral.'

'He doesn't want me there. He's so jealous of me he can't stand to be in the same room.'

'He's not jealous – he just knows you hate them, him and his *queer friends.*'

'Well he's right about that.'

'Bobby, come with me to the funeral. I know you went to see Jason before you left London. This is a chance to say goodbye to him.'

'He wouldn't see me when I visited his flat.'

'I know. He was sorry about that.'

'I really can't face them, Nina. Besides, the church will be so full I won't be missed.'

'I'll miss you.'

He laughed bitterly. After a moment he said, 'I think Hugh will follow you to London when he's well.'

'That's up to him.' She picked up the cabbage and deftly cut it in half. 'Set the table, Bobby. Supper will be ready soon.'

Chapter Sixteen

Nina stood on Thorp Station, her suitcase at her feet, Bobby and Hugh on either side. She glanced at Hugh, worried about how pale he looked although he had insisted he was well enough to see her off. Earlier that morning he had come into her room as she'd packed and pulled her into his arms for the first time since the night they'd arrived. 'I'll miss you.' He kissed her, urgent with desire. 'Don't go. I don't think I can stand you going.'

She'd pushed him away gently.

The station was deserted but for the three of them and a porter who stood checking his watch a little further along the platform. Bobby turned to her.

'I've sent a wreath from us both, so you don't have to worry about that. It was expensive so let me know if I got my money's worth.'

Hugh snorted. Ignoring him Bobby said, 'Nina, I'll say goodbye now. You'll be all right, won't you? Tell Davey how sorry I am.' He kissed her cheek. 'Goodbye sweetheart.' To Hugh he said, 'I'll wait for you in the car.'

As soon as he began to walk away Hugh pulled her towards him. 'Should I come with you?'

'Don't be ridiculous, Hugh. You're barely well enough to be out of bed.'

'You know I'll be on the next train, don't you?'

She stepped away from him. She wished the train would come, she wished she was already on it and far away. She need to be away from Hugh for a while to gather her thoughts. Most of her thoughts were of how attracted she was to him, but she had to think more clearly – impossible when he was around her. She wondered if he really would follow her straight away, if he would find his way to the funeral and be shocked by Jason's friends. She remembered how uneasy he had been around even a homosexual man as mild and unaffected as Henry Vickers. Some of Jason's more flamboyant lovers would appal him; he would wonder even more what type of girl she was to be associated with such men.

Anxiously she said, 'Hugh, you mustn't come to London – not for a few days at least, until you're really better. Promise me.'

'A few days – I can't promise to keep away any longer.'

The train whistle sounded. Hugh held her tightly, only drawing away to kiss her. Holding her face between his palms he said, 'I do love you. I feel crazy with love for you. I'm not crazy, am I?'

She looked toward the train. 'I have to go, Hugh.'

He kissed her again, his tongue searching out hers until lust weakened her resolve and she pressed her body against his. She felt as though she could never get close enough to him and she stood on her toes and wrapped her arms around his neck, his strong, powerful bulk exciting her as it had from the moment that she saw him. He threw his head back and laughed, lifting her off her feet and crushing her still closer. With his lips close to her ear he whispered, 'I want to fuck you so much it hurts.'

She pushed away from him at once. Her legs felt shaky and she stumbled a little. Hugh caught her elbow. 'Steady!' There was laughter in his voice still and she looked at him angrily. Frowning he said, 'What's the matter?'

'Don't talk to me like I'm a whore. Don't ever use that word in front of me!'

The guard called out, 'All aboard.'

Panicked, Hugh said, 'My God, Nina, don't be angry with me now. I'm sorry. Really – it was just you make me feel so –' He shook his head, glancing away as though exasperated. Suddenly he snatched her bag up and got on to the train. He stowed it above an empty seat and turned to look at her. 'I'm sorry ... if you don't want to see me again –'

Quickly she said, 'I do! But you must go, Hugh, now, before the train leaves with you on it.'

He walked beside the train as it moved off, then ran to keep up. At the end of the station he stopped and waved to her until she could no longer see him. In the carriage her fellow passengers smiled at the romance of it.

Hugh slumped on to a bench outside the waiting room and lit a cigarette. He felt exhausted, the tightness in his chest worse than ever. He wondered how much of the pain was caused by her leaving and how much by the fear that his own idiot clumsiness might keep her away from him. He had never met anyone so difficult to understand; being with Nina was like being lost in the middle of the Atlantic without a compass, without sun or moon or stars. She made him feel afraid of a future without her.

Bobby came and sat beside him. He didn't speak, only lit his own cigarette. They smoked in a silence punctuated by Hugh's coughing.

At last Hugh said, 'We'll go.'

Bobby stood up, crushing his cigarette out beneath his shoe as he took his car keys from his pocket.

The rehearsal had started badly and disintegrated into farce. Jane watched in dismay as the boys fluffed their lines and missed their cues, their concentration totally shot by the appearance of the awkward young man sitting at the back of the hall. He had come in so quietly she hadn't noticed him at first. It was obvious he didn't want to draw any attention to himself. He sat on the edge of his seat, hunched forward as though listening intently. Jane sighed as Mark Redpath stammered over a line she thought he had learnt perfectly. Stepping on to the stage she clapped her hands.

'All right. Let's call it a day, shall we? And all of you – I want to see an improvement. The day will soon be here when you're doing this for real.'

Mark Redpath approached her. His face was flushed with embarrassment. Sorry for him, she said lightly, 'Is that your

390

brother, Mark?'

'Yes, Miss.'

They both stepped down from the stage and Mark looked towards the back of the hall where his brother had got up and was walking towards them. Jane began to feel afraid of how she might react to his disfigurement and found herself standing up straighter and smoothing back her hair.

Mark said, 'Mrs Mason, I'd like you to meet Bobby Harris, my brother.'

He said it with such pride that the young man laughed. He held out his hand to her. 'Hello. I hope you don't mind me turning up like this.'

Shaking his hand she said, 'No, of course not. I'm very pleased to meet you at last, Mark has told me a lot about you.'

She was smiling too broadly. Although she hardly ever blushed, she felt her cheeks colour. She glanced away towards the stage. 'I'm afraid you didn't catch us at our best.'

'Well, sometimes an unexpected audience can put a spanner in the works.' Turning to Mark he said, 'Mark, why don't you catch up with the others?'

He looked relieved to get away and there was an awkward silence as they both watched him leave. When he was out of earshot Bobby said, 'Mrs Mason, please say if you don't think this is a good idea. I don't know what Mark thinks I can do to help – besides, I'm quite sure you don't actually need my help. Don't feel you have to put up with me when you'd really rather not.'

He had the loveliest voice she had ever heard. Too taken up with listening to him she'd hardly taken any notice of what he'd actually said. There was a pause and she realised he expected her to respond. She opened her mouth to speak, only to close it again, at a loss to know what to say. At last she stammered, 'Mr Harris, really – I don't mind ...'

'If you're sure.' He turned to the stage. 'What are you doing for props and scenery?'

Pulling herself together she said, 'Not much. Pretty minimal, really – there's the question of money, and of course the stage directions in the play itself.'

'Of course. I seem to remember all we had was a makeshift table and a couple of broken chairs.'

'Yes. That's about it, really.' Too quickly she said, 'Your brother is very good, normally.'

'I did rather unsettle him, didn't I? All of them, in fact.' Smiling, he added, 'I have that effect on people.'

'It must be difficult for you.' As soon as the words were out she wondered if it was better left unsaid, but he only nodded.

'Some days are better than others.' For the first time he looked at her directly. 'I crashed my plane. My own fault – a second's lack of concentration and boom! Suddenly I was flying straight into a field.'

'I'm sorry.'

'What are you doing now?'

She must have looked puzzled because he became awkward suddenly.

He said, 'Sorry – I just wondered if you were going home or had to stay on … sorry.'

'No, it's all right. I was going home, actually.'

'Would you like a lift? You could tell me about how you think the play is coming along as I drive.'

In the car Bobby said, 'The car's been stood in a garage for months. She seems to be behaving herself but keep your fingers crossed.'

'I don't know much about cars – I've always found trams to be extremely reliable.'

Bobby laughed, turning the key in the ignition. 'Too old-fashioned.'

She smiled that odd smile she had, as though she was secretly amused by something. Looking straight ahead she said, 'Well, I'm older than you are, Mr Harris. I like old-fashioned.'

'Call me Bob. And I'm probably older than you think.'

'That sounds as if you don't know how old you are. What you meant was you're older than I probably think you are. I think.' She glanced at him. 'Sorry. Correcting people is a bad schoolteacher habit.'

She looked straight ahead again, her hand clasping a battered leather briefcase on her knee. It looked heavy but when he'd offered to carry it for her she'd declined quickly, glancing at his hands. She obviously though he looked incapable of managing a bag and he'd felt the familiar awkward atmosphere his injuries caused. Until that moment he'd thought she might be someone who could be more relaxed around him than most.

The car picked up speed. She stared out of the window, as though Thorp's dull streets looked more interesting from the seat of a car, and he took his eyes from the road to look at her. Despite what she said she looked young and fresh-faced. Jane Mason glanced at him.

'You should take the next left at these traffic lights.'

The lights showed red. Stopping, he pulled on the hand brake and fumbled in his pockets for his cigarettes. The lights turned green before he had a chance to strike a match and Jane reached across and took the cigarettes and matches from him. She lit one and handed it over.

'Thanks. Please, take one yourself.'

'I don't smoke.' After a moment she said, 'Mark told me you knew Michael Morgan.'

She sounded impressed and curious at the same time and he drew on the cigarette, fighting back the urge to be rude about him. Evenly he said, 'I knew him when I was a child, his son and I were – are – friends. When I joined the RAF we lost touch.'

'Did he live up to his image?'

'His image?'

'You know – a rough diamond, a working man's hero.'

Bobby thought of Mick Morgan's expensive tastes and impeccable, worldly manners. 'I didn't know people thought of him like that.'

'But his poetry suggests it, even if you haven't read the stuff they write about him.'

'I don't read his poetry.'

She smiled to herself. 'Some of it is rather emotive.'

393

He looked at her. 'Tell me what that means.'

'It manipulates your feelings. The famous poems tell you what to think instead of making you think.'

'Really? I've never met anyone who didn't think his stuff was marvellous.'

'There are a few of us about.' She glanced out of the window. 'My husband, for one.'

'Is the play emotive?'

'*Theory of Angels*? It's more honest, I think. And in an all boys school it's one of the easier productions to stage.' She smiled at him. 'No one has to wear a dress.'

He laughed. They came to a crossroads and he stopped and asked, 'Which way?'

'Oh – left. Sorry, I should've been paying attention.'

For a moment their eyes met and he was aware suddenly that for the last few minutes he'd felt normal and unselfconscious. He looked away quickly, knowing that the feeling could disintegrate if she betrayed the slightest bit of pity.

'Left, then,' he said, and shoved the car into gear.

He stopped in front of her house and Jane heard herself say brightly, 'Right. Here we are then. Thank you for the lift.'

'We didn't talk about the play or what you'd like me to do.'

'Do you feel you'd like to be involved?'

'Yes, I think so.'

'All right. The next rehearsal is on Thursday, four-fifteen, after school. How's that?'

'I'll be there.' Glancing towards her house he smiled. 'Your husband's seen us.'

Adam stood in the bay window, holding the curtain to one side. He was frowning and she sighed, not wanting to go in and face his interrogation. Getting out of the car she said, 'Thanks again for the lift. I'll see you on Thursday.'

She watched from the pavement as he drove away. He held a hand up in the rear view mirror in a farewell salute and she smiled, holding up her own hand in response. She was still smiling as she walked into the house. Adam came out into the hall to meet her.

'Who on earth was that?'

She brushed past him into the kitchen. Putting her bag down she took the kettle from the stove and filled it. He watched her from the doorway. At last he said, 'Well? Anyone I know?'

Lighting the gas Jane said, 'You knew his father, or so you said.'

'*That* was Bobby Harris?'

'You know, he was nothing like I expected.' Going to fetch milk from the pantry she looked at Adam, affecting a coolness she didn't feel. 'Nothing at all.'

Sitting down at the table he said curtly, 'And what did you expect?'

'Oh, you know what RAF types are like.'

'No, I don't.' He sniffed, frowning. 'You stink of cigarettes. I suppose he smokes like a chimney, does he? His father lived on the things.' He tugged off his glasses and polished them vigorously on a corner of his handkerchief. 'So, is he going to help with the play?'

'Yes.'

'How?'

'What?'

'*How*'s he going to help? You don't want to be undermined in front of the boys.'

'He won't undermine me. Do you want a cup of tea?'

He put his glasses back on and met her gaze. The lenses caught the evening sunlight and glinted. Not for the first time she felt for the boys who were sent to his study to be disciplined. Adam didn't use the cane, he prided himself on that, but he knew how to make someone feel worthless and ashamed, as though he made notes on everyone's quirks and faults to use against them should he need to. He went on looking at her, his eyes cold. When she looked away he said, 'Don't make a fool of yourself, Jane.'

She laughed, a silly, high-pitched noise. 'I don't know what you mean.'

'I saw you grinning after him. And then you come in here

smiling like a girl who's just had her first kiss. Try to be a little more dignified, please, if only to stop the neighbours gossiping.'

He walked out, closing the door behind him softly. Still holding a bottle of milk, Jane set it down. She closed her eyes, deflated. Adam was right; she had allowed herself to be carried away, pathetically flattered by the smallest amount of attention. Turning off the gas beneath the kettle she went upstairs to run a bath, making as much noise as she could to somehow prove to Adam that she wasn't hurt.

Chapter Seventeen

In Jason's flat Nina said, 'I'm so sorry, Davey. I know how much you loved him.'

The flat seemed less theatrical now Jason no longer occupied centre stage. Davey blew his nose. His eyes were swollen from crying and fresh tears ran down his face. Nina took his hand.

He said, 'I'm pleased you're here. He would have wanted you to be here.' He laughed brokenly. 'A big turnout at the funeral, that's what he wanted. All his friends – enemies too. Everyone he ever said hello to. And lots and lots of flowers.' He began to cry again and Nina pulled him into her arms. At once he pulled away and made an effort to sit up straighter as though he was composing himself for one of Jason's photographs.

Wiping his eyes he said, 'Is he coming?'

She smiled at the way he could never bring himself to speak Bobby's name. 'No.'

He looked vindicated. Bobby's absence from the funeral was more evidence of his thoughtlessness. All the same he pretended surprise. 'He's not? Oh well. We'll say he's not up to facing people. We'll say he's indisposed. Everyone will understand.'

'He sends you his condolences.'

Davey snorted. 'Would you like a drink, Nina? Sherry?'

As he poured their drinks he said, 'Do you have an escort for the funeral? Perhaps that wonderful man I saw you with? Hugh Morgan! I suppose having a father as famous as Michael Morgan makes him a celebrity by default, wouldn't you say?'

He handed her a schooner of sherry. Nina sipped at it as

Davey waited eagerly for her response. It would be easy to gossip with him about Hugh. They could have one of their bright, bitchy conversations that took apart their victim and reduced him to a set of affected mannerisms. But Hugh was her secret; to speak about him at all would be a betrayal. She couldn't allow Hugh to be exposed to the particular light Davey would shine on him: he might become ordinary again and the man she'd left waving at Thorp Station someone she'd invented.

Davey said, 'He doesn't write poetry too, does he?'

She laughed, thinking of Hugh and his hatred of his father's work. 'No, he doesn't.'

'No. Didn't look the type. He looked like a man of action, to me. Will he be coming with you to the funeral?'

'No.' She met his gaze. 'He's in Thorp, with Bobby. The two of them are old friends.'

His eyes widened. 'No! He's knows him? They're friends? I can't believe a man like him would be even associated with a man like Bobby Harris.'

She looked down at her drink. Already she felt as though she'd said too much. Davey looked amazed, his grief temporarily forgotten as he seemed to consider all the questions he might ask her. Nina said quickly, 'If there's anything you'd like me to do, Davey, any arrangements to be made, I'd be happy to help.'

His eyes lingered on her face as though he was appreciating a much-valued possession. His gaze swept over her, taking in her silk stockings, the dark suit she'd chosen so carefully for its sombre modesty, the little veiled hat made from sleek, oil-black feathers. His smile puckered. 'Look at you. So smart. I remember when Jason introduced us. Little waif, he called you, little Irish ragamuffin. He told me how he found you in that dreadful little café on Percy Street without the price of a cup of tea. You were so …' He frowned. At last he said, 'Unspoilt. Then you met Bobby Harris. Only this morning I was looking at pictures of you and Bobby and remembering how he used to correct the way you spoke, the way you walked, even the way you dressed. You're his product, Nina, I always thought he made you someone you're not meant to be. Even Jason regretted introducing the two of you.'

She remembered Jason saying, 'Bobby's something of a worry to me.'

It was the spring of 1940. They had been strolling through Regent's Park, Jason stopping occasionally to photograph the ducks or the small boys pushing boats out on to the water. She remembered how sunny it had been, the trees newly in leaf, and that she'd worn a pale green silk dress that draped softly and made her feel like a shapely, elegant woman with hips and breasts rather than a stick-thin child. Bobby had chosen the dress, holding it against her in the shop and explaining why the colour suited her.

As they'd walked towards the park gates Jason had said, 'You do know Bobby's not right in the head, don't you?'

Outraged, she'd laughed and immediately he snapped her picture. Lowering the camera he gave her a triumphant smile only to frown thoughtfully. 'No, Bobby's definitely not right. Damaged – I think that's the word.'

She remembered how he'd taken her hands. 'You're so lovely, my darling. Don't let him make you think you're as damaged as he is.'

Davey got up suddenly. 'Listen – there is something you can do for me. Some old acquaintance of Jason's is arriving at Waterloo this afternoon. Would you meet him?'

Every time he returned to England his faith in his long ago decision to leave was re-born. He hated the cold and the damp and the fog. He hated the hostility of strangers, their pinched, closed-in expressions and their look-twice suspicions. But if he hated England, England had hated him in return.

Standing outside Waterloo Station, beside the flower seller where Jason's lover had told him to wait, the cold of the pavement seeped through the soles of his shoes and rain began to spit from a gun grey sky. He looked up at the dense clouds, thinking of Samir and his longing to see London, how he had begged to be allowed to accompany him. He tried to imagine the boy's brown feet on the filthy pavement, unable to picture him in shoes. On the streets at home Samir wore sandals and his feet bore a tide mark of white, sandy dust. Here in England the boy would freeze to death, or else wear the heavy boots he himself had worn at his age: army boots, made weightier by Flanders' mud. He closed his eyes and felt the rain on his face. He couldn't bear to see the boy subjected to this country.

The Easter-time scent of daffodils competed with that of exhaust fumes and he thought of buying flowers for Davey, a bunch each of daffodils and iris, a contrast Jason would have appreciated. He wondered about the etiquette of flowers in England, if a man could be seen carrying them on the street without being jeered. He sighed at his paranoia and wilful distrust of his once fellow countrymen. Men like him were hated wherever they went, whether they carried flowers or not. He had to remind himself that it was really only the weather in England that was crueller.

The woman behind the flower stall said, 'What would you like, sir?'

He suspected she smiled at him only because he looked like someone who would buy two dozen roses. He wore a black cashmere coat over a Savile Row suit, a silk tie in the deep, velvet blue of violets. His shoes were handmade. Lately flecks of grey had appeared in his hair so that Samir said he looked wise as Solomon. He felt old suddenly, England's weariness creeping into his bones.

The flower seller was looking at him expectantly, smiling still. He thought of Davey and his love of flamboyance and bought an armful of yellow roses.

Davey had said, 'His name's Francis Law. I don't think it's his real name.' He smiled at Nina enigmatically. 'I think he's a spy.'

Francis Law was waiting exactly where Davey had told her. He had described him accurately: a slight, elegant man who carried himself like a general and looked as though he might own the world. Only the roses were a surprise. He cradled the flowers in one arm and she saw him glance at his watch as she approached. Nina quickened her pace, all at once feeling nervous; she was late and he obviously wasn't the type used to being kept waiting.

Breathlessly she said, 'Mr Law? Hello – I'm Nina. Davey sent me to meet you.'

Shifting the roses from his right arm to his left he held out his hand to her. 'Nina. Hello. I'm Francis.'

His hand was hard and dry. She noticed how tanned he was and how striking he looked amongst the pasty-faced commuters leaving the station. He smiled at her, drawing his hand away. 'Nina, Davey very kindly invited me to stay at Jason's flat. But I think it might be considerate to stay at a hotel given the circumstances. I usually stay at a hotel very near here. I know you must have had a tiresome journey across London so perhaps you'd care to have lunch with me there?'

In the hotel the roses were given to a porter to be put in water and Law frowned as he watched the boy carry them away. 'They seem inappropriate now.'

'Jason loved roses.'

'I should have telephoned Davey and insisted that I stay in a hotel. I feel I've wasted your time.'

'Not at all.'

'Well, I hope lunch makes up for your inconvenience.'

They followed a waiter into the dining room. Only a handful of tables were occupied, all the diners men. Heads turned towards her as the waiter pulled out her chair, a few eyebrows raised in mild disapproval. As she sat down Francis Law smiled at her as though they were fellow conspirators.

He took out a silver cigarette case and held it out to her. When she declined he slipped the case back into his pocket. The waiter had handed them menus and he glanced at his cursorily. 'I hear the rationing is still very bad?'

'Yes.'

'I haven't been to England since before the war. I live in Tangiers – I suppose Davey told you?'

'No, he didn't.' He had hardly told her anything at all, only that Jason had always been mysterious about this man. But Jason liked secrets, real or invented. 'Did you know Jason

401

well?' Nina asked.

'Yes, we met before the war. We were good friends – pen friends on the whole, although he and Davey visited me late last year, before he became ill.' He looked at the menu again. 'The roast beef, I think. I'd recommend it, Nina.'

She realised how hungry she was and her stomach rumbled a little. He grinned and suddenly he looked boyish, all of his seriousness falling away. 'I think we'll have something to start as well, and pudding and cheese,' he said. 'We'll get the better of this rationing business, eh?'

Over coffee he said, 'Where do you and your husband live, Nina?'

'I'm not married.'

'Oh – forgive me. I noticed your ring.'

She looked down at the thin gold band on her finger. 'I'm a widow. Nick was killed in 1940. He was a fighter pilot.'

'I'm sorry.' After a moment he said, 'Was he a friend of Bobby's?'

She had told him about Bobby as part of the long story of how she knew Jason. He'd listened attentively as she told him how Jason had encouraged Bobby to learn to fly, how she suspected he had paid for the lessons because Bobby wanted them so badly and he could never bear to see him denied anything. Now she wondered why she had told him all about Bobby and so little about herself.

Francis was watching her, his first cigarette of the afternoon sending pale wisps of sweet, expensive smoke up to the high ceiling. Meeting his gaze she said, 'Bobby introduced me to Nick. They were in the same squadron. Bobby said we were made for each other.' She looked down at her coffee cup. 'I don't know whether we were or not. Time would have told, I suppose.' Quickly she said, 'I don't think I miss him as much as I should. Bobby –' She stopped herself. 'May I have a cigarette?'

As he lit her cigarette Francis said, 'I saw Bobby's portraits in Jason's studio before the war.' When she looked at him in surprise he said, 'More than attending the funeral, my reason for being here is to see him.'

For the first time since they met she saw him as the kind of man Bobby would despise, the kind who would walk into Jason's studio to buy one of the artful photographs Bobby posed for. She thought of the photograph that he would be most likely to choose: Bobby sitting naked on a bed, sideways to the camera, a sheet barely covering his groin. He was leaning back, the weight of his body resting on his splayed hands. His head was bowed in submission. Disappearing into shadow, the bed was skilfully disordered, a pillow placed casually at Bobby's feet. A moment after Jason had taken the shot Bobby had looked up at her, his eyes blank as a sleepwalker's.

Her coffee was cold now, too strong and bitter but she sipped at it anyway, wanting to avoid this man's eye. She imagined him holding Bobby's likeness to the light. He would admire it in private before hiding it away to be shown only to those he thought discerning enough. She hated him suddenly; she wished she could leave without appearing rude.

Law stubbed out his cigarette. 'I didn't go to the studio for the reasons you think, Nina.'

She set her cup down gently. 'In that case how do you know what I'm thinking?'

He signalled to a waiter for the bill. 'Nina, shall we sit in the lounge? It's a more private place to talk.'

Chapter Eighteen

Every lunchtime before pudding was served Jane left the clattering, controlled chaos of the school dining hall and walked into town. She needed this escape. Outside the confines of the school she could take a break from the tight-lipped, too-stern school marm she became the moment she stepped through Thorp Grammar's gates. Even so, the smell of the school clung to her and the sweaty plimsoll stink was made worse today by the smell of baked fish dished up for lunch. The smell seemed trapped in her clothes and hair; she felt tainted by it; it seemed to be a mark of her failure to be desirable.

Desirable! She smiled bitterly as she walked along the High Street. Since she'd met Bobby Harris she had become obsessed with her own plainness. She thought of all the glamorous women he must have known and how even the most gorgeous of them must have thrown themselves at his feet. She pictured him dancing to some slow, sentimental song with an aristocratic girl in his arms. The girl would be as incandescently lovely as one of Arthur Rackham's fairies; she would be called Annabel or Diana and would be madly in love with him and swoon when he kissed her. In his uniform he would look brave and vulnerable at once and Diana would be terrified for him every moment they were apart.

Jane turned down one of the alleys that ran off the High Street. She stopped outside Mellor's Curiosity Shop and gazed at her ghostly reflection in the window. She could make more of herself, she supposed. She could wear more feminine clothes and have her hair styled. Her figure was still good, she didn't have the round belly and heavy breasts that made most women her age appear matronly. She was as slim as a girl and like a girl she had never borne a child, she had never even felt a man's hand on her thigh as his eyes questioned hers. Inexperience made her as brittle and insubstantial as a blown egg.

A group of women from the sugar factory approached her on their way back to work. They wore their hair in turbans, their overalls showing below the hem of their coats. They laughed, a loud burst of raucous noise, and Jane stepped closer to the shop window and drew her arms into her body in an effort to become smaller. The women jostled past in the narrow space, trailing the scent of spun sugar. She glanced after them. Perhaps if she had left school at fifteen and taken work in a factory she would be married to a man who gave her his pay packet each Friday afternoon and took her to bed every Saturday night. By now they would have half-grown children about to leave school themselves. She would be one of the sugar girls, reeking of sweetness and buoyed by camaraderie. Jane sighed, touching her hair that was drawn back too severely beneath her mouse-brown felt hat. Perhaps she would buy herself a lipstick in a bright, bold colour.

Jane waited in the school hall for her actors to arrive. She glanced at her watch then up to the clock above the stage. They were late and she went to the hall doors and looked up and down the corridor. A few minutes ago the school had been full of boys jostling each other to leave as quickly as possible, now the corridors were empty. Her footsteps echoed as she walked back into the hall.

She sat down on a chair in front of the stage. Taking a compact from her handbag she flicked it open and peered at its mirror. She should have known better; the mirror was too small, smudged with fingerprints and dull with old face powder, and her reflection was unflattering. She snapped the compact closed. If Bobby Harris turned up he could take her as he found her. He was just a boy anyway, younger than her by ten years at least. She had romanticised him because of his lovely voice and shy manner and because in the war he had been brave and his courage had damaged him so badly. But he was still only a boy, even if she couldn't stop thinking about him.

Behind her a voice said, 'Hello again.'

She leapt up at once. Bobby Harris smiled at her. Looking to the empty stage he said, 'Am I too early?'

'No – the boys are late. Sometimes a master keeps them back for one reason or another. Some of my colleagues think the school play is too frivolous to be taken very seriously, especially when the fifth form has exams coming up ...' She trailed off, aware that she was gabbling. He was still looking at the stage as though he was afraid he would have to perform on it. About to say something, he stopped as the boys clattered into the hall.

Mark Redpath only glanced at his brother and she guessed he didn't want to set himself outside the group by being over-friendly. Instead he looked afraid that inviting Bobby might not have been such a good idea after all. Jane smiled at Mark reassuringly but her own nervousness made the smile thin and sickly.

Bobby Harris sat down next to her. Mark took centre stage and his brother watched him intently. To her surprise Mark seemed to gain confidence from this. His major speech about the girl he left at home was performed directly to Bobby Harris, word perfect. The other boys picked up on Mark's confidence and the scene became charged with emotion so that Jane felt a thrill of excitement. At the end of the act she stood up and applauded enthusiastically.

'Well done, boys! All of you!' Grinning, she glanced over her shoulder at Bobby Harris. 'What did you think?'

He stood up. 'Mrs Mason, would you excuse me?'

He turned and walked out of the hall. Jane looked at Mark. He was frowning, concern mixing with disappointment. He made to get down from the stage but she motioned that he should stay where he was. 'Start on the next act,' she said. 'I won't be long.'

She found him outside. He was sitting on the steps leading up to the main entrance, a cigarette ignored between his fingers, his head bowed. She stepped towards him cautiously. He seemed to radiate unhappiness and she almost turned back into the school, afraid of the infectious depth of his despair. On the brink of turning away he looked up at her. It seemed as though he'd been crying.

Carefully she asked, 'Are you all right?'

He nodded. Drawing on his cigarette he said, 'Will you apologise to the boys for me? I think I should go home.'

She sat down beside him. Across the school drive boys played tennis and from time to time their shouts rang out as a point was disputed. Jane concentrated on their game, wanting to give Mark's brother time to compose himself.

As the ball was hit into the net, he said, 'I get into a state, sometimes.' He tapped cigarette ash on to the ground between his feet. 'I should have known better but I didn't want to let Mark down.'

'He'll understand.'

'Maybe.' Suddenly he said, 'He's very good, isn't he? I don't think he needs any advice from me.'

She watched the tennis players resume their game. In a moment, when his cigarette was finished, she knew he would go and she couldn't think of a single thing to say that would make him stay. She would probably never see him again. Her disappointment felt silly; she wondered what high expectations she must have had to suddenly be so miserable. Deciding she had nothing to lose she said, 'Mark may not need your advice but perhaps I do.' She glanced at him. 'Do you have any photographs of your school's production? Perhaps I could steal some ideas.'

She thought he hadn't heard her. Her heart began to beat faster; all her oblique, ill-formed hopes relied on his answer. Her mouth felt dry as she prepared to speak, but his look silenced her.

'I don't have any photographs.' He stood up, crushing his cigarette stub out beneath his foot. She was still seated and for a moment he stood over her. He looked as though he couldn't understand why he was here, talking to a spinsterish teacher on a flight of stone steps. Feeling foolish, she scrambled to her feet, stumbling as she caught her heel in her skirt. He grasped her elbow and for a moment his face was close enough to kiss. She stepped away from him quickly.

'I should get back to the boys.'

'I'm sorry I couldn't be of more use, Mrs Mason.'

She nodded. Afraid of giving her disappointment away she hurried inside the school.

In Parkwood Bobby stood in the attic room where trunks and tea chests were stored. Cobwebs stretched across the window and there was a scattering of desiccated flies on the sill; the dry smell of dust made him sneeze and he reached into his pocket for his handkerchief. He thought of Jane Mason and the way her eyes had met his as she stumbled on the school steps. Beneath his grasp her arm had felt fragile, she seemed weightless as a bird. Mark had told him that they called her Stony Mason, naming her as cruelly and inaccurately as only adolescent boys could.

When she had asked him about photographs of his school's production of *Theory of Angels* his first thought was that of course he had none, although other boys' parents had come to the first night and taken pictures. They had been proud and enthusiastic as they herded their sons into stagey groups for their cameras. He had been in several of these group photos, standing between Andrew Hill and Stuart Johnson, his sergeant and corporal in the play. He had smiled dutifully when asked to say cheese, all the while thinking that Palmer should not smile; there was, and should not be, any record of the captain looking anything but deadly serious. Saying cheese was beneath his dignity, but he did it all the same. The mothers smiled back at him, aware as mothers usually were, that his own mother was absent, that there was no representative from his family to embarrass him as the others were embarrassed. Johnson had said how he envied him as he wiped a smudge of maternal lipstick from his cheek. Johnson's father, laughing, had slapped his son on his back and said, 'Shall we send you a picture, Harris?' His camera hung round his neck and he tapped it with his finger. 'A memento of tonight.'

The photographs had arrived just before the end of term. By then his plan to run away to London was already fully formed, detailed and precise. He believed the plans made him strong, that he had taken back control of his life after Vickers and that Mr Johnson's snaps would hardly affect him at all. He couldn't risk it, though. Unopened, he put the envelope they had arrived in inside another envelope and addressed it to his grandfather.

Bobby knelt in front of the chest, afraid to open it. The photos were of a boy that had died on the last night of the play, just as Palmer had died, cut off suddenly from any number of lives he might have lived. Looking at his picture would be like exhuming a corpse: there was a terrible fascination to it. Realising he couldn't stop himself he lifted the chest's lid.

The envelope, addressed in his cramped, slanting handwriting, was beneath a folder full of his school reports. He lifted it out and ran his finger over his grandfather's name. He remembered that he had almost wept as he wrote it, making him realise that he had only imagined himself to be strong and that his control was as breakable as the fake barbed wire Palmer sacrificed himself on. But he hadn't cried. He had bit down hard on his lip so that it bled and forced himself to feel nothing but the sting of the wound. He would make himself immune to the pain and humiliation of what had happened, even if it killed him.

From downstairs he heard Hugh call, 'Bob? Bob, are you up there?' He heard Hugh's surprisingly light tread on the stairs, imagined him bounding up two steps at a time, impatient as ever. Bobby stood up, holding the envelope casually so that Hugh might not notice it. The chest gaped open, breathing out the smell of camphor; he wasn't quick enough to close it before Hugh was standing in the attic door way.

Hugh said, 'What are you doing up here?'

'Nothing.' His voice had an edge to it, angry and defensive at once, a tone he recognised as typical of the man he had

409

become.

Hugh glanced at the envelope and the open chest. He seemed to consider and decide against any more questions. 'I was wondering if you fancied going for a drink.'

'No.'

'Oh, come on, Bob! I'm bored out of my head.'

'I'm not stopping you going.'

'Look, you miserable bastard, I want to buy you a drink, all right? A goodbye-thanks-for-having-me-drink.'

That morning Hugh had sheepishly told him he was going to London the following day. He had said, 'Bob – do you think I'm making a fool of myself over her?' He hadn't been able to bring himself to answer and Hugh had laughed awkwardly. 'OK, so I'm a fool. So what?'

Slipping the envelope into his jacket pocket Bobby said, 'Where would we go for a drink?'

'Somewhere quiet?'

'Dark?' Bobby smiled at him. 'The Red Lion? It's pretty dim in there.'

Chapter Nineteen

The Red Lion was dim. It smelt of coal fires and was warm as a Sunday morning bed. The barmaid was peroxide blonde with a dark, tiger-stripe of roots showing along her parting. Her neckline was low, her skin creamy; when she smiled at him Hugh imagined propositioning her. Since meeting Nina he wanted to fuck any half-decent looking woman he saw. He was a sex god, horny as the devil. He had never felt like this in life before. He glanced at Bob who had seated himself in the gloomiest corner of the pub, and wondered if he too had felt like this when he'd met her.

He carried their pints to the table where Bob was unwinding his scarf and taking off his gloves. Hugh thought of this process as Bobby shedding his skin, leaving himself vulnerable for the time it took for others to be shocked and then pretend not to be.

Immediately Hugh set his drink on the table Bobby took a long drink. He put the glass down and fumbled in his pockets for cigarettes. Unable to bear seeing him struggling with matches Hugh took out a lighter in preparation. As Bob put the cigarette between his lips he flicked the lighter open.

Accepting the light Bobby said, 'Will you come back to Thorp?'

'I don't know. Maybe.'

'I'll miss you.'

Surprised, Hugh said, 'Will you?'

Bobby rolled his cigarette around the edge of the tin ashtray in the centre of the table and Hugh sensed that he was about to give something of himself away. But he remained silent, his cigarette forming a pointed head of ash as he rolled it back and forth. At last he said, 'I should start looking for a job – does that bank you mentioned need a filing clerk?'

'Why don't you come back to London with me? Don't you have friends there? What did you do before the war?'

Bobby laughed oddly. Finishing his drink in one long swallow he looked towards the bar. 'Do you want another?'

'Should I get them?'

Bobby looked up from patting his pockets for his wallet. 'You bought the last round.'

'I know, but –'

'Do you want to make eyes at that barmaid again?' He stood up, touching his shoulder lightly as he edged past him. 'It's all right, Hugh. I can screw up enough courage to buy you a drink.'

When he returned with their drinks they drank in silence and Bobby seemed to retreat into himself as though he had become shy of him suddenly. Hugh found himself considering topics for small talk, until he realised they had nothing in common that would be easy and safe to talk about. All conversations would lead to a minefield of memories and ultimately to Nina because all he could think about was her. He pictured her in her room, undressing for bed, unclipping her suspenders and rolling her stocking down past her knee as her hair fell across her face; he thought about her breasts, how her nipples hardened beneath the stroke of his thumb. He sighed and Bobby looked at him piercingly as though he read his thoughts.

Feeling as if he'd been caught masturbating, Hugh tried to make his voice light. He said, 'What were you doing in the attic?'

For a while he thought Bobby wasn't going to answer and he shifted uncomfortably, wishing that he could be alone with his dirty thoughts. At last Bobby took an envelope from his pocket and placed it on the table between them.

'I was looking for this.'

Hugh picked the envelope up, glancing at Bobby questioningly.

'Open it. It's only photos.'

The photos were of a group of boys in army uniform, looking as though they'd just stepped out of the trenches. Hugh frowned at the first picture, puzzled by it. He held it up to the light and squinted at the image of the boy in the centre of the picture. It was Bobby, his cap shading his eyes, his smile forced and self-conscious. The others seemed to be laughing so that Bobby looked like the outsider, reminding Hugh of Bobby as a child, always a step away from the group. He shuffled through the other photos; in each picture the eye was drawn to Bob.

'Your school play?'

'*Theory of Angels*.'

Hugh snorted. 'What else?' He remembered his own school's production and the excruciating embarrassment of being deferred to by the young drama teacher who seemed infatuated with his father and his works. He looked down at the photos again.

'You were the star, eh?' He frowned, remembering suddenly. 'Didn't my father go and see you in the play? It was just before you ran away to London, wasn't it? Without a word to anyone.'

Remembering how bitter he'd felt then, Hugh shoved the photos back inside the envelope and pushed them across the table. He lit a cigarette, glancing towards the bar and watching the barmaid pull a pint. She smiled at him; all he would have to do was ask. She might have a room somewhere. From the corner of his eye he saw Bobby slip the envelope into his pocket and reach out for his drink only to put it down again and trail his finger down its side. Bobby cleared his throat as if to speak, and smiled as shyly as the six-year-old boy Hugh had sat next to in Miss Grey's infant class.

Awkwardly Bobby said, 'Hugh, I'm sorry about what happened – about how we lost touch. I'm sorry.'

'Doesn't matter. I suppose your running away to London was inevitable; you didn't really fit in anywhere else, did you?' He could hear how angry he sounded, a hangover from the hurt he had felt at the time. Less sharply he said, 'Maybe I would have done the same in your shoes.'

Bobby looked down, turning his packet of cigarettes over and over on the table until Hugh's irritation got the better of him and he snatched the packet away.

Clearing his throat Bobby said, 'Mark's about to play Palmer. It's why I dug the photos out. His drama teacher was interested in seeing them. Although I don't think they'll be much use.'

'It's not Mr Rogers, is it? He used to teach drama when I was there – he adored Dad's work. Had a crush on him, I think.'

'No. Her name's Mason. Jane –'

'Pretty?'

'She's nice. I liked her.'

'Oh? So maybe you could use the photographs as an excuse – go and see her after school, take her an apple as well.'

'She's married.'

Thoughtfully Hugh said, 'Jane Mason. A Mr Mason taught me at that school. English Master. Sadistic bastard. Everyone hated his guts. She's not married to him, is she?'

'I don't know.'

'We were convinced he was queer.'

Sharply Bobby said, 'Then she probably isn't married to him.'

Hugh laughed, regarding him carefully. 'You do like her, don't you? Is she game, do you think?'

'For God's sake!'

'Come on, Bob! Married women are usually the most obliging – you know that.'

'Do I?'

'You fly boys were fighting the women off.'

'Aren't you confusing us with the Americans?' After a while he said, 'I think those photos were an excuse to see her again. A bit pathetic, really.'

'I don't think so.'

After a moment Bobby said, 'I almost got engaged to a girl during the war. She was in the WRAF. Kate Hammond. She used to sing at dances – the first time I saw her she was singing. Singing right at me.' He smiled, trailing his finger

414

down the side of his glass again. 'She was lovely. Jolly – you know? She came from a great big family of jolly people, terribly posh, terribly nice. Spending the weekend at her family's house was like sinking into a feather bed and being fed cream cakes whilst everyone told you how wonderful you were.'

'Sounds too good to be true. What happened?'

'Nick was killed.' Bobby looked at him. Hugh deliberately kept his face blank, deciding that trying to be impassive was the best way of keeping his jealousy in check. After a moment Bobby said, 'Nina didn't have anyone else. Kate said I should choose between them and that was the end of that. I heard she married an army chaplain.'

Dryly Hugh said, 'Quite a sacrifice, giving up all those cakes and feather beds.'

'Well, maybe we weren't all that suited when it came down to it. And Nina was pregnant, I couldn't let her cope alone.'

Hugh looked down at his drink. He hated that Bobby and Nina had been together, brought up her little girl together; he hated that she had returned to London, to a place that was full of memories she shared with Harris. On top of that he missed her; he missed her as much as he missed the sea.

All day, when he hadn't been thinking about Nina, he'd been thinking about the sea. All day the ground beneath his feet had felt too solid and too still, as through he'd become rooted to it. He felt weary and hoped that it was only the after-effects of his illness rather than the dismay he felt at leaving the Navy growing more unbearable. He looked at Bob and wondered if he missed the fury of flying just as he missed the ocean. Bobby caught his eye and smiled shyly. At once Hugh felt sorry for him and his jealousy seemed petty and childish.

Bobby said, 'Those married women you mentioned …?'

Hugh sighed. 'You know adultery is wrong, don't you?' He stood up. 'I'll buy you another drink.'

Chapter Twenty

Francis Law said, 'Bobby may not want to see me. I would understand if he didn't.'

She was standing beside him at Jason's grave. The other mourners were walking back towards the funeral cars, one of them supporting Davey who was weeping noisily. A single yellow rose lay on the coffin, a splatter of dry earth partly obscuring the brass plaque bearing Jason's name and dates. Nina fixed her gaze on the rose, imagining its rapid decay beneath the heavy London clay. She couldn't look at Law. She had told him too much. She felt panicky with betrayal. In her mind's eye she saw Bobby's Spitfire plummeting from the sky trailing the fire no one could save him from. Law rested his hand lightly on her arm.

'Nina?'

She shrugged him off, her flesh creeping where he'd touched her. 'I don't want him to know we met.'

'As you wish.'

She turned away, hurrying to catch up with the others. She felt her heels sink into the cemetery's soft earth and stumbled. Looking back she saw Law still standing at the graveside, his head bowed as though he was praying.

In her flat Nina took off her funeral dress and lay down on the bed. She placed her hands over her concave stomach, felt her hip bones jutting sharp as a dress shop mannequin's. Jason insisted on her thinness; he needed her to be only straight lines and hollows; there should be no comfortable flesh to soften his compositions. She became used to hunger and stopped menstruating, breaking the rule that women must be in thrall to

416

their bodies. She felt hard and powerful as an outlaw; she began to believe that women with breasts and bellies and thighs were indolent and weak. As she became thinner Bobby made love to her less often and took her out to dinner instead. She would catch him watching her as she ate her morsels of steak and string beans, but she would watch him, too, note with satisfaction his concern for her. During those meals he looked less like Jason's creation. In his RAF uniform tie and collar he looked like a boy who had behaved well all his life.

Once, just before he'd introduced her to Nick, she had asked Bobby if his mother would approve of her. She'd stood naked in front of the mirror on her wardrobe door, angling it so that he could see her reflection from the bed and she could see his. His cock nestled against his thigh, vulnerable and exhausted, the johnny he was always so careful to use flaccid on the floor. He'd pressed both his hands to his face like an appalled child and she'd looked away, ashamed for him. Inside the wardrobe they'd once shared, his clothes still hung: expensive, beautiful clothes Jason had chosen, and then there was his uniform, surprisingly exotic beside his civilian suits. She'd picked a thread of cotton from the blue sleeve and wrapped it around her wedding ring finger. Even then she'd wondered if she loved him and if lust could be so badly confused. There were times when he seemed strange enough to be repellent. All the same she'd asked him, 'Would you marry me?'

Would you, could you, if you cared. They were the words of a song Jason sang, a nonsense song. And Jason was dead now, along with Nick, and Bobby, in his way. Lying on her bed she moved her hands up to her breasts and cupped them.

When Joan was a few days old Bobby asked her, 'Would you marry me?'

She had smelt boldly of blood and sweat and milk. He was shy of her. When she answered no she had felt triumphant for an hour or two. *Would you, could you, if you cared.* She remembered Jason's intensity when he took Bobby's photograph. Only afterwards, in his darkroom, would he sing, as though through capturing Bobby's image he had been released.

She had told Francis Law too much; when she remembered how much she'd told him she felt frightened. Unable to keep still she sat up and placed her feet firmly on the floor. She imagined pacing because this was a busy agitating fear, the type she imagined the condemned felt. Francis Law, who was handsome and kind as the good kings in fairytales, was at this moment travelling on a train to Thorp, his head full of her stories. She stood up. Across the corridor Cathy began to cry. Sinking down on to the bed again she curled on to her side and covered her ears with her hands.

Jane had drawn the picture of the soldier from memory and only when it was finished had she taken Adam's bible down from its high shelf and compared her drawing to the photograph hidden between its pages. She'd spent a few moments studying the photo and, despite herself, found she was touched by how young the boy was, hardly older than the boys in her play. Her drawing resembled him only a little. She had remembered him as arrogant as Palmer and just as vapid. Her memories had been coloured by jealousy, of course. She had put the picture back in the bible, feeling ashamed of herself.

Her drawing was on the kitchen table and she stood looking down at it as Adam came in from the garden. Taking off his muddy wellington boots he said, 'I think slugs are immortal. Perhaps slugs are actually gods and we've all been looking in the wrong direction for our deities. What do you think?'

She glanced at him absently before returning to the drawing. Adam came to stand beside her and she smelt the cold of garden soil and his own faint, clean scent. No matter how hard Adam worked he didn't sweat, he was always dry as kindling. He took off his glasses and polished them swiftly with his handkerchief. Hooking them over his ears again he said, 'What have we got here?'

'My picture for the cover of the play's programme.'

They both stood looking down at it. She hardly dared glance at him, although she knew her copy was nothing like

418

the original. All the same, she felt anxious as he picked the drawing up and studied it more closely.

'Captain Palmer, I presume?'

'Yes. Supposed to be.'

'It's very good.' Placing it down again he said, 'Rehearsals coming along all right?'

'Yes.'

'And that boy. Harris. Did he turn up to offer his advice?'

'Yes.'

She thought of Bobby Harris on the school steps, the firmness of his grip on her elbow as he steadied her. She had imagined he would be frailer but there had seemed to be a wiry strength to him. Lately she had begun to imagine him naked, his body, unmarked by the fire that had ruined his face, lean and hard and muscular.

His eyes on the drawing, Adam said, 'Did Harris have anything useful to say?'

'He didn't stay very long. The boys put on such a good show for him he probably thought there was nothing he could add.'

She tried to imagine the real reason why he had walked out of the rehearsal so abruptly. She remembered how shocked he had looked, as though what had been performed was particularly disturbing. There seemed to be nothing in the scene that could have caused such distress. Palmer's speech was about the girl he'd left in England. Perhaps that was it: Bobby Harris missed some girl; it seemed an inadequate explanation for such a display of misery.

Adam said, 'I'm going out tonight.'

She turned away, deliberately ignoring him.

'Jane?' She glanced at him and he smiled weakly. 'It's just a meeting of the school governors. I may be a little late – you know how these things drag on. I'll take my key, of course.'

'Of course.' She waited. In a moment, if she held her nerve and stayed silent, he would leave her be and go upstairs to bathe.

In a rush he said, 'You should go out too, to the pictures, or somewhere –'

She laughed. 'Who with?'

'Betty Ryan? You used to go out with her – the two of you had some pleasant evenings together.'

Betty, the school secretary, had become engaged at the end of the war. He had forgotten, just as he forgot most things she told him, that Betty wanted to spend every waking hour with Bill, her fiancée, that Betty believed too much time had been stolen from them already. She wished she could have been scornful of Betty's excuse not to see her rather than understanding it quite so much.

Adam said, 'Perhaps you and I could go out, later in the week. *Henry V* is showing at the cinema, I heard.'

'If you want.'

He sighed. 'I'll go and get changed.'

When Adam had left for his meeting Jane took out the bar of Fry's Chocolate Cream she'd hidden behind the bread bin and lay down on the sofa with a library copy of *Jane Eyre*. The gas fire spluttered companionably. Rain began, splattering heavily on the tar roof of the bay. She hoped Adam would be soaked and she glanced towards the window, which rattled in the wind. It was a fifteen-minute walk to the school, if that was where he was truly going. When he had come to say goodbye she'd noticed how carefully he'd dressed and shaved and combed his hair. He'd used cologne, the expensive, sandalwood scent he bought and concealed in his sock drawer. She wondered who he thought it was that put his socks away. The sock fairy. She smiled grimly, turning a page, the story so familiar it didn't matter that she'd lost concentration.

She unwrapped the chocolate, exposing only the first section, intending as usual to eat it slowly. Each bite would melt in her mouth in its own time even as she wondered how it would feel to strip the entire wrapper away and gobble the bar down in a few seconds. There was no one to stop her, no one to share with or to be shocked by her uninhibited greed. She knew that, unwrapped, the chocolate would look decadent; as it was the chocolate became a furtive pleasure and such furtiveness seemed fitting.

She became absorbed in her book, so calmed and comforted by the sweetness of the chocolate and the satisfying ending the novel was leading to that at first she mistook the knock on the door for the wind's rattling. When the knock came again she looked up, frowning, holding herself still to listen more intently. The knock was repeated, the same patient rat-a-tat-tat.

Jane stood up, ashamed of the way her heart had begun to beat too quickly. She had become timid as an old lady, all callers a potential threat. Hesitantly she went to the window and lifted aside the curtain. A muffled figure stood at the door, a man. He stepped back and looked up at the house. She watched as the man glanced back towards the road as if about to give up. Following his gaze she saw the car parked opposite the gate and at once she realised who her caller was. She almost ran to the door.

She swung the door open too quickly so that he stepped back as though startled by her sudden appearance. Jane's hand went to her throat and she smiled broadly, hating the absurd breathlessness in her voice as she said, 'Mr Harris. Hello again – this is a surprise.'

'I hope I'm not disturbing you –'

She cut in at once. 'No! No, of course.' Holding the door open even wider she stepped aside. 'Come in. Out of the rain. Come in.'

He thought, 'What am I doing here?' He thought of Hugh, who would smirk if he knew, and of Nina who would only be puzzled and certainly not jealous. Nina would have only been jealous if his face was still intact. He sighed and fumbled in his pockets for his cigarettes.

Jane had scurried away into the kitchen, insisting on making him tea. He must have a hot drink to warm him, although he'd only been caught in the rain for the time it took for him to walk up her path from the car. She had taken her time answering his knock. He had seen the curtain twitch and he realised that unexpected callers were rare enough to cause alarm. Her husband was out. He didn't know whether to be relieved or not.

Lighting a cigarette he glanced around the room for an ashtray. There wasn't one, and he edged along the sofa, ready to flick the ash into the fire. He noticed a book lying open on the rug and picked it up. *Jane Eyre.* He smiled and put it down again, careful to make it look as though it hadn't been disturbed. A chocolate wrapper lay beside it, the kind of dark, sickly stuff he often craved. He picked the empty wrapper up and held it to his nose, inhaling greedily, only to drop it as Jane bumped the door open with her hip, both hands holding a tray set with tea and biscuits. He got up, going quickly to hold the door.

'It's all right! I can manage.' Her smile was as bright and embarrassed as her voice. 'Do take off your coat. You mustn't sit around in a wet coat.'

He did as he was told and she took it from him, having set the tray down on a side table. Draping it over the back of a chair she said, 'Rain was forecast. They get it right, sometimes.'

She was wearing dark slacks and a pale green blouse buttoned to the throat, a cardigan in the same green draped around her shoulders. Her feet were bare, her toes short and snub. He had never seen an otherwise clothed woman with bare feet. No woman he had met had ever been so casual with him. Disconcerted, he glanced away from her.

'Oh – you need an ashtray!' She had been about to sit down in the chair on the other side of the fire but she leapt up and went to the sideboard. Rummaging inside she finally produced a scallop shell, its pale pink interior painted with Greetings from Scarborough. She smiled. 'I'm afraid it's the only suitable thing I have. We don't smoke, you see.'

'I'm sorry – would you like me to put it out?'

'No, please don't. I don't mind, really.'

He balanced the shell in one hand and as she poured the tea he glanced around, taking in the boxy, red moquette three piece suite and plain, utility sideboard. Above the beige tile fireplace was a print of Constable's *Hay Wain.* There were no framed photographs, no ornaments. Apart from the book on the floor the room was unnaturally tidy.

'Do you take milk and sugar?'

'Just milk, please.'

'Have a biscuit.' She held out a plate of custard creams but he shook his head. 'No? I suppose it is rather a lot to juggle – why don't you put the shell down? Here.' Once again she got up and placed the smallest of a nest of tables beside him and put his cup of tea on it. The cup and saucer were pink as the inside of the shell and almost translucently fine. He noticed how delicate the cup's handle was and knew his fingers couldn't grasp it safely. The tea would have to be ignored to avoid embarrassment.

The photographs were in his jacket pocket, still in the envelope addressed to his grandfather. He had glanced at them only when Hugh had taken them out in the pub. He knew they were all more or less the same, that they would hardly be of any use. They were his excuse for calling on her; she would guess that and wonder what to make of him but he had decided to risk appearing foolish. All day, since dropping Hugh off at the station, he had thought about Jane Mason. When he'd caught her arm on the school steps he had recognised the look in her eyes; it was the look women used to give him before he was disfigured.

He took the photographs from his pocket and held them out to her. 'I found these. I don't think they'll be much use but I thought you might like to see them.'

'Oh, yes – of course! How interesting.' Taking the photographs from him she began to shift through them. After a moment she held one out to him.

As he took it she said, 'That's you – in the centre of the group as Captain Palmer?' She hesitated then said, 'You don't look like him – my idea of him, that is.' She put the photographs back in their envelope. 'Thank you for letting me see them.'

He felt as though he was being dismissed. He was still holding the photograph she'd handed to him and he looked down at it. She was right – he didn't look like a man as bold and sure of himself as Palmer was written to be. He looked

423

like a self-conscious boy. She handed back the envelope and he slipped the photograph inside.

She sipped her tea and he remembered his own tea cooling beside him. Deciding to be straight with her he said, 'I'm afraid I might break your cup. My hands are clumsy.'

'Of course, how thoughtless of me. I'll fetch you another one.' About to get up she said, 'Unless you'd like a drink? We have some whisky left over from Christmas.'

'Tea is fine, thank you.'

She left the room, reappearing a few moments later with a thick, brown mug. Decanting his tea into she said, 'It's hardly wet its sides! Should I top it up with some hot from the pot?' She laughed self-consciously. 'I'm fussing aren't I? My husband says I'm inclined to flap.'

She coloured a little, as though mentioning her husband was breaking a taboo. She busied herself with pouring more tea into the mug but her blush spread to her neck and chest. When she sat down she said shyly, 'Adam – my husband – has gone to a school governors' meeting. You only just missed him, actually.'

'Is he a teacher too?'

'Headmaster. You'll meet him, if you come along to see the play.' Carefully she said, 'Will you come and see the finished production?'

He stubbed his cigarette out, not wanting to meet her gaze and feel compelled to answer. He placed the makeshift ashtray down and it rocked a little, the cigarette ash drifting into the grooves the lettering had made in the shiny, pearl-like interior. Mick Morgan had taken him and Hugh to Scarborough once. In Peaseholme Park he had pushed the poet's wheelchair along by the lake while Hugh and his mother had trailed behind eating ice cream. He had felt proud of the companionable silence there was between Morgan and himself. But then Morgan always did have the ability to make him feel more grown up than he actually was.

She said, 'Mr Harris? Might you come and see Mark in the play – I know he would really like you to …'

'I'm sure he would.' After a moment he said, 'Please – call

me Bob.'

'Yes, of course. Sorry.'

An embarrassed silence hung between them. Bobby shifted uncomfortably, wishing he'd stayed at home. But since Hugh had left the house seemed even emptier than when he'd first arrived; he imagined he might go mad if he didn't go out. And he'd thought a lot about Jane Mason, her no-nonsense kindness. She was attractive, too, in a way that intrigued him – not obviously pretty, but undeniably sexy.

Trying to think of a way to break the uneasy silence he remembered what Hugh had said about a teacher called Mason. Needing to know if her husband was the same man Hugh had disliked so much he said, 'Was your husband an English teacher at Thorp Grammar before he became headmaster?'

'Yes.'

'Has he been there a long time?'

'A very long time, yes. Why?'

'A friend mentioned that a Mr Mason taught him. I wondered if it was the same man.'

'I should think so. It's not such a common name.'

Her manner had become colder. After a while she said brusquely, 'Thank you for bringing the photographs to show me, Mr Harris, and for the interest you've shown in the play.'

This time he knew that he had been dismissed. Surprised at the disappointment he felt, he stood up. 'I'm sorry I couldn't have been more help. I hope the rehearsals continue to go well.'

She stood up too and picked up his coat from the chair, only to put it down again. Without looking at him she said, 'I'm sorry. Don't go yet.' She glanced at him. 'Are you sure you don't want a drink?'

'A whisky and soda would be nice.'

She smiled as though relieved. 'I keep it in the pantry. Come through into the kitchen.'

Chapter Twenty One

Sitting in the bar of the Grand Hotel, Francis Law took out the postcard he had bought that evening at Thorp Station and laid it on the table next to his gin and tonic. The picture was sepia but the corporation geraniums that grew in the flowerbeds around the war memorial had been touched up with a bright, unnatural red, matching the wreath of poppies at the memorial's base.

Tossing the postcard down on the table Francis sipped his gin. The good-looking boy behind the bar had been generous with the measure even as he regretted the lack of ice and sliced lemons, although Francis had told him that really it didn't matter. The boy had smiled at him so sweetly he thought his heart might break.

He picked up the postcard again and looked at it more closely. His spectacles were in their case in his pocket but he didn't want to put them on, not yet. Instead he squinted, as though that might help him read the indistinguishable names carved into the memorial's obelisk. He would know some of the boys whose names were immortalised, only one or two, of course; he had been born in Thorp but had never really lived here for more than a few months at a time. Adam knew many more of them. These names, now listed according to rank and in alphabetical order, had been those of Adam's school friends and neighbours. One or two of them Adam had mourned deeply, sometimes asking him too casually if he had ever come across this boy or that, as though Flanders was a gigantic social club.

Turning the postcard over he took out his pen. He'd addressed the card in his room, but a message had evaded him.

What could he say except that he was here, and that truly he wished he were not alone, that after all he needed the support he had decided so foolishly to do without. His gaze lingered on the name and address he had written so carefully, afraid that the card might go astray in the post. Then, after a moment's hesitation, he wrote swiftly, *Arrived safely. I'm shocked by the cold and the greyness – just as you said I would be. I miss you, of course.*

Of course. He missed him. They had been together for twenty years and in all that time had barely been apart. Tonight he would write a long letter; he would write about the war memorial, how he had stood before it in the dusk as the market traders packed up their stalls around him and how the light was too poor to read the names. The poppies were no longer there, nor the gaudy geraniums. Daffodils broke the bare soil of the flowerbeds, their scent reminding him fittingly of Easter. He would write that he had thought of him and no one else, not even the dead, who anyway had their memorial and their poppies on Armistice Day. Standing in the memorial's shadow his exile had seemed more complete than ever.

He signed his name and slipped the card back into his pocket. In a moment Adam would arrive; he had never known him to be late for anything. Glancing at his watch he saw how close the moment was and his nervousness made his heart race. It crossed his mind that Adam might not recognise him and that there would be some awkward scene in which the boy behind the bar would have to point him out. He lit a cigarette, his hands trembling a little. He had loved Adam once. Now he was afraid of him.

The door leading from the reception into the bar opened and Adam walked in. Francis stood up at once, stepping around the table and holding out his hand for Adam to shake. He knew he was smiling too broadly, making too much of a show of himself to hide his nerves and sudden shyness. He was almost fifty and felt fifteen, as bashful as he was the day they'd first met.

Adam took his offered hand and shook it briefly, barely

able to hold his gaze before glancing away towards the bar. 'Shall I get us a drink?'

Francis said, 'Allow me. What would you like?'

'What are you having?'

'Gin.'

'I'll have a lemonade.'

Returning from the bar with their drinks Francis saw that Adam had chosen to sit facing away from the rest of the room in a high-backed, wing chair, effectively hidden from anyone but the most curious. He had to expect furtiveness but all the same he felt angry, remembering how it had sometimes seemed that Adam revelled in his sense of shame, no matter how innocent the situation. He drew breath in an effort to quell his anger, reminding himself that Adam had a right to protect himself from gossip.

Setting a tumbler of lemonade in front of him he said, 'No ice, I'm afraid. The boy was very apologetic.'

'Ice? Where do you think you are – Casablanca?' He laughed scathingly. 'Ice!'

Francis sat down and lit a cigarette, taking his time so that he might seem unperturbed by Adam's hostility.

Adam said, 'You've hardly changed.'

Placing his lighter down Francis said, 'Neither have you. You look well.'

'I am, thanks.'

'Thank you for meeting me.'

'Did you think I wouldn't? I was much too curious.'

Francis felt as though he was appraising him and finding him offensive. Adam's eyes had fixed on the plain gold band on his finger and he knew that it was this symbol of fidelity that had offended him the most. He drew on his cigarette, determined to resist the urge to hide his left hand beneath the table.

'So,' Adam said, 'You're back in Thorp.'

'Yes.'

'I must say I was surprised when you telephoned. Quite a shock.'

'I'm sorry – I should have given you more warning.'

'I'm still not sure why you want to see me. Old time's sake?'

'Old friendship's sake, I hope.'

'Were we ever friends? It was more – I don't know – what did you used to call it? Fucking?' Adam looked at him steadily, eyebrows raised in mock enquiry. Francis knew that this was the type of treatment he meted out to the boys in his care – mock patience edged with sarcasm that could all too quickly turn nasty. Adam was a ruthless interrogator: lies had to be unearthed and truth established no matter how painful the process was. Francis realised that the fingers of his right hand had gone to hide the ring on his left.

Adam snorted. 'You don't change. Why don't you tell me to piss off – stand up for yourself! It was always your trouble – turn the other cheek or run away. Whatever was easiest.'

'Easiest?' He frowned. 'You think it was easy?'

'Running away usually is.' He nodded his head at the ring on his finger. 'How is Patrick? I presume you're still together?'

'He's well, and yes – we're still together.'

'And you wear his ring. Does he wear yours or are things not quite that equal?'

'I'm not here to talk about him.'

'No. Pity. I still have my fantasies about him – he was so gorgeous – and hung! My god! I only wonder how you cope!'

'Adam –' He stopped himself, too tired to remonstrate. He thought of his room upstairs and its private bath deep enough to drown in. He would soak in it until the water grew cold and his skin wrinkled. A hot bath was something to look forward to even though he knew that he would go over and over this conversation, marring the pleasure of it.

Drawing on his cigarette he said, 'You're headmaster now? Congratulations.'

'Well, it isn't much compared to what you've achieved. I saw an exhibition of your paintings in London, just before the war. I made a special journey.'

'Did you like them?'

'Like? Are we meant to like them? They're horrible. Dead

429

soldiers. Painting what you know, eh?'

'I've started painting flowers. Pansies, mainly.'

Adam laughed. His expression softened. 'I thought the paintings were very powerful. They surprised me. *You* surprised me. Your stand against the war.'

'It didn't make me very popular after 1939.'

'I knew you weren't an appeaser.'

Wanting to change the subject, Francis asked, 'Do you still teach or is it all administration as Head?'

'I teach the sixth form. Now, are you here just to make small talk, to catch up? I don't believe it.'

'I wanted to see you.'

'Why? Don't be disingenuous. I know why you're here and it's not to quiz me about my career. Well, I'll save you some time. I haven't seen him. The last time I saw him was about 1940 – yes,'40 – just before the air raids began in the autumn. He was walking along the High Street. I must say he looked marvellous in his uniform. Very young, though. Much too young.'

Francis thought of the photograph he had of Bobby dressed in the RAF uniform. His first thought when it dropped from the envelope was that this was another dressing up, a joke of Jason's in poor taste. It wasn't a joke, but rather in such deadly earnest that he had hidden the photograph away and gone outside. It was midday and even in the shade of their walled garden the sun was merciless. The rest of the household slept in the cool, tiled rooms. He remembered the sound the fountain made, how he had scooped up the water to cool his face and disguise that he had been crying. He didn't feel entitled to tears, although he knew he would have been allowed them. When he went inside he found that Samir had woken and had made him coffee. The boy had only been working for them for a few weeks and his anxiety had touched him. He was grateful, too, that he'd had the tact not to wake Patrick.

Francis stubbed his cigarette out. He downed his drink and glanced towards the bar where the handsome barman was chatting to a young couple. The girl laughed and her partner slipped his arm around her waist, possessive and unsmiling. Catching Francis's eye, the barman smiled as though he shared the joke. Francis looked away quickly, only to find Adam watching him.

'Francis –' He snorted. 'I can't get used to calling you that! Francis, are you going to visit him?'

'Yes.'

'Do you think you should? I mean, think of the upset you'll cause.'

'I need to see him.'

'Why? Why after all this time? And what does he need? Peace, I would imagine, after all he's been through.'

'Peace!' Unexpected anger rose inside Francis. He lit another cigarette in an attempt to be calmer but it was too much for him. He wanted to let go of all the rage he'd suppressed for so long; but Adam was the wrong man to vent it on. He drew on the cigarette, dragging smoke deep into his lungs until he could feel it working. At last he said flatly, 'Adam, everyone believes that things should go on as they are and that I should accept it – as I have all these years, meekly. But I can't accept it any more. I can't.'

'It will hurt him.'

Francis looked down at the tip of his cigarette. The night before he left Tangiers he had lain sleepless until finally he had got up and taken Bobby's photograph down from the shelf in his studio. He'd thought he had left Patrick sleeping but he turned to find him standing in the doorway. 'Don't go,' Patrick said. 'Let him be.'

'You still smoke too much.' Adam had ducked his head to smile at him. 'Listen, I know what happened was unjust – terribly unjust and you didn't deserve it, not at all. But that boy –' He sighed, sitting back in his seat. 'Oh, I don't know. What would I do if I were you? I don't know.'

Francis made himself look at Adam properly for the first time. He had aged, his once thick, dark hair was grey and thin, his delicate expressive hands beginning to show signs of arthritis. He would make one of those wiry old men, keeping his strength and impatient quickness until he shrank too tightly

431

against his bones and gave in. He would make an inoffensive corpse. Francis sipped his drink, trying to banish the image.

Adam said, 'Are you really painting flowers now?' He had seemed to make the effort to keep his voice light, as though they could make small talk and that their friendship wasn't broken beyond repair.

'I stopped painting the war years ago.'

'You used to draw in the margins of the letters you sent me from France. Do you remember? I never thought those doodles might be valuable some day.' Softly he said, 'If I could turn the clock back ...'

Quickly Francis said, 'Would you like another drink? Something stronger this time, eh?'

In his room Francis undressed, hanging his clothes carefully. He could leave his shoes outside to be polished by the night porter but it seemed too much effort, too much fuss. Going into the bathroom he studied himself in the mirror. He hadn't aged as Adam had, gradually and with grace, but suddenly and frighteningly, his own mortality showing itself so starkly he wondered why others weren't in awe of him. He thought of the beautiful girl who had met him outside Waterloo Station. She had flirted with him. He smiled at the memory, his smiled fading as he remembered how she'd shunned him at Jason's funeral. She had known all about him by then and everything he had told her he knew she found incomprehensible. At the graveside she could barely bring herself to look at him.

Over lunch the previous day, when she had still been inclined to be flirtatious, Nina had told him about Bobby, imaging that this young man she seemed to adore was a stranger to him, that her stories could be believed or not and it wouldn't matter, as the stories of strangers' didn't. She had laughed a lot; even when she told him about the baby that had died she'd smiled as she described how Bobby had held this child and played with her and thought of her as his own. He had listened, encouraging her to go on; he felt compelled to, such was his longing to hear everything. Everything: truth or lie or distortion. He had begun to fall in love with this girl and

432

had to draw himself back. He noticed that she watched him with speculative interest.

There was a knock on his bedroom door. Taking one of the neatly folded towels draped over the side of the bath he wrapped it around his waist and went to answer. He expected the porter with the tea he had ordered, instead the barman stood there, grinning as he held up a tray.

'Your tea, sir.'

The boy stepped round him, going to the side table and placing the tray down. Turning to him he made an obvious show of looking him over, frowning a little like a tailor about to alter the hem of a client's jacket. He put his hand on his hip, the other hand went to his mouth; he exhaled softly. 'White towelling sets off your tan.'

Francis laughed, despite himself.

'No – really. You have a beautiful tan. Where did you acquire it?'

Going to the table where he had left his loose change Francis picked up a few coins and held them out. 'Thank you for bringing me the tea. Would you ask at reception if I might have a call in the morning at eight o'clock?'

'Perhaps you won't need a call.'

'No? Why not?'

'I must say how much I admire your work. All those male bodies –'

'What's your name?'

'Stephen.'

'Well, Stephen, I was just about to bathe, if you'd excuse me.'

The boy stood his ground. Francis expected him to carry on his absurdly camp act, was almost prepared to be entertained by it for the few moments it took him to hold the door open and say goodnight. But suddenly the boy slumped down on the bed, defeated. He glanced up at him.

'I'm sorry, Mr Law. I just wanted to talk to you. It was the towel. The towel threw me.'

Leaving a careful space, Francis sat beside him. He was less handsome than he'd seemed to be behind the dimly lit bar with its glamorous display of bottles and cocktail glasses. He looked younger too; acne scarred his cheek and neck. He smelt of cigarettes and alcohol, as though the spirits he served had soaked into his skin. His fingernails were raggedly bitten. Francis overcame the urge to take his hand to comfort him.

Stephen said, 'I do admire your paintings. I love them, their realism. When I saw your name in the guest book, when I saw you at the bar – I used to have a poster of *The Machine Gunner* on the wall of my room.' After a moment he said, 'I was at art school, before I was called up. Somehow I can't bring myself to go back to it.'

Francis thought of the words he might say to encourage him, all of them useless. The boy would go his own way no matter what he said. He pictured *The Machine Gunner* curling its corners away from the walls in the boy's room. It had been one of his earliest works; he thought of it as crude and too shocking, too full of the hate he'd felt at the time. He wished the boy had chosen another of his pictures to pin up, except that most of his popular, early works were like Gunner. At least he had made the machine gunner beautiful, surreally so, he'd thought.

Stephen said, 'You want me to go.' He made to get up but Francis touched his hand, stopping him.

'I don't want to talk,' Francis said. 'Do you still want to stay?'

The boy nodded, already silenced. Lying down, Francis held out his arms.

Chapter Twenty Two

Bobby sipped the whisky Jane had handed him, pretending to study the plates and servers and tureens displayed on the Welsh dresser in her kitchen. Pouring herself a drink Jane said, 'I collect porcelain. Very dull, I'm afraid.'

He turned to her. Without thinking he said, 'My mother collects china figurines.'

'Oh?'

Quickly he said, 'But these are more interesting. They have a purpose, at least.'

'I don't use them.'

'No? Oh well …' He went on looking at the display, knowing how awkward he must look as he searched for something to say that wasn't tactless or idiotic or both. At last he said, 'I had a friend who loved Wedgwood – that blue and white classical Greek stuff. I bought him a plate with a border of Greek warriors fighting with swords.' He smiled, remembering Jason's pleasure in the plate.

'Was he in the RAF too, your friend?'

'Jason? No. He was someone I knew in London. We met before the war.'

She sat down at the kitchen table and motioned that he should sit as well. The table was only large enough to seat two. As he sat his knees brushed hers and she coloured, sipping her drink as if to hide her embarrassment. She said, 'What were you doing in London?'

'Oh, you know. Learning to fly, mainly.'

'Mainly?'

Quickly he said, 'Have you always lived in Thorp?'

'No, I came here when I was offered a job at the school.

What else did you do in London?'

He imagined telling her the whole, indecent truth. He wondered how shocked she would be. She seemed to want to be shocked, as though she guessed he was hiding something he was ashamed of. Deciding to test her he said, 'I worked for Jason in London – as a model. He was a photographer, although he didn't have to do it for a living, he was terribly wealthy. I used to ask how much money he had but he would just laugh. He was always surrounded by others like him: second sons of dukes; the daughters of bishops caught with their knickers down once too often, the telephone numbers of abortionists in their handbags.'

He paused, trying to gauge her reaction. She looked back at him, impassive, and he went on, 'They'd all known each other for years – there was an air of incest about the way they bed-hopped. It was a revelation to me that such people existed: a tight circle of mad, immoral people, although they loved outsiders – the type of outsider who was interesting in the right way.'

'Not outsiders at all, then?'

Surprised by her astuteness he said, 'No, I suppose not.' After a moment he said, 'Jason picked me up in a café. In return for being his model he offered to pay for my flying lessons. Sometimes he and a group of his friends would drive to the airfield with a picnic hamper filled with bottles of champagne and crystal flutes. They'd spread a rug on the field beside the runway and stand up to cheer as my plane bumped down, rushing to tell me how marvellously brave and clever I was. My instructor was bemused. He thought Jason was my father and I was ashamed of how embarrassed I was that he should think such a thing. Not that Jason wanted to be my father – well, perhaps occasionally he did. I know he worried that I might kill myself in what he called those plywood box kites.'

'It sounds like he loved you.'

He remembered how often Jason would say just how much he loved him. 'I know he didn't want anything to get in the way of his taking my photograph. He said finding me was like

436

finding the key to his creativity. He said I was a screen he could project anything on to. I didn't really understand, but it didn't matter. He took his pictures of me and I posed as I was told to, but in my mind I was flying, doing everything I'd been taught during my last flight. During my next lesson my instructor would tell me I was a quick learner.'

Uncomfortably aware that he'd talked for too long he said, 'So, that's what I did in London before the war.'

'It sounds exciting.'

'Flying is.' He smiled. 'As for photographers, cameras, modelling – that's all so boring you'd think your brains had fallen through a hole in the floor.'

She laughed and he imagined reaching across the table and taking her hand and wondered what she would do if he did. The way she looked at him was puzzling; it gave him the idea that adultery was nothing to her. And yet she seemed shy, was awkward around him in a way that had nothing to do with the way he looked. Gathering his courage he covered her hand with his own.

She remained still, ignoring his touch. At last, as he was about to draw away and apologise she said, 'My life hasn't been nearly so exciting. In fact sometimes I think it's passed me by and I did nothing to stop it, just observed its going.' Hesitantly she said, 'I'm thirty-four. That's a lot older than you, isn't it?'

'Nine years, that's all.'

'All!' She looked down at his hand on hers. 'My husband often goes out on his own. Often he doesn't come home until very late, three or four in the morning. He has his own life and I have mine, such as it is.' After a moment she looked up at him. 'You have the most lovely voice, did you know that? I bet women have told you that.'

'No, you're the first.' He smiled but she avoided his gaze and glanced towards the clock on the dresser.

'I suppose you have to go?'

'I don't have to. Would you prefer it if I did?'

She laughed desperately. 'This is so silly isn't it? All this pussy-footing around. I should be brave and say what I want, shouldn't I?'

'Yes.'

'I can't. You'll think I'm ridiculous.'

He held her hand more tightly. 'Say it, Jane.'

'I want you to stay. There. I think you're lovely and I want you to stay.'

Still holding her hand he stood up. She stood too, stepping around the little table and leading him upstairs.

At her bedroom door he hesitated. 'It's not your and your husband's bed, is it?'

She shook her head, not daring to look at him. He still held her hand and she knew that if he left now she would feel his touch for days, her body unable to forget how much she ached for him. She expected him to go, had expected all evening that he would leave as soon as he politely could; she'd imagined him sighing with relief as he drove away. But he had stayed and in his beautiful voice he had said enough to make her think he was seducing her. She had never been seduced, and perhaps she was wrong, perhaps it wasn't even his words but the timbre of his voice and the humour in his eyes that made her forget her propriety. Her propriety! That was an Adam word; thinking how much he influenced her she remembered how impressionable she was. Angry with her own silliness she said, 'I'm being foolish!'

He let go of her hand and stepped back as though giving her the space to decide what to do next. When she managed to look at him he smiled, kindly, she thought. He was being kind to her. She looked away, humiliated.

He said, 'Jane, I think you're lovely, too. I think you're the loveliest woman I've ever met.' He held out his hand to her. 'Look at me.'

She did and he laughed brokenly. 'Maybe you shouldn't look. I should go.'

'Please don't.'

'Your husband –'

She kissed him and at once he was pulling her into his arms. He held her tightly; she could feel how slight he was.

438

She wondered how he would look naked and felt her insides soften with want.

She said, 'Lie down on the bed with me, let me undress you.'

He held her face between his hands. 'Are you sure?'

She nodded. 'Quickly. We should be quick.'

Nina was singing *Paper Moon*, spot-lit on an empty stage. Beside him one of the Gestapo officers stood up suddenly and began applauding, his hands ostentatiously high. The officer stopped and turned to look at him, frowning as though considering the solution to a problem. At last he said, 'I think we shall burn you.'

The other officer laughed, delighted. 'At the stake, like Joan of Arc!'

Nina stopped singing. She smiled from the stage and an unseen audience threw flowers. The pyre was lit at his feet. His hands were tied; he panicked and fumbled and struggled and wept, but suddenly there was nothing but sky beneath him; he couldn't understand where the fire came from. Nina watched him from the ground, far below, her head tilted, her hand shading her eyes against the bright flames.

'Bobby. Bobby ... hush now, hush ...'

Jane Mason knelt beside him. He stared at her, so disorientated for a moment he thought that this was some new twist on the familiar nightmares. He was sitting up and she held his shoulders, her face close to his. She smiled and her eyes were soft with concern. 'It's all right. Just dreams. Just dreams.'

He lay down and turned his head away from her, ashamed of what she'd witnessed. He had begged for his life, he knew, begged and pleaded and made promises, the entire time struggling to open the Spitfire's canopy as the fire leapt around him. God became real, capable of saving him, God and Christ and all the angels and saints. He had begun his own litany as his plane spun and the canopy opened. How scared he had been, how shamingly afraid.

Jane still knelt beside him. He could sense her watching

him, her concern. Forcing himself to look at her he attempted to smile. 'Did I scare you? I'm sorry.'

'You didn't scare me.' Reaching out she pushed back a strand of his hair that had fallen across his forehead. 'Is Nina your girl?'

'No. Not any more.'

She lay down on her back and pulled up the sheet to cover her breasts. Earlier he had taken the grips from her hair and now it was dishevelled, a mass of wild curls framing her face. He remembered how her hair had surprised him as it fell about her shoulders, that there had seemed too much of it to be contained so neatly in the chignon she wore. Both naked on her bed, he had pushed his fingers through the curls until they pressed against her scalp and she had groaned and arched her neck and body, so responsive he had felt his own excitement quicken and become impatient. Too soon he had cupped her breast and felt her whole body stiffen. It was as though she was afraid of some pain to come and he drew back, resting his hand on the soft mound of her belly. Until that moment she had kept her eyes closed but she had met his gaze then.

'I'm a virgin,' she'd whispered.

He'd had to go over her words in his head. Understanding, he was ashamed of the new intensity of want he felt: he wanted to take her at once, roughly so he could feel her tear. It would be over quickly and then he could start again and make good.

Instead he had asked, 'Do you want to stop?'

'No. I don't know. What if you can't ... if I can't ...'

'I'll be slow,' he said. He wondered how much coercion there was in his voice, how much desperation. He was so hard; he had never been so hard, he wondered if this was how rapists felt and if he could stop himself spreading her thighs and breaking into her. He rested his forehead against her astonishing hair and felt her hand on his hip.

She whispered, 'I do want to.' She was crying and he lifted her hand away and held it as gently as he could. Not wanting to, he thought of Nina, the way she flung back her head when she straddled him, the slow way she licked her lips and closed her eyes and pressed her hands against her breasts and groaned with such satisfaction, like a man. He exhaled sharply. It had been so long since anyone other than doctors and nurses had touched him. In his mind's eye Nina smiled wantonly, play-acting the whore. He couldn't bear it any longer. Guiding Jane's hand he closed her fingers around his erection.

She was tentative at first but then her grip tightened, her whole fist closing around him. She would bring him to climax too soon with a jerk of her wrist, and he was just about to lift her hand away when she released him. She knelt and her hair fell to hide her face as she bowed her head and took him into her mouth.

He gasped in surprise. Blindly she reached up and took his hand as her lips and tongue worked with such exquisite delicacy that he pulled his hand away from hers and grasped the sheets, arching his body to thrust deeper. He was beyond care for her, for anything but his own release. Raising himself on one elbow he grasped her head. He came, bucking against her, his orgasm going on and on and annihilating him.

He had fallen back, throwing his arm across his face. His fingers grasped the metal bars of her bed frame. His chest had heaved like that of a man saved from the sea. Unforgivably, briefly, he had slept and his nightmares had disturbed her and brought Nina openly into bed with them.

They lay side by side, both staring at the ceiling. He tried to think of something to say that would make him feel less disgusted with himself. Sorry was all he could come up with. He felt she would be slighted by an apology.

She broke the silence. 'We have to get dressed. He may be back soon.'

'Jane –' He looked at her. 'You were so wonderful – incredible ...'

She sat up and rested her cheek on her raised knees, meeting his gaze. Her curved spine displayed its bumps; she looked pale and delicate and he thought of the sprites in Arthur Rackham drawings. Despite his guilt he had an urge to reach out and stroke her but the steadiness of her gaze stopped him. Eventually she said, 'You were shocked by what I did.'

'Yes.'

'No girl has done that to you before.'

'No.'

'Good. It seemed natural. A natural thing to do.'

'I lost control.'

'I wanted you to. I wanted you not to have to worry about me or about being careful, after what I told you. Perhaps I shouldn't have told you. I should have kept quiet.'

He sat up. Needing to reassure her he said vehemently, 'No – you were right to tell me if you were afraid.'

'I was ashamed.'

He was filled with such a feeling of tenderness for her that he had to look away in case she thought he pitied her. He caught sight of his reflection in her dressing table mirror and looked away quickly. He had forgotten himself for a moment; he didn't need such an ugly reminder.

He thought of her husband, undoubtedly queer, as Hugh and his school friends had guessed. He wondered if he had told her before they married, if some arrangement had been worked out between them, or if his failure to consummate their marriage had been a total humiliation. Either way he felt angry. Queers should be killed; they should be rounded up and gassed like vermin. He thought of Jason, the exception, and clenched his fists. His anger was so childish, so bitter and full of hurt. He wished he could leave it in his childhood where it belonged.

'Bobby?'

She had moved across the bed to kneel behind him and he turned to look at her.

'Please don't call me Bobby. Mark calls me that – my family. I hate it. Bob, I prefer Bob.'

'All right.' Gently she said, 'We have to get dressed.'

When they'd dressed and she stood with him at the front door, he kissed her impulsively, tasting his own dark scent. Holding her face between his hands he said, 'Will you be all right?'

She nodded. 'He won't guess anything.'

'I don't care about him!' He let his hands fall, exasperated

442

with his inability to articulate how he felt. He needed a cigarette to calm himself, he needed to seem strong and confident so that she would know she could rely on him. Instead he was desperate to be in her bed again, mindlessly making love to her. He wanted to find her husband and smash his teeth down his throat. Agitated, his hand went to her face and she turned to kiss his palm.

'I want to make love to you,' he said. 'I want to make you feel as I did.'

The hallway was dark and he searched her face to try to discover what she might be thinking. He couldn't tell and so he said too quickly, 'Come to my house tomorrow after you've finished at the school.'

'Yes. All right.' She smiled shyly. 'Go now. I'm afraid he'll find you here.'

Chapter Twenty Three

Nina woke from a dream that someone was knocking on her door. Sleepily she peered at her alarm clock. It was almost midnight. The knocking went on, real and gently insistent. Her heart began to hammer as she tried to imagine what emergency there could be for someone to call so late. She sat up, staring at the door. After a moment she called out, 'Who is it?'

'It's me, Nina. Hugh.'

Tossing the bedcovers aside she got up and went to the door. Just for a moment she hesitated before drawing back the chain and bolt and turning the key. He could wait, long enough to know that she wouldn't rush for him, but also so that she might compose herself. He mustn't see that she had been frightened.

As soon as she opened the door he was hugging her. He smelt of the cold outside, of stale train carriages and too many cigarettes. His coat was rough against her sleep-warm cheek. Suddenly she remembered that the night-dress she wore was horribly matronly, its flower-sprigged flannel covering her voluminously from her throat to her ankles. Even Bobby had never seen her in it. She pushed away from him, turning her back and picking up her dressing gown from the bed. Putting it on she said, 'I didn't think you were coming until tomorrow.'

'I couldn't wait. I caught the first train going to King's Cross.' He laughed, sounding exhausted. Rubbing his hand across his unshaved chin he said, 'It stopped at every station. I think I could have walked faster.' He grinned. 'It was worth it, though. Every minute.'

'Would you like a cup of tea?'

He nodded.

'Toast? I have some bread, it's only a day old.'

Again he nodded. He seemed unable to take his eyes off her, or speak in case that might break his concentrated looking. She sighed. 'Hugh, put your bag down, take off your coat. We can go to bed after you've eaten.'

Driving him to Thorp Station Bobby had said, 'You won't come back, will you? Will you go to Cornwall?'

'I don't know.' Impulsively Hugh said, 'The cottage is empty – why don't you take a holiday there? It's so quiet this time of year – you'll have the beach to yourself –'

'So no danger of frightening any tourists, eh?'

Hugh sighed. 'I didn't mean that.' Frowning he said, 'You don't look so bad, you know.'

He snorted. 'Don't I?'

'It's easy to feel sorry for yourself, Bob.'

'And you think skulking on a Cornish beach is going to make me feel good about myself?'

Exasperated, Hugh turned away. They were passing the cemetery and he watched as its rooks were startled into the air by some unseen presence. Lighting two cigarettes he handed one to Bobby. 'We had some good times at the cottage when we were kids.'

'Yes,' Bobby changed down gears as they approached a junction. He smiled slightly. 'We did.'

'Do you remember going out in that little fishing boat, the time Dad was so seasick? Christ, he was angry with himself!' He laughed, remembering how green Mick had become. It was the first time he remembered thinking he could do something that his father couldn't. The pride he had felt in his own sea legs had stayed with him for days. Suddenly he realised that the only other holidaymaker on that boat who hadn't thrown up was Bob. At the time Bob had been more concerned for Mick than he was, enforcing his belief that Bob was more suited than he was to the role of Mick's son.

Carefully Hugh said, 'I'll visit Dad when I'm in London. He's beginning to ride high again with this new collection.'

Without taking his eyes off the road Bobby said, 'Nina told me.'

'He asked about you when I saw him last.'

Bobby shook his head, smiling bitterly. 'Liar.'

'Why should I lie about that?'

'I don't know, Hugh, it's your lie.'

'For Christ's sake! You're right, I lied. He didn't ask about you. He's still angry with you, though, about something or other.'

He watched Bobby, waiting for an explanation at last. His running away had caused a flurry of gossip amongst his parents' friends. Of course everyone had known all along that Redpath had beaten his stepson, had actually seemed to hate him. Of course everyone had felt sorry for the boy – and he was so beautiful, wasn't he? So courteous and bright – who wouldn't be proud of him? Instead, Redpath had driven him away to God knows what dangers such vulnerable boys could find themselves in.

But Hugh had known that it wasn't anything to do with Redpath. Bob had become immune to his stepfather's bullying; he treated him with such contemptuous detachment that Hugh had been awed. Hugh knew Bob's absence had everything to do with Mick. Whenever one of his parents' friends speculated about Bobby, Mick would go into one of his thin-lipped, hard-eyed silences that Hugh so dreaded.

They had almost reached the station and Bobby had remained silent, the atmosphere between them in the car so oppressive that Hugh couldn't stand it any longer. Hugh cleared his throat and Bobby glanced at him.

Bobby said, 'You know why I ran away, Hugh. School had finished, I wasn't clever enough to stay there any longer and I couldn't face going back to live at home. Simple as that.'

'So why didn't you write to me?'

'I don't know. Why didn't you write to me?'

'I didn't know where you were! And anyway –'

'And anyway what, Hugh? Listen, I'm sorry I behaved like a shit when I was sixteen. All right?' After a moment he had said, 'I'll write to you at Nina's. I'll ask you to invite me to the

446

cottage – maybe we could hire the *La Fillette* again and go fishing.'

It was only when he was on the train that Hugh realised that *La Fillette* was the name of the boat on which Mick had been so seasick. He'd realised too that it had been their last holiday together. He and Bobby had been sixteen, close as brothers. A few months later Bobby had gone and he was telling himself it was unmanly to miss him so much.

Lying beside Nina in her bed, Hugh rolled on to his side to look at her. Asleep she looked younger, more like the innocent girl he imagined she was when Bobby first met her. She had told him she was seventeen when she first saw Bobby. She had told him she had fallen in love with him at once – because everyone did. Everyone did! She'd said it as though it was so patently obvious and unremarkable it amused her that he was so ignorant. He didn't say that he was well aware of Bobby's charm. He didn't say that he thought Bobby had corrupted her. He wasn't even sure why he thought this, except that there were times when she seemed too much like him; she possessed the same hard-edged independence he had, as though other people and their untidy feelings were nothing to them.

Nina stirred and opened her eyes. She frowned at him sleepily. 'Hugh?' She exhaled softly and he felt her warm breath on his face. 'Hugh! I'd forgotten …'

'Forgotten me? Already?' He pulled her into his arms. 'Good morning, gorgeous.'

'What time is it?'

He glanced at his watch. 'Eight o'clock.'

'Oh God!' She struggled from his embrace and threw the covers aside. 'I'll be late for work!'

'You're not really going to that shop, are you?'

She grabbed a pair of knickers from a drawer. 'That shop is where I earn money, Hugh. Money – you know – to live on?'

'I know – but …'

'Will you make me some tea while I get ready? I don't want anything to eat.'

He got up reluctantly and filled the kettle at her chipped and drip-stained sink. Through the window he could see the terraces of tall, Victorian tenements just like the one he was stood in; washing lines were strung from window to window, men's combinations flapping in the breeze like headless, grubby, paper dolls. He hadn't realised what a slum she lived in. He supposed he'd seen it through the eyes of one blinded by love-sickness. He was sick in a way: he felt feverish with want for her. Lighting the gas beneath the kettle he said, 'Nina, don't go to work. You don't have to –'

She laughed, looking up at him from rolling on a stocking. 'Of course I do! I need the money, Hugh. Besides, I can't let Elizabeth down.'

'What about letting me down?'

'I'll be back by six. You can take me to dinner.'

He made tea, at the same time watching her dress and apply her make up. She rolled her hair into a net snood then straightened her stocking seams, twisting her body to see the backs of her legs reflected in her wardrobe mirror. Watching her, thinking about their love-making, he said, 'Will you marry me?'

She laughed.

'I'm serious. Will you?'

'Oh, Hugh – not now. I have to go to work.'

'I only need you to say yes. It won't take a minute.'

For a moment she said nothing but stood looking at him until he became self-conscious and glanced away. Through the window he could see smoke rising from the huddled, rain-shiny chimneys into a thick, sulphurous sky. A dog barked over and over. In the next flat a baby began to cry.

He said, 'I want to take care of you. I want to do everything that it says in the marriage service – love and cherish and honour you.'

She bowed her head and her fingers went to the wedding band on her finger. Slowly she began to twist it until it lay in her palm. Turning away she placed it on her bedside table. She touched it gently and he thought she was about to slip it back on her finger. He found he was holding his breath.

Quietly she said, 'Honour me?'

He stepped forward, only to stop himself, afraid that

448

showing too much would startle her and break the spell he had somehow managed to conjure. He had to be still and quiet, as though she was a rare bird he had to hide himself from. She couldn't escape. He wanted her to himself so badly, to be able to say *this is my wife*. He couldn't let her see how much he wanted to possess her.

She repeated, 'Would you honour me, respect me –'

'Yes.'

'Despite what you know?'

'What do I know? Nothing. Only that I love you.'

'You won't change your mind?'

'No!' He crossed the small space between them and pulled her into his arms. For a moment she held herself stiffly only to relax against him. Her head rested on his shoulder; he thought how well their bodies fitted.

He kissed her head and she looked up at him. 'I don't want to wait, Hugh.'

'As long as it takes to get a licence, that's all.'

She nodded. 'I should go to work now.'

'Let me walk you there.'

'No. Have the day to yourself.' She kissed his mouth swiftly before fetching her coat and putting on her hat in front of the mirror. She smiled at his reflection then left so quickly the door swung open behind her. Going out to the landing, Hugh leaned over the banister and watched her run down the stairs.

Chapter Twenty Four

Jane took the day off work. That morning she'd told Adam she suspected she was coming down with 'flu and he had frowned at her for a while, reassuring himself that she was indeed too ill to go into school. He had reminded her of her father when she was a little girl, always on the look out for those who might be taking advantage of him.

At last he'd said, 'You do look pale. I heard you get up in the night, didn't you sleep well?'

Unable to look at him she had sat down at the kitchen table and covered her face with her hands to feign tiredness. She heard him sigh and snap his briefcase closed. 'You'd better go back to bed, Jane. Is there anything you need? Something I can bring you from the chemist?'

She'd shaken her head. A moment later she felt his hand on her shoulder, a quick squeeze and he was gone. At once she'd run upstairs.

Naked, she stood in front of her bedroom mirror and regarded her reflection with as much cool criticism as she could. She had bathed, pouring too much bath oil in the running water. Now her skin felt slippery, lubricated. The bath water had formed globules on her skin as she'd raised her legs and arms to shave the soft, innocent hair that until last night no one else had ever seen. She had shaved to the very top of her thighs, even nicked at her pubic curls to tidy them.

Years ago, she had read in a book on women's health that the night before her wedding a girl should, whilst bathing, push two of her fingers inside her vagina, allowing the warmth of the water to relax her as she became used to the invasion. The book had said that this technique would help to know

450

what to expect from sexual intercourse; a girl would feel less frigid if she knew and understood her body.

She hadn't followed the book's instructions. She already knew and understood her body. She had learned how to bring herself to orgasm, she didn't need to explore the soft, tight folds inside her. Her frigidity had nothing to do with the fear of pain but of humiliation, the belief that a man like Bobby wouldn't want to have anything to do with her once the sex was over. She couldn't shake the thought that men laughed behind the backs of such desperate women.

Late last night, when Bobby had gone and Adam hadn't yet returned, she had taken out the silk underwear she'd bought for her honeymoon and laid it against her crumpled sheets. The bra and cami-knickers, the slip and suspender belt all in what the shop assistant had told her was the finest oyster silk. She had been invited to run her fingers over the slip to appreciate its smoothness. The dry skin of her finger had snagged on the silk, lending credibility to her idea that she wasn't the type to wear such garments. They would make her feel as though she was pretending to be someone she wasn't. The shop assistant had been persuasive, though, and suddenly she'd decided that they were only clothes, best clothes that might give her confidence, as all best clothes should. She had bought the whole set happily, feeling audacious as she walked out of the shop carrying the bag in which the underwear was folded in tissue paper and packed secretly in a box.

Laid out on her bed the underwear looked like relics that might be displayed in a museum. They had been worn only once, for a few hours, and had been washed and returned to their tissue paper and box as soon as she'd returned from her honeymoon. She remembered how quickly she had washed them in the sink, the hasty way she had put them away as soon as they were dry enough. She couldn't bring herself to look at them, they were so foolish. Last night, taking them out again, her heart had hammered in anticipation. But they had looked as though they belonged to someone who had lived and died years before the hardening experience of the war. She had put them away again, unable to decide if her superstitions would allow her to wear them.

But she had nothing else, nothing but ordinary white cotton knickers and bras. She needed the confidence that oyster silk would give her. She began to dress. The silk slithered over her newly depilated skin and she gasped at the thrill of it, as though his hands were stroking her. She closed her eyes as she remembered the experienced lightness of his touch. He would have had many lovers. She worried whether he thought of them as conquests.

She chose a summer dress rather than one of her school-marm suits. In the mirror she looked as if she was about to serve tea at a garden fete and immediately took the dress off again. In the back of her wardrobe was a plain black dress she had last worn to a cousin's funeral. She remembered how grown up she had felt in it, that its simple cut lent her a measure of sophistication. She would wear the black dress with a string of pearls and the high-heeled black court shoes that had been so impractical at her cousin's graveside but gave her height and tautened her calves. She would wear the little pillbox hat with its net veil folded back. Her cool silk underwear would calm the heat that spread over her skin whenever she thought about him.

Downstairs, Jane covered her black dress with her everyday coat and checked her appearance in the hall mirror. Her lipstick was a shade too bright and she blotted it on her handkerchief. Stepping closer to the mirror she smiled experimentally and was appalled by how frightened she looked. For a moment she wondered if she could go through with it, only to remember how, as he was about to get into his car, he had stopped and hurried back to where she was watching him from the doorstep. He'd taken out a pen and written down a telephone number on the inside cover of a book of matches. 'Call me if you need to, if anything happens, if you need me –' Holding out the matches he'd said awkwardly, 'Take it, anyway.'

She guessed he wondered at the strangeness of her marriage and that he believed its strangeness was somehow dangerous. He had looked so concerned she had wanted to reassure him but there was nothing she could say, no way to explain that strangeness was sometimes safe.

She looked down at the phone on the table beneath the mirror. Heart pounding, she took the book of matches from her handbag and re-read the neat, bold number although she knew it by heart. Her hands shook as she picked up the receiver and waited for the operator's voice.

Bobby placed the receiver down and stood looking at it. A minute ago he had been full of purpose, now he was at a loss. He was still in his pyjamas and dressing gown. The frustratingly long time it took him to dress correctly meant that he wouldn't have time to change the sheets on his bed, to clean the bathroom or to place the daffodils he'd been about to pick from the garden in a vase on the hallway table. The flowers would have been something ordinary to fix on as he showed her into the house. She would have commented on them and he would have told her that they grew like weeds in the garden and would she like to see? In the garden the extraordinary desire he had for her might have been subdued for a while, inhibited by the blank-eyed stare of his neighbour's windows. He might even have been able to tell her that she should go home to her husband, for her own sake: he would eat her alive if she stayed.

He hesitated, torn between daffodils and dressing. Dressing had to take priority. He couldn't allow her to see him like this or to smell the thick blunt scent of sleep on him. In a few minutes when she pressed the doorbell he would be dressed, albeit swiftly and casually. He smiled, remembering her bare feet and thinking that perhaps he might leave his own feet bare to save the time wasted struggling with socks and shoelaces.

In the hotel restaurant Francis lingered over his coffee, the last guest to leave. The other guests were mainly single men, like himself, although unlike him they all had work to go to, work that involved dressing in suits and ties and carrying briefcases. Most of them had an air of steadiness that had Francis guessing at how dull their jobs might be. He remembered how unsuited he'd been to the work that other men did to support their families. The indefatigability of his fellow guests made him feel ashamed.

The coffee was weak and tasted more strongly of the chicory it had been adulterated with. He wouldn't think of it as coffee but as a beverage peculiar only to the English and that way he wouldn't feel slighted by it. He was determined not to take England personally, a petulance he knew he'd been guilty of since stepping off the boat. Even that boy Stephen had noticed it, laughing as he lay naked beside him on his bed, smoking his cigarettes.

'I've never seen anyone actually shudder at a plate of fried egg and bacon before,' Stephen had said. 'This morning, when I saw you in the restaurant, shuddering, it clinched it for me, I just knew you were queer.' Casually he'd asked, 'Who was that man you were with in the bar?'

When he didn't answer Stephen went on, 'An ex-lover. But he still loves you and you're sad that you don't love him.'

'Get dressed now.'

He'd said it gently enough but the boy had looked hurt. Stephen said, 'I haven't fucked you yet. Turn and turn about, it's only fair.'

Francis laughed. 'I haven't the energy. Get dressed.'

'Can I finish smoking this?' The boy looked down at the tip of the cigarette. 'They're foreign, aren't they? Sweet. Fairy cigarettes.'

'Put it out if you don't like it.'

'Then I'd have to go. I don't want to go.' After a moment he said, 'I read that you were mentioned in dispatches during the first war?'

During a raid on a German trench he had killed their machine-gunner at point-blank range. Like an executioner, Patrick had said later, and without meaning to he had made him feel scared. He couldn't remember the details of the killing; he'd had to take Patrick's word for it along with the testimony of the men. He had executed a man. His cold-bloodedness chimed with what he knew about himself and had wanted to keep hidden. But its revelation hadn't surprised

454

Patrick, only made him want him more. He should have been ashamed of such lust.

The boy was watching him curiously, waiting to be told whether what he'd read was truth or fiction and so Francis said, 'Lots of men were mentioned in dispatches.'

'I was in Italy during the war.' Stephen's lip curled contemptuously. 'Bloody Eyeties. Not one of them gave a shit about anything. Couldn't fucking care less.' Stubbing his cigarette out he said, 'I had an easy war. Lucky bugger, eh?'

The boy got up and began to dress. Francis couldn't stop himself watching him, noting how lean he was, how pale. He'd wondered if he'd become tanned by the Italian sun, if his mousy hair had become lighter until it seemed England had lessened its grip on him. He doubted it.

Sitting in the restaurant now, Francis considered settling his bill and finding another hotel. He couldn't face the boy again, couldn't be bothered with any awkwardness or expectation. And if the boy behaved as if nothing had happened he would feel even more of a fool than he already did. He thought how hurt Patrick would be if he discovered his unfaithfulness but how stoically resigned too. Patrick expected him to behave badly. Patrick made allowances for him. It was infuriating, and that fury was something he had learnt to hide.

He thought about ordering more coffee, of delaying decisions already put off until he was beginning to feel a panicky urgency. He couldn't panic; he felt sure Bobby would despise such lack of control. Bobby. He closed his eyes, his breathing quickening as the familiar pain closed around his heart. He stood, too agitated to remain still, as though the pain could be placated by action. He would walk by the river; he would walk and think and decide. He paused just long enough for his breathing to steady before making his way out of the hotel.

Chapter Twenty Five

Bobby whispered, 'If only my hands –'

Jane covered his mouth with her fingers. They lay side by side, his arms wrapped tightly around her. He could feel her breasts against his chest, her nipples soft now. Remembering how they had hardened at his touch, he kissed her mouth. 'I didn't hurt you, did I?'

'No.'

He could hear the smile in her voice and he drew away a little to look at her. 'Can you stay for a while?'

'If you want me to.'

'*If.*' He grinned. 'Did you think I'd want you to leave?'

'I thought you'd kick me out before carving another notch on the bedpost.'

'Another?'

She sighed and closed her eyes. 'I could sleep now, I feel so relaxed.'

'Then sleep.'

'No. I don't want to waste my time with you sleeping!' She laughed. 'I don't want to waste a minute of our time together.'

She wriggled down the bed a little until her head rested on his chest. He stroked her hair, thinking that he could just as easily sleep, that like her he felt loose-limbed and lazy. He smiled, realising that for the first time in his life he felt content.

After a while she said carefully, 'It was a joke – what I said about the notch on the bedpost. I was joking.'

'I know you were.'

'I didn't offend you?'

'No!' He tipped her chin back so that she met his gaze.

'Before you there was really only one girl. And before you I thought she would be the only one ever.'

'You still love her.'

'No. Jane –' He sighed. 'No, I don't.'

'Last night, during your nightmare, when you called her name out …'

His feeling of contentment was destroyed by the memory of the nightmare. He believed he was more scared in the dream than during the crash, that in reality he had been calmer. Braver, he supposed, the kind of bravery that came from having so little idea of what was in store for him.

He said, 'That dream – it's one I often have. It doesn't mean anything. She doesn't mean anything any more.'

She was silent for a while. Eventually she said, 'I wasn't sure what to do – whether to wake you or not. What shall I do next time?'

'Next time?' He smiled at her. 'You'd need to spend the night with me. What excuse could you give him?'

'I could tell him I'm going to my mother's.'

'This weekend?'

She nodded. There was such desire in her eyes he became hard again and thought of a whole weekend with her in his bed. They could retreat behind the locked door and closed curtains; he would take the phone off its hook. They needn't dress; they could bathe together and eat picnic meals in bed. No one would disturb them. Imagining it he smiled and she kissed his mouth gently.

She said, 'I'd worry he would find out.'

'He wouldn't.'

'But if he did –'

'Would he care so much?'

'Of course!'

'Does he have a right to?'

She moved away from him a little. 'He cares for me, I think.'

'Not like I do.'

'This is too quick.'

'I don't know how long it's supposed to take.'

'You don't know me – I don't know you!' She laughed but he could see that she was on the edge of tears.

Quickly he said, 'My name is Robert Harris. I'm twenty-six, almost. For five years I was a pilot in the RAF, until 1944 when I was shot down. I was in hospital for two years – blah blah blah. Last month my grandfather died and left me this house and a comfortable amount of money. I'm in sound mind and body, fit even, apart from my clumsy hands.' After a moment he said, 'I hate looking at myself in the mirror but I do, often, because I'm probably the vainest man you'll ever meet and I want to reassure myself. Of what, I don't know. Maybe I'm trying to get used to it.'

She closed her eyes and tears spilled out over her cheeks.

Wiping them away with his fingers he said, 'Why are you crying?'

'I don't know!' She sounded exasperated. 'I don't cry very often. I'm sensible and careful. Timid.' She looked at him. 'My name is Jane Mason. My maiden name is Castleton. I still think of myself as Miss Castleton, often. I'm not married, not really, not in any meaningful sense. Is that an excuse? Because I am married. Whatever it feels like, I am married.'

'Do you love him?'

She gazed at him so long that he held her face between his hands and asked her again. At last she said, 'No. I think I love you.'

Still holding her face he kissed her. Drawing back he said, 'Don't go home tonight.'

'Bob – I must. I'll lose my job, everything –'

'You'll have me.'

For a while she said nothing. He felt his smile freeze on his face until it felt absurd and still she went on watching him, silent and anxious, so he blurted out, 'I think I love you.'

She exhaled softly. 'Let's not talk. Make love to me again.'

Pretending to be asleep, Jane heard him get up and go to the bathroom. She heard the lavatory flush and a tap turned on, she heard him draw back the bolt on the door and go downstairs. She rolled on to her back and ran her hand over his side of the bed where the sheets retained the heat from his body. Hesitantly her other hand went between her legs; she was tender and sore despite his gentleness.

His size had surprised her, her body resisting him so that he'd sucked his fingers to wet them and carefully pushed them inside her. 'Relax,' he'd whispered and for a moment he seemed impatient, but then he withdrew, brushing her mouth with his as he found that place she had discovered for herself. He smiled, his gaze holding hers as his fingers rubbed and stroked and pressed against her, harder and faster until she was arching her back and opening herself for him, so wide open, so blatant with want. When he pushed inside her she gave easily, orgasmic still and crying out words she had never used before.

Listening to him move about in the kitchen downstairs she curled on to her side. Earlier he had drawn the curtains but an oblong of sun slanted through a gap he had left and lit a patch of frayed carpet. The room was quite bare, only a wardrobe and a chair beside the bed. There were no pictures or books, no toys or games left over from his childhood. He would have hidden such childish things away, she was sure, all too aware that his childhood was less distant than hers was. He was a kind, thoughtful man; his voice was beautiful and his eyes made her forget herself so that she became confidently sluttish whenever he looked at her. She smiled, only for her smile to slip away. He was kind and thoughtful and his voice made her weak-kneed. His eyes were beautiful. And he was strange.

There was something not right about this man, as though a part of him was too badly damaged and corroding. She thought of him burning, the terror of it. Perhaps such pain had killed something in his mind, something that if left to survive would make it impossible to go on. She closed her eyes against the sudden fear that she was no longer safe. All her dull, comfortable security had been sacrificed to a boy whose fragility she should have recognised from the start. She drew her knees up, hugging them to her chest. She deserved this fear, the numbing shock of it; her foolish horror of dying a virgin had wrecked her life.

And yet the sex had been better than all the days of her life

459

so far. Even now when she thought of him inside her she wanted him again. He could be quick and hard or slow, too slow and teasing, knowing how greedy she was for him. She had thought of him flying, so brave and ruthless, and she had groaned with lust, shocking herself. She had been thrilled by the idea of a man in uniform: she thought she had been above such silliness.

There was wetness between her legs and she drew her hand away and inspected it, expecting to see her deflowering blood. Instead there was mucus-like whiteness, a smell like thin flour-and-water-paste. She stared at it fearfully. He had made her pregnant. Of course he had.

From the doorway he said, 'Tea, madam.'

She heard him set a tray down on the table at his side of the bed, felt the mattress dip as he climbed into bed beside her. She expected him to pull her into his arms, but she only felt his hand on her shoulder. Gently he said, 'Jane? Are you asleep?'

She couldn't bring herself to answer him. Ludicrously she thought of the snoring noises children made when they pretended to sleep. She clutched the bedcovers more tightly beneath her chin, smelling his sperm on her fingers so that she suppressed a sob.

'Jane?' He sounded anxious and he moved closer to her. 'Jane, is there something wrong?'

'No. I'm tired, that's all. I should go soon.' She was surprised at how calm she sounded, the shock, she supposed, kept her steady.

'You're going?'

'I must.'

'All right.' After a while he said, 'You'll come back though, won't you?'

'I don't know.'

She felt him move away and get up. He began to pick her clothes from the floor, laying them over the chair before gathering his own clothes and beginning to dress. She watched him. Looking up from the awkward business of buttoning his shirt he caught her eye.

Timidly she said, 'I'm sorry.'

'About?' His voice was hard, his eyes dark and unreadable. Lifting his collar he draped his tie around his neck and began to knot it. 'Perhaps you should dress now.'

She hesitated, not wanting to expose her nakedness to his hurt and anger. He would see her as she was, older, skinny, her breasts sagging. He would wonder what she was doing in his bedroom. She realised suddenly that if he was strange, she was stranger, just because she wanted him so much. She was indecent with want. As he sat down at the foot of the bed to put on his socks she said, 'I'll come back, if you want me to.'

At first she thought he was deliberately ignoring her. Eventually he said, 'If I want you to? What about you, Jane? What do you want?'

'You.'

He laughed shortly. 'Me. You don't want much, do you?' He looked at her at last. 'You'd leave your husband for me? Give up your job – I'd suppose you'd probably have to? How would you feel walking down the street with me – people stare, you know, children point and ask their mothers what's wrong with that man's face. And I dream – my god, you haven't heard the half of my nightmares …' He had been talking too quickly, breathlessly, and he breathed in deeply. He gazed down at the shoes he'd been about to put on. 'Listen to me. I'm such an idiot. All I want to do is beg you not to go but I end up giving you a reason to leave.' Looking at her he said, 'I'm not really as odd as you must think.'

'I don't think that!'

He smiled bleakly. 'No? You look scared of me, sometimes, wary. I think I was in hospital too long; I've forgotten how to behave amongst the well.'

She reached out to touch his arm. 'Lie down. Talk to me.'

'What shall I talk about?'

'Hospital?'

'Hospital?' He smiled. 'That's boring.'

After a moment he lay down and took his cigarettes from his pocket. He lit one, keeping his eyes fixed on the ceiling. She kept quiet; aware that she was holding her breath she

461

breathed out softly and he glanced at her.

Looking away again he said, 'I was in a hospital where everyone was burnt like me – some worse, poor buggers. The senior MO there had wangled it so we didn't have to wear our uniforms – they were too stiff and chaffing, too many buttons – so we could wear what we liked.' He laughed as though at some bad joke. 'I wanted to wear my uniform. Vain eh? The others lolled about, gossiping and drinking beer – another concession the MO had fought for – but I just wanted to be on my own, sober and on my own. I wanted my life back, my face back, my hands. All the others were just walking reminders of what I'd become.'

He blew a smoke ring into the air. Watching it he said, 'The doctors said I was depressed. Properly depressed, not just angry and sad and frightened like all the others. They threatened me with an asylum if I didn't buck up. They called my parents and when I heard they were coming to see me I went out into the town and got drunk. It was the first time I'd been out on my own – although they were always encouraging us to go out. I was scared stiff, but it was easier than facing them.

'They waited for me, my mother and stepfather. When I came back, drunk, I was sick over his shoes. He told me I should be ashamed of myself. I haven't seen him since.'

Carefully she asked, 'Did they send you to the asylum?'

'Jane, are you worried I'm mad?' Rolling on his side he looked at her closely, frowning a little. After a while he said, 'I bucked up. Pulled myself together. I don't think they were serious about the loony bin, just bored with my silence.' He smiled, reaching out to hook a strand of her hair behind her ear. She shivered.

'Are you cold?'

'No, not cold.'

'The tea will be stewed. Did you want a cup of tea? I could make some fresh?'

'No, thank you.'

He sat on the edge of the bed and stubbed his cigarette out. Somehow he looked frailer dressed, the soft grey shirt he wore

462

making him appear boyish. She remembered the scars on his body where they had plundered undamaged skin to graft on to his hands and face. She had kissed them and he had smiled self-consciously, obviously wanting her to stop. For a moment she had felt awkward and too sentimental, the only time he had made her feel anything other than cherished.

She thought of his semen leaking between her legs and unable to resist the nagging worry she said, 'Were you careful?'

He frowned at her over his shoulder. For a moment she thought she would have to explain what she meant but then he said, 'I'm sorry – I meant to withdraw.' He exhaled sharply. 'Oh Christ.'

'Yes. Oh Christ.'

'It doesn't necessarily mean – what I mean is …'

'I might not be pregnant.'

'Yes. You might not be.'

Hesitantly she said, 'But if I was?'

'Would you marry me?'

'I'm married.'

'After your divorce.'

She laughed miserably. 'It would take years. Bob junior would be a bastard.'

'He'd be yours. Yours and mine.' He knelt beside her. 'I want you to be pregnant. I think you should lie still, perhaps lift you legs up in the air so the little buggers are given a fighting chance.' He grinned. 'What shall we call him? Not Bob – bloody awful name.'

'It might be a girl.'

'Maybe.' Gazing at her he said, 'I think you're blooming already.'

She looked away from him and the blatant look of love in his eyes. She felt dazed by the speed of what had happened between them. If he went on looking at her like that they would make love again. She was reminded of how young he was, how insatiable, how his appetite for her seemed to feed hers for him. She laughed shortly; he might just as well have brained her for all the sense she could make of it.

He lay down and placed his hand gently over her belly. For a while they didn't speak and gradually she sensed that he was waiting for her to come to some decision. The words formed in her mind, she rehearsed them, fine-tuning and re-phrasing, wanting to be sure he wouldn't misunderstand.

'I'll go now,' she said. 'I'll pretend to him that I've spent the day at home and tomorrow I'll go back to school. The play is staged on Thursday, the boys have worked so hard I can't let them down. But after the play I'll hand in my notice. I'll leave Adam. I'll come here, if you'll have me.'

'Are you sure?'

'Are you?'

'Yes.'

She turned her head on the pillow to look at him. 'We'll be the talk of the town.'

'Do you care?'

'No.'

He kissed her. 'Are you hungry?'

'Yes.'

Getting up he said, 'I'll go and make you something to eat while you dress.'

Chapter Twenty Six

Francis sat by the river on a bench carved with a heart and intertwining initials. He ran his fingers along the indentations. Perhaps C&W were still together, married with children; perhaps they sometimes came back here and traced the outline of the enclosing heart. Perhaps C was dead, killed in this recent war, and W mourned, believing him to be the only one, her true, lost love. She may have forgotten him. It seemed more likely. Everyone was forgotten, in the end.

Francis closed his hands into fists. His bitterness, even after so many years, still made him feel unhinged, as though he could seize a stranger by his lapels and beg him to agree how unfairly he'd been treated, how terribly wronged. He could tell this stranger the whole story, he could rant and weep and say 'This was done to me! Do you think I deserved such treatment?' The stranger would, of course, say no, because even a mad man who had accosted him on the street deserved to be treated kindly.

Until lately he had always managed to keep this agitating bitterness to himself. Even Patrick, who knew most of it, didn't understand how deeply he'd been hurt. Patrick believed he had come to terms with the past and was relieved because he couldn't bear him to be sad or to think that he missed any part of his old life. Patrick wanted all to be well if only because he loved him so badly.

Lately, however, he'd decided that Patrick should recognise his hurt, should be made to see it and understand. One morning, during a breakfast of figs from their tree, he had found himself watching Patrick as he ate. Catching his eye, Patrick had smiled at him.

'Will you finish your picture today?'

Francis thought of the painting he was working on, how badly it had failed to show what he wanted it to. He had decided that he was a fraud and would stop painting. He hadn't told Patrick this. Patrick would think he was craving attention.

Pouring coffee for them both, Patrick said, 'Samir thinks you're angry with him.'

'I'm not.'

Ignoring him Patrick went on, 'Odd, really, that he should think so, because actually I've been thinking that you're angry with me.' Setting the coffee pot down he said, 'What have we done to upset you?'

He was such a beautiful man, so fuckable still. Often the only place he wanted to be was in bed with him, his weight pinning him down during the kind of hard, silent sex that Patrick allowed him sometimes. Patrick, who was gentle and careful and wanted only to make love to him, half understood his need to be fucked with the kind of violent force that would make him groan with the shock of it and come too quickly. Francis suspected that Patrick was ashamed of him after such sessions, ashamed of himself too for so easily becoming his bit of rough.

Patrick had said, 'Francis?'

He'd realised he'd been staring at him, as though trying to memorise his face. He had an idea that he would be changed by what he was about to say. Resisting the urge to touch his mouth to silence any words that might come, he said, 'I'm going to England. I have to see him, Pat. I have to. I'm sorry.'

'Will you come back?'

'Yes.' To assure him he had taken his hand. 'Yes, of course.'

He had drawn his hand away. 'What if he hates you?'

'What if he doesn't?'

Looking out over the oily River Tees, Francis remembered how Patrick had frowned at him until he had felt like a spoiled child about to be reasoned with. Eventually Patrick had said, 'Shall I come with you?'

466

Francis had almost wept then and he hadn't wept for years, not since that day in prison when he read the letter that told him he wouldn't be allowed to see Bobby again.

He lit a cigarette and drew smoke deep inside him. In Durham Gaol he had made himself think of his imprisonment as just an extension of the war, except there were no snipers aiming for his head, no bombardments to shatter his nerves. His gaolers could do their worst but at least he would survive his three years' hard labour for buggering a stranger in a public toilet. His lawyer had pleaded for leniency: his client was a veteran of the war who had lost an eye fighting for his country. There had seemed something comical about that; there were sniggers in court as though a one-eyed queer was the punch line to a dirty joke the judge wouldn't get. The judge said gravely that he was a disgrace and that his fine war record had been nullified by such a depraved, disgusting act. His father had shouted from the public gallery that this was not justice, that there was no justice any more. For his own part he had bowed his head, meekly accepting. He had always known that fucking men would lead him to this.

In Durham Gaol he didn't expect his wife to visit him. He expected the divorce papers, her only response to his letters. When the letter came advising him that Bobby was to be adopted by his new stepfather he had cried for days, openly and without inhibition. During his next visit his father said, 'Perhaps it's for the best – imagine how the child would feel if he knew the truth about you.'

The truth was that he was a homosexual, a queer, a fairy, a shirt-lifter, a sodomite. That stranger in the public convenience had a sweet, lost expression, and he had looked young, even younger than he was. There had been something irresistible about such innocence.

Francis crushed his cigarette beneath his shoe. He remembered how Patrick had waited for him outside the prison gates, how he had silently taken his small suitcase from him and helped him into the cab. Together they left England the next day, crossing the Channel to Calais just as if the war still raged and they were returning to their platoon. Throughout the long journey to Tangier, Patrick broke into his silences to speak of his house with its tiled floors and shutters to keep out the heat, its courtyard where the fountain cooled the jasmine scented air. The sun would heal him, Patrick said, it would make him strong again. On his first night of exile in his new country, in Patrick's tiny, whitewashed house that smelt of heat trapped in stone, Patrick had wept as he'd undressed him, tenderly exposing his skinniness, his deathly prison pallor. They hadn't made love for years, and wouldn't for months; he stank of fear, he was frail and sickly and repellent and thought of no one but himself. Even Bobby was forgotten for a while.

For a long time all he did was sit in Patrick's courtyard, watching the shadows lengthen. The light was different here; he found himself stirred by its intensity. As he became stronger he began to draw the little birds that came to drink from the fountain's edge. Without comment, Patrick bought him paper and paints and brushes. He painted the birds over and over and thought of prison, of a particularly sadistic guard who had such an imagination when it came to the sexual humiliation of his prisoners. The birds became tamer, he would throw down crumbs and they would hop around his feet. Patrick began to call him Saint Francis, smiling so that he might smile too.

One day he'd told Patrick, 'I don't want to be called Paul any more. They've decided Paul Harris is dead – well, so be it.'

He'd taken his mother's maiden name and the Christian name Patrick had chosen for him. Francis Law. It was the name on the first painting he sold, a portrait of Patrick half-naked and asleep on their bed. Other buyers came forward; he sold the pictures of the birds, and those of the young servant boy who cooked and cleaned for them. He began to gain a reputation amongst his fellow ex-pats for painting decorative pictures, perfect for their tasteful, modern homes. He painted beautiful pictures of Patrick and the boy and the little birds and all the time he remembered the prison guard and the men he'd killed and seen killed on the battlefields of France. The memories were too vivid to be ignored. He began to paint them in dull, realistic colours. In these paintings the men were even more beautiful than Patrick was and some of them were dead, and some of them were Paul, painted by Francis.

To his surprise these paintings sold. In England Mick Morgan's war poetry had become so popular that people queued outside bookshops to hear him read. Morgan's play about the war ran for years in the West End and Francis's paintings were seen by some as the antidote to Morgan's popularisation. It became chic to own a Francis Law; whereas Morgan was read by the masses, Law was appreciated by the discerning few. These few paid large sums to prove how unsentimental they were.

After his first exhibition in London one cold spring afternoon in 1930 he walked from the gallery where all his paintings had been sold and found himself at the door of Morgan's Kensington flat.

For a while he'd hesitated, even walking back along the street, believing that his courage had failed. But he had to do this and he'd turned back again. Before he could change his mind he pushed hard on the bell above Morgan's name. He made himself think of Patrick, who would only be exasperated by his nervousness, but all the same he jumped as the door opened.

A man smiled at him. Francis had heard him laughing before he opened the door and he was still smiling, his voice bright as he said, 'Hello! What can we do for you?'

'Is Mr Morgan in?'

'I'm afraid he doesn't see anyone without an appointment.'

'He'll see me.'

'Will he?' The man raised his eyebrows. 'And who are you?'

Behind the man's back Mick Morgan said, 'It's all right, Henry. I know him.'

Henry looked put out. After a deliberate hesitation he stood to one side.

In Morgan's living room Henry said, 'Are you going to introduce us, Mick?'

Morgan turned to Francis. Without bothering to keep the

contempt from his voice he asked, 'What do you prefer to be called nowadays?'

'Francis.'

'This is Francis, Henry. The man who lives with my brother.'

'So you're Francis! The artist everyone is talking about! Well – pleased to meet you, at last.'

Francis said, 'I'd like to talk to you alone.'

'Well – don't mind me, I'm sure!'

Mick sighed. 'Henry, just give us a few minutes, eh?'

When he'd gone Mick said, 'You have two minutes. Say what you have to and go.'

Francis ignored him. Going to the window he watched Henry walk along the street before turning to Mick. 'Why are you living with a queer?'

'I don't live with him! For Christ's sake! He's my assistant – a bloody good one too. He's not usually so silly – I should imagine you brought out the worst in him – you usually have that effect.'

'May I sit down?'

'Do what the hell you want.'

Francis sat. Anxiously he asked, 'Do you still go home to Thorp?'

'I'm not about to abandon my family like you did.'

'So you go home often?'

'Why?'

Taking a deep breath to steady his nerve Francis said, 'I'm worried about Bobby.'

Mick snorted. 'Are you? Rather late in the day to be concerned, isn't it? How old is he now, nine? Ten?'

'I heard his stepfather treats him badly.'

'I wouldn't know about that.'

'I know!' Trying to keep his anger in check he repeated more calmly, 'I know. My father writes to me.'

'Then perhaps your father should do something about it.'

'He can't deal with this. He's quite frail now.'

Francis thought of George, his father, and how badly he had aged since 1918. It was frightening how enfeebled he had

470

become, a fate Francis could envisage for himself were it not for Patrick. Reading his father's letters had always made him feel ashamed of himself but lately they had disturbed him. He wrote how withdrawn Bobby had become, how his stepfather treated him cruelly. In his last letter he'd written that he'd noticed bruises on Bobby's arms. Reading the letter Francis had felt sick with rage. He had wanted to leave for England immediately and confront Redpath. Patrick had persuaded him to stay, to do nothing that might hurt Bobby further. Patrick had said, 'Perhaps Mick could help.' Francis had seized on the idea that Patrick's brother could help him. Now, sitting in Mick's flat, he felt indecently exposed to his contempt.

Mick said, 'I've met his stepfather – what's his name – Redpath, briefly. I didn't like the man.'

'Would he hurt Bobby, do you think?'

Mick avoided his gaze. 'I don't know. I'm sorry.'

'Would you go and see Bobby? If Redpath knew Bobby was watched over –'

'You want me to look out for your son?'

'Yes.'

'Why don't you go and see him for yourself?'

'You know I can't.'

'Can't? No one would keep me from my son!'

'They've told him I'm dead.'

Mick laughed in disbelief. 'They told him what?'

'They decided it was better than telling him I was in prison.'

'Jesus.'

'I thought you knew. I thought Patrick had told you.'

'Patrick and I have lost touch – you should know that, given it's your fault.' He shook his head as though trying to make sense of what he'd been told. 'So – they told him you were dead? And you just allowed them to?'

'I wanted to see him, when I was released, but I was ill then, and Patrick … Pat …' He remembered how Patrick had persuaded him that it would be wrong to disrupt Bobby's life, and that he had allowed himself to be persuaded. After three years in prison he had felt incapable of standing up to anyone, not even this man who loved him so much. Redpath would have demolished him completely.

Mick said, 'Don't bring Patrick into this. If you blame any of it on him I won't help you.'

'Will you help me? Not me, but Bobby? I know it's a lot to ask –'

'Does Pat know about this?'

'Yes.'

'How is Pat?'

'You should write to him.'

'And endorse the filthy life he's living?'

Francis exhaled sharply. 'Mick, my son needs someone to watch out for him. Please help me.'

'I'll help for the boy's sake. He's a good boy – well-mannered.'

'Is he?'

'Don't smile like that – you've no right to claim any credit for him.'

Francis stubbed out his cigarette and stood up. 'Will you write to me from time to time, let me know how he's getting on?'

Grudgingly he said, 'Yes, all right.'

As he was about to leave Mick said, 'Will you tell Pat you've seen me?'

'Do you want me to?'

He looked away. After a moment he said, 'Remind him he has a nephew he should visit.'

Beside the river Francis remembered how he had waited anxiously for Mick Morgan's first letter. It arrived after several weeks telling him that Bobby had been sent away to boarding school and that it was better that he should be away from Redpath. He included a photograph of two small boys in swimming trunks standing shoulder to shoulder on a beach, their hair wet from the sea, both of them grinning for the camera. On the photo's reverse Mick had written only *Hugh and Bobby – August 1930*.

Francis stood up. A few yards ahead of him a flight of

stone steps led from the river path to Thorp High Street. From the High Street it was only a few minutes walk to the house were he was born and where his son now lived alone. His son. He wondered what he would say to him.

The stone steps had a handrail. He held on to it, shaky as an old man. As he crossed the High Street the sun came out. Grateful for the excuse he disguised himself behind sunglasses.

Chapter Twenty Seven

Jane had kissed his scars, those where the surgeon had harvested skin to graft on to his face and hands, and Bobby had squirmed, embarrassed, wanting her to pretend not to notice. He wanted to be perfect for her, handsome. He wanted to show her a picture of himself in uniform, standing beside his Spitfire. 'This is me,' he would say, 'as I was.' No such picture existed.

She hadn't wanted to eat with him, afraid to stay too long in case her husband suspected something. He had kissed her goodbye and she had slipped out the back door furtively. He had wished she hadn't looked so guilty, as though she felt she really was betraying her useless, disgusting husband.

In the kitchen Bobby threw the cold, stewed tea down the sink and swilled out the pot. He opened a tin of pilchards, filleting the strip of bones from each fish and feeding them to the kitten weaving between his legs. He made a sandwich and ate it ravenously, messily. It seemed a long time since he'd felt hungry like this. On his lap the kitten purred loud as a generator; he held out his damaged fingers for her to lick. Like Jane it seemed the little cat didn't mind about his ugly hands.

In the second hospital they sent him to he had asked the surgeon, 'I'm going to lose my fingers, aren't I?'

The surgeon had looked up from examining Bobby's left hand. 'Not if I can help it.''

His hand lay on its sterile pillow, newly unwrapped from its bandages and stinking of green meat. Despite the stench the doctor smiled, pleased with his handiwork. 'Most of the grafts have taken. You're lucky – so no more defeatist talk.'

Waiting to soak his hand in a saline bath, the nurse covered her mouth and nose with a surgical mask against the stench. He was freezing suddenly, saliva watering his mouth. Fighting back his rising nausea he'd closed his eyes and felt the doctor's light touch on his shoulder. 'We'll take the stitches out tomorrow. Try and rest.'

The kitten curled on his knee. He began to stroke her and she settled trustingly to sleep. He closed his eyes, thinking of Jane and the lies she would have to tell to her husband. Inevitably, pessimistically, he imagined that she would change her mind about leaving Adam Mason, a man who had a career that could support her, who could face up to the world and not be scared of his own shadow. A man who wasn't so sickeningly damaged.

He looked down at his hands and remembered the nurse who had covered her mouth and nose against his stink. As she'd dressed his hand after the saline bath, he'd caught her eye and she'd lowered her mask.

'You're going to be all right, you know. Other pilots have left here to fly again.'

He tried to imagine climbing into a cockpit and being on standby, strapped in and ready and waiting for an instant departure. He would have taken a discreet piss beside the plane but, all the same, nervousness would make him feel the need to go again. But he was strapped in and one of the ground crew had helpfully arranged the parachute over his shoulders – how astonished the man would be if he unbuckled himself and ran away! He would have to sit tight. Soon an arm would signal from the commander's cockpit and that would be that.

He thought of those other pilots the nurse had mentioned – those men who, guessing his otherness, had kept their distance from him. He imagined them climbing into their planes again happily – scornful of being told they were only fit for ground duties, and remembered his terror as he scrambled from his burning plane; the torturous agony as his burnt hands struggled to pull the ripcord that would open his parachute. The mere idea of flying again had made him want to cry with fear.

The nurse had said, 'Lieutenant Harris? You will fly again, you mustn't worry that you won't.'

Knowing she expected some response he said, 'Perhaps the war will be over soon.' It was the best he could do. All he could think of was the pain to come, the sensation of red-hot needles being forced beneath his fingernails. As he had during other procedures on his hands he would think of Christ enduring the torture of the crucifixion, but that would make him whimper, softly at first, and then, to his shame, more loudly. He was sure the nurses thought he was more cowardly than the other men were.

He lifted the kitten from his knee and got up. He made tea and carried his cup out into the garden, the little cat following him, pouncing at a leaf tumbling across the lawn.

Despite Mark's efforts the garden appeared overgrown and so long neglected he wondered if it could ever be tamed. He looked back at the house and saw that the guttering had finally fallen away. There was not enough money to fix all that was wrong with Parkwood, but even if there was he had no will to restore it. The house had never truly been his home. Lately he had come to feel like the forgotten caretaker of a building that had outlived its usefulness.

He sat down on the bench that ran around the base of the horse chestnut tree and lit a cigarette. Jane would be home now. He checked his watch and saw that it was almost five o'clock; her husband would be back from the school. He had an urge to go to their house and ask him how he could have been so cruel to marry a woman like Jane, but he knew he would end up making a fool of himself. All he had left were anger and frustration; he imagined how incoherent his rage would make him. Mason would think he was an idiot; worse, Jane would realise he was no more grown up than the boys she taught.

But he had been a husband and a father, both in all but name. When Joan died the pain he felt made him believe he had actually become ill. At her funeral he had carried her little coffin into church and was sure that when he set it down in front of the altar his heart would explode inside his chest and he would drop dead. After the funeral tea, when Nina had retreated to bed and all the other mourners had left, Jason had made him stop clearing up and sit down.

Jason took his hands in his. 'I wish you were my son, Bobby. I wish I could make you understand how much I want to help you through this.'

He had been unable to speak in case he should start to cry. He wouldn't be able to stop crying if he started. He drew his hands away and searched through his tunic pockets for his cigarettes. 'I've been refused leave.'

'They can't refuse! My God, Bobby! They must give you compassionate leave for this!'

He'd laughed tearfully. 'Perhaps if she'd been my real daughter.'

'Real! Of course she was yours! Go sick – tell them you're sick to death –'

'I can't.' He'd managed to smile. 'I'm absolutely indispensable to the war effort, apparently.' Tears stung the back of his throat. He had an idea that he would walk out into the lanes that surrounded Nina's cottage and howl with pain. Only the cows would hear him.

Jason said, 'This will pass, Bobby. The pain will lessen in time –'

'I think my heart –' He stopped himself saying it. Admitting to a broken heart sounded like a line from a cheap song. Besides, his heart didn't feel broken; it went on beating, treacherously keeping him alive. The pain encompassed all of him. He wondered if he curled up tight and breathed carefully it might let up a little.

He'd lit a cigarette. Eventually he'd said, 'Flying will help. I can't think about anything else when I'm flying.'

The next week he had been shot down. He remembered the farmer running across his field towards him, the burst of flames as his plane crashed beyond the man's barn. For a moment he'd imagined the farmer was about to berate him for destroying his crop but there was only horror on his face. He must have looked a sight, he supposed, even then, before his body realised properly what had happened to it.

The kitten leapt up to sit beside him and companionably they gazed out over the garden. If Joan had lived she would have been almost six; he would have hung a swing from one of the trees for her and built a Wendy House. If Joan had lived he would have asked Nina to marry him. If he hadn't been burnt she might have said yes.

He heard someone clear their throat behind him and he sprang to his feet, surprise making his heart beat too quickly.

A middle-aged man stepped towards him. He was wearing a pair of dark glasses. No one wore dark glasses in Thorp, they were absurd, and despite his surprise at being disturbed he suppressed a smile as he wondered if this stranger had been mistaken for a blind man and helped across roads. Curtly Bobby said, 'Were you looking for someone?'

Francis heard himself say, 'I was looking for Doctor Harris.'

Bobby drew on his cigarette. Exhaling he said, 'Doctor Harris died.'

Francis nodded. He was shaking. He had always expected to recognise Bobby no matter what; now, standing in front of him, he realised he would have walked right past him in the street and only felt the fleeting pity he would feel for a stranger whose life was so ruined. He wondered if perhaps this wasn't Bobby after all, but some friend he had met in a hospital that cared for burn victims. Burn victims! Francis felt ashamed that he could think so abstractly about him.

Carefully Francis said, 'Are you Doctor Harris's grandson?'

'Yes. Did you know my grandfather?'

'Quite well.'

Bobby held out his hand. 'Bob Harris. How do you do, sir?'

'Francis Law.' He shook his hand.

'I'm sorry if I broke the news of my grandfather's death abruptly.' He glanced towards the house, only to smile at him shyly. 'Would you like a cup of tea? I've just made some.'

'Then yes, thank you.'

Stepping inside the dark, untidy kitchen was like stepping back into his own past. Francis half expected his father to be sitting in the chair by the fire, ready to tell him that he smoked too much, or, in a more oblique way, that the life he was living was all wrong.

Francis took off his sunglasses and looked around. The kitchen was unchanged – it even smelled the same, making his memories all the more vivid. He might have only walked out an hour ago. He sat down, the grief he had refused to acknowledge over his father's death suddenly overwhelming.

Bobby said, 'Are you all right, sir?'

'Yes, I'm fine.' He managed to smile. 'Could I have a glass of water, perhaps?'

He noticed that Bobby allowed the tap to run for a while before filling a glass and remembered that the first flow of water in this house was always brackish. As he handed him the glass Bobby said, 'You weren't expecting to see my grandfather as a patient, were you?'

'Do I look ill?'

'Yes, in all honesty.'

Francis sipped at the freezing water. Although it was a speech he had been rehearsing all day his voice quavered as he said, 'Actually I came here to see you, Bobby. Your grandfather wrote to me and asked that if ever I was in Thorp I was to look in on you.'

Bobby laughed. 'To make sure I was behaving myself and not playing with matches? I don't think granddad ever thought of me as older than ten.' He sat down in the armchair opposite. 'Are you Francis Law the painter?'

'Yes, I am.'

He didn't seem surprised. 'Granddad mentioned you once or twice. He had one of your paintings.' He glanced up at the square of less faded wallpaper above the fireplace. 'He took it to his bank at the start of the war. He told me he wanted to make sure it was kept safe – I think he thought there would be more bombing in Thorp. I'm afraid I haven't got around to fetching it back.'

'Sell it.'

Bobby raised his eyebrows. 'Do you think I should?' After a moment he said awkwardly, 'Do you think it might be valuable?'

'Immodestly, yes.' Francis smiled and found himself studying Bobby's face, wanting to see if any likeness remained. He remembered how beautiful he had been as a baby; there had been times when he would crouch beside his cot just to watch him sleep. He had carried a photograph of him in his wallet and when he'd been arrested it had been taken away from him, never to be returned.

He must have been staring too hard at him because Bobby became self-conscious, lighting a cigarette and drawing on it deeply before clearing his throat.

'Your painting – the one granddad had – it was of a soldier on his bunk.'

Francis nodded. He remembered sending the picture to his father after his first London exhibition, all the time wondering what he would make of it. The soldier lay on his back, one arm dangling over the side of his narrow bed, a cigarette smoking between his fingers. In the foreground was a table on which an oil lamp cast a mustard-yellow glow. Beside the lamp was a pile of letters. He'd called the painting *Letters Home*. He'd wanted his father to look at the picture and think of him not as its creator but as its subject. He'd wanted his father to understand that there were times when the trenches were quiet, times when he could smoke and think in peace.

Bobby said, 'I don't know if I should sell the painting – he loved it so much it would seem wrong, somehow. I think it reminded him of his sons. They fought in the first war.' After a moment he said, 'How did you know my grandfather?'

'I was raised in Thorp.'

'Was he your doctor?'

'Yes.' It wasn't a lie, not really, but it must have sounded like one because Bobby looked at him suspiciously.

'Granddad talked about you sometimes. He admired your paintings a great deal.'

'Did he? That means a lot to me.'

'Will you paint this last war?'

'No, I don't think so.'

'Not your fight, eh?'

'That's right.'

Too lightly Bobby said, 'I heard you were a pacifist?'

'Do you think that was wrong of me?'

'Terribly.' Flicking cigarette ash at the fire he said, 'Do all painters stare at people?'

'No, I'm sorry.'

'Well, at least you do it openly. If you're curious I was a Spitfire pilot. I didn't bail out quick enough.'

'It must have been very frightening.'

Briskly Bobby said, 'I should ask for your autograph or something, shouldn't I? Aren't you very famous?'

Francis realised Bobby wasn't about to recognise him, as, in his wilder moments, he had hoped he would. But why should he? Bobby truly believed his father was dead. No one expected dead men to climb out of their graves and introduce themselves.

Bobby said, 'What brings you back to Thorp?'

'As I said – to see you.'

'Honestly? Why? Did my grandfather really tell you what a hopeless case I am?'

'He was concerned for you.'

'Yes, well. He needn't have worried. I'm all right.' He smiled, dropping some of his curtness. 'I may even have turned a corner.'

'That's good.'

'I've met a girl – she's …' He trailed off as though he'd said too much.

'She's …?'

Bobby tossed his cigarette stub into the fire. 'She's very nice.' Standing up he said, 'I'm sure you don't want me to keep you, Mr Law. Although it was very kind of you to come and see me.'

Hurriedly Francis said, 'Bobby, if there's anything I can do for you, if there's anything you need –'

Bobby seemed puzzled. After a moment he sat down again. 'Mr Law, I don't know what my grandfather told you, but if you're looking for a charity case I'm sure there are many more deserving than me.'

'I know you don't need charity.'

'Then what are you offering?' As if he'd come to a sudden understanding he said, 'Do you want to paint me? I could be your muse – I have the experience.' His voice was heavy with sarcasm. Angrily he said, 'Why not just come straight out with it? You think I'd make a bloody good subject for one of your anti-war pictures. Well, I'm not anti war – the last war or any other. I won't be used.'

'I didn't come here to ask to paint you, Bobby.'

'Stop using my name like that! No one calls me Bobby unless they've known me all my life.'

'I'm sorry. I didn't mean to upset you.'

Bobby looked ashamed of his outburst and Francis said gently, 'If I was to paint you – and I would like to – it wouldn't be because I wanted to make some political point.'

'What other point would there be?'

Francis attempted to smile. 'No point at all, I suppose – art for art's sake?'

'Christ!' Lighting another cigarette he said, 'You sound like Jason Hargreaves.' Glancing at him from shaking out his match he said, 'He was a photographer – I modelled for him.'

Francis said, 'Would you model for me?'

'You really want to paint my portrait?'

'It would be a great honour.'

Bobby laughed as though embarrassed. 'Would you make me look as I am or more idealised?'

'I'd paint what I see. A courageous man.'

Looking away Bobby said, 'Would I have to go to London?'

'No. My studio is in Tangier.' He smiled. 'You could treat it as a holiday.'

'I don't know.'

'I would pay your expenses, of course.'

'And if I wanted someone to come with me?'

'Then I would pay for her, too.'

He drew on his cigarette, seeming to consider. Eventually he said, 'I won't go unless she wants to.'

Francis stood up. The idea of Bobby in his studio, in his house, was overwhelming and he needed to be alone to think about it. 'I should go,' he said. 'Perhaps if I come back tomorrow for your decision?'

Chapter Twenty Eight

After school the next day Jane said, 'I thought I'd go to the cinema.'

Adam looked up from the exercise book he was marking. 'Do you want me to go with you?'

Putting on her coat she said, 'It's only a romantic comedy, it wouldn't be your cup of tea.'

Adam returned to his student's work. 'I wouldn't have thought it was yours, either.'

'You think I'm not romantic?'

Adam sighed. 'I didn't say that.' He took off his glasses and pushed his palms against his eyes. 'Jane, has something happened?'

Trying not to sound too guilty she said, 'Happened? What could have happened?'

Dropping his hands away from his face he said, 'Jane, please. I know you weren't ill yesterday. I came home at lunchtime to see how you were and you weren't here. Your room smelt of perfume.'

'I felt better – I went out to cheer myself up.'

'Wearing perfume?'

'Why not?' Angrily she said, 'Why shouldn't I dress up occasionally and feel feminine?'

'No reason at all.' Gently he said, 'Take your coat off, sit down.'

'Why?'

'Please, Jane.' He attempted to smile. 'I can talk to my wife, can't I?'

She sat down opposite him, keeping her coat on as a small act of defiance.

Closing the exercise book Adam pushed it away. 'Sometimes I think I love my work too much. I think it means more to me than anything else in my life, ever. Do you think that's pathetic?'

'I don't think anything about you is pathetic.'

'No? I haven't been a husband to you, though, have I?'

'And do you want to start being my husband?'

He avoided her gaze. At last he said, 'How's the play coming along? First night on Thursday – are they ready?'

'I think so.'

'And that boy – Bobby Harris? Has he helped at all?' When she didn't answer he said, 'Is he a bit of a dead loss?'

'No!' She frowned at him. 'It just turned out that –'

'What? Wasn't he very interested?'

Coldly she said, 'No, he wasn't interested. He's a grown man – why would he want to spend his time with schoolboys?'

'Or their teacher. Of course he wouldn't. I was only surprised he consented to it in the first place.'

Jane stood up. 'I'm going. I don't want to miss the start of the film.'

As she was about to leave he called after her, 'Jane, let me know what the film is like – I might want to see it myself after all.'

In bed with Hugh, Nina rested her head on his chest and concentrated on the strong beat of his heart. She'd thought he was asleep but she felt his hand on her head, his fingers gently curling into her hair. Quietly he said, 'I adore you. You know that, don't you?'

She held her breath. There was something he wasn't able to bring himself to say – words that seemed like a weight suspended above her, about to fall. She would be killed, her heart crushed. His heart went on steadily.

Eventually he said, 'I miss the sea.'

She breathed out. His hand was heavy on her head, its restless stroking finished with. She thought of the battleships that sometimes appeared in newsreels; the grey, industrial bulk of them had always made her feel afraid. The sea was a bleak, cold waste, and the metal ships seemed as unforgiving of human frailty as giant machines. She'd heard how their boilers exploded and scalded men to death, how their blasted holds flooded to drown trapped men. Ships that looked invincible gave up too soon and sank with all hands. She thought of the saying Jason used when his day was going badly: 'Worse things happen at sea.' She never doubted it.

Hugh said, 'Nina?' He lifted his head from the pillow to look at her. 'You're not asleep are you?'

'No.'

'If I re-joined the navy –' more quietly he said, 'I can't settle on shore. I've tried.'

She wanted to tell him that he hadn't tried hard enough, for long enough, that he should keep trying because she didn't want him out of her sight for more than a few hours a day. She didn't want to see him wearing a uniform, or hear him call another man sir and salute. She thought of Nick's funeral, the senior officers following his coffin that they'd had draped in the Canadian flag. Beside her, Bobby was not Bobby but an RAF officer, stiff and correct as a tin soldier.

She got up and put on her dressing gown, wrapping it tightly around her. Sitting on the edge of the bed she said, 'I want a baby, Hugh.'

He scrambled across the bed to kneel at her side. 'Of course! I want children too. It won't stop us having children –'

'But if you're not here with me –'

He pulled her to him. 'I'll make you pregnant before I go.'

'That's what Nick did.'

She stood up and went to the sink to fill the kettle. She could feel him watching her. When she caught his gaze he said, 'I won't be killed, Nina. I'll always come home to you.'

'Yes. Of course.'

'I will!' He sprang up. Naked he stood in front of her. 'I'll have a career – a real job that I'm good at. I'll be a captain – I'll have my own ship.' He smiled. 'I'll have you piped aboard, you and our six kids.'

'I just want an ordinary life, Hugh.'

'You'll have it. I'll make you proud of me –'

'Proud! I was proud of Nick, of Bobby – I've grown out of being proud of men in uniform wanting to kill each other!'

'I'm not a soldier, Nina.'

She stepped away from him. They had made love all afternoon, their bodies smelt of each other's; one of her long blonde hairs caught in the dark hairs on his chest. She picked it off tenderly. His body was beautiful, like the painting of the muscular figure of Christ about to be flogged that hung in the convent's hall. The tattoo on Hugh's arm seemed to glow red and gold in the dim light, the fire-breathing dragon a jewelled, magical creature, his talisman against ill fortune. She touched the dragon's curving tail.

'The war's over,' he said.

She nodded, watching her finger trace the dragon's spine. She looked up at him. 'You'll be safe?'

He caught her hand and pressed it to his mouth. 'Come back to bed,' he said. 'I'll hold you while you sleep.'

Chapter Twenty Nine

In his hotel room Francis wrote to Patrick.

He began, *I've been absent from you too long. I miss you so badly and yet this being apart makes me realise you're not simply the faithful man who loves me so astonishingly well, but an angel, sent for some unfathomable reason to look out for me. I should have realised this truth years ago because you are so extraordinary, so unlike other men, so unlike me, this weak, vain, faithless creature you have been so intent on saving from himself. I should have realised from the first moment I saw you in that trench, when I fell so badly in love with you and hoped you wouldn't notice. Or perhaps not then, but later, when you saved my life so often just by lending me courage when I was half-mad from fear. How much courage you had to spare – I will never forget. But angels are courageous, aren't they? I should know. I have never understood why I deserved such grace.*

I don't have your faith, Patrick, or your love of God. I am uncertain and afraid, I wish you were with me now, not just in spirit, as I know you are and always have been, but here in body. I need to cower behind you, because if God is real He might be kinder knowing you loved me.

If angels need to pray, pray for me. I love you.

It was not the letter he had intended to write. He had intended to write only that he was coming home in a few days, and that Bobby might be with him. All the letters and postcards he had written since he left contained only the bare facts like this, his way of keeping at bay the homesickness that made England seem so much more miserable than it really was. But seeing

Bobby had reminded him painfully of the frightened boy that Patrick had rescued. He had found himself wanting to put into words how much he owed him: his life, in fact.

Before he left for England he had been to see his doctor who showed him the x-ray of his lungs and pointed out the shadows. Because he was his friend as well as his doctor he had told him that he should make his peace with the world, that if he had left some things undone they should be attended to. Francis had asked how long he had, not believing a time limit could be put on his life, believing still in his own immortality. 'A year, perhaps,' the doctor said. 'It's difficult to be accurate with cancer.'

He'd asked, 'How long will I be able to keep it from Patrick?'

'For a while, at least.' The doctor had frowned, his first betrayal of concern. 'Tell him today, Francis. Allow him to help you through this.'

So far he'd told Patrick nothing; it seemed impossible to tell him such a thing when he could barely believe it himself.

He looked at the letter he'd written to Patrick. It was too sentimental, too trite. He should write the truth, that he was dying and afraid his life had been nothing because he had lost his son.

After his father had written to him telling him that Bobby had run away to London, he had hired a private detective to find him. The search hadn't taken long. As soon as he knew where Bobby was, Francis left for England, ignoring Patrick's fear that there would be a war in Europe and he would be stranded there. As soon as he'd arrived in London he'd gone to the address the detective had given him. Jason Hargreaves had been alone in his studio. Setting up a camera, Hargreaves had looked up at him impatiently.

'Can I help you?'

'Are you Jason Hargreaves?'

'Depends who's asking.' He'd smiled, beginning to take more notice of him. 'I probably am, to you.'

'My name is Francis Law.'

'*The* Francis Law? The artist?'

'Yes.'

Hargreaves abandoned the camera and tripod and stepped towards him. Shaking his hand he said, 'I'm honoured. I can't tell you how much I adore your work.' He cleared a pile of clothes from a purple velvet couch, a feather boa trailing across his arm to the floor as he said, 'Look – sit down. Will you have a drink? Can I take your coat? What brings you to see me? Oh – listen to me – what a flap! You can tell I don't meet many bona-fide celebrities, can't you?'

Francis glanced around the studio. There was a Chinese lacquered screen in one corner, golden lilies etched on the deepest, reflective black. More clothes were draped over it, dresses that were no more than scraps of lace and organza trimmed with feathers and tassels. On the walls were pictures of Bobby. He went to look at them more closely, his heart pounding.

He hardly recognised him as the same boy that smiled from the snaps his father sent him. In these pictures Bobby didn't smile; he looked remote and aloof, like the men he painted from memory, like his portrait of himself as a soldier. Bobby's eyes were blank, as though he had just placed his pistol to the machine gunner's head. He was naked, drapery carefully arranged to conceal just enough to make the photographs artful rather than shocking. All the same he was shocked. His child's body had become that of a man's, powerful, the muscles of his chest and arms clearly defined. So strong, he looked, and dangerous, as though he hated the men who would want most to look at his picture.

Hargreaves said, 'He's marvellous, isn't he?'

Francis turned away from the photograph. 'I'll buy them all. Every picture you have of him.'

'All right.'

'And I want your word that there won't be any more copies printed and that you'll stop using him as a model.'

Hargreaves laughed. 'That's quite a lot of wants.'

'Will you agree to them?'

'Of course not!'

'I'll pay whatever you want.'

490

'Jesus!' He looked at Francis speculatively. 'Pay whatever price, eh? You shouldn't wear your heart on your sleeve so – it's rather unwise these days.' More gently he said, 'Look, do you want to meet him? If you saw him in the flesh you might get over such ... ardour. He's quite ordinary, really. And straight. Horribly, disappointingly straight.'

'I just want the photographs and their negatives.' He took out his chequebook. 'How much do you want for them.'

'I've just decided they're not for sale. Who the hell do you think you are anyway? I think you should go.'

'Not until I have the pictures.'

Hargreaves shook his head. He laughed wearily. 'Fuck off, Mr Law, would you? Don't forget to close the door as you leave.'

Francis lifted one of the photographs of Bobby from the wall. He smashed it to the floor, shattering its glass. Tearing the photograph from its frame he ripped it in two.

Hargreaves stared at him. Dryly he said, 'Feel any better for that?' He sighed. 'You've cut yourself. You're dripping blood.' He stepped past the broken glass and grasped his wrist, inspecting the cut across his palm. Glancing up at him he said, 'It's quite deep. You best sit down. Over here.'

Still holding his wrist he led him to the couch. 'You're shaking,' Hargreaves said. 'Do you feel faint? I'll fetch a bandage. I have a first-aid kit somewhere ...'

Francis felt an overwhelming sense of foolishness; he had intended to be calm, to make a deal with this man to stop Bobby's exploitation. But he had lost his temper, something he did so rarely it felt even more like he had let Bobby down.

Sitting beside him, Hargreaves inspected the cut before dabbing on iodine with a piece of cotton wool. Pushing the skin together he began to wrap a crepe bandage around his hand. 'I haven't done this since the war, so you'll have to excuse me if I've lost my touch.'

Feeling he should say something Francis offered, 'Were you in France?'

'Oh, you weren't the only one out there, you know!' He smiled, looking at him briefly before lowering his eyes to his

491

hand again. 'I was a stretcher bearer.'

'I was –'

Fastening the bandage deftly, Hargreaves interrupted him. 'Everyone knows what you were – hero of the hour. There,' he said. 'All mended. Now the only thing left is for you to ask the doctor if you'll ever be able to play the piano again.'

Francis said, 'I'm sorry.'

'That's all right. No harm done. Well, not much, anyway. Besides, it'll make a good story – I can dine out on it for years.'

'I don't want anyone to know I've been here.'

'No.' Hargreaves sighed. 'I'm sure you don't.' After a moment he said, 'You can have the pictures, if you feel so strongly.'

'Will you stop taking his photograph?'

'Would you, if you were me? Of course not. Why, anyway? Do you want him for yourself?'

'Are all the photographs of him like the ones on the walls?'

'Some are just head and shoulder portraits.' He smiled slightly. 'In some he's even dressed. Those are private, though, I don't show them.'

'I was told you were a pornographer.'

Hargreaves laughed. 'Were you now? Well, I'm not.' Bitterly he said, 'I'd say you were more of a pornographer than I am. I portray beautiful young men's bodies more honestly than you do.'

Getting up, Hargreaves began sweeping the broken glass into a dustpan. He picked up the torn photograph and without looking at it crumpled the pieces and tossed them into the coal fire. The flames leapt around them. Turning to him Hargreaves said, 'You're some relation of his, aren't you? I can see the likeness – in your manner, too. You've got the same funny little ways. Who are you, then? An uncle, cousin?'

'I'm his father.'

Hargreaves stared at him. At last he said, 'Well, fancy that. I'm surprised – you don't look like a shit. But there you are, even artists like me can be taken in by a pretty face. Now, I think you should go. He may be back soon. I don't want him upset by a waste of space like you.'

'You've no right to judge me.'

'No? Maybe not – all I know is if I hadn't found him when I did he'd probably be dead by now. He was too scared to go home to you, too innocent to last five minutes on the streets. I've seen what happens to boys like him. You should be thanking me for saving him rather than coming in here making a bloody fool of yourself.'

Francis said, 'Is he well?'

'He's all right.' He crouched down to put more coal on the fire. Glancing at him he said, 'When did you see him last?'

'He was two.'

Hargreaves snorted. 'That explains why he's never mentioned you.'

'It doesn't mean I don't care about him. I do '

He straightened up and brushed coal dust from his hands. 'Odd way of showing you care, if you ask me.'

'You don't know anything about it!'

'No. Do you want to explain?'

To his surprise Francis had done just that.

The words came haltingly at first, but Jason Hargreaves listened attentively and he began to tell him details even Patrick didn't know, that he had been raped in prison. He had been raped over and over for years until he felt stupefied, so degraded he was nothing more than a body, an obscene, filthy receptacle. He'd had to stop talking then. Hargreaves had waited silently for him to collect himself. Eventually when he could speak again he told Hargreaves that sometimes he looked at Patrick and wondered how he had ended up with him, in such an alien country, his life so bizarrely different to what he had expected as a young man, before prison. He wasn't like Patrick, so sure of his queerness. He thought of other lives he could have lived. He thought of Bobby every day.

When he'd finished speaking Hargreaves said, 'Do you think I should feel sorry for you?'

'No.'

'I do.' He'd been sitting opposite him and he stood up.

'Have you eaten? I'd like to take you out for dinner.'

In his hotel room, Francis remembered that Jason had taken him to a Greek restaurant and that it was the first time he had eaten olives in England. Jason lined their stones along the rim of his plate as he told him his own story, that his father owned coal mines in South Yorkshire, that thank God he had brothers to take on the business and not mind that he was odd. Jason had smiled. 'They like my oddness – I'm their artistic pet. Their wives think I'm wonderful, especially when they come up to town and I take them shopping in Harrods.' He had served as a stretcher-bearer for the last year of the war. The first time he set eyes on Bobby he knew that all he wanted to do was to photograph him. He'd looked down at his circle of olive stones. 'All he wants to do is fly.'

It was the first time Francis had heard about Bobby's flying lessons. He'd thought of Patrick's predictions of war and felt sick with fear.

That night he and Jason had made love with unsatisfactory tenderness, both of them realising how unsuited they were to each other. Afterwards Jason had said, 'I suppose I want men who fuck me like they're going to kick my head in afterwards.'

Francis had laughed. 'Then you'd like Patrick. The first time I saw him –' He stopped himself, ashamed of his disloyalty and faithlessness.

Jason patted his hand. 'It's all right, sweetheart. Best pretend tonight never happened, eh?' He'd smiled at him wryly. 'Shall we be pen pals?'

They'd written to each other until Jason became too ill. In his last letter he wrote, *Bobby needs you – someone who will love him unconditionally*.

Jason's letter set the seal on his decision. He would go home to England and tell Bobby who he was. He had felt brave at the time. Face to face with Bobby he found that his courage had failed.

He picked up the letter he had written to Patrick. He hadn't even mentioned that he'd seen his son and he imagined Patrick reading the letter and wondering if perhaps he had changed his mind, hoping that he had. He hadn't. Decisive suddenly, he tossed the letter down and walked out.

Chapter Thirty

Jane slept. Quietly, so as not to wake her, Bobby got up and pulled on trousers and a jumper. In bare feet he went downstairs and into the kitchen where the photograph of his father stood on the mantelpiece. He picked it up and studied it closely. He was such a handsome man – if handsome was the right word. Nina, looking at this picture, had called him beautiful. 'You're like him,' she'd said. Everyone said that, although he couldn't see the likeness himself.

He set the picture down again, thinking of his visitor yesterday, the creeping sense he'd had that he recognised him. At first he thought he must have seen his photograph lately in a newspaper and he'd even gone through the pile of papers he'd saved for lighting the fire, looking for the article that bore his picture. There was nothing. When Jane arrived he'd pushed it out of his mind but the nagging idea that he'd seen Francis Law before kept returning.

Nick had said once, 'You don't talk about your people.'

He'd laughed. 'My people?'

'OK – your family.'

They'd been sitting in a pub, a tiny beer and sawdust place in an unremarkable village he'd found whilst out driving. No one else in the squadron knew of it. He drove there whenever he wanted to get away from the forced joviality of The King's Head with its tankards hanging from a beam above the bar and the piano where more often than not the others gathered to sing filthy songs. The King's Head reminded him of boarding school, he had the same sense of being excluded, the odd one out that the others only tolerated. Those boys at school and the drunken pilots around the piano all had families they talked about. So did Nick. Nick never seemed to tire of talking about his family. That evening Nick had suddenly seemed aware that he'd talked about them too much. So, sheepishly, he'd asked about his.

Bobby remembered being flippant. 'I don't have a family.'

'Yes you do! Come on, Bob – don't give me that, I know you write to your mother.'

It was true, he did, stilted, formal letters in reply to hers. His mother wrote once a week, dutifully. Dutifully, he wrote back.

Bobby took a long drink and wiped beer froth from his mouth. Glancing at Nick he said, 'My father's dead. My mother re-married so I have a stepfather and two half sisters and a little brother, Mark.'

'So why'd you say you had no one?' Nick shook his head. 'Jesus, Bob, it's like you're disowning them or something.'

He wanted to say that they'd disowned him, but it seemed too pathetic. 'I don't see much of them. I was sent away to school when I was ten – as soon as the school would take me. I haven't seen much of them since.'

'Truly?' He looked so surprised that Bobby had laughed. Meeting Nick's gaze he thought again how sweet he was, all the love Nick had been brought up with like an aura around him. No wonder he wanted to be close to this easy man, as though some of that aura might rub off on him and make him more acceptable. He'd realised then how perfect he would be for Nina.

In Parkwood's kitchen Bobby picked up his father's photograph again. He turned it over and took out the piece of card holding it in place. On its reverse his father had written To Dad, with all my love, Paul. He remembered how his grandfather had talked to him of Paul as though he was a secret they shared.

Francis Law looked like Paul. Bobby frowned, putting the photo down only to pick it up again. He remembered Law's voice, how it had the same gentleness as his grandfather's, the same wry humour. They were related in some way – he was a cousin, perhaps. Bobby wondered why he hadn't mentioned it.

Perhaps he thought he already knew.

Bobby went into the larder and brought out a tin of tomato soup and half a loaf of bread. It wasn't much of a supper and he only had apples for pudding. He hoped she wouldn't rush off this evening but stay and eat with him. He wished he could serve her steak and salad and tiny new potatoes, a crème caramel with freshly brewed coffee and dark mints to follow, the kind of meal Jason would treat him to before the war. He was a growing boy, Jason would tell him, and smile indulgently as he watched him eat. Sometimes Jason would pretend to the waiters that he was his son.

As he opened the can of soup he heard a knock on the back door. Guessing it was Mark he called out, 'Come in.'

He turned away to pour the soup into a pan. 'Since when did you start knocking, Mark?'

Behind him Francis Law said, 'It's not Mark, Bobby.'

Bobby spun round. 'Mr Law – I'm sorry, I thought you were my brother.'

Law gazed at him. At last he said, 'I heard you had a half-brother. Are you close to him?'

Bobby shifted uncomfortably under his intense gaze. 'Fairly close.'

Law nodded. 'That's good.' He looked around the kitchen as if seeing it for the first time. Catching sight of the photograph on the mantelpiece he looked away quickly. Bobby became aware of a change in him. Carefully he said, 'Would you like to sit down?'

'You're about to have supper – I'm disturbing you.'

'No, not at all.'

Law sat down. Bobby watched him curiously, reminded of his likeness to his father. He thought how ill Law looked, so pale he seemed afraid. As he was about to speak Bobby cut in, 'I probably should know this but you're not related to us, are you?'

Law opened his mouth to speak again only to stop. After a moment he said quickly, 'When you were a baby ... I loved you so much, I have no excuse for what I did. Every moment of my life since I've regretted it –'

Bobby sat down opposite him. He became aware of the clock ticking, of the other man's laboured breathing. Seconds passed. He thought of how his grandfather talked about his father, always stopping himself short as if he'd said too much. He had always puzzled over the feeling that he was being deceived. He couldn't explain it until now.

Feeling the kind of disconnected calm he'd felt when he'd witnessed Nick's plane shot down, he said, 'You're Paul, aren't you?'

'Yes.'

Bobby shook his head in disbelief and Law sat forward, closing the gap between them. At once Bobby sat further back. Painfully Law said, 'Bob, if I could have stayed with you and your mother I would have. You meant everything to me –'

'Where did you go?'

'What?'

'If you weren't dead, where did you go – if I meant so much, what stopped you coming back?'

Law looked down. 'I was in prison. I was sent to prison.'

'Why would they send you to prison – you were a war hero –'

Law laughed bleakly. 'Did my father tell you that?'

'What did you do? Steal, murder?' Bobby heard his voice rising and struggled to keep calm. 'Tell me what you did.'

'I was caught with a man –'

'Caught doing what?'

'Bobby …'

'Don't call me that!' He shouted so loudly that Law cringed. He found himself on his feet. Furiously he said, 'You and this other man –' He stopped, not needing to go on, the truth suddenly so obvious he felt like a fool for not understanding sooner. 'You're queer.'

'Yes.'

'Get out of my house.'

'Bob, please –'

'I don't want you anywhere near me! Men like you – you're disgusting! Filthy and disgusting –' His heart was racing, a thread of spittle hanging from his mouth. He wiped it away; his mouth seemed full of the stuff, drowning any coherent words. He felt possessed by rage, a shrieking, infant devil that would have him stamp and scream. Horrified that he was crying he shouted, 'Get out! I'll kill you if you don't get out!'

He began to weep, great, gasping sobs that felt as if all the air was being burnt from his lungs. He thought of Henry Vickers telling him how good he was as he raped him. He had been good. Somehow he had encouraged a man to have sex with him and he had been good.

He sank down on to the chair and covered his face with his hands. His face was wet with tears and snot; he imagined the work of the surgeons disintegrating, the face they had reconstructed melting on to the floor and he drew breath, afraid of crying like this. He lowered his hands. He wiped his eyes with his fingers and searched in his pockets for a hanky. He didn't have one. Law stood up. Stepping towards him he held out his own, neatly folded handkerchief. 'Here,' he said gently. 'Use this.'

The handkerchief smelt of his grandfather. The shock of smelling his scent again caused the crying to stop. He thought of Joan, how he would lift her from her cot and at once her screaming would become only hiccuping noises. He felt like a baby to be comforted by so little, as though his tears had been nothing.

Law said, 'Your grandfather always made sure I had a clean handkerchief. He even used to send them in food parcels when I was in France.'

Bobby's throat felt raw. He was trembling, too close to the onset of another bout of crying. To prevent it he cleared his throat and made himself say, 'I want you to go.'

'No, please Bob … let me talk to you.'

'About? What could you have to say to me?' He heard his voice rising hysterically but didn't care any more. He just wanted him out of his sight. 'Get out! Go now before I throw you out.'

'Then throw me out. I won't walk away from you again.'

Bobby stepped towards him, his fists clenched, but Law

stood his ground as though he guessed that he wouldn't be able to bring himself to touch him. The idea of touching Law was repellent. All he could do was stand there, puffed up and ridiculous with impotent rage, the atmosphere charged with it so that he wondered how long he could go on without breaking down again and making an even bigger fool of himself.

Gently Law said, 'Bob, why don't we sit down?' He reached out and touched his arm.

Bobby stepped back. 'Don't touch me!' He felt his lip curl in disgust and knew how ugly he must look. 'You filthy bloody queer! I won't have you touching me! Christ – when I think of what you are it makes me want to throw up! Do you have any idea how much I detest men like you? Even Hitler was right about what should be done with queers!'

Calmly Law said, 'You don't mean that.'

'No? Why not? Why shouldn't I mean it? What did you expect from me? Acceptance?' He felt his anger like a surge of agitating power. He grabbed his father's photograph from the mantelpiece and threw it at the wall so hard one of the frame's metal corners made a tear in the wallpaper. It fell to the floor, its glass shattering. Bobby went to it and snatched the photograph up from the wreckage. He shoved it under Law's nose. 'You see this? This is the man I was meant to admire! This is the man my grandfather kept reminding me was so brave and clever and wonderful! No one could live up to you! Not me – certainly not me! My own grandfather could hardly bear to look at me! I must have reminded him too much of you – the lies he had to tell to cover up your disgusting behaviour! My God! No wonder they told me you were dead – the only pity is you weren't!'

Law took the photograph from him. He was white and the picture trembled in his hand; he seemed to gasp for breath, stepping back, fumbling behind him for the chair. Bobby stood over him, his own breath coming in short bursts as though he'd just scrambled for immediate take off. His heart was pumping just as it did as he waited for the final clearance, only now there was no where to channel his fearful energy. There was only this frail, suddenly old-looking man. Bobby stepped back from him. Coldly he said, 'You are dead to me. You always have been and nothing's changed. I want you to go and I don't ever want to see or hear from you again.'

Law seemed not to hear him. He closed his eyes as though concentrating on each breath he took; his face creased with pain. Bobby knew enough about pain to know this wasn't just the shame of humiliation but real, physical agony. The photograph slipped from Law's fingers to drift to the floor, the beautiful, familiar face lay at his foot, gazing up at him.

The room grew still, his own breathing returned to normal; Bobby felt some of his anger slip away, replaced by a creeping sense of shame that he quickly suppressed. He had nothing to be ashamed of. He had every right to be angry. All the same it seemed most of his anger had spent itself, burnt out quick as petrol on a fire. He could never sustain anger, never rant and rave for hours as men like Mick Morgan could, as though it was more a show of force than any real emotion.

Stiffly he said, 'Will you leave now?'

Law looked up at him. He seemed unable to speak. He closed his eyes again, his hands clenched together so tightly his knuckles were white. There was no colour in him. He reminded Bobby of corpses laid out on bombed airfields; the same shocked, agonised expression on his face had been on the faces of the dead, too.

Bobby shifted uncomfortably. He stooped to pick up the photograph and as he straightened up Law caught his eye and said painfully, 'Could I have a drink?'

Bobby fetched him a glass of water. He thrust it at him.

Law sipped at the over-filled glass; his hand was still shaking and he slopped some of it on his lap. Eventually he managed to say, 'I just need to catch my breath.'

'And then you'll go?'

Law closed his eyes as though he despaired of his heartlessness. 'For pity's sake. You don't have to stand over me.'

'I'll stand where I want – this is my house.'

'Is it? Perhaps you'll find it's mine.'

Bobby laughed, outraged. 'Is that why you're here? To

502

claim your inheritance? Jesus Christ! Are you going to throw me on the street now? Well, I don't want this bloody house! Do you imagine I was ever happy here? You have it! I'd rather have nothing than keep anything that was his!'

'His?' Law frowned at him. 'You mean your grandfather's? Hate me, by all means, but he loved you. Show him the respect his memory deserves.'

'Deserves? He lied to me! Not only that he just stood by while my stepfather ...' He couldn't bring himself to say that Redpath beat and humiliated him. Even the memory of it was enough to make him begin crying weak, disgusting tears. He had to do something, anything but show himself up again. He went to the cupboard under the sink. Taking out a dustpan and brush he began to sweep up the glass, so aware of Law's eyes on him his flesh crawled. He dropped the bent metal picture frame into the dustpan.

As he stood up straight Law said, 'Your grandfather was a good man. If he seemed weak to you it was because he'd had too much grief in his life, more grief than most. I won't have you criticise him for my mistakes.'

'Mistakes? Buggering another man and getting caught was a mistake was it? Not simply vile and filthy and degenerate, but a mistake?'

'For God's sake, Bobby!' Law gazed at him, a little of the colour returning to his face. Angrily he said, 'I'm queer – as you call it. I'm not much bothered what you think about that and I won't apologise for it. Do you imagine this childish disgust hurts me? I've had your kind of contempt and bullying all my life, I've become immune. Hate me for abandoning you, by all means, but don't demean yourself like this.'

'I don't need your reasons to hate you.'

'No, I can see that.' He took another sip of water, his face creasing in pain once more. After a moment he said, 'I knew you'd hate me.'

'So why are you here?'

'You're my son.' He gazed at him steadily. 'Every day of my life since my arrest I have wanted to see you.'

'Why? To apologise? To explain? Yes, why don't you

explain?' Bobby sat down. 'Explain what made you do the filthy thing that got you arrested.'

'I can't. You're my son. How could I talk about such a thing to my son?'

'I'm a stranger. A grown man. So – man to man – tell me. What made you want to leave a young wife and baby to have sex with a man?'

'Bobby, please. Are you always so relentless?'

'Did you think this would be easy? That I'd just say never mind, I forgive you?'

'No. I don't know what I thought.'

'I would have kept away if I were you. I would have been ashamed to show my face.'

'Shame doesn't matter as much as other things.'

'Such as?'

'Love. I never stopped loving you.'

'Well you can stop now.'

'Oh Bobby! Do you think I can just turn my feelings off like a tap?'

Bobby glanced away. 'Stop calling me Bobby.'

'It's what I've always called you.'

Unable to sit still, Bobby stood up. He felt like pacing, the anger that was building inside him making him want to lash out. He turned on Law.

'You should have been at your father's funeral.'

'Yes, I should have. I was too cowardly.'

'Really? He used to tell me you were brave. He told me you faced up to losing your eye courageously. I used to wonder how you would have looked with only one eye. It's hardly noticeable is it? Got off lightly really, didn't you, compared to some of us?'

Law said, 'Yes, I was lucky. I'm only half blind.' He shook his head. 'Bob, are we bickering? For goodness sake! Imagine what your grandfather would say if he could hear us! He was so proud of you – of everything you did.'

'He wasn't! All he ever did was compare me to you! I couldn't do anything as well as you! There was one thing I could do though – fly, and he hated that, he did every thing to

504

discourage me –'

'He was terrified for you! Couldn't you see that? God knows what losing you would have done to him, and to me. We just wanted you safe … not putting yourself up for danger, volunteering for it … and flying was so dangerous …'

'Unlike sitting in a trench waiting to be blown up?' Hating the sneer that had crept in to his voice he said, 'I had an idea of you –' He stopped himself from finishing what he was about to say, not wanting to admit to this man how much he'd missed his father. His anger subsided into self-pity. He began to cry again and it felt ridiculous and demeaning. He wanted to hide from him.

Law said gently, 'Bob, please don't cry. I've cried enough for both of us over the years.'

Bobby blew his nose. 'I get it from you, then, all this bloody self pity?'

'I'm afraid when I was your age I cried at the drop of a tin hat.'

'You were shell-shocked.'

He smiled slightly. 'Making an excuse for me? I was in an asylum for a while, after the war, it wasn't shell shock – I'd seen shell-shocked men. I was just mad.' After a moment he said, 'When I heard you'd been hurt I wanted so badly to be with you. I would have sat at your bedside day and night if it had been possible.'

'But it wasn't possible, was it? You were dead. My mother had told me you were dead.' He remembered his mother's reluctance to answer his questions about Paul. Those childish queries about *my real Daddy* must have terrified her. She must have known that one day he would find her out. Her lies explained a lot about her relationship with him. It was all so understandable, in retrospect, it made him think that anyone with half a brain would have guessed her secret.

Thinking of Margot, that plump, unremarkable woman, he frowned at Law. 'Why did you have anything to do with my mother? You must have known what you were.'

'I loved her.'

'How could you love her, imagine that you loved her? I

505

know men like you, they never even look at women.'

For a while he said nothing and Bobby found himself looking at him thinking, 'This is my father.' It seemed surreal, and yet he was so recognisably his flesh and blood. He said, 'I know I was a mistake, that she was pregnant when you married her. Were you experimenting? An experiment that went wrong – landed you with a baby.'

'It wasn't quite like that.'

'Then what was it like?'

Law looked down at his hands.

Bobby said, 'I had a child. I would have given up anything, everything, to keep her safe. In the end I couldn't keep her safe enough. She died. I would have died in her place happily.' He lit a cigarette. Exhaling he said, 'My daughter was called Joan. No one could have taken her from me, least of all a man like my stepfather.'

'I'm sorry.'

'Is that what you came here to say? Do you feel better now? You know I didn't cry when Joan died. And yet here I am, crying for myself. I feel ashamed. You've made me feel ashamed. I'd like you to go.'

'Bob, please let me talk to you.'

Bobby looked at him. He thought how handsome Law was, his clothes well cut and expensive looking, his voice measured and gentle so that he sounded like his grandfather, making it so impossible to keep the tears in check. He tried to imagine what it would have been like to have been brought up by this man and if such an upbringing would have made him a better person.

He said, 'When I was growing up I used to escape to this house and pretend that my grandfather was actually my father. But he wasn't, and he kept reminding me he wasn't – telling me about you, showing me your picture. He'd tell me how bright you were, what a good soldier you'd been. He made you into a saint. And then I'd go home and my stepfather would tell me how useless I was, that I would only ever go to the bad.'

He got up to fetch an ashtray. Sensing Law's eyes on him

he said, 'You don't want to explain or to apologise. You just want me to forgive you.'

'I'd have to give you a reason to forgive.'

'That you were young and stupid and let your dick rule your head?'

Law avoided his gaze. After a moment he said, 'You're right, I do want your forgiveness and I have no excuse other than those you've just given me which really are no excuses at all. In the trenches I surprised myself – I didn't mind what other men seemed to mind so much. I don't know where that courage – that madness it seems to me now – came from, but as soon as the war was over it melted away. Being a civilian was too hard for me. I tried, I tried for your sake, but as much as I loved you I felt my life had ended. Prison was almost a relief in some ways – I didn't have to try any more.'

'And when you were released? You could have come back, you could have claimed me.'

'Yes, I could have. You were five years old. My father sent me a photograph of you. I couldn't believe that you were so big, not the baby I'd left sleeping in his cot the day I was arrested. I couldn't imagine what I'd say to you, couldn't imagine that you would accept me. With the photograph Dad wrote to me saying it would be best if I kept away from you.'

'Are you blaming him now?'

'No.' He exhaled. 'I don't know! Perhaps! I trusted his judgement – I thought he knew what would be best!' His voice rose as he said vehemently, 'I just wanted what was best for you! And I was ill and scared and utterly beaten and I couldn't face a five-year-old boy to tell him his mother had lied to him so horribly.'

'But now, now when I'm twenty-five?'

'I just wanted to see you. I wanted you to see me and know the truth. I want to make it up to you if I can, to help you.' He looked around the shabby, dark room. 'I always hated this house. It's so dark and cold, so full of my father's grief for my mother and brother, for me, I suppose. I hate to think of you alone here.'

'I'm not alone. And I can cope with being a civilian. I'm

not like you.' He heard a noise from upstairs and realised that he had forgotten about Jane. He looked towards the door.

Law said, 'Is there someone upstairs?'

Bobby ignored him, listening to her footsteps in the room above them. Looking at him he said, 'I want you to go now. I don't want to see you again.'

'Please, Bob. Please don't be like this …'

To Bobby's horror Law began to cry. As coldly as he could he said, 'Stop it. You can't behave like this – you've no right…'

'No. No … of course I haven't …' He seemed to make a great effort to pull himself together, wiping his eyes quickly with his fingers. Bobby stood up and held out his handkerchief but Law shook his head, refusing it.

'I'm sorry,' Bobby said. 'But you should have come back sooner. I'll show you out. I don't want my friend to see you.'

On the doorstep Bobby held out his hand but Law stepped forward and pulled him into his arms. He held him tightly and Bobby felt how frail he was beneath the expensive clothes. Law stepped back and smiled awkwardly, 'Forgive me, but I have wanted to do that for such a long time. All that time I imagined a little child in my arms but you're so strong, a grown man.' He touched his face gently. 'Goodbye, Bob.'

Bobby watched him walk away. He realised he was still clutching his handkerchief. He shoved it in to his pocket, a damp, snotty ball.

Jane wrapped herself in Bobby's dressing gown and went downstairs. From the kitchen doorway she said, 'I should go home, before he wonders where I've got to.'

Bobby was standing at the sink, smoking and staring out over the garden. She went to him. Slipping her arms around his waist she pressed her cheek to his back. The pullover he wore had been washed too many times, its wool felt matted. Breathing in his clean, soap smell she smiled, wondering if they had time to go to bed again.

Her hands were clasped just below his heart and he covered them with his own. Hugging him closer she said, 'Perhaps I

508

don't have to go yet.'

He remained silent and after a while she said cautiously, 'Bob?'

He breathed out sharply. 'I think you should go.' Disentangling himself from her embrace he turned to face her. 'I don't want him to be suspicious.'

She frowned, studying him. 'There's something wrong.' Anxiously she said, 'Tell me what's wrong.'

'Nothing!' He smiled and touched her face. 'Nothing, really.'

He'd been crying, it was obvious. Because she was too afraid to ask why and be told the truth she smiled back at him. 'You're right, I should go. School tomorrow.'

She went upstairs and began to dress. As she buttoned her blouse she looked up to find him watching her from the doorway.

Taking a step towards her he said, 'It's the first night of the play tomorrow, isn't it?' He attempted to smile. 'I hope Mark's not too nervous.'

'I'm sure he'll be fine.' Gently she said, 'Why don't you come and see the play – Mark would be so pleased if you did.'

He took out a handkerchief and blew his nose. Crumpling it back in his pocket he said, 'Would you like me to be there?'

'Of course! Bob, you know I would!'

Tears rolled down his face and he pressed his lips together as though to stop any sound escaping. Still holding his hand Jane led him to the bed. Lying down beside him she pulled him into her arms.

At dawn Bobby got up and went downstairs to smoke. In the kitchen he saw that his father's photograph was still on the floor. He picked it up and considered tearing it into pieces. He stared at it and saw himself as he was when he first walked into Jason's studio, naïve and vulnerable and too young to be out in the world alone.

Jason had said, 'If you take your clothes off I'll pay you far more.'

The cost of the flying lessons had been nothing to Jason.

509

After one lesson he had returned to the studio and found another boy there smoking Jason's cigarettes, an ordinary, dull-faced boy who had looked at him shyly but with a kind of hunger too. The boy was wearing the Japanese garden robe; he looked like a half-hearted transvestite who couldn't be bothered to do his hair and make-up. He was naked beneath the robe, the beginnings of an erection showing through the thin silk.

'You'd only be pretending, Bobby!' Jason had laughed at his outrage. 'I've told him you're not queer! God forbid anyone should think that of you!'

The boy had sniggered. Dressed by then, he had witnessed Bobby's rage, the panic that had him almost on the brink of tears. As the boy was leaving he blew Bobby a kiss and it took all of Jason's strength to stop him chasing after him to smash his teeth down his throat.

Bobby tossed his father's photograph down. He gazed up from the table and he turned it over so he wouldn't have to look at him. He couldn't help reading the message on its back, *To Dad, with all my love, Paul*. Paul had been eighteen, his grandfather had told him, eighteen, and desperate to join his brother at the front. He had wanted to prove himself, his grandfather said, and so he did. 'And oh! But he loved you!' His grandfather held Paul's picture out to him. 'He loved you more than anything in the world!' Bobby had been proud that Paul had loved him so much.

His grandfather had talked of Francis Law the great artist who had painted the picture that hung above the fireplace. If Law had an exhibition in London his grandfather would travel to see it. Once he had taken him. He'd been ten and the paintings of soldiers living and dying and killing each other had scared him and he had vowed to himself that he would never join the army, would never be so vulnerable and frightened and vicious as the men Law depicted. His grandfather had wept when he saw the paintings; lots of men of his generation did – those fathers of the dead. Even as a ten-year-old child he had thought Law wrong to show so much.

Law had wanted to paint him. His father had wanted to

paint him, as he was now, with his face all changed and ugly, only his eyes the same and recognisably his. He remembered the first time they had allowed him to see himself in a mirror. He had looked worse than he did now, the flesh still angry and livid, and he had believed he would never be able to face anyone ever again without his good looks to hide behind. How vain he was! Far more vain than the other men, who seemed braver and more stoical than he could ever be. He had set himself apart from these men, the worst vanity of all.

He went outside into the garden where the birds had just begun to sing. His feet were bare and the grass felt cool and soft, the dew darkening the hem of his trousers. The sky was clear, the day promised to be warm, the kind of day that always made him feel ashamed to be hiding away. He thought of Jane who had left a note on the pillow beside him telling him how much she loved him. He wondered if she could be pregnant. Afraid suddenly, he sat down on the bench beneath the horse-chestnut tree and tossed his cigarette stub down.

Nick told him Nina was pregnant as they sat side by side in deckchairs, their faces to the warm sun, off duty for once in that summer of 1940. Through half-closed eyes he'd been watching Simpson work on his Spitfire a few dozen yards away and he'd wanted to go and talk to the man, to remind him, badger him about something or other, there was always something he felt he had to bring to the ground crew's attention. But it was hot, there was a heat haze on the horizon, he felt deeply weary and anxious and couldn't be bothered to move, not even to tell Simpson something that might save his life. He'd been thinking about fate, wondering if he could let go of the worry and be a fatalist. Of course he couldn't; he knew that in a moment he would get up and go and breathe over Simpson's resigned shoulder. But then Nick said, 'Bob? Are you awake?'

Nick imagined that he could sleep; he didn't know him very well. He'd smiled, pretending to be dozy. 'Not really asleep.'

Nick shifted uncomfortably. 'Bob … Jesus – I don't know how to say this! You've always been such a good friend to me

– the best. Like a brother …'

He'd looked at him, surprised. He remembered smiling self-consciously. Nick had looked away, towards the busy scene of men clambering over planes. He'd looked angry, as though he hated the sight of him and Bobby had felt himself become afraid.

At last Nick said, 'Nina wants you to drop by the cottage and have supper with us.' He turned to him, still angry. 'I don't want you to. I want you to stay away from her.'

Bobby had avoided Nick's gaze, the way he looked at him as though he was unclean. He remembered fumbling for his cigarettes, and that his hands had shook as he said, 'I've always stayed away.'

'I know.' Nick had sighed. 'Bob – I know how you feel about her and I know for sure she still feels something for you…I hate it. It's got so I can't stand being around you …'

Watching Simpson walk away from his plane he said, 'Then go, Nick. Go and sit with the others. I understand.'

'I need to tell you something first.' He drew breath as if summoning courage. 'Nina's pregnant.' He looked at him. 'She's very happy, we both are. But I need you to stay away from us. I want her to forget all about you.'

Before he could speak, Nick was on his feet and was walking towards a group of their fellow pilots who were sprawled on the grass playing cards. He remembered that Nick kept his back to him, seemed stiff with the effort of not looking in his direction. He heard the others laugh. One of them caught his eye only to look away again as though his bloody, disgusting past was etched into his face. He had hardly spoken to Nick again. A week later he was dead.

Sitting beneath the tree Bobby bowed his head, remembering how sometimes he would look at Joan and see Nick in her, bringing him up short. He had vowed to himself that one day he would tell her all about her real Daddy, knowing that he would make Nick sound like a character in a book, remote and saint-like as his own father had been. It would be a kind of revenge; the thought of it made him feel ashamed.

512

He watched as a thrush pulled a worm from the lawn. He had to think of something else and his thoughts returned to Law, how Law had held him so tightly. No man had ever held him like that, not even his grandfather, who always seemed so lost in grief. Law had touched his cheek and he had felt that touch for hours afterwards. He remembered the raw expression of love in his eyes. He wondered how he could do without such unconditional love, how he could have spurned it. He remembered his pride. Pride had always been important to him, even as it made him feel hollow and brittle as bird bones.

He got up. He went inside the house and shoved his bare feet into shoes. He shrugged on a jacket. He tried not to think of anything at all as he walked out of the house towards town.

Bobby told the porter it was an emergency and that he needed to speak to Mr Law urgently. He watched him as he went to the switchboard and dialled his room. It seemed Law answered at once and Bobby felt his nervousness intensify. He almost turned around and left but the porter was already turning to him saying, 'Go straight up, sir. Room 323.'

Law was standing in the open doorway. He made no move to embrace him again, just stood back, holding the door open. He smiled at him, a careful smile, Bobby thought, as though afraid of showing too much of his feelings. He was dressed in shirt and trousers but his hair was messy from sleep, his face haggard. His bed was a tangle of sheets and blankets and Bobby looked away from it quickly. He felt as though he had breached some code of intimacy between father and son and at once he felt awkward, hating the way he seemed to radiate shyness. He had wanted to feel grown up and in control of his emotions even as he recognised that such coolness would be impossible, but he felt like a child, a timid, inarticulate one at that, true to himself, at least.

Law said, 'Would you like to sit down?' He indicated the only chair in the room.

Bobby remained standing; he would have to brush past Law too closely in the narrow space between the wall and the bed to get to the chair. Stiffly he asked, 'Did I wake you?'

'No. I was awake.'

'I haven't slept much.'

'No, I can understand that. I haven't slept much, either.' He sat down on the edge of the bed and his gaze went to the open suitcase beside the wardrobe. 'I thought I would start packing rather than go on chasing sleep.'

'You're going?'

'Yes. I'm going home. England's much too cold for me.'

In a rush Bobby said, 'I'm sorry. I behaved terribly badly. I don't want you to think I'm such an idiot …'

Law held his hand out to him. 'Sit down, Bob. Sit down here with me.'

He sat beside him, leaving a small space. His skin prickled, whether because he wanted his father to hold him or because he was afraid that he might, he didn't know. Awkwardly he said, 'I'm sorry, anyway. Those things I said…'

Law took his hand and held it gently. After a while he said, 'All night I've been thinking how wrong I was to come here, to tell you who I am. But I had to see you, I had to make sure that you were all right …' He held his hand more tightly. 'And when I saw you, well … I just wanted to hold you, to keep you safe … all I've ever wanted to do. You don't need to apologise to me, I will love you no matter what.'

'I wish you'd come back … when I was a child, I wish you'd come back then …'

'I know, I'm sorry.'

Bobby drew his hand away from his and wiped his eyes. 'You could have taken me away with you, I wouldn't have minded …'

Law laughed a little and Bobby could hear the tears in his voice as he said, 'If only I had. Too many if onlys and all of them too painful to think about. But here you are now, a strong, courageous man … we must look to the future.'

After a while Bobby said, 'I've been thinking …' He cleared his throat and made an effort not to sound so tearful. 'I've been thinking I would like to go home with you.'

Carefully Law said, 'To Tangier?'

'Yes. I want to get away from here … the woman I'm

seeing, Jane, she's married … we need to get away from the gossip and the scandal … would that be all right?'

'Of course.' After a moment he said, 'There is just one thing you should know before you decide. I live with someone, a man. His name is Patrick, we've been together many years.'

'I don't mind about that.' He managed to look at him directly for the first time. 'I'm not a bigot … I'm not, honestly.' Anxiously he said, 'Does he know about me?'

'Yes.'

'And he wouldn't mind, me arriving on his doorstep …?'

'He wants what's best for you, Bob. We both do.'

Bobby blew his nose. He laughed painfully. 'Jane has to direct her school play this evening. *Theory of Angels*. I played the lead when my school put it on – Captain Palmer. I thought of you as I was acting it … and afterwards, I thought of you and what you must have gone through …'

He began to cry. Cautiously Law put his arm around his shoulders. Bobby didn't resist him and Law held him tighter, stroking his head as he wept. He thought of Henry Vickers, how he had made him feel so small and filthy and used, how he had wanted a father then, even as he realised he never would have been able to tell him what had happened. He would have kept it to himself just the same, perhaps run away just the same.

He felt Law kiss his head. He had made his shirt wet with his crying; all the same Law rocked him in his arms, murmuring soft, comforting words as if he was a baby again.

Chapter Thirty One

He'd been to see his mother and told her, 'Paul came to see me.'

She'd frowned. 'Paul? Is he a friend of yours, dear?'

Later, when she'd realised exactly who he meant, after she'd cried a little and asked him to forgive her, she'd said, 'You were always more his than mine.'

He'd gone to Francis's hotel, waiting self-consciously for him in the bar. When he came down from his room Bobby had stood up at once.

Francis had smiled. There was such an expression of love on his face that Bobby felt the same sense of being protected he had almost failed to recognise the day before. That morning he had polished his shoes and pressed his best suit and chosen his tie carefully. He'd been to the barbers and his hair was as short as the day he joined the RAF. He had wanted to impress this man, to show him that he had survived. And, needing his support, he had asked him to the opening night of Mark's school play.

Sitting at the back of the school hall Bobby kept his head bowed as groups of parents, grandparents and siblings took their seats, chatting and greeting friends and neighbours. It felt as though the whole of Thorp was here, at least that section of it that mixed with his parents. He dreaded anyone catching his eye and approaching him with their curiosity dressed up as concern. They might even ask to be introduced to the man sitting beside him.

Evenly Francis said, 'Are you nervous for your brother?'

'Yes.' Grateful for the excuse, Bobby smiled at him. 'Almost as if I was the one about to go on stage.'

'Will your mother be here tonight?'

'No. They're going tomorrow night.'

Francis looked relieved and Bobby realised he wasn't the only one who was nervous.

The orchestra began to tune up. A schoolboy wearing a German infantry cap poked his head through a gap in the stage curtains and seemed to assess the size of the audience. Francis laughed. 'Poor mite.'

'Yes, he did look scared'

'And having to play the German too – such an ignominious part!'

'Do you know the play?'

'Well, it is very famous.'

Bobby was silenced. Somehow he'd imagined that Francis wouldn't know Mick Morgan's work, that living abroad it would have passed him by. He had wanted him not to know the play; Francis should be untainted by it, totally separate. Hesitantly he said, 'Do you know Morgan's poems, too?'

Francis looked at him. He seemed to consider his answer before saying, 'I know some of them, the early ones. The good, true soldier in the poems is Patrick, the man I live with, and I know he can't bear to read a single one of them.'

Before he could say anything the headmaster walked on to the stage and announced the evening's entertainment.

As the curtain came down on the first act Bobby said, 'Apparently there's tea and biscuits in the refectory.'

Francis said, 'Would you mind if I stayed here and minded my own business? Listen, why don't you go back-stage and tell your brother what a good job he's doing?' He nodded towards the stage. 'Looks like someone's trying to catch your attention, anyway.'

Bobby followed his gaze and saw Mark signalling to him. He breathed out, anxiously aware of how much Mark resembled him when he played Captain Palmer.

Francis touched his arm gently. 'Tell him from me I think he's doing brilliantly.'

Bobby went over to the boy. Mark said breathlessly, 'What

do you think? Are they enjoying it?'

Bobby smiled at him, wishing he had a cigarette to distract himself with. A few yards away Jane was directing boys shifting scenery. She caught his eye and looked away quickly, pushing a strand of her hair from her eyes. She looked hot and flustered; patches of sweat darkened her dress beneath her arms. She had become a school marm, not the lithe, sexy woman who made love to him so astonishingly. He found himself watching as she bossed the boys, wanting to see more of this side of her, until Mark said, 'Bobby?'

He turned to him. 'You're doing very well – everyone's enjoying it.'

'Do you think so?' Mark took off his captain's cap and wiped his brow. 'Really?'

'Really.' Bobby took an envelope from his pocket. 'Here, this is for you, to read after the play.'

Mark frowned at the envelope, then at him. 'You've written me a letter?'

'A note, to say what a good brother you are.'

Mark laughed, embarrassed. 'What else does it say?'

'Read it after the play, when you get home and you can't sleep because your head's buzzing. Will you remember to?'

Mark thrust the letter into his pocket. 'Of course.' He smiled. 'You don't have to write to me, you know.' He glanced over his shoulder as Jane approached them. 'Miss, Bob thinks everyone's enjoying it so far.'

Jane said, 'Hello again, Mr Harris.'

'Hello.' He must have looked at her too adoringly because she said sharply, 'Redpath, would you go and help Anderson and Smith?'

When he'd gone she said anxiously, 'How are you?'

'Fine. I'm sorry about last night. I don't cry normally.'

'It's all right! You don't have to apologise.' She glanced towards the boys moving scenery. As if they could hear her, she lowered her voice. 'I've been so worried about you.'

'Don't worry about me.'

She frowned, still concerned after the show he'd made of himself last night after Francis had gone. Gently she said, 'I

518

have to go – I'll see you after the play.'

Before the end of the final act, Bobby whispered his excuses to Francis and went outside, unable to watch the closing scene in which Palmer gives his grand speech and goes out to die on the wire. Morgan had written it so that Palmer was seen to suffer and Bobby knew his own weakness in the face of such pain. He had a feeling he would cry and he'd done enough of that lately.

That afternoon he'd agonised over his letter to Mark. In the end he'd written, *I hope that you won't be too angry at my leaving like this, so suddenly. I seem always to be going away, never getting the chance to get to know you as well as I would like. But recently I've felt that we're becoming friends as well as brothers – can we remain friends, no matter how many miles there are between us? I'm sure we can, with all the practice we've had. For now, though, I need to go before I become too scared to do anything and become so odd and eccentric in my odd, eccentric house that no one will want to come anywhere near me, not even you. I'll send you postcards. When I come back you can buy me a beer. (I've left the key to the back door under the plant pot – would you take care of the little cat?) My fondest love, Bobby.*

Bobby sat down on the school steps and lit a cigarette. He thought of Jane and the way she smiled after she kissed him as though he was particularly delicious; she would touch his cheek and smile into his eyes and he'd have such a feeling of happiness that he would laugh. He laughed more when he was with her than he could ever remember, making him realise all the joy he'd missed out on by being too serious and afraid. He thought of asking her to go abroad with him and was terrified. He hoped she would see it as a way out of their predicament, and not think of how bizarre it all was.

Behind him, Jane said 'What are you doing out here?'

He stood up at once. 'I'm sorry – the ending …'

'Yes. It is rather emotional.'

'All the same, I should go back inside, now – I shouldn't let Mark down.'

'He'll understand. Stay out here with me.'

'Don't you need to be watching from the wings or something?'

'They can manage.' She sat down. 'Who's that man you're with?'

'A friend.' He sat beside her. 'Do you think the play's gone well?'

She looked at him. 'Why are you going away without telling me?'

'I'm not –'

'Please don't lie, Bob. Mark read your letter, he told me. He was upset.' She laughed tearfully. 'I had to comfort him! Buck him up so he could go back on stage! I wanted to bawl my eyes out! How ridiculous, eh? What a silly woman you must think I am!'

He frowned at her. 'Why are you so willing to think badly of me? Do you really think I would just walk away from you after everything I've said?'

'I don't know –'

'Tell me who you think I am, Jane. Tell me honestly.'

'I don't know you well enough. That's the point.' After a moment she said, 'I think of you during the war, if you want me to be honest. I think of all the girls you must have known. I think of you dancing with them. In bed with them … I think you must miss all that.'

He thought of the few girls he had actually been to bed with before Joan was born; for most of them he had been one of a number. There had even been one particular girl who seemed to have slept with him for a bet. She had laughed afterwards as they'd dressed. 'Everyone said the only thing that made your heart beat faster had two wings and an engine. Well, I think we've debunked that particular piece of misinformation, don't you?'

It seemed ironic that Jane should think he was a womaniser. He thought of Joan falling asleep in his arms as he read to her. She hadn't allowed him to change out of his uniform but had thrust her storybook at him the moment he walked through the door. As he'd gathered her into his arms she'd taken his cap and placed it on her own head so that it fell over her eyes. He exhaled sharply against the pain of missing her.

Jane sat down beside him. He looked at her. 'Nina and I had a child,' he said. 'Her name was Joan. Her real father was a Canadian pilot, Nick – he was killed before she was born so I was the only father she knew. She called me Daddy. She died, a little while before I was shot down.' He laughed painfully. 'Joan made me forget myself. Whenever I was with her I was just her Daddy and that was that. At the beginning I used to think about Nick and try and keep a small distance from her because she wasn't mine and Nick deserved to be remembered and not have me fill his place in her heart so completely. But I found that I couldn't hold myself back like that. She was mine, my little girl and I was her father. I felt guilty but I couldn't help myself. Nothing mattered but Joan. Everything that has happened to me feels like nothing compared to losing her.' After a moment he said, 'So I wasn't out dancing or bedding women. I spent most leaves with Joan and her mother, idiotically not realising how happy I was.'

Jane took his hand. 'I'm sorry.'

'I should have told you earlier. Such a huge thing to come out with, there never seemed to be the right, proper moment. It's only been lately that I could bring myself to talk about her.'

'You must miss her.'

'Yes.'

'And Nina, too.'

He touched her face, gently making her meet his gaze. 'There's nothing between us any more. Memories, I suppose, that's all. I love you, Jane.'

'But you're going away.'

'I want you to come with me. Tomorrow.'

She stared at him. 'I can't –'

'Can't? Why? What have we to stay here for?'

'Where are you going?'

'Tangiers.'

'Why?'

'It's where he lives – that man who's with me tonight. He's an artist, he wants to paint me.' He thought of Francis, how he would have to explain the truth to her eventually, but not tonight, not until he was used to the truth himself.

'Jane, I know this is sudden –'

'Sudden! Why can't you wait? A few days, that's all, let me think about it …'

'Do you need to think about being with me?'

'No!'

'Then come with me.' He took her hands. 'I love you.'

'I know you think you do –'

He let go of her at once. 'I think I do?'

'Bob – it's been such a short time. You don't know me or I you, really …'

'You've changed your mind about me.'

'No – it's not that. It's just … my job, my whole life …'

He looked away, afraid to push her too quickly into making a decision. He saw that the moon was full, clouds scuttling across its bright face. He remembered the song he used to sing to Joan, *Paper Moon*, a song about make-believe and pretence and longing. He wished he could banish it from his memory forever.

He turned to her. 'I can't stay in Thorp, Jane. I thought I'd feel safe here but I don't, I feel more of a freak show than ever. At least in London …' Realising how self-pitying he must sound he said briskly, 'Anyway, it's best I stop hiding away and face up to things.'

'If you stayed here I would help you …'

He smiled, resisting the urge to beg her to come with him. He would seem pathetic, she would say yes out of pity for him. Taking the programme for *Theory of Angels* from his pocket he wrote down an address on its back and handed it to her. 'It's a flat above a photographer's studio. I'll wait for you there for two weeks.'

She took the programme. From inside the school hall came the sound of applause. Jane turned towards it. 'I should go in – they'll wonder where I've gone …' She shoved the programme into her pocket. 'Bob –'

'Don't say anything now.' He touched her face. 'I'll wait for you to make the right decision.'

Chapter Thirty Two

Two weeks later

Bobby hired a red MG and tied white ribbons from its bonnet to the windscreen. The sun shone and so he put the car's top down and as he pulled up outside Nina's flat children left the bomb site they'd been playing on and gathered around, exclaiming and begging rides. He handed out sweets and told them to wait as a guard of honour to see the bride off. The children agreed solemnly.

Bobby looked up at Nina's flat. She had promised to be ready and waiting when he arrived, reassuring him she wouldn't be late. But Nina was never on time, always infuriating him with her lateness. He worried about Hugh waiting in the church, afraid she had stood him up.

Hugh had said, 'I'd ask you to be my best man, Bob, but Nina wants you to give her away.'

Bobby laughed. 'I've never been so popular.'

Hesitantly Hugh said, 'You don't mind, do you? No hard feelings?'

'I'm happy for you both.'

He was happy for them. Nina looked more radiant than he had ever seen her, her excitement as always bringing out the remnants of her Irish accent and making her indiscreet. Taking both his hands she'd laughed. 'I think I might be pregnant, Bobby! It's marvellous, isn't it?'

He had only just arrived in her flat, hadn't even taken off his coat. He'd smiled, wanting to hide his shock and the sudden, surprising bitterness he felt. He'd hugged her. 'Congratulations.'

Too quickly she had stepped away from him. 'Don't say

524

anything to Hugh. I haven't told him yet.'

Bobby ran up the stairs to her flat and knocked on the open door. At once Nina's neighbour's baby was thrust into his arms.

Irene said, 'Thank Christ you're here! Hold Cathy while I fix madam's hair.'

Cathy patted at his face amiably. She smelt of turning milk and rusk and he kissed the top of her head where a ribbon tied up her limp curls. Nina sat at her dressing table in a satin slip. She smiled at him in the mirror.

'I'll be two minutes. Honestly. Two!'

'You're not even dressed, Nina –'

She laughed. 'You look handsome.'

He was wearing a new suit and a dark blue tie. There was a cream rose in his buttonhole. Cathy closed her hand around the flower and he gently lifted it away again. 'Should I wait outside?'

Irene looked at him. 'You've seen it all before, Bobby. Besides, if you put Cathy down she'll scream blue murder again.'

'I'll take her down to the car.'

'No – I'm ready!' Nina stood up. She took a pale blue dress from its hanger and slipped it over her head. She smoothed the silk over her hips and thrust her feet into pale blue shoes. 'There!' She grinned. 'How do I look?'

Irene took Cathy from his arms. 'I'll go and wait downstairs.'

When they were alone Nina said, 'Will I do, Bobby?'

'You know you will.'

'Thank you for being here today, for doing this …'

He picked up her bouquet of cream roses and blue silk forget-me-nots. Holding it out to her he said, 'Come on, let's not keep Hugh waiting.'

The wedding reception was in the church hall. After sandwiches and cakes the bride and groom were toasted with champagne. Bobby made a speech, an ordinary, short speech about how lovely Nina was and what a perfect match she and

Hugh were. He had been applauded loudly, as though everyone was relieved he had got through it. He supposed they expected him to be as shy and nervous as he looked. As he'd sat down beside Nina he had caught Mick Morgan's eye. Bobby had held his gaze steadily before Morgan looked away.

He had expected Hugh's father to be at the wedding, but he hadn't expected Henry Vickers to be with him. As he'd walked Nina down the aisle he had seen Mick's wheelchair at the front of the church. The man standing beside it, just like the rest of the congregation, had turned to watch the bride, and Bobby had recognised him at once. He had almost stopped, almost turned and run away. Sensing his hesitation, Nina had smiled at him, no doubt presuming he felt intimidated by so many strangers. He forced himself to carry on escorting her to the front of the church, to stand a few feet away from Vickers.

At the reception Irene said, 'Hold the baby, Bobby love, while I nip to the loo.'

Once again Cathy was thrust into his arms. She smiled at him from chewing on Blue Bunny and he used one of the rabbit's floppy ears to wipe away the teething-drool from her chin.

'That's a pretty child.'

Startled, Bobby looked up. Mick Morgan tore his gaze from Cathy to him. 'How are you, Bobby?'

Bobby felt his as though his legs might give way. Ashamed of his cowardice he said curtly, 'Fine.'

Morgan nodded. 'Good.' He held out his hand to Cathy but she buried her face in Bobby's shoulder.

'She's shy,' Bobby said.

'She's not yours, is she?'

'No.'

Morgan cleared his throat, 'Bobby, Hugh told me how you looked after him when he was in Thorp. I'd like to thank you for that. You always were a good friend to him.'

Desperate to get away, Bobby shifted Cathy to his other arm. 'Would you excuse me? I feel Cathy and I should be circulating.'

'Bobby –' Morgan sighed. 'I just wanted to say –'

'I'm sorry. I really should go and talk to the other guests.'

Vickers approached them, smiling, a champagne glass in hand. Bobby found himself holding Cathy tighter so that she squirmed and protested. She dropped Blue Bunny; flustered, Bobby crouched to retrieve the toy.

As he straightened up Vickers smiled at him and held out his hand. 'Hello. We haven't b…b…been introduced. Henry Vickers.'

Bobby turned to Mick. Hotly he said, 'Didn't you tell him I'd be here?'

'I didn't know – Hugh thought you'd stay in Thorp…'

Bobby felt a physical pain from the effort of not looking at Vickers, his whole body tense and ready to run. The baby squirmed in his arms, sensing his anxiety.

Mick Morgan said, 'Henry, why don't you go and talk to Hugh?'

'What's going on, Mick?' Turning to Bobby, Vickers said, 'I don't think there's any need for rudeness, young m…m…man.'

'Oh for Christ's sake, Henry!' Mick looked at the man angrily. 'This is Bobby Harris! I thought you might have had the wit to recognise him!'

Even without looking at him, Bobby could sense Vickers's shock. Cathy began to cry and he jogged her up and down, hushing her and forcing a smile into his voice. She made him feel calmer, a grown-up, and he forced himself to look at Vickers. He seemed more afraid than he himself was. Vickers's face was pale; he looked old and small as though age had shrunk him. Bobby found himself staring, trying to make sense of the fact that this was the same man who had instigated such a dramatic change in his life. Vickers fumbled in his pockets to bring out a cigarette case. Bobby noticed how badly his hands shook.

Still crying, Cathy patted Bobby's face to regain his attention. Hugh's navy friends burst into loud, filthy laughter. One of them sat down at the ancient-looking upright piano and began to play *The Lambeth Walk*. He saw Hugh lead Nina on to the dance floor. They danced, making up silly steps and

527

laughing. Hugh spun her around. Her silk dress shimmered and flared around her knees. Bobby thought of the day he first saw her and how much he had wanted to prove he wasn't what Vickers had believed him to be.

Irene came back and began to dance with the bride and groom. She signalled that he should join them, too. Watching them dance he thought of Jane, how, if she didn't come to London he would go back to Thorp and fetch her. He wouldn't give up; coming face to face with Vickers had made him realise he was stronger than he'd imagined.

To Mick, Bobby said, 'Would you excuse me?' He carried Cathy on to the dance floor and danced with her and her mother.

Jane sat on the low wall surrounding the churchyard. From the church hall she could hear music and laughter. A young, beautiful woman in a blue dress came out and kissed a tall, handsome man. The man lifted the woman off her feet, crushing her to him. They kissed long and deeply. Jane looked away. She knew this was Nina and Hugh.

Adam had said, 'You're really going.'

She had been folding clothes into a suitcase. Earlier she had told him about Bobby. He hadn't lost his temper as she thought he might. Instead he'd said flatly, 'I guessed. From the day you came home in his car I knew he'd take you from me.'

Going to her drawers, Jane had lifted out knickers and slips and stockings and tossed them in the case, not caring any more how neatly she packed, wanting only to get away. Stepping towards her Adam said, 'Please don't leave.'

'I'm pregnant, Adam.'

She wasn't certain if it was true or not, only that her period, usually so persistently on time, was a week late. Her breasts had begun to feel too tight for their skin. She had begun to accept the idea of Bobby's child growing inside her with a kind of subdued excitement, mixed with terror. He might not love her enough; he might have already left for that distant country. He was so young and frail: it was this that terrified her most.

Adam stepped towards her. 'I'll adopt it. I'll be its father –'

'No, Adam.' More gently she said, 'I couldn't do that to him.'

'What will I say to people?'

'That I left you. No one will blame you, Adam. Let them blame me all they like.'

He sank down on to her bed. 'I feel ashamed.'

'Don't. It's over, now.' She sat down beside him. For the first time in years she took his hand. 'I think he's a good man.'

Adam laughed bleakly. 'The Harris men are. A bit pompous, maybe. They should laugh more, I think.' He squeezed her hand before drawing his own away. 'I'm not sorry I married you, Jane. These last few years, well, I've felt a little safer, I suppose. That's terrible, I know, using you to hide behind.'

Carefully she said, 'Do you have anyone now?'

'There's a man I see. All very furtive …'

'Do you love him?'

'Love. Are women obsessed with love? I think we should all be more careful over how many people we love.'

Sitting on the churchyard wall Jane curled her fingers into the soft pads of lichen growing in the wall's cracks. She remembered how Adam had called a taxi for her, how, on the doorstep of the house they'd shared for seven years he'd handed her an envelope. 'Money, for the journey. If he lets you down, call me. Come back, if you need to, I'll always be here for you.' He'd smiled sadly, 'Very much second best, I know.'

The piano playing in the church hall stopped suddenly to roars of disappointment. Almost at once it started up again. A girl began to sing *Paper Moon*. She thought of Bobby, his sweet, slow kisses, and the way he cupped her face in his hand and smiled into her eyes. Desire for him was always with her, a constant nag, as though her body was afraid of becoming celibate again. She missed his tenderness.

A man sat down beside her. He said, 'Hello, Mrs Mason.' He smiled. 'We were introduced at your school, after the play. Francis Law.'

'Of course, hello again.'

He nodded towards the church hall. 'Are you waiting for Bob, too?'

'Yes.'

'It's a wedding. Old friends of his.'

'I know.' He'd left a note pinned to the door of the address he'd given her, telling her where he was. At the end of the note he'd written, I love you – Bob.

She wondered if he left a note on the door every time he went out. She had smiled with relief when she read it. He loved her. Seeing it written down in his neat, bold hand helped to quell her doubts.

Francis Law said, 'I feel rather shy of going in there, almost like a gatecrasher – although I was invited. Perhaps if we go in together?'

'I wasn't invited.'

'Would you like me to find Bobby and let him know you're here?'

'Not yet.' Nervously she said, 'They sound like they're having a good time, anyway.'

'I hope so.' He took a cigarette case from his pocket. 'Do you smoke?'

'No, thank you.'

'Good. Horrible habit. Perhaps you could persuade Bobby to give up the dreadful things.'

She felt herself blush and Law smiled at her. 'He talks about you a lot. This last fortnight Bobby has been my London tour guide; we've done all the galleries and museums and I tried to teach him a little about art but I think his mind was elsewhere, with you.'

'Do you think so?' They were sitting side by side and she turned to meet his gaze for the first time. She found herself looking into the face of the boy in Adam's photograph, aged and more gaunt but still recognisable, still beautiful.

She went on gazing at him, hardly able to believe that this was the man she had once thought of as a rival. She had been naïve then. She wondered if she was naïve still to imagine that a man as lovely as Bobby would want to spend his life with her. Realising she was staring she looked away, all the doubts she had about being here creeping back, swift as startled snakes.

Francis said, 'I'm going inside. Won't you come in with me?'

She shook her head, too anxious now to face a hall full of strangers.

'I'll let Bob know you're waiting.'

Jane watched Bobby leave the hall and look around. There seemed to be a look of panic on his face, as though he believed she'd already run away. Perhaps Francis had told him how nervous she was, like a schoolgirl on her first date frightened of making a fool of herself. When he saw her he grinned. Jane stood up and he ran the few yards towards her and swept her into his arms. He spun her round, hugging her tightly.

Putting her down he held her face between his hands. 'Have you left him?'

'Yes.'

'And you'll come away with me?'

She laughed, excited by the joy in his eyes. 'Yes!'

He kissed her again, a long, deep kiss. She pressed her body against his, wanting to wrap herself around him, to become entwined so they'd never be separated. She remembered the possible life inside her. She wouldn't tell him yet, not until she was sure.

Breaking away from her he grinned. 'They're dancing in there. Will you dance with me?'

'Of course.'

He took her hand and turned, only to hesitate. 'You'll marry me, won't you?'

She nodded. 'Now,' she said, 'let's dance.'

Nina watched Bobby dance with the woman he had introduced to her with such excitement. She wasn't very pretty; she was slim and had good legs. The two of them laughed a lot together; for an hour they had been dancing and laughing with eyes only for each other. It was odd how much he seemed to adore this plain, older woman.

Hugh slipped his arm around her waist. His eyes followed hers. After a moment he said, 'Are you jealous?'

'No!' She looked at him, horrified that he had guessed.

He laughed a little, his eyes on Bobby still. 'Do you see the way he's looking at Jane?' He turned to her. 'That's the way I feel about you.'

The hall had become too warm and Hugh had loosened his tie and undone his collar. Earlier he had taken off his jacket and the white shirt he wore showed off his broad chest and muscular arms. The dragon showed faintly through the thin cloth. He was so handsome, it thrilled her how handsome he was. She found herself grinning, wanting him. 'Let's go home.'

He grinned back at her. 'You really do love me, don't you?'

'Yes,' she said. 'I really do.'

Later, in his hotel room, Francis found the letter he'd written to Patrick a fortnight earlier. He read it again before tearing it into pieces. Taking a piece of the hotel's notepaper he wrote quickly *I'm coming home with Bobby and the lovely girl he's to marry. I've missed you. My love always, Francis.*

THE END

Marion Husband

Marion was the winner of the first Andrea Badenoch Prize for Fiction, in 2005, for *Paper Moon,*
Her first novel, *The Boy I Love*, was published in July 2005 to much critical acclaim.
Paper Moon was followed in 2007 by *Say You Love Me* and *The Good Father*.
Marion graduated with distinction and won the Blackwell Prize for Best Performance for the MA in Creative Writing at Northumbria University in 2003. She currently teaches creative writing through the Open College of the Arts and has had poems and short stories published, most recently a pamphlet of poetry about her father and childhood entitled *Service*. Marion is 43, married with two children and lives in the Tees Valley

www.marionhusband.com

The Good Father

When Peter Wright's father dies he leaves his entire fortune to Peter's best friend Jack. Over a few weeks in the summer of 1959 the consequences of the old man's legacy seriously affect three men's lives, Jack, who has brought up his three children alone since his wife was killed, Wright's solicitor Harry, who is trying to rebuild his relationship with his estranged son Guy, and Peter himself, whose friendship with Jack is threatened by his father's death and the terrible secrets he has kept since his return from the Japanese POW camps.

The Good Father explores the nature of fatherhood and the bonds between fathers and their children in a gripping story of love, betrayal and adultery.

ISBN 9781906125035

Price £7.99

Say You Love Me

This is a powerful, sensitive yet shocking, exploration of the long-lasting traumas caused by parental sexual abuse. Marion Husband's superbly drawn, multi-dimensional characters, loving and hating freely, both fascinate and repel.

Ben Walker sets out to trace his father and discover the truth about his adoption in 1968. But the past holds secrets that his brother Mark is desperate to keep.

Old hatreds between the brothers are rekindled and their adopted father is made to face his own guilt over the events of that spring of 1968.

Pulling no punches, this enthralling, disturbing novel gives the reader a real insight into familial abuse.

ISBN 9781905170869

Price £7.99

For more information about our books please visit
www.accentpress.co.uk